# THIS CASE IS GONNA KILL ME

# THIS CASE IS
# GONNA KILL ME

## phillipa bornikova

TOR®

a tom doherty associates book

new york

THIS CASE IS GONNA KILL ME

Copyright © 2012 by Melinda Snodgrass

A Tor Book
Published by Tom Doherty Associates, LLC
175 Fifth Avenue
New York, NY 10010

www.tor-forge.com

Tor® is a registered trademark of Tom Doherty Associates, LLC.

Library of Congress Cataloging-in-Publication Data

Bornikova, Phillipa.
    This case is gonna kill me / Phillipa Bornikova.—1st ed.
      p. cm.
    "A Tom Doherty Associates book."
    ISBN 978-0-7653-3389-6 (hardcover)
    ISBN 978-0-7653-2682-9 (trade paperback)
    ISBN 978-1-4299-7791-3 (e-book)
    I. Title.
  PS3602.O765T48 2012
  813'.6—dc23

                         2012011473

First Edition: September 2012

Printed in the United States of America

0  9  8  7  6  5  4  3  2  1

*This one is for Christy Carbon-Gaul,*
*attorney extraordinaire, friend, advisor,*
*and an all-around smart, pushy, modern woman.*

# Acknowledgments

I couldn't have written this book without the aid of Daniel Abraham, Ty Franck, Walter Jon Williams, and Ian Tregillis, who helped with the initial plotting. Walter Jon for the kick-ass title. And special thanks to Ian Tregillis, who had so many great ideas about the world and the mythology that I have shamelessly incorporated.

# THIS CASE IS GONNA KILL ME

# 1

"This case is gonna kill me."

I stared down at Chip Westin and tried to think of an appropriate response. Actually, I would have been happy with *any* response, but nothing came to mind. This was my immediate boss, and these were the first private words he said to me after McGillary, one of the senior partners at Ishmael, McGillary and Gold, had introduced us.

*What does that* mean? I thought miserably.

Westin looked to be in his early fifties, balding, wearing an expensive suit that had probably looked good when he was thirty pounds lighter. His complexion was pasty, but he wasn't a vampire. His cluttered office's one window was blocked by a stack of books and files, and I suspected he didn't get out much. His jowls looked like they were melting toward his collar, but this seemed to be caused less by gravity than by bone-grinding weariness and frustration.

Thus far my first day at Ishmael, McGillary and Gold, one of the premier White-Fang law firms, had consisted of signing my insurance and pension papers, designating who would receive said pension should I die while still employed by the firm, being shown my small cubbyhole of an office, and being introduced to Westin. "You'll be helping with his cases," McGillary had said as he led me toward Westin's office. Then he'd amended that, adding in a peculiar tone of voice, "Well, one in particular." I could only assume Westin's prediction of imminent death was related to that case.

"Okay. Maybe you should tell me about it," I said. I would have liked to sit down, but there was no available surface that wasn't covered with papers, books, and files.

"It's a probate case. Back in sixty-eight, Captain Henry Abercrombie was serving in Vietnam when a werewolf went rogue and bit him. That was just after the spooks went public, and the military had to admit how many hounds were actually serving in the armed forces."

I blanched a bit at the pejorative term but let it pass. After all, I'd just met the man. Westin continued.

"Anyway, he had a wife and three kids back in Newport News, and shortly after he came home on medical leave he separated from his wife, Marlene. He didn't divorce her because of the kids, and he kept helping with expenses, but he never lived with them again. Then three years later, he left the marines and founded a company, Securitech."

I choked. Securitech was the largest private military force in the world, worth close to a billion dollars. They had serious clout. The last time Securitech had been in the news was when they'd received a thirty-million-dollar, no-bid contract from the DOD. A crusading senator from Minnesota had tried to reopen the negotiations, but the investigation was closed down by the White House and the Justice Department, and the senator abruptly resigned from Congress, stating the ever-popular need to *spend more time with his family*.

Westin continued. "In 1980, Abercrombie decided to sire a werewolf heir, and he picked his second in command, Daniel

Deegan. At this point the kids were grown up, so Abercrombie divorced Marlene. Then seventeen years ago Abercrombie was killed in a car wreck in Somalia. His human ex-wife, Marlene, and the kids—though they're not really kids any longer, they're in their fifties—retained us to challenge the will that left the company to Deegan.

"In the beginning we raised the issue of the wording about progeny in the will. The lawyer who drafted the will for Abercrombie threw the word *natural* in front of progeny. We wanted to argue that sex resulting in pregnancy and birth is more 'natural' "—he made quote marks with his fingers—"than biting somebody."

A Supreme Court decision came floating to the front of my mind. *Geisler* had established that *progeny* could mean the werewolf or vampire the testator had sired. In fact, the court had contended, that relationship was closer than the relationship with children produced by sex and birth, because the act of Making showed such a high level of intent.

"But *Geisler*—"

Mr. Westin nodded. "Yeah, kicked us right in the nuts. Sometimes I wonder if there's a secret spook on the high court."

There it was again—the pejorative term for vampires, werewolves, and Álfar being used by a lawyer working at a White-Fang law firm. I assumed he had as-yet-undiscovered talents that made him valuable to the senior partners despite his atttitude. Judging by the piles of papers in the room, he was probably the firm's resident research monkey, a highly esteemed position since most lawyers hated the role. Then I wondered if he had any idea that I had been fostered in a vampire household and that *I* might find this offensive. Again, I hid my reaction. Calling my boss out for being a bigot was not a smart move the first day on the job.

"So, where does that leave us?" I asked. It felt good using the plural. *Our case.* It made me feel like a real lawyer.

"In arbitration," Chip said.

"*Geisler* was years ago."

"Yeah, we've been in arbitration for seventeen years."

I stared around at the paper towers and felt my gut sinking toward the soles of my feet. "So all this . . ." I gestured.

"Depositions. Interrogatories. Transcripts of arbitrations. I got a few other smaller cases . . ."

His voice trailed away and he looked around the office with the air of a confused dog. I was reminded of the old basset hound my foster liege, Mr. Bainbridge, had owned. Dilbert constantly forgot where he'd hidden his bones. Mr. Bainbridge had spent many a night out with a flashlight, Dilly lumbering alongside and tripping over his ears while his well-trained owner searched for the lost bone.

I pulled Mr. Westin back to the *Abercrombie* case. "Why is this still going on?" I asked.

The response was blunt. "Because our clients are crazy. The wife and kids are demanding the entire company."

"And the court hasn't shut this down?"

"They don't give a shit. As long as we're in arbitration it's not their problem." He picked up a stack of papers and set it down. Picked up a file, flipped through it, set it aside. "We're about to start another round, and I yelled for help. One of our witnesses died last month, and Deegan's lawyers are challenging his deposition. I need somebody to help me prepare for this meeting."

"And that would be me?"

"Yep. Your lucky day, huh?" Westin suddenly realized I'd been standing for a long time. "Oh, I'm sorry."

He left his chair, hurried around the desk, lifted a stack of folders off the client's chair, and offered it to me. He then stood looking around. Once again I was reminded of Dilly. Westin tried to find a place for the stack of folders. There wasn't one. I stood back up and he set the folders back down on the chair. Even that much exertion left him short of breath. Pants punctuated each word as he said, "Sorry my office is a mess. Maybe now that you're here I can start to dig out. I'm really, really happy to have you on board."

"Thank you, I'm very excited to be here," I said, and it wasn't a lie.

Or at least I wasn't lying about my pleasure at having been hired by this particular firm. Only Gunther, Piedmont, Spann and Engelberg down in Washington, DC, had a better rep, but my folks—my real folks, not my vampire foster liege—hadn't wanted me to go that far away from home this early in my career.

"I'll need you to read through everything and see if you can think of any other witnesses or arguments we can use to bolster the idea that Abercrombie actually loved his wife and kids and wouldn't have cut them out without a dime."

"Despite abandoning them," I said somewhat acidly.

"No, no, no. He left them because he loved them too much to risk them, or warp his children by having them grow up with a werewolf daddy. It's all in the presentation." He gave me a grin that made him look like a delighted, fat-faced baby. "Our job is to present bullshit like it's filet mignon."

I decided I could work with him despite his prejudice, and I made a conscious effort to start thinking of him as Chip rather than Mr. Westin.

Chip rooted through the office, gathering up papers and files and piling them in my arms. When the stack was almost up to my chin, he said, "This should give you a sense of where we've been and where we're at."

"Great. I'll get started reading."

"We'll drop those in your office, and then I'll give you the dime tour. Also, I could use a snack, and the food's better up in teak heaven."

It took me a second to figure out what he was saying. We were on the seventieth floor, where the human associates resided. On the seventy-third floor was where the partners dwelled. Things were fancier up where the partners worked.

People said that working for a White-Fang firm was like stepping back to the sixties, but since I wasn't alive back then, I couldn't attest to the accuracy of the statement. I just noticed as we made our way across the common area housing the assistants that I didn't see a single male secretary, and it seemed that the male associates had the nicer, larger offices on the outer walls.

Chip kept leading us in and out of offices, as I tottered along behind like a pack mule with a precariously balanced load and he tossed out names like confetti. I have a terrible time remembering people's names unless I can pin the name to a face, but the only way I could see their faces was if I peered around my stack.

Only a couple of introductions stuck, because I was so worried about dropping the papers and causing a humiliating mess. One was Caroline Despopolis—blonde, tall, slender, and beautiful. We were both wearing Yves Saint Laurent skirts and jackets, but on her it looked fabulous while on me it looked dowdy. I wondered if the sage green jacket really complemented my black hair.

The only other introduction that made an impact was David Sullivan, and that was because he was a vampire. His luminous white skin made his eyes look like dark brown velvet. His taffy-colored hair was carefully styled into casual disarray, and it was pretty clear his suit had never hung on a rack. Definitely bespoke. But here he was down on the human floor. Vampires were partners. Partners didn't have offices on a human floor. Which meant he'd screwed up majorly to get banished like this. He saw my mental wheels turning as I did the analysis and reached my conclusion, and he rewarded me with a look that would have killed me on the spot if vampires really had that power.

But he still had the intimidation thing down pat, and since I'd grown up in a vampire household I immediately reacted, offering a submissive and wordless apology by tilting my head to the side and shaking my hair off my neck. Not that he would ever have bitten a woman, but Sullivan neither accepted nor acknowledged the apology. He just snorted and disappeared into his office.

The door to my office beckoned, and I managed to get through the door and deposit the stack just before the top files went sliding like the leading edge of an avalanche. As Chip helped me gather up the files he asked, in a too-casual tone, "That thing you did." He cocked his head awkwardly to the side. "That's like spook etiquette, right?"

I cringed and Chip looked contrite. "I don't mean any harm. It's just the way I was raised. My mom worked here, but my dad never did like it, and didn't much like the"—he made the mental correction and used the politically correct term—"powers, either. I hope you won't mention that I used that term."

I wondered if Chip would also say his use of the n-word didn't mean anything, and that it was just his background. But I didn't want to start out my tenure by ratting out a coworker. "Sure. No problem."

"I heard from Shade that you were fostered in a spook—er, vampire household. Is that true?"

"Yes, I was."

"How does a parent swing something like that?" Chip asked.

"I'm not exactly sure. My family's been pretty closely allied with the Powers since 1963. My grandfather was a lawyer, and he helped with the integration after the Powers came out—went public. However you want to put it."

"Sure does help your profile if you can establish that kind of relationship." Chip ran a hand across his face. "I sure would like my kids to have that advantage, even if it meant that the boys might turn into inhuman creatures."

I gave a mental sigh and decided that this was a habit Chip wasn't going to break easily. I also had to wonder why he was working in a vampire-run law firm, given his feelings. Had to be the mother thing. Vampires took loyalty to servants very seriously.

I gave a noncommittal answer. "I'll ask my dad. See if I can give you any pointers." But I doubted it would do much good. If there's one thing that can be said for the Powers, it's that they're snobs, and I had a feeling that neither Chip nor his offspring would pass muster with those households. I wasn't exactly sure how we had rated. Maybe it had to do with my family's illustrious past rather than our rather mundane present.

We once again passed through the reception area on our way to the elevators, and I noticed that the secretaries and assistants went into a huddle after we passed. Maybe the word had spread further than Chip that I had been fostered in a vampire household. That would inevitably result in them thinking I had gotten the job through connections, which I had—sort of. All of this meant I was going to have to work that much harder just to prove I deserved to be here.

I could feel the determination settling into my jaw as we stepped into the elevator. I almost suggested we take the stairs, but then I remembered how moving files and walking to my office had winded Chip and decided against it. Killing my boss on the first day was not a way to impress.

The seventieth floor was nice. Mahogany and cherry wood, slate tiles, green glass partitions to separate the assistants, private offices for the attorneys. The seventy-third was opulent. Teak furniture, polished Carrera marble floors softened by elaborate oriental rugs, an antique sideboard where an attractive and obsequious assistant would mix the beverage of your choice. A client might have to wait, but they would have a cocktail to sip while they waited.

And if said client wasn't tempted by the wide selection of magazines, both foreign and American, they could drift to the wall of windows (all carefully treated with heavy UV screens for the protection of the vampires) and look out across the shimmering patch of green that was Central Park. Right now the early morning sun danced on the skyscrapers on the far side of the park and Columbus Circle, turning them into crystal spires and pulling rainbow colors from their windows.

The receptionist looked to be all of twenty, and he was gorgeous in that pouty way that only a really handsome male can achieve. He ran a bored eye over me, and I could see the rejection. I tried to figure out why. *Because I'm not seventeen? My outfit is dowdy?* Then I caught his expression as his eyes drifted over to Chip. *I'm with Chip. That's why I'm being dismissed.*

"Anybody in the conference room?" Chip asked, pointing toward the heavy, carved-wood double doors.

"No. I guess you can go in there, but be quick about it." The kid's tone was curt to the point of being rude. The level of disdain set off my alarm bells. Chip might not be a vampire, but he was still an associate in the firm.

We stepped through the doors and were in a long hallway with offices to either side. The aroma of coffee hit my nose and my stomach gave a loud growl. I had been too nervous to eat this morning. Chip walked through a doorway on our left, and we were in a kitchen.

The fluorescent lights glittered on stainless-steel appliances and granite countertops. My apartment didn't have a kitchen this nice. A young woman was toasting a bagel.

Leaning casually against a counter and wolfing down a

powdered-sugar donut was a stunningly handsome man dressed in blue jeans, a silk polo shirt, and a blue blazer. His hair was a mix of white, gold, and black streaks of varying widths, as if a hairdresser had gone mad during a highlighting session. His eyes were green and he sported a spectacular shiner.

Now that I was looking more closely, I realized he had a long grease stain across the back of his coat, which had one elbow ripped out. He was also pretty clearly an Álfar. Among all the Powers, only the fey folk possessed such devastating beauty.

". . . saw me taking a scraping off the bumper, and came flying out the front door and down the steps. He threw back the screen so hard he broke it," the man was saying, punctuating his words with little puffs of powdered sugar.

"What did you do?" the woman asked, pausing from smearing cream cheese on her bagel.

"Ran like hell, but he was fast for such a fat guy. He tackled me." The man ruefully regarded the rip in his coat. "He tried to grab the Baggie with the sample, but I had it someplace safe." The Álfar patted the front of his pants and leered at the woman. She blushed. "He popped me once, but he got the worst of the encounter," he concluded with satisfaction.

"Oh, you poor thing. Would you like to come over tonight? I can make dinner."

"Sorry, but Jennifer has already offered tea and sympathy."

Chip chuckled and slapped the man on the shoulder. "John, stop telling tales of your derring-do and pitching woo to all the secretaries, and come meet our new associate." Said secretary blushed and slipped through the door. "Linnet Ellery, John O'Shea. Linnet comes to us by way of Radcliffe and Yale."

We shook hands, and I found myself studying his. Despite a scrape on the knuckles, they were beautiful, with long tapered fingers, manicured nails, and powerful muscles across the back.

I am a sucker for hands. I have capable hands made even wider from years of riding horseback, but no one would describe them as elegant.

We murmured our how-do-you-dos, and I wondered why he'd assumed the human name. O'Shea was smiling in a way that made me catch my breath. I knew that smile was fool's gold; in addition to inhuman beauty, the Álfar are also known for devastating charm and short attention spans.

"John's our P.I. If you need anything investigated, photographed, stolen, or staked out, he's your guy," Chip continued.

I was startled and decided to say so. "Not the usual role for an Álfar. You're usually in the entertainment industry."

"I'm not your usual Álfar." He gave me a genuine smile this time. "Most of the Fair and Crazy Folk couldn't hold down a real job."

I was startled by his dismissive tone, and I would have loved to talk more with him, but I wasn't sure if the desire was from actual intellectual interest or if he was throwing a glamour on me. If it was a glamour, I decided to start breaking the spell. The best way is to perform a mundane activity, so I began to prepare my own bagel. Chip was rummaging through the big Sub-Zero refrigerator.

"There's lox," he said, and emerged with a package of thin-sliced salmon.

"I'll leave you folks to it," O'Shea said. "I'm going to go put in a requisition for a new blazer. Nice meeting you," he added.

"And you," I said, putting the finishing touches on my bagel.

Chip pulled down plates from a cabinet. It was real bone china, Wedgwood. No paper plates at Ishmael, McGillary and Gold.

"What's his story?" I gestured toward the door and the now departed O'Shea. "O'Shea isn't exactly an Álfar name."

"It's not. He is a changeling. Raised by humans, lived with humans, worked with humans. He was actually a policeman before he opened his own detective agency and we put him on retainer. I'm surprised more Álfar haven't done that, or become really good crooks. They've got that whole walk-through-Fairyland thing they can do. When John's on your tail, he's almost impossible to spot."

"Wow." I really couldn't think of anything else to say to this remarkable story, and now I really wanted another chance to talk with John O'Shea.

Armed with food and cups of coffee, Chip and I continued to the end of the hall, where five conference rooms occupied the far wall. The center one was magnificent, with an inlaid-wood round table and high-backed chairs.

"This is where the big boys meet," he said, and I could hear the envy.

"Where's the law library?" I asked.

"Just below us. They took out the floor between seventy-one and seventy-two to accommodate the shelves. Walkways and ladders everywhere so you can reach the top shelves." He paused to gauge my reaction.

It was one of pure lust. I love books, especially old books. There's a smell and a feel to old paper that makes me feel like I am shaking hands with people across time. Law firms measure their wealth in the quality of their research library, and it's always a real point of pride in a White-Fang firm. During one of my summer internships while I was in school, the senior partner loved to wander by, notice what book I was perusing, and casually mention that he'd acquired the tome back in 1715.

I have the same reaction to portraits. Whenever I walked through a museum, I was always drawn to the walls of faces. I actually preferred the unknown subjects to the famous people. I'd look at the young girl playing with a puppy, or the young man wearing his dignity like a cloak, his hand resting on the sword hilt in a way that clearly said, *don't laugh at me.*

I'd weave stories about them and wonder about their lives. And then I would look over at my foster liege and realize that Mr. Bainbridge had become a vampire during the Renaissance. The past had been walking among us every day, and it was only in the past forty years that most humans had learned of it.

"Want to see the library?" Chip asked, pulling me out of my reverie. I nodded in enthusiastic assent. We finished off our bagels and coffee, dropped off the china in the kitchen, and rode the elevator down one floor.

There were twelve-foot-tall wood and glass double doors to the left of the elevator bank. Chip pushed one open and allowed me to precede him into the muted light thrown by glass-shaded brass lamps. It was so quiet that I could hear someone turning a page in a secluded carrel.

For my high school graduation present, my folks had treated me to a trip to Europe. The only other place I had seen a library like this was at Blenheim Castle. Stairs led to a catwalk at the level where the seventy-second floor would have been. On both levels the walls were covered with floor-to-ceiling shelves and rolling ladders were available to reach the upper volumes. There were desks scattered among the standing shelves, carpet underfoot, a beautiful inlaid round conference table, and even a large gas fireplace topped with a carved marble mantle to add to the sense of comfort.

Only one thing was missing. There were no computers. Instead, the index files were kept in an enormous antique file cabinet, and a table held a large stack of legal pads and pens. At least there was a copier so you wouldn't have to hand-copy every citation you found.

I sighed, but I wasn't surprised. Vampires were conservative. If something worked well in 1847, why wouldn't it work just fine in the twenty-first century? It was something I had endured growing up in the Bainbridge house. If I'd wanted to surf the net, I had to make a trip into town and find the nearest Internet cafe. A laptop was no help because there was no Internet service. Eventually the neighbors put in Wi-Fi, and I discovered that if I sat near the edge of the Bainbridge property I could bootleg their signal.

Chip and I were just turning to head back to the door when a tall, silver-haired man in a rich gray-and-blue Canali suit emerged from between the stacks. He was frowning down at the open page of a book. Shade Shadrach Ishmael was one of the founding partners of the firm. He was close friends with my foster father, Meredith Bainbridge, and had often been a guest in the Sag Harbor house. Over the years we'd shared a number of rambling conversations about music, history, and law. I suspected Shade was the reason I had been asked to interview at Ishmael, McGillary and Gold.

"Linnet, my dear. Welcome."

He bent, making the motion seem more like a bow. Vampires were so damn graceful, it made me feel all the more like a klutz. He kissed my cheek, and his lips were cold against my skin. Like most vampires, he wore a lot of aftershave and made sure to use mouthwash four or five times a day, but nothing completely masked the faint scent of blood that hung around him.

Deep inside, I felt that primal shiver of fear. Intellectually, I knew it was unwarranted. I was in no danger. I was a woman, and vampires didn't bite women. I had also been raised in a vampire household. I had watched Mr. Bainbridge feed every night from the time I was eight until I graduated from high school. But the old lizard brain that had kept us safe when we first swung down from the trees was convinced that I was prey and that I was standing way too close to a predator.

"Thank you, Mr. Ishmael, I'm very happy to be here."

He stared down at me, puzzled, and shook his head. "So formal, Linnet?"

I smiled. "I work for you now. I need to be respectful."

He threw back his head and gave a sharp laugh. "I have a hard time reconciling that with the little girl I watched grow up. When I think of you, I think impertinent, cocky, brash—"

"Pert, flippant, cheeky, insolent, saucy, sassy, smart-alecky." I broke off and gave him a quick grin. "I can play Thesaurus too."

Shade laughed again and glanced at Chip. "You see what you have to contend with? You are forewarned."

Chip had gone from looking aghast to grinning. He nodded. "I think we're going to get along fine."

Shade patted me on the shoulder. "You're in good hands. Chip is the most meticulous lawyer I've ever known."

An image of his cluttered office flashed through my head. Shade seemed to read my mind. "Don't be fooled by his surroundings. He keeps everything." Shade tapped his temple. "Up here."

As we walked back to the elevator, I said softly to Chip, "Don't get hit by a bus. At least not until I know where all the bodies are buried."

I spent the rest of the day beginning to read through seventeen years of pleadings, depositions, and interrogatories. Chip packed it in around seven o'clock. I hung on until eight p.m. and felt I'd made the right choice. Most of the human associates were just leaving.

The assistants' desks, wooden ramparts guarding the doors to the lawyers' offices, were unmanned at this time of the night, but the central reception area was awash with departing lawyers. Expensive suits and snap-brim fedoras on the men, pencil skirts and elegant jackets for the women. Goodbyes were exchanged; a few people made plans to meet for drinks. There didn't appear to be a lot of office romances, either brewing or actually up and running. If you were male and hoped to make partner and be made a vampire, you knew marriage and a family weren't in your future.

If you were male and weren't interested in making partner, you probably lacked the ambition to be hired at a White-Fang firm. Thus, most of the women attorneys knew their male coworkers were a bad bet.

David Sullivan stood in the doorway of his office and watched the humans mill with an expression of sublime indifference. He caught me looking at him, turned on his heel, and closed the door of the office. I joined the mass exodus and stood in a clump of people awaiting the arrival of an elevator. The moment of Briefcase Comparison had arrived—the ultimate legal version of dick measuring, or whatever the female equivalent would be.

There were Forzieri and Brunelleschi cases with leather like butter. Caroline had a pale green leather Dior bag that she had thrown nonchalantly over her shoulder. She looked poised and elegant. Mine was a roller bag that held my small MacBook, up to four files, a legal pad, pens, a book to read at lunch, and sometimes a lunch. I looked like a geek.

The elevator arrived with a melodic *ding*. People crowded in. I tried to follow. "I don't think there's room for the both of you," Caroline said with a nod at my roller bag, and she let the door to the elevator close in front of my nose. I could hear the laughter as the elevator began to descend.

Why did there have to be one like that in every office?

# 2

As I walked from the subway, I realized I didn't want to cook. There was a hole-in-the-wall Thai restaurant just around the corner from my apartment, so I stopped there for takeout. I didn't bother to check the mailbox in the entryway. I had moved in three days ago. There wouldn't be any bills yet, and who wrote letters anymore? Then I thought about my foster liege, and his meticulously maintained fountain pens and heavy, creamy stationery embossed with his initials. Okay, vampires still wrote letters, and tried to get you to take notes in longhand, which meant I made a sharp turn and returned to the wall box to find a letter from my vampire liege/foster father. I hooked the bag with my dinner over the handle of the roller bag and read the letter as the ancient elevator wheezed its way to the seventh floor.

*Dearest Linnet, first day on the job. I hope it wasn't too daunting. I was thinking of you, and the entire household is very proud of you. Love, Meredith.*

I kicked off my heels, dropped the sack of food on the coffee table, and headed to the windows. The July heat made the place stifling. I resolved to get to a hardware store over the weekend and buy a window air conditioner. I had to stand on a chair to unhook the window latch, and while I was up there I paused to take a look at the Hudson River. The rays of the setting sun danced on the water, making it look like a river of glass. The view was why I had rented the apartment, though I had to stand on a chair and cock my head to actually see the river. It was small, but I did have an actual bedroom, and I loved the old ten-story redbrick building that had been erected in the 1920s. It had leaded-glass cabinets in the tiny kitchen, the wrought-iron radiators were heavily decorated, and the floor was hardwood.

The smell of lemongrass and chili made me remember I was hungry, and I jumped down as the last of the light faded. I located a plate for the pad thai, a bowl for the tom yum soup, and a fork and a spoon, then pulled out my cell phone and called my best friend, Ray. He wouldn't mind if I chewed in his ear, and he'd want to hear how my first day had gone. I knew he'd be home. It was a Monday night, and the show in which he was currently dancing was dark on Mondays.

"Hey, Munchkin," he said in his soft baritone. "I've been thinking about you all day. How was it?"

"Fine. My new boss seems nice. . . ." My voice trailed away.

"I hear the paranoia," Ray said.

"I can't help thinking I just got the job because Shade knew me."

"Please—you were third in your class at Yale. You did all that crap good little law students do. . . ."

"Law Review and Moot Court," I mumbled around a mouthful of pad thai.

"Which is why I cannot take another month of you working through the emotional trauma of getting the job."

"Hey!" I tried to interrupt, but he was on a roll.

"Last month, you were sure you blew the interview. I had to listen to six days of you replaying all the things you should have said. Then there was the week where you tried to figure out what you'd do if you didn't get this job. Then there was ice cream therapy when the depression hit because you just so knew you weren't going to get this job—"

"And you were no help," I grumbled. "You kept eating Tofutti while I was pigging out on Ben and Jerry's."

"Hey, I have to keep my girlish figure." I made a rude noise. "And I'm lactose intolerant. So, come on, tell me there was some moment of joy before you returned to your usual habit of looking for the black lining in every cloud."

I smiled, relishing a memory. "I did send gloating e-mails to everyone on my law school LISTSERV after I landed the job. And I made damn sure my worst enemies received the e-mail."

"Now that's what I like to hear. Petty vengeance is the very best kind." I heard Gregory, Ray's partner, calling loudly in the background. "That's the dinner bell," Ray said. "Gotta go. Brunch on Saturday?"

I agreed. Ray hung up, and I sat in my dark apartment and realized that right then all my clouds were silver and bright.

By Friday, my clouds had turned into thunderheads. During the past week, I had read through eight years of arbitrations—just nine more to go—and the files were getting thicker with each passing year. The takeaway from all my reading was that Chip was right: Our clients were crazy. After reading Marlene Abercrombie's depositions, I decided that if I'd been Henry I would have left her too. And her kids were just as irrational, grasping, and greedy as their mother. I dreaded meeting them in the flesh.

I mentioned this to Chip, and he looked at me with an expression I couldn't really identify. "Yeah, and we're trying to put the most powerful private army in the world in the hands of these people. Kinda makes you wonder what we're doing." He didn't elaborate, and I didn't follow up. One of the first things you learn in law school is that the law isn't necessarily about justice. It's about process. And you try not to make value judgments about your clients. That's not your job. Of course, that's honored more in theory than in practice. We're human beings, not robots, and we have emotional reactions. We just have to try to keep them under control when we're in front of a judge.

By the second week, it was clear that Chip was definitely not in any kind of loop when it came to the firm. Most lawyers handle lots of cases. It seemed like Chip just had *Abercrombie v. Deegan*, because we never talked about, and I never worked on, anything but *Abercrombie, Abercrombie,* and more *Abercrombie.*

At first I had thought it was because *Abercrombie v. Deegan* was so important, but it wasn't. It was small potatoes when compared to the contract negotiations that McGillary was undertaking on behalf of one of our clients. They were going to be *taking over power generation for Argentina.* Caroline was assisting Gold on a massive and potentially very lucrative class-action tort case about long-term use of Botox.

And I had the crazy-people case.

It only took a day for me to notice that my fellow associates went off to lunch in groups of three and four. At first that level of camaraderie encouraged me. In a lot of White-Fang firms the competition between the human associates is so fierce that it precludes friendship, and can even tip over into outright warfare. I thought the fact these folks socialized together was great. I took to loitering in central reception at lunchtime, but an invitation was never extended. Instead I "overheard" remarks about "drones," and classmates who were just wonderfully qualified and really ought to be working at IMG, followed by pointed looks. Then, on Friday, Caroline's bosom buddy Jane had mused about the

THIS CASE IS GONNA KILL ME

hiring policies at the firm. One of the male associates, Doug McCallister, had smirked at me and said loudly, "Every firm has the legacy or the patronage hire." Caroline delivered the coup de grâce when she said, "And you just hope they realize they're out of their league sooner rather than later, and seek their own level." That was when I stopped hanging around the lobby looking to be included.

My stomach growled. I looked up from the file, rubbed my burning eyes, and realized it was 1:15. Definitely time for lunch. I kicked off and sent my ball chair rolling back from the desk. It didn't have far to roll—the room was tiny. I came up hard against the back wall of my office and nearly lost my balance on the ball. The framed print from the Santa Fe Opera, a time-lapse photo of stars over the theater, shivered on its hanger. I quickly rolled forward again. The way things were going, the picture was going to come down off the wall and brain me.

I left my office and headed toward the kitchen on the seventieth floor. It wasn't as nice as the one up in teak heaven—the plates were paper and the utensils plastic—but we did have an espresso machine and a big fridge. There was also a sunny and pleasant break room off the kitchen where the secretaries tended to eat. I had eaten there on Wednesday, but it was very clear I was not welcome. I couldn't really blame them. It was their only chance to dish about the attorneys. After that I had taken to just eating at my desk.

I snatched my brown bag out of the refrigerator, grabbed a plastic spoon, and hurried past the door to the break room. The whispers from the secretaries pursued me. I returned to my postage stamp–sized office. I pulled out an apple and a carton of yogurt from the bag, then found that my appetite had vanished. I stared morosely into the unblinking stare of my tiny wind-up toy Godzilla. He staked out a corner of my desk, ready to fight off any monsters that might threaten me. I wound him up and set him marching toward the tower of *Abercrombie* folders. He walked into them and promptly fell over. *Abercrombie* had defeated even the mighty Godzilla.

I pulled back the foil top on the yogurt and thrust in the spoon as the odor of pineapple and banana washed up and crashed against my nose. It was gross. Whatever had possessed me to buy such a disgusting yogurt flavor? I jiggled the little container in my hand, then decided, to hell with it, I'd treat myself to lunch out. I would save the apple for a mid-afternoon snack.

I decided to try to entice Chip to join me, so I stopped by his office. His door was closed, and his secretary, Norma, was in the break room eating. Chip's basically sweet nature had won me over, and after two weeks we had pretty much stopped standing on ceremony with each other, so after a quick knock I opened the door and walked in.

Chip was on the phone, studying a piece of paper, and I heard him say, "Of course it's convenient, but there's one more angle—" He broke off abruptly and muttered into the phone, "Gotta go." He hung up and quickly shoved the paper deep into one of the piles on his desk.

"Sorry, I didn't mean—"

He waved off the apology. "No problem." He grabbed an ice cream sandwich, unwrapped it, and took a bite. "Going out?" he asked.

"Yeah. Want to join me?"

"Nah, but thanks. I bought lunch from the Sandwich Girl," he said, making it into a title.

"Well, I guess that qualifies as a sandwich, "I said.

He looked startled, glanced at the ice cream sandwich, then laughed and picked up a white paper-wrapped sandwich from the desk with his other hand. I smelled the greasy, garlicky scent of pastrami.

"Life is short, eat dessert first. That's my motto. Have fun," he said, and turned back to the files.

I gathered my courage and asked, "Chip, do we have any other cases other than *Abercrombie* that I might work on?" He looked up at me with an expression that clearly said he found the question baffling.

"Why?"

"Well, I just feel like I'm sort of wasting the firm's money. I'm just going over the same ground, and I'll never be as up to date on this case as you. So, I thought maybe I could take some . . . other case . . . off your plate." I wound down, suddenly, desperately afraid I would discover that he didn't have any other cases. *But he had told me he did*, I reminded myself.

"Let me think about that." Chip crammed the remaining third of his ice cream into his mouth. "Maybe after we get past this latest hearing. That witness dying really screwed us, and I like the idea of fresh eyes on the problem. You may see something I've missed. Let's talk about it after you've read through all the files and helped me prepare."

"Okay."

I was feeling so low that I almost abandoned my plan to go out for lunch. But another glance into my office, where my ficus was dying from lack of light, made me head for the elevators.

I'd seen this small seafood restaurant a block from the skyscraper that housed our firm. Seafood was good for you, and more to the point, I liked it. I wasn't big on sandwiches, and salads always left me starving by late afternoon. Since I didn't normally get dinner until nine or later, I wanted some real food.

The heat shimmered off the concrete sidewalks as I walked

over, and the city was ripe with the aroma of rotting refuse rising off the black garbage sacks set out for collection. Added to that was the smell of exhaust, hot dogs being hocked by street vendors, and sweaty people bustling along, accompanied by the music of blaring car horns, jackhammers, and a thousand conversations in a hundred different languages. It was New York. It was a grand, if somewhat dissonant symphony, and I loved it.

I stepped into air-conditioned bliss and breathed in the smell of lemon, garlic, butter, and fish. Saliva burst in my mouth, and my stomach gave a loud growl. Then I noticed the table for seven off to one side. Six associates from my firm sat there, among them Caroline and Jane, and a man with his back to me. Caroline stared at me like I was one of those bags of rotting garbage and leaned over to Jane to share a remark. Jane laughed, and I felt my guts writhing.

There were two options. One: Pretend I was looking for someone, and in a nicely audible voice ask the waiter if So and So (pick sexy-sounding male name) had arrived. When the waiter said no, ask the name of the restaurant and then declare (loudly) that I was in the wrong place. Leave.

Option Two: Slink back out the door like a kicked dog without uttering the cover story. That was probably going to end up being the option, because my mind was a whirling blank, and I couldn't summon up a single male name.

Then the maître d' asked, "Are you alone, miss?" in that snotty tone that seems to be reserved for waitstaff in nicer New York restaurants, and which guarantees you are going to get a table by the bathrooms or the kitchen.

Option Three appeared, arriving courtesy of the temper my father had warned me against. I decided, what the hell. My coworkers couldn't treat me any worse. *Wanna bet?* the cautious Linnet asked, but I ignored her and went with furious Linnet. I nodded toward the table.

"No, I'm with them. I was just running late. They must have forgotten to mention it. If you'll get another chair." I threw the order over my shoulder as I started walking toward them.

The man with his back to me turned at the sound of my heels on the stained concrete floor. He was a partner. Not one of the named partners, but nonetheless a real, honest-to-God partner. There's a tension in law firms between the founding partners whose names appear on the letterhead and the partners added later whose names don't appear. Some lawyers don't give a damn, but if you have ambitions beyond litigation—like sitting on the boards of powerful corporations or advising presidents—you like to have your name chiseled into the building and printed on the stationery.

The fact that I was crashing a partner's luncheon made my steps falter, and I was about to give up on my "damn the torpedoes" approach and fall back on slinking away, but Ryan Winchester gave me a careful vampire smile that didn't reveal the canines, and said, "Linnet, how lovely, please, join us."

The waiter, who had been ignoring my order for a chair, now leaped into motion. By the time I reached the table, he'd brought a chair and set another place next to Ryan.

I had met Ryan Winchester a couple of times over the past two weeks, which was the only reason I went ahead and sat down. Ryan had been friendly. He had actually come down to my office to welcome me to the firm, and two days ago we'd run into each other in the library. I had been standing at the foot of a ladder, gazing up at a top shelf that held the book I was seeking. He'd offered to climb up and get it for me, for which I was eternally grateful. Heights were not my friend.

Ryan had blond-streaked brown hair that women spent two hundred dollars to achieve, and blue eyes that he focused on you in rapt attention when you talked. I tried to tell myself it was just a technique, but it really felt genuine with Ryan. Ryan and the four human males all stood up. Vampires are all about the courtesy, and they insisted on the same old-fashioned manners from the male humans around them. Ryan pulled out my chair.

"Linnet, I'm so glad you came in today. You've just been locked in your office working far too hard. Now I'll have a chance to get to know you away from school, so to speak." He gave me a warm smile, and this time I got a flash of tooth.

I noted the frowns from my fellow associates, and I responded with a great big smile. I turned back to Ryan. "Well, I'm trying to get up to speed," and I heard a muffled snort of suppressed laughter off to my left.

I took a quick look, but couldn't identify who was responsible. My guess was Doug McAllister, who was always making little digs at Chip, to which Chip seemed oblivious.

I met Caroline's cool gaze. She was above cutting remarks. She just existed, and that was enough to establish her superiority. For a moment, the therapist in the back of my head rummaged through my neuroses.

*Why are you so insecure?*

*Because she's tall and cool and elegant, and she knows the ropes. I hate not understanding the rules. And she reeks of money.*

*And you're from an old New England family with money and respect.*

"Linnet?"

"Hmmm?" Ryan's face was only inches from mine. It was a handsome face that looked totally normal, and those facts helped push back the involuntary shudder.

"I said, I heard you're quite the horsewoman," Ryan said.

"Ah, yes. Have been. Hard to do now. Here in the city." The words emerged in tiny, disjointed sentences.

"Well, I have a weekend place in the Hamptons, and a stable full of fat and lazy horses. Please feel free to come out and ride any time you like."

"Tha . . . thank you," I stammered. "That's very kind."

"No, it's not. I have an ulterior motive." He smiled. "I was hoping you'd give me some tips."

"I would be delighted." I hoped Ryan had a good seat, because that whole predator/prey thing is amplified with horses. Before cars, most vampires had humans to handle their horses, and they rode in carriages rather than riding astride.

But that was a problem for another day, and one that might never materialize. Right now it was time to savor my triumph. I looked down the table. The men were looking annoyed, but the women's reactions were very different. Jane was looking down and away, almost hiding behind the swing of her long brown hair. Caroline stared at me. Her expression was harder to identify. I almost thought it was pity, but then it was gone, and I wondered if I'd imagined it. Perhaps I was stepping into a situation I didn't understand. Maybe Ryan and Caroline had been an item? Though that would have been dangerous, since it's drilled into a newly made vampire not to fraternize too closely with women. I needed to find a source of gossip in the office.

The waiter came by with the others' orders. It all looked wonderful. The baked seafood that Joseph was having smelled amazing, but I calculated the calories and settled on the bay scallops in a white wine and lemon sauce. Ryan wasn't eating. The manager came over and leaned down to say softly, "We have a lovely organic-fed host in the back. A swimmer. Very healthy."

Ryan smiled up at him and nodded his appreciation. "Thank you, but I dined rather well last night. I'll be fine."

The real money in the restaurant business is made in booze and hosts. Since it was noon, none of us was drinking, and Ryan wasn't eating. The manager nodded and walked away, looking disappointed.

The kitchen rushed out my meal (though it didn't taste rushed; it was delicious) so I could eat with the others. The conversation was mostly about the firm, about cases that could be discussed without violating attorney/client privilege, about politics—we were approaching another presidential election—and Labor Day vacation plans. For the first time since I'd started at Ishmael, McGillary and Gold, I felt like I belonged.

As we walked back to the office, the group fell into discrete clumps. Ryan, umbrella unfurled against the sun, fedora firmly in place, was flanked by Doug and Tom. Jane and Caroline walked together, and the final two associates, Sam and Paul, orbited the triumvirate in the front and tried to attract Ryan's attention. I followed behind, feeling like the sick gazelle trailing the herd and wondering when a lion would pounce.

I thought the guys looked like perfect idiots, capering jesters trying to attract the attention of the king. In some ways I couldn't blame them. Being male, they actually had a chance to make partner with all the benefits (i.e., becoming a vampire). The few women who made partner only got to hold that exalted position just for their lifespan. They never got their names chiseled on buildings or placed on the stationery.

There were a few wolf whistles from some construction workers on a nearby building. I decided to include myself in the whistles, because construction guys aren't normally discriminating. I fall into the cute category, and that can be very disheartening when you're surrounded by beautiful people. My dad says I have charisma, loads of it, but charisma only has practical application if you're a politician or have power and want to wield it. I'm not the former, and don't have the latter. All I have is a slim though short physique, jet black hair that I keep at chin length so it's more comfortable under a riding helmet, and dark gray eyes.

We reached the building. The doorman held the door and nodded respectfully to Ryan. We all trooped in after him, little human ducklings led by a raptor. Ryan closed his umbrella, and there was a scrum of people waiting at the elevators. Clashing scents of Coco Mademoiselle and Frédéric Malle and Chrome and even the occasional whiff of tobacco swirled around me. It was just dumb luck that left me alone on an elevator with Doug.

Glances into his office had revealed diplomas from Harvard, and break room gossip had filled in a bit more. He came from an old Charleston family, and from a long line of lawyers. His suits were all Italian, and he'd been at pains to tell people he had his shoes made in London because he had such narrow feet. He was also going bald and tried to hide it.

He leaned against the mirrored wall of the elevator as we whizzed up seventy floors and my stomach dropped slowly toward my heels. Just as the elevator began decelerating, he suddenly drawled in his warm molasses accent, "I work for Gold. He black-balled you. You only got in because of your family connections. Have a nice day."

The doors opened and he stepped out.

I was so shocked I just stood there and ended up riding the elevator back down to the lobby level. I rode up and down three more times while I tried to gather my thoughts and my courage. I fought off the temptation to run home, crawl into bed, and pull the covers over my head. *But if you run, you'll never stop running,* I thought on one of the rides up the length of the building.

*You've let them push you around too much already,* was the thought on the second ride.

The concluding thought on the third and final ride was, *If you don't stand up you're going to end up a smear on the bottom of their shoes.*

I got off the elevator and stopped first at Doug's office. I stuck my head in the door, gave him a brittle little smile, and said, "You know, I've never seen a bald vampire. Better hurry." He came half out of his chair, face twisting in anger. I waved, left, and headed upstairs to confront Shade.

"I was third in my class. I did Law Review and Moot Court. I passed the bar on the first try. Not just the New York Bar, but the Connecticut and Rhode Island Bars too. I petitioned and was accepted to the Federal Bar. What's wrong with me?" I wanted to sound pissed and proud, but instead it came out as the wail of a lost and hurt child.

"Nothing," Shade said. He sighed and leaned back in his chair, rubbed his eyes, and pinched the bridge of his nose. "You're getting caught up in a battle between two partners. It's never a good place for a human to be."

"Gold," I said, and dropped into one of the high wing chairs on the other side of Shade's polished cherrywood desk.

The office was spectacular, offering a view of the Brooklyn Bridge and the sparkling water beyond. All the furnishings were beautiful Art Deco pieces, and the art interspersed with Shade's diplomas and awards tended toward the soft, pastel, and impressionistic. The only odd note was the prie-dieu in one corner. The purple velvet cushion looked pretty worn. I tried to picture Shade kneeling there praying. It didn't compute.

Shade pulled me back. "He wants to take the firm in a certain direction—"

"Would that be backward?" I asked waspishly.

"I suppose you could put it that way. I'm resisting. McGillary is being pulled between us. Blackballing you was just an act of pettiness on Gold's part. But in an effort to protect you I've put you in . . . well . . . a . . . a . . . how to say this? A less than vital position. If I had given you any real authority, it would have made you a target, and it might have ruined your future opportunities."

I gulped and stared at him. "Less than vital? I think this is a total dead-end job. And why are we still messing with this case? You could have told the Abercrombies years ago to accept a rational settlement, or find other representation."

Shade sighed. "This case generates billable hours, works to Chip's strengths, and helps me fulfill a promise I made to his mother. She was my secretary back"—he waved vaguely—"in the day. I have a responsibility to her child."

"Yeah, okay, I get that . . . but getting back to me. Look, I like Chip, don't get me wrong, but you've as good as said he's a loser, and this is a dead-end assignment, but somehow you think this is going to help me? I'd hate to see what you'd do if you wanted to hurt me."

"Trust me, being roadkill in a fight between me and Gold would be far, far worse."

"Is there anything I can do?"

"Keep your head down. Work hard. Don't make waves. And hope I come out on top in the power struggle."

"And how long might this take?" I asked.

"Oh, years. We're vampires."

# 3

"I hate this case. I hate this case. I hate this case."

The mantra didn't make me feel any better. Some of my discomfort was my outfit—a very tight short skirt that gripped my hips and upper thighs. It wasn't designed for sitting. It was designed for dancing. In addition to the skirt I wore a bright cobalt blue silk blouse with a plunging décolletage and a waist that emulated a corset. It only looked good if I wore a push-up strapless bra, which was also really uncomfortable.

I had accessorized the ensemble with a wide choker necklace that drew attention to my best feature—a long, swan-like Audrey Hepburn neck—and a wide metal bracelet set with small seed pearls. I had finished it all with a pair of drop-dead gorgeous Manolo Blahnik shoes that had set me back eight hundred dollars.

I'd had a date—a first date, with a cute guy I'd met at the health club. This was a big step for me. I hadn't been out on a date since I'd ended my engagement. Or had it been ended by mutual consent? I wasn't sure anymore. The only thing I was sure about was that I felt very ambivalent about the whole thing. Devon was a good guy and a brilliant architect, but he had expected me to follow him as he moved around the world. First stop: Dubai. I had nothing against Dubai, except that I couldn't practice law there, and I was about to finish three years in law school. I wasn't willing to put my career aside before I even started. Thoughts about the ex made it hard to concentrate on the Abercrombie pleadings, and then it was eight thirty and I had no choice but to call Pete and tell him there was no way I was going to be able to meet him at Citrus. So, now I pictured Pete sipping G & Ts and dancing with a bevy of tall, beautiful, long-legged girls while I was stuck at the office on the Fourth of July holiday with only Chip to keep me company.

I had worked until one o'clock this morning, gone home for a few hours of sleep, and come into the office at seven thirty—and Chip had still beaten me in. I had run out at six to grab a salad for me and a calzone for him, then stopped at home to change into my date clothes because I was still hoping to get away in time to meet Pete.

It wasn't like my bitching showed any courage. There was no one to hear me but my sad little ficus. Chip was in his office preparing to argue that the dead witness's deposition should remain part of the record. Harold Meyers had been a good friend to Henry Abercrombie, and he had given us a nice quote about how Henry had said that he never wanted to hurt Marlene or his kids and wanted to look after them all, during a card game at the Elks club. But now Harold was dead, and Gunther, Piedmont, et al. had smelled blood. Meyers was one of our better arguments for forcing Securitech into giving Marlene and her grown-up kids a boatload of money, but he was dead and couldn't be cross-examined. Which was the argument from the other side.

We had dredged up another poker buddy from the Elks Lodge, Jonathan Gelb, who had been present at that card game, and we just had to hope he remembered things the same way as poor dead Harold. But that hadn't been enough for Chip. He had me tracking down every member of the club from that period, trying to find the other men who'd been at that fateful poker game. Naturally, Jonathan, who was seventy-eight, couldn't remember any of the others except for Henry Abercrombie. I had this horrible feeling that we would get into the deposition meeting and Jonathan would forget he had ever been an Elk.

Chip had decided that since I'd gone to Yale and done Law Review, I had to be a better lawyer than he was. I pointed out to him that I had no actual experience, and had never run a deposition, but he wanted me to lead, so here I was frantically typing up questions, trying to think of possible ways our opponents would twist and confuse the issues and listening to the music of my favorite band—Crooked Man—on my iPod, instead of live at Citrus while dancing with a really cute guy.

I stared at the question I'd just written and realized it was just another way to phrase the same question I'd asked three times before.

I leaned too far back, and my Evolution ball chair nearly tipped me onto my ass. I righted myself only because the heel of my shoe, skittering wildly across the slate tile floor, lodged in a grout seam. Why had I ever asked for this dumb chair anyway? I practically had to do sit-ups all day long to stay balanced. I should have just gone with a big cushy leather chair and to hell with my stomach muscles. It didn't matter anyway. Twenty years from now, when Chip retired, I'd get his office, this case would still be pending, and I'd be fat and forty-five, single, childless, and married to my dead-end job.

I suddenly laughed because my level of self-pity had just gotten too deep. It was one night. If Pete couldn't understand work pressures, then I didn't want to be with him anyway, and Crooked Man was playing for another four nights. I'd hear them before they headed on to Boston. And since I was giving up my entire holiday to Ishmael, McGillary and Gold, I figured I could have one weeknight when I left the office at six.

I leaned forward and hooked my coffee mug with one finger. I started to sip, realized it had been a long time since my last sip, and looked down, swirling the cold caramel-colored dregs. Time for a fresh cup.

I stopped by Chip's office on my way to the kitchen. He looked up, and his jowls seemed as long as a basset hound's ears. His eyes were red rimmed, and his hair was so oily that the combover had become separate clumps of hair with pink scalp peeking through.

"Good God, Chip, you look like hell," I said before I could bite back the words.

"I didn't go home last night," he mumbled, then coughed to clear the fatigue.

"You said you were leaving right after me," I said.

"I meant to, but I found some interesting responses in some interrogatories from . . ." His voice trailed away.

"Well, then you're stupid."

I was beyond caring about being rude. Maybe I'd get really lucky and they'd fire me. And I actually did like Chip, even if he was the millstone that was going to sink my career. I leaned across the desk and took the wireless mouse from his flaccid hand. I shook it in his face as I said, "Look, tomorrow is the Fourth. We can work all day, and it should be nice and quiet since everyone has taken off. Go home, get some sleep. I'll finish up what I'm doing, and we can reconvene at eight a.m. tomorrow. How about that?"

He rubbed a hand across his face. "Yeah, maybe you're right." He stood up and got a funny look like a colicky baby. "I think I forgot to pee today."

I laughed. "Well, you better take care of that, pronto. I'm going to go get a cup of coffee."

"You don't mind me leaving you?" he asked as we moved into the lobby area.

"No. I left you last night, and then you didn't go home."

"You'll go home, won't you?" Chip asked anxiously.

"Yes, I'll go home. I work better when I've had some sleep."

"You must think I'm awfully dumb," he said, and there was something about the way he said it that made me realize he wasn't just talking about this case, or this night, but maybe about his career as a lawyer.

"No," I said gently. "I think you're really dedicated, and the firm is lucky to have you."

He gave me a grateful little smile and headed off to the men's room while I walked to the kitchen. The Jura-Capresso busily ground beans, then groaned as it dispensed a double espresso into my cup. It finished, and I realized that what I had thought was just the coffee machine was actually the hum of the elevator coming to rest on the seventieth floor.

I glanced at my watch—12:23. Who on earth would be coming by at this time of night on a long holiday weekend? It was silly, but I felt nervous. My rational mind took control. Chip had to call the elevator to go home. God, I was being stupid. Then I heard the distant hollow sound of a toilet flushing. My unease returned. I snagged my coffee and headed out of the kitchen.

"Oh, Jesus . . . shit!" It was Chip's voice, rising into an almost soprano range and cracking with terror.

The tinkling of broken ceramic as my cup hit the slate floor was swallowed in sounds of rending and splintering wood. Two conflicting emotions warred for control.

Retreat—run back into the kitchen and hide in a cabinet.

Rescue—go to Chip's aid.

Chip was still shouting, so whatever was tearing through furniture hadn't gotten to him yet. Then he screamed, a horrible sound like a dying rabbit. It was stupid. I couldn't help it. I ran to help.

The outer office, with its star-like arrangement of secretaries' desks in front of the doors of the lawyers' offices, was in shambles. Desks had been upended. One had been reduced to matchsticks. The musky, wild scent of werewolf filled the room. There was another smell too, sharp and coppery. The smell of blood.

Looming in the midst of the rubble was a werewolf, huge and gray-brown. Chip was staggering backward. His left arm hung uselessly at his side, and blood poured from a gaping wound on his shoulder and upper arm. His coat and shirt were in tatters. So was his flesh. I could see the white flash of bone through the blood.

"Linnet! Run!" he yelled.

I loved him in that moment for thinking of me, but hated him because now the wolf knew I was in the room. Granted he would have known soon enough, but I might have had a few seconds to flee. I was still wondering if I'd actually run when the creature turned. The amber-colored eyes, set close to a long, wicked muzzle, were filled with a mad light.

Beyond being terrifying, werewolves are disturbing. They remain bipedal, though hunched and twisted. They use their arms to help propel themselves, but they don't have paws so much as hairy hands tipped with fearsome claws.

He launched himself at me. I darted sideways, and he came up short because the hind claws on his back foot got tangled in the phone, cable, and Internet wires, which caused him to fall full length on the stone floor.

I ran to Chip's side, my absurdly high heels making it hard to balance. I got my shoulder under his good arm, and we fell more than stepped through the door into the office behind us. I slammed shut the door and threw the lock. Chip's face had gone the color of fresh dough, and he was starting to shiver from shock and blood loss, but I couldn't deal with that right now. I threw myself across the desk and grabbed the phone. There was no dial tone.

"Shit!" I screamed, and jabbed futilely at the buttons. Then I remembered the torn and tangled wires in the outer office. There would be no call for rescue.

*Cell phone!* My cell phone was in my purse . . . which was back in my office.

Tears of terror and desperation tightened my throat. The office door gave a *boom* like a wooden gong, and a fist punched through the panel. The werewolf began tearing apart the door like a greedy child ripping paper off a Christmas present.

Chip gave a moan of despair. I grabbed him, and we tottered through the connecting door into the next office. The werewolf just kept coming. Doors merely slowed him down. They looked like they were going through a wood chipper as the thing's claws ripped them to pieces. I knew I needed to get out of my shoes, but there were buckles on the ankle straps and the werewolf wasn't giving me time to unhook them.

At the fourth office, the wolf seemed to lose all patience. He kicked into a run as he saw me closing the door. I got it shut and threw the lock, but the werewolf just came through it.

Chip and I were cowering behind the desk. I smelled the faint whiff of Frédéric Malle. This was Caroline's office. I yanked out the bottom drawer of the desk. Her small makeup kit was there, along with a bottle of hair spray.

I straightened up and looked into slavering jaws. I closed my eyes and held down the plunger. My eyes snapped open at the scream of fury and outrage. The wolf was snarling and spitting, red tongue lolling out of its mouth. Apparently I'd sent the spray right down his throat. I took the opportunity to pick a different target. The mist shot into those maddened eyes. The wolf screamed and pressed his hands against his watering eyes.

I dropped my pathetic weapon and grabbed Chip, and we headed back into the reception area. If the elevator was still there, we could get on and reach the ground floor. There was security at the building's front desk. But why would they have let a werewolf onto the elevator? Because the guard was dead? Or maybe because our attacker hadn't been in wolf form when it entered the building? He might have transformed in the elevator.

It was crazy that my mind was concerned with these stupid issues—or maybe that was the only way I could keep from becoming catatonic with fear. Chip was resting more and more of his weight on me. I could feel my legs buckling, and then the weight was suddenly gone. Chip screamed. I looked back. The werewolf had reared up onto its legs and held Chip between his hands. The claws penetrated Chip's body. He screamed again as the wolf yanked his claws in opposite directions. Internal organs spilled from the gaping tears in Chip's body and onto the floor. Blood fountained from torn arteries, splashing on the desks, walls, and even the ceiling.

The room reeked of blood and feces, overlaid with the scent of the calzone Chip had eaten for dinner. I vomited, then started screaming as I ran full out for the bank of elevators. I was dully aware of the agony in my toes as they were driven deep into the pointed tips of my shoes. I could hear the thud of paws hitting the floor behind me, getting closer and closer. I was sobbing now, I had no breath left to scream, and my mouth tasted of bile.

There were four elevators. I had no idea which one had delivered the killer to my floor, and I realized I wasn't going to have time to find out. I could feel the werewolf's hot, rancid breath on my neck. I glanced back. His arms were outstretched, his claws ready to tear me apart. He gathered himself and leaped.

Suddenly the heel on my right shoe broke. I pitched toward the floor, but I managed to throw out my hands to keep from face-planting. The gray-and-brown body flew over me. The massive fur-covered form hit the metal doors of the elevator, and they popped open. Not a lot, but it was enough to allow the werewolf to fall through.

I heard an almost human cry of terror. One hand scrabbled at the edge of the hole, then there was a rapidly receding wailing cry. I lay panting on the floor for a few more seconds, then cautiously crawled over to the sprung doors and looked down.

The werewolf had rolled snake eyes. Service lights threw shadows down the long, empty shaft. The heavy cables that pulled the elevator were vibrating softly. I could picture that falling body, hands reaching out desperately to grip the cables, trying to stop the plunge down seventy stories.

I hoped he'd gone splat.

"You were incredibly lucky, miss." The speaker was Lucius Washington, a NYPD homicide detective.

It was almost two a.m. I was seated in the conference room on the seventy-third floor sipping a hot tea spiked with a bit of brandy from Shade's office, and wrapped in a coat someone had left in coat check back in the winter. It was July, but I was freezing. Shade stood just behind my chair, and he kept rubbing my shoulder when I shuddered. It wasn't actually helping, because he was a vampire and his hand was really *cold*.

Lieutenant Washington was African-American, tall, and slim in that way runners and swimmers are slim. His skin was the color of rich caramel and there was the hint of an epicanthic fold to his warm brown eyes. He also had a voice like dark velvet. The overall impression he projected was calm. It was incredibly comforting after the chaos on the seventieth floor.

After the werewolf had taken a swan dive down the elevator shaft, I had managed to get back to my office and my cell phone. It was horrible, because there was no way to avoid going past the mess of blood, muscle, and viscera that had once been Chip. After my call to 911, I'd called my dad. It had taken him a few minutes to understand because I was crying so hard. After making Soothing Daddy Noises he asked if I'd called the police. I said I had. Then he asked, "Linnie, is Shade likely to bring in a Hunter?"

The strangeness of the question had broken me momentarily out of my shock. "No, why would he?" And then I shrieked at him, "I know what killed Chip! It was a werewolf! I saw him kill Chip!"

"Miss?"

"Huh? What?"

"I said, you're lucky to be alive."

"Yes, I know." I lifted up my foot and looked at the ragged tear where the heel of my shoe had been. "I think I must have weakened my shoe when I almost fell off my chair. I caught myself on the heel."

Nothing changed in Lieutenant Washington's expression, but I had a feeling he thought I was an idiot if I could fall out of a chair. I hurried to explain. "I have this weird ball chair. Not a normal chair . . . It can be . . . tippy."

*Tippy? Tippy?* Now he *knew* I was an idiot. I stared up at him and wished the floor would open up and swallow me.

"That's okay. Whatever the cause, it's a real good thing your heel broke. It saved your life." I shuddered and took another sip of tea, and Washington laid a hand lightly on my wrist. His touch was a good deal warmer and more comforting than Shade's. "Any idea who the wolf might have been?" he asked.

I shook my head. "He wasn't exactly wearing ID."

Washington gave me a strange look. I pressed a hand to my forehead as if I could squeeze out the headache that was forming behind my eyes and push back the dumbass remarks that fluttered on my tongue like maddened butterflies.

"I'm sorry," I mumbled. "I don't mean to be flippant, but that may be the only thing that's keeping me from retreating into gibbering hysteria."

"That's okay," he said again. "People deal with stress in different ways. There is no right way. Now, do you think the wolf was after you, or Mr. Westin?"

"I'm not sure. I think Chip."

Washington stood. "I better get downstairs and see what Forensics has for me," he said to Shade.

But something in our exchange finally jump-started my traumatized brain cells. "Wait," I called before he reached the door. Washington looked back. "The big case we're working on involves werewolves."

"What kind of case?" Washington asked.

A page in The Code of Professional Responsibility concerning lawyer/client confidentiality came floating past my mind's eye. I had probably said too much already, but what the hell, in for a penny, in for a pound. "It's an estate dispute between our clients and Securitech." I figured he would have heard of Securitech. A lot of cops and military went to work for them after they retired.

I was right, because Washington gave a soundless whistle and wrote it down. The policeman left. I looked up at Shade. He was frowning at me.

"You shouldn't have mentioned the case."

"I know. I'm sorry. But the filings are public record, and it's been going on almost as long as I've been alive. And it doesn't seem to be high on the priorities list with Ishmael, McGillary and Gold. And Chip's been murdered, which I think should reset the table."

"You've pulled Securitech into a police investigation. Someone will leak it to the press, and Gunther, Piedmont, Spann and Engelberg will accuse us of dragging Securitech into a sordid murder purely in an attempt to damage their client's reputation with the arbitrator."

"Shade, don't you care that Chip's been killed?"

"Of course—"

But before he could say more there was a preemptory knock. Without a pause the door opened. A gaggle of partners trooped in, led by Gold with McGillary a step behind. The lesser partners marched behind like mourners at a New Orleans funeral. Ryan was among them, and he gave me an encouraging smile.

Gold strode up to me. Shade again laid his hand on my shoulder, and he and Gold glared at each other. I was between them, and as the tension sparked I felt like a small, squeaking rodent trapped between mastodons.

Gold loomed over me. "What do you know about this?" He had curly black hair, intense black eyes, and a powerful build, and if he hadn't been dead his face would probably have been brick red.

Shade interposed himself between us, and his tall, lean form seemed fragile next to Gold's bulk, but there was nothing timid in his expression. McGillary, hovering on the outskirts of the confrontation, looked like he wished he were invisible, which would be tough given his carrot-colored red hair.

"Leave her be," Shade said.

"I demand an answer," was Gold's response. "Chip worked here for twenty-eight years. Then she arrives, and this happens."

"No way are you blaming this on me," I shot back. I was still shaky, but this amount of 'tude after what I'd been through was starting to piss me off. "I just graduated in May, and while Yale is cutthroat, it doesn't usually produce enemies who want to *kill* you!" I realized I had stood up, and was shouting at him. Gold blinked at me and actually took a step back. I raged on.

"No, that wolf had to be after Chip. If I hadn't run out of the kitchen when I heard Chip scream, he might not have known I was there. I could have just hidden until it was all over. And it has to be about one of his cases, because I'm pretty damn sure a werewolf didn't attack him because of his kid's soccer games, or because he and his wife liked to play bingo at church on Wednesday nights. And . . . and Chip didn't deserve to die like that." And suddenly I was wailing like a lost five-year-old.

It struck me that I had transitioned from raging harridan to sniveling child in the space of about three seconds. They probably thought I was certifiable. *Way to go, Ellery. Way to impress your bosses.* My knees turned to rubber and I sat back down. And suddenly I was horribly aware that I had vampires on three sides of me, and I couldn't retreat because I was trapped in a chair.

"She has the right of it," I heard Shade say as if from a great distance. "Chip was my *súbdito de casa*. I will see justice done."

My mind provided the translation. *Subject or servant of the house.* And in that moment I had a total understanding of the relationship between the vampires and the humans. Despite having been fostered in a vampire household where I felt like I belonged, I was hit with the disheartening thought that Mr. Bainbridge probably described me that way to his guests. *"Yes, Linnet is a delightful little thing. My súbdita de casa."*

"We need to discuss how to handle this," Gold said, and then the three partners were gone, and I began to cry again. Mostly for Chip, but some of the tears were for me. Someone laid a hand on my shoulder. I squeaked, jumped, and looked around. Ryan was standing next to my chair.

"Let me take you home," he said softly.

"I can take a cab—"

"No." He got a hand under my arm, and helped me to my feet. We made our way slowly toward the door. "And for what it's worth . . . I think you're absolutely right. It had to be something Chip was working on." He paused and looked down at me. "Don't you dare come in tomorrow . . ." He broke off and checked his watch. "Today. You stay home and get some rest."

We rode down the elevator and stepped out into the lobby. It had become a crime scene too. Yellow tape blocked the door. There was a lot of blood behind the security officer's desk, and a few random splashes on the marble walls. There was no security guard present. Just a black body bag with a human-sized bump. Evidence techs, dressed in white jumpsuits with booties covering their shoes, were taking swabs and samples. One of them lifted the tape to allow us out of the elevator and guided us around the edge of the lobby, where there was no blood.

We stepped through the front doors, and an explosion of light struck my tear-sore eyes. Light glinted off the lenses of television cameras, transforming them into cyclopean monsters. The fourth estate had arrived; in force and with a vengeance.

"Who died?"

"Was it a werewolf?"

"Was it a vampire ritual?"

"How did you survive?"

"I hear you killed the attacker."

"How?"

Ryan put his arm around my shoulders and stiff-armed the ravening hoard.

"Ow!"

"Jesus Christ, guy!"

"Back off!" Ryan roared, and such is the power of the vampire that they obeyed.

A limo was idling curbside. A driver jumped out and yanked open the back door. I tumbled in, my entrance speeded along with a boost from Ryan. The door fell shut with a heavy clunk, cutting off the hysterically shouted questions. The car shot away, merging quickly into the flow of traffic on Park Avenue. I yanked my blouse back up onto my shoulder.

Ryan took my hand and stroked the back of it like a man gentling a terrified horse. "Sorry about that. If I'd known they'd already arrived, I would have taken you out the back way."

"It's okay." Exhaustion dragged at my muscles, and it felt like my bones had disappeared. "I'm going to get blood in your nice car."

"Don't worry about that. Stephenson will clean it. Let's just get you home. What's your address?"

I gave it, and the driver turned past Columbus Circle so he could get on the right side of the park, then headed uptown.

"Your condo is closer, sir," the driver called back.

Ryan cocked a questioning eyebrow at me. "What do you say? You want to go to my place?"

I shook my head. "I really just want to be alone."

Ryan backed off immediately. "I understand. Let's just make sure there's nobody waiting at your place."

The thought chilled me, and I almost reconsidered his offer. But I had no clothes, and I wanted to throw away the ones I was wearing.

"Would you check the place for me? In case it was about me and not Chip," I quavered.

"Of course."

At three thirty a.m. there wasn't much traffic—for New York.

We reached my building in fifteen minutes. The driver unlimbered a tire iron from the trunk, and we all rode up in the elevator.

Ryan and Stephenson checked all three rooms and the closet while I waited in the hall. There were no werewolves lurking.

After they left, I jammed every stitch of clothing I had been wearing into a garbage bag. Wrapped in a robe with slippers on my sore feet, I padded down the hall to the garbage chute. Returning to my apartment, I filled the old claw-footed tub to the rim with the hottest water I could stand and crawled in. But I still smelled Chip's blood even after I'd washed my hair three times and frenziedly scrubbed my body with a loofah. When my toes and the tips of my fingers looked like pink, wrinkled raisins, I finally got out. Just before I climbed into bed, I called my dad, but he didn't answer.

My dreams were filled with blood.

# 4

I slept into the afternoon and woke up feeling like I hadn't slept at all. In addition to dreams about rivers and fountains of blood, I'd spent the night running—first from the werewolf and then from a Hunter. Unlike most dreams, these didn't fade. I staggered into the bathroom and splashed cold water on my face. *Thanks, Dad, for letting one of those faceless, slug-like creatures invade my psyche.*

The hairbrush caught in the snarls in my hair, formed by my desperate thrashing. Padding into the kitchen, I opened the fridge and immediately choked on bile. I closed it and retreated into the living room. It was probably time to turn the cell phone back on. I snagged it out of my purse and turned it on. It chimed, indicating new voice mail. I tapped on the phone icon and saw the number 36 floating over the voice mail icon.

The phone rang even as I was staring at it. I almost answered, but I stopped myself when the caller ID read *Inquirer*. I let it ring. A few seconds later, the number of voice mails changed to thirty-seven. The phone rang again. *New York Post.*

Hugging my robe tight around me, I started pacing. The phone kept ringing. I realized my feet hurt. I settled on the couch and studied my toes. They were bruised and swollen, and my baby toes had raw places where my shoes had rubbed off the skin. While I undertook the podiatry investigation, the phone rang another three times.

"Stupid shoes," I muttered. "All that money and the heel breaks—"

Which took me right back to a vision of blood-smeared muzzle and red teeth as the werewolf leaped at me. I shuddered and tears burned my eyes. Snatching up the phone, I called my parents' house. Still no answer. That could only mean Dad was on an airplane coming to me. That made me feel a little better, but I wanted to talk to somebody.

I called Mom. She and my little brother were in Paris on Charlie's Congratulations! You Graduated From High School trip.

"Linnet, *hello*," my mother's odd intonations and emphasis on the wrong syllables came through the phone.

"Mommy." The word emerged thick and tear filled. "I'm okay."

"Well, why wouldn't you be? My big grown-*up* girl with a *job*."

I wasn't feeling teary any longer. I was remembering why my mother drove me crazy. "Didn't Daddy call you?"

"Yes, and called and called, but Charlie and I were *exploring* the flesh *pots*, and I didn't want to be disturbed, so I didn't *answer*."

I tried to figure out what "exploring the flesh pots" meant and then decided I didn't really want to know.

"Did something wonderful *happen*?" my mother trilled.

"No, something horrib—"

"Paris is *won*derful, darling. You should have postponed *starting* work, and come with us."

"Mommy, listen!"

"I am listening, dear. OH WAITER, ANOTHER CHAMPAGNE, *si'l vous plait*."

"My boss was murdered last night. I almost got killed." I was shouting into the phone. This was always how things ended up between us. Why had I called?

"Oh, my dear, *how* terrible for you. Let's not *dwell. We'll* talk of pleasant things. The new *exhibit* at the Louvre is wonderful."

"I don't care about that!"

"Linnet, really. What do you *expect* me to do? We *can't* just pack *up* and come home. This is your brother's graduation present. *How* selfish of you."

Charles Grantham Ellery. Little brother. Big pain. The beloved male heir. He had been born eight months before I was sent away to the Bainbridge house. In those first lonely weeks in the Sag Harbor house, I had wondered if my parents had given me away because now they had a boy. I was older now, and intellectually I knew that was silly, but that little girl deep inside me still felt like I was second best.

"He's going to be eighteen in three weeks," I muttered resentfully. "He could manage on his own. In fact he'd probably be glad not to have his mother along."

"Which is precisely *why* I can't *leave*," my mother said in an odd moment of clarity. I had to admit she had a point. For the golden child, Charlie managed to fall into shit piles with astonishing regularity. "Oh, here, your brother wants to talk to you. Should we get a little tray of olives?"

"What?" And then I realized she wasn't talking to me.

Charlie came on the line. "Hey, sis, what's up? Are you once more a chaos magnet?" His cheerful voice crossing thousands of miles had me torn between wanting to cry and wanting to bite his head off—it wasn't fair that he was having fun.

The snark won out over family affection. Somebody needed to suffer as much as I was, and my mother was clueless. "Charlie, it wasn't like that. I was so scared and it was so awful. He was literally torn apart. There was so much blood." My voice started shaking and my words were thick with tears. What had started out as spite became an actual need for comfort.

"Whoa, whoa, whoa, what happened?"

"My boss was killed. I was there. I saw it."

There was a long silence on the French end of the call, and my baby brother surprised me by saying in an astonishingly adult voice, "I think we should come home. I'll tell Mom."

I was touched, and despite our rivalry I realized I loved this kid. "No, you stay. Finish the trip. I got my European trip after high school. You shouldn't lose out on yours."

"All right, but if you change your mind . . ."

"Believe me, I'll tell you."

I toggled through the rest of the messages, erasing all the ones from the press. I listened to only two.

The first was from Shade. "Linnet, I hope you're recovering. The police will want to talk to you again after the holiday, and you *must not* mention any of our cases. Gold is on the warpath, threatening to fire you and report you to the ethics committee. Don't worry, I'll handle this, but please don't make any more waves."

*Don't worry.* Yeah, right. I was shaking again, chilled to my core.

The second message was from Pete. "Hey, Linnet . . . wow. When you said things had come up at work, I thought you meant, like . . . well, work. This is weird, no offense, but I don't think I can deal with this kind of thing in my life right now."

And now I really didn't mind missing the date. I wondered if I might hear from Devon. If he was already in Dubai, he wouldn't see the news unless someone sent a link to him. I wished he would call. I wished somebody who cared about me would call.

I headed back to the bath and hot water.

———

After this second, long bath, I realized I was hungry. I didn't want to be alone, so I called Ray. Gregory answered.

"Hi, I was calling to see if you and Ray wanted to have late lunch or early dinner."

"Linnet, my God, are you all right? It's all over the papers. My God."

"Papers?" I repeated dully.

"Oh, honey, you sound wasted. I wish we could, but Ray's doing a matinee."

"Oh," I said, and felt my throat tighten again with unshed tears.

"I'd offer my poor self as a substitute, but I have a date with my old professor, and I've got to catch the train out to Long Island." He hesitated. "I could cancel."

"No, no. You go. I'll be okay."

"Well, I don't know how. You get yourself onto a couch, sweetie. I can give you the name of my therapist if you don't have one."

"Thanks, Gregory, that's really sweet. I'll think about it." And I hung up before I actually burst into tears. I tried Dad again. Again no answer.

Gregory's mention of the papers sent me to my computer. I brought up both the *New York Times* and the *New York Post*. The *Times* had the headline below the fold on the front page, and it was an appropriately gray statement of fact. MURDER AT LAW FIRM. I noted that the name of the deceased had not been made public pending "notification of next of kin."

The *Post* was less discreet. My picture was plastered across the front page. I was huddled against Ryan, and they had used a shot that showed a flash of bosom because my beautiful blouse had been pulled aside by Ryan's arm, and the photographer was shooting from the side. The headline screamed SEXY ASSOCIATE

SURVIVES BIZARRE DEATH RITUAL! I laid my head down on the table next to the laptop and moaned.

A knock at the door brought my head up like a gazelle that had heard a lion cough. Stiff legged, my gut shivering like Jell-O, I approached the door. I pictured ravening claws and slavering jaws.

*Don't be an idiot. Killers don't normally knock.*

My voice quavered as I called, "Who is it?"

"Linnet, dear heart, it's all right." Meredith Bainbridge's reedy voice was muffled by the door, but unmistakable.

I threw it open and fell into his cold but welcome embrace. After the initial hug, he pushed an embroidered handkerchief into my hands and escorted me back inside the apartment. He removed his wraparound sunglasses and wide-brimmed panama hat. Placing firm but gentle hands on my shoulders, he sat me down on the sofa.

Bainbridge wasn't what people picture when they think *vampire*. Movies push the image of tall, brooding, slender, smoky, sexy vampires, and indeed they often are. Vampires are attracted to attractive people just like people are attracted to attractive people. Bainbridge, however, was more like Mr. Fezziwig from *A Christmas Carol*, and *jolly* was the only word that applied. He had twinkling blue eyes, a short, rotund frame, and curly nut-brown hair. Rather than downplay his belly, he wore loud vests as if trying to draw attention to it.

He pulled over a chair from the dinette table and sat down in front of me. "All right, now tell me what happened," he ordered.

"I really don't want to talk about it."

"Yes, yes, you really do. Freud and I had some long conversations about the dangers of repression. Horrific events lose power if they're acknowledged."

The casual way he threw out the name of the father of modern psychoanalysis made me snort with laughter. "That's better," he said gently, and wiped a tear off my cheek with his thumb.

So, haltingly, I recounted the events of the night before while my stupid phone rang and buzzed and danced on the table. I ended the tale by saying, "And I got in trouble with the partners for mentioning a case. But the police asked me what might have been behind the killing, and it was a werewolf that killed him, and Securitech is owned by a werewolf and employs lots of were-wolves. . . . Oh God, I did it again."

He patted me as if I were a terrified puppy. "It's all right. If there's one thing a vampire knows how to be, it's discreet. Is that infernal thing never going to shut up?" he asked, referring to the cell phone.

"Let me turn it off." I went to the table and shut down the phone. Then I slowly turned back to face him. "Mr. Bainbridge. I know you put your prestige behind me to get me this job, but I just don't know if I can go back into that office."

He waved it off, then asked, "If you don't go back, what will you do?"

"I don't know."

"What's important to you right now?"

I remembered Chip's screams of terror and agony. "Seeing that Chip gets justice."

"Then do that." Meredith gave the tight vampire smile. "And you truly have absorbed the vampiric code."

"Grasshopper," I added.

This time Meredith didn't bother with the polite vampire smirk. He grinned at me. "Yes, I have taught you well, young Skywalker."

"Let's not confuse our pop culture references," I said, and we shared a laugh.

"Keep that sense of humor, Linnet—it's going to get you

through this," Meredith said as he stood and put his hat and glasses back on.

"Or get me fired," I said as I walked him to the door.

"If you need a bolt-hole for a few days, you know you can come home."

"I know that, and thank you. I just want to stay close so Dad can find me."

"There are these things called phones, much as I hate them," Meredith said.

"I know, but he hasn't been answering, and I just want . . ." But I wasn't sure what I wanted, so my voice trailed away.

"I understand. You want human contact. Nothing wrong with that. I'll be in touch, and don't worry about Gold. The day I can't intimidate that youngster . . ." He kissed me on the forehead, his lips cold but comforting. "Now go take a walk. It will make you feel better. It's a beautiful day and you're not dead."

"Yeah, the not dead thing. That's a good thing, right?"

"Yes, it's a good thing."

He left and I turned the phone back on. It rang. It was the *New York Post* again. I donned a big straw hat and Greta Garbo sunglasses and, looking like a vampire myself, I fled the apartment. Central Park on a holiday weekend would be crawling with people, and I could lose myself among them.


I was sitting by the carousel, flicking my eyes between the monotonous rise and fall of the horses and nervously scanning the crowds for werewolves. The nasal toot of the calliope playing a spritely waltz was an odd counterpoint to the shrieks of joy or terror erupting from the urchins on the prancing horses. Somewhere nearby, a Jamaican steel drum band was playing, and in another direction I heard the breathy sound of a Peruvian flute.

Food vendors pushed their carts along the paved paths of the park. The smells of pretzels and hotdogs warred for primacy. Added to that was the pungent smell of horse manure from the carriage horses waiting patiently at the curbs and clopping slowly through the park, as the drivers cranked around and gave their spiels to the tourists riding behind them.

My phone rang. An hour ago, the constant calls from the press had stopped. There had either been another salacious murder or sex scandal to replace mine, or the reporters had given up. They were probably writing that I'd been implicated in Chip's murder, out of spite.

But this call was from a friend. Ray was on the line. "What are you doing?" he asked.

"Watching the carousel go round and round."

"Well, get over to our place."

"I thought you were performing?"

"I called in sick and convinced Greg to put off Dr. Findle. Dinner on the roof, and fireworks to follow. You know we have a great view from our place."

"What can I bring?" I asked automatically.

"Don't be an idiot. Just yourself, of course."

He hung up. I put away my phone and headed for the edge of the park and taxis. I hadn't heard from my father, which made me feel teary all over again. Where was he? Well, he could find me at Ray and Gregory's. With cell phones no one was really ever out of touch. Unless they were in Dubai.

# 5

Ray handed me another mojito. I'd started with a margarita, but Ray had insisted I try his "fabulous" mojitos. He was making them with saki, rum, and fresh mint plucked from the pots that dotted the rooftop garden. Traffic sounds floated up from the streets seventeen stories below us. It was a clear night, and I could see Jupiter even through the city's light haze.

Gregory and Ray lived on the edge of Wall Street in a top-floor apartment. They had been given permission by the building owner to put up a cedar fence on one quarter of the roof, which they turned into a garden. Most rooftop gardens in Manhattan are paltry affairs: a table and two chairs, a few potted plants, and a hibachi. Ray and Gregory had thrown themselves into the project. It didn't hurt that Gregory came from money, and the money flowed to him so long as he stayed far, far away from the rest of his rock-ribbed Republican family back in Kansas.

Dwarf orange trees grew in large pots, and small, sparkling white lights had been strung through their branches. A row of box planters held herbs—mint, sage, oregano, basil, thyme, dill, tarragon, parsley, chives, and rosemary. Gregory was quite the chef, and he heaped scorn on my little turntable of bottled herbs.

Another box held tomatoes, the branches heavy with green fruit tied to poles. The shape of the poles made them look like tomato teepees. Other pots and planters held a riot of flowers—deep red geraniums, dusty miller, vinca, petunias, Canterbury bells, and lavender.

The table was set with china and flatware, and a candle flickering in a Chinese lantern provided area lighting. There was the occasional sizzle and hiss from the leg of lamb on the grill. The smell of roasting meat marinated in olive oil and herbs mingled with the scent of foil-wrapped corn roasting in the coals and the cinnamon-and-fruit smell from the freshly baked apple pie that sat on a small serving table.

I was stretched out on a lounge chair. Gregory huddled over the Weber grill, sipping a scotch on the rocks, and Ray handled bar duties—which was why I now held his signature mojito. I took a sip. The soda water laid a pleasant fizz across my tongue, and the alcohol and mint wrapped themselves around my taste buds. It was incredibly refreshing, and it tasted wonderful. The rest of the city might be baking, but here near the water swirling winds set the candle flames dancing, and I had even donned one of Ray's shirts over my halter top.

Ray stared at me with the air of a whippet hoping for a walk. "Well, what do you think?" he asked.

"Delicious," I said.

"But you're still not smiling."

"I'm not drunk enough to forget," I replied.

"Dinner," Gregory called.

Ray offered his hand and pulled me out of the lounge. As we all settled around the table, I said, "I feel like I'm a horrible person."

"You're not—" Ray began, but Gregory glared at him.

"Don't. You always do that. You always shut off a person when they're working through something important. You do it because you can't stand raw emotion and emotional pain."

Ray bristled. "I do it because I don't like to see my friends hurting, and I can't treat people like a lab specimen the way *you* do."

"Excuse me." I held up my hand. "I'm the one who's just endured the trauma. You guys can work out your personal glitches on your own time, and not when I need to be the center of attention."

Everyone laughed, including me, but the effort of being glib and cheerful seemed to have sucked all the strength out of me. It was exhausting to lift a forkful of food to my mouth.

"How are things at the firm?" Gregory asked. "Are they giving you time off?" I shook my head. "Bastards."

"No, I don't want to take any time off because I'm afraid they wouldn't let me come back. I'm in big trouble because I talked about a case to the police. One of the big bosses wants me fired. And that's why I feel like an awful person—because I've been thinking more about keeping my job then I have about poor Chip. I feel like a bug on a pin. I want to help the police, but I have obligations as a lawyer, and if I get fired after only two weeks . . ." Tears burned my eyes. "God, how can I face everybody? Especially my dad. I mean my human dad. It meant so much to him that I become a lawyer, and work for a big firm."

Ray and Gregory got out of their chairs, made a manwich, and gave me a hug. For a few moments I let them, then I straightened and pushed them away. "Your dinners are getting cold."

For a few minutes we all ate in silence. I was reaching for the salt when Gregory said, "Try squeezing lemon juice on the corn. It's orgasmically good." He was right, and I savored the explosion of sweet, yeasty flavor as the kernels crunched between my teeth.

"I feel like Nero Wolfe," I said. "Well not in size," I hastened to add at Gregory's look of horror.

"Who's Nero Wolfe?" Ray asked.

"The enormously fat hero in a series of detective novels," Gregory said. "He grew orchids and was a notable gourmand."

"He liked fresh corn on the cob," I added. "That's what made me think of him. . . ."

"What?" Ray asked as my voice trailed away.

"We have a detective at the firm."

"Okay," Gregory drawled. "And this is relevant how?"

I stood up and paced. "He works for the firm. I can give him information about Chip's cases, and I won't be violating confidentiality. He can follow up on any leads. That way I'll be helping Chip, and I won't feel like such a shit."

"And protecting your job. Wins all around," Ray said.

I suddenly felt better and hungry. I returned to my chair and started to eat—and dropped my fork when a loud *BOOM* echoed across the water. The night sky flared red, then blue, then white.

"The fireworks are starting," Ray cried with the joy of an eight-year-old.

Gregory shook his head at this statement of the obvious, but he smiled as he watched Ray rush over to the side of the building facing New York Harbor. Gregory stood and offered me his arm. "Shall we join him?"

"Absolutely."

Off to our right the Macy's fireworks display thundered off barges in the Hudson River, but the president had decided to provide a federal display on Liberty Island. Sparks fell past Liberty's shoulders.

"Trust the president to kick off his reelection campaign by wrapping himself in the flag until he chokes," Gregory said.

"I know that's probably true, but don't be a cynic. Not tonight," Ray said.

The wind off the water faintly carried the notes of "Stars and Stripes." I'm a sentimental sap, and my umpty-ump great-grandfather, William Ellery, had been a signer of the Declaration of Independence, so I had tears in my eyes. Gregory threw up his hands.

"God, I'm surrounded."

Ray twined his arms behind Gregory's neck. "Admit it. That's why you love me. Because I'm sincere."

The older man smiled down at him. "Well, that's one reason." They embraced. I looked away.

Their love made me feel so horribly alone. Once again, I questioned the wisdom of ending things with Devon. When you share your life with someone, the good times are better and the bad times are less bad. I sternly warned myself not to romanticize my time with Devon. Toward the end, it hadn't been all unicorns, rainbows, and cotton candy. It had been about competing goals and who yielded to the other. I hated power games, so I'd taken my ball and gone home. Except I wasn't sure which home I belonged in, the vampire one or the human one.

The grand finale was starting. Some of the secondary explosions looked like spinning galaxies out over the water, and Lady Liberty seemed to be wearing a crown of stars. It reminded me of a statue of the Virgin I'd seen in the Basilica of St. Francis of Assisi. My father loved the Virgin Mother, and he always lit a candle in any Lady Chapel he entered. I had adopted the habit, but in my case the candle was always for him. So, *where the hell was he?*

I turned my back to the figure in the harbor. Was it trauma

that made every train of thought take me back to the men who were in (or out) of my life?

The trip home required a decision—subway or taxi? A taxi was potentially safer, but there was also safety in numbers, and the subways had police on duty who had guns. My vivid imagination made me picture being stuck in traffic when a werewolf ripped the door off the cab, yanked me out, and tore . . . I cut off that line of thought and decided on the subway.

I walked toward the green globe glowing on the corner, past the windows and doors of restaurants spilling light, conversations, and the clink of silverware on china onto the sidewalk. They were a pleasant contrast to the dark, blank shutters of the neighboring stores. Above the stores were offices and apartments. From the apartments came the sounds of televisions, radios, voices, and children's laughter.

The lonesome sound of a saxophone floated up the stairs as I descended to the station. The musician was an elderly African-American man. I threw five dollars into his instrument case as I passed, and he nodded his thanks.

The platform was filled with people heading home from various Fourth of July celebrations. The mood was exuberant, so the nervous couple alternatively huddled against and studying the subway map hung on the tiled wall stood out like gazelles in . . . well, in New York. I debated walking over and speaking to them, but New York teaches you to keep to yourself. Zones of privacy are really important when you have over eight million people living in about three hundred square miles.

The woman made the decision for me. She sidled over to me, eyes flicking nervously from side to side as more people drifted down the stairs and gathered on the platform.

"Excuse me, my husband and I are tryin' to get back to our hotel." The distinctive drawl of the South flattened every vowel. She fumbled in her purse and pulled out a card. "It's the Amsterdam Inn on West Seventy-sixth street. Are we in the right place?"

"Yes, this train is going uptown. I'm going past there, so I'll signal you when to get off."

"Oh, thank you." She motioned vigorously to her husband to join us. As he lumbered over, I reflected that he looked like a high school or college football player now gone to middle-aged seed. "This nice young lady says we're in the right place, honey."

He gave me a big, warm smile. "Thanks. This place is a little overwhelming."

"Where are you from?" I asked, resigned to conversation during the ride.

"Muscle Shoals, Alabama. I know, I know, funny name, but we've got some real history. W. C. Handy, Father of the Blues"—the pride in his voice provided the capital letters—"and Helen Keller were all from Muscle Shoals. I own a chain of family restaurants, Yummy's. Debbie, here, wanted to celebrate her birthday in New York City, so here we are." He thrust out a hand. "Todd Bingham."

"Pleased to meet you, and welcome."

"Are you from here?" Debbie asked. "I thought you must be, a little thing like you, riding the subway all by yourself at night."

"Actually, I'm originally from Rhode Island. I moved down here a month ago from Connecticut, where I went to school."

"And you're not scared?" Debbie asked.

"Uh-uh." I gave her a smile. "The city isn't that dangerous." The husband gave me a look that suggested I was on crack. "Of course, there are places I don't go, but they're few and far between. Basically you just have to avoid looking like a victim, and you'll be fine."

In a world where werewolves, vampires, and Álfar had stepped out of the shadows and taken power, that really was the trick for an ordinary human. It was like Debbie read my mind, because she leaned in close and whispered, "I think I've seen *three* vampires while we've been here."

"You probably have."

She shivered, and I couldn't tell if it was due to delight or alarm. She said, "We don't have them down our way. It just kind of adds to the excitement of New York."

"Well, they better leave my girl alone," Todd said, and gave his wife a quick hug. "And I gotta say, the werewolves bother me more. To think somebody who looks human can just turn like that. Creepy."

And that, I thought, was why the Powers tended to congregate in major metropolitan areas—New York, Los Angeles, Washington, DC, London, Paris. People in urban areas were generally more accepting of different lifestyles. But until the Powers started living in places like Muscle Shoals, they were never going to be fully accepted. They were going to continue to be a source of titillation and dread, as evidenced by the Binghams.

The train's arrival was heralded by a gust of warm air. The subway rumbled into the station, brakes squeaking as it slowed and came to a stop. The doors opened with a sucking sound, and we stepped aboard.

I got the Binghams off at their stop, and was surprised and touched when Todd gave me his business card and promised me a free meal at Yummy's if I ever got to Muscle Shoals.

I then half-closed my eyes and scanned my fellow riders. Rocking with the swaying of the car, lulled by the clatter of the wheels, I watched a young Hispanic couple cuddling across from me. He was trying valiantly to grow a mustache, but right now he just looked like he had a dirty upper lip. The girl was gorgeous, with a tumbled mane of black hair and gold jewelry that glowed against her amber-colored skin.

In the front of the car, a bearded Hasidic man in his black suit, hat, and *payot* sat reading. Not Proust, but the summer's latest potboiler. Its lurid cover seemed to pulse under the flickering lights. It was a perfect antidote to cliché.

Best of all, none of them looked like werewolves.

At 181st Street, I got off and headed up to the sidewalk. My phone chimed. I had a message. It was my dad. And he had sent a car for me.

The driver pulled up at the door of the Sofitel. The doorman opened the door and assisted me out of the car. The bell captain had instructions to bring me directly up to my father's room. The care was so extreme that I almost expected the bell captain to place me on a luggage cart and roll me up to the room so I wouldn't have to walk.

A discreet knock, and the door flew open. My dad held out his arms. I raced into his embrace and burst into tears. The bell captain closed the door on our emotional reunion.

Daddy provided me with a handkerchief. The way his first action echoed Meredith's was sort of disconcerting, but I wiped my eyes, blew my nose, and allowed him to lead me over to the sofa in the room. His eyes were red rimmed and his features slack with exhaustion. His jet-black hair, frosted with silver at the temples, was tousled. I touched his cheek.

"Daddy?"

"It's all right, honey. Everything is all right now."

"They're going to fire me."

"No, they're not. That's why I didn't come to you right away. I went to see Bainbridge. He called Gold and McGillary and told them he would take it as a personal affront if his fosterling was dismissed. Your job is safe."

I blinked in confusion. "But I just saw Meredith. Well, a few hours ago. He came to my apartment."

There was a brief moment of silence, then he said, "Yeah, he said he was going to."

"But he hadn't talked to the partners then."

"He called me and told me what he'd done."

"Oh, okay."

Respect is a big deal with vampires, and Bainbridge had just warned the partners that I was still under his protection. It should have been a relief, but I was still confused. "You went first to Meredith before you came to me?"

"It couldn't wait. If they actually fired you, their sense of honor would never permit them to hire you back." He hugged me again. "I'm sorry, honey, but this was important."

"And how is it that my job is more important than my mental health?"

He smiled at me. "I know you. If you'd lost this job your mental health would be in a far worse state. You're too competitive."

"And who made me that way?" He swayed, pretending my fist bump to the shoulder had rocked him back.

"Guilty as charged."

My smile died and I shook my head. "I can't get it out of my head. I just keep remembering . . ."

"You won't forget, but the horror will fade. And you're an Ellery. We don't quit. You'll make me proud. You always do."

We sat silent for a few moments. I gave myself a shake. "You're right. I have to go back. I've got to find out why this happened."

"Linnet, it's not your job to solve murders. That's a job for the police. You let them do their job and you do yours. You keep your head down and just be a lawyer."

It was good advice. Which I probably wasn't going to follow.

# 6

When I reached home late on Sunday night, there was a message that all associates were to return to work on Tuesday—which gave me Monday to start my investigations.

I started with a Google search to see if there were any angry debtors bitching about Chip. I didn't find any. Next I checked for open civil or criminal cases. Again, nothing. So maybe he had a secret life in Atlantic City, or a mistress stashed in Jersey—though how I was going to find that was unclear.

I decided to try the direct approach and go to his house. My computer skills were sufficient to garner an address, and soon I was riding the subway out to Brooklyn. I located the apartment building, then got cold feet. How could I impose on a recent widow? I knew Chip had kids. They'd be there too. I walked nervously down the street, noting the plethora of Italian restaurants and an Italian bakery. I considered Chip's waistline, then entered the bakery. There were three women wearing crisp white aprons over their street clothes, and hair nets securing their red, black, and gray hair. I ordered an amaretto macaroon and took a bite of chewy coconut goodness. I then asked casually if Mr. Westin was a customer.

A wall of suspicion went up. "Why? Are you one of those ass-hole journalists?" the gray-haired woman demanded.

"No, no." I held up placating hands. "I worked with Chip. I'm an officer of the court." (Not a lie.) "And I've been asked to make a few inquiries. We're all devastated by what's happened, and we want to get to the bottom of this."

"Well, okay." The three women exchanged glances. *Here it comes*, I thought, *I'm going to find out something disreputable. Something that will shed light on the killing.*

"Mr. Westin was just the best. We've provided the cakes for every one of his kids' birthdays."

"Do you know if Chip made trips out of town, particularly on weekends?" I was pursuing my notion of Chip as rogue gambler.

"No, he came in every day to buy a coffee and a danish before he headed to the subway, and on weekends the whole family came in. Saturdays were cookie days, and on Sundays it was chocolate and almond croissants," said the red-haired woman.

The image of Chip as secret swinger vanished with a pop. "Well, thanks. And I'll take a dozen of those macaroons. They're amazing."

Provided with a white box neatly tied with a string, I headed back onto the street and spent the next few hours talking with the pharmacist at the drug store, the guys at the shoe repair store, and the clerks at the toy store. I ducked in and out of restaurants and sandwich stands. Everyone knew Chip. Everyone liked Chip. Everyone was worried about the family. I ended up eating a late lunch at one of Chip's haunts and doodling around the map of Italy printed on the paper placemat. I had meant to make notes summarizing my research, but it boiled down to this: Chip was a really nice guy who had spent his life either at the office or at home with his family.

I finished my ravioli, paid, and started back toward the subway.

As I passed the apartment building, I realized there was a funeral parlor, Purelli and Sons, directly across from the front doors of the apartment. There was still one last question to be asked. Maybe Chip and his wife had presented a normal facade to the world, but had crazy, dangerous visitors.

There was a man in a rather too snappily cut black suit loitering in the door of the funeral parlor and smoking a cigarette. He had slicked-back black hair and a long face, and looked to be around forty. I crossed the street and realized he was watching my approach with a knowing smile.

"Hello, Nancy Drew," he said as I stepped up on the curb.

"I beg your pardon?"

"Nancy Drew, girl sleuth. You've been asking about Chip all around the neighborhood."

"And how would you know that?" I demanded.

The man gave me a smile and a wink as he tapped the side of his nose. "There's not a lot that goes on in this neighborhood that we don't know about."

I looked up again at the name of the funeral home. "Don't tell me. You're the mob funeral parlor." He just gave me another smile and flicked ash onto the sidewalk. "Okay, I may as well cross every T. Did Chip and his wife have strange guests or wild parties?"

"They played canasta on Friday nights. Does that qualify?" I just stared at him. My feet were tired, it was hot, and I was beginning to face the reality that the reason for Chip's murder had originated at the law firm. I had been working with Chip on the only big case he had, ergo . . . I looked nervously over my shoulder.

Something in my expression must have penetrated, because the grinning undertaker stopped smiling. "Look, kid, Chip was a decent guy and a good neighbor. We're providing the casket, the hearse, everything. Now, I really hope you're not going to bother the family, because Susie and the kids don't need that." I nodded and started to walk away. "You were smarter than the cops, though. You talked to the neighborhood, not just the immediate neighbors in the building."

I nodded and almost ran to the subway. I wondered how many locks I could add to my apartment door. Then I remembered the hound bursting through the office doors. Locks weren't going to help.

The lobby was still a crime scene. A burly cop, with more gut than was probably strictly regulation, waved all the tenants toward the delivery entrance in the back of the building. Another cop guided us onto the freight elevators. I had dispensed with the hat, but I was still wearing the Garbo glasses. Whispers pursued me, but no one spoke to me directly, as if murder might be catching. I had been an outcast before. Now I was a pariah.

The seventieth floor was also off-limits. All the associates, secretaries, and legal secretaries ended up milling around in the library. The senior partners made a call to One Police Plaza and a few hours later a group of cops, under the supervision of the vampire partners, boxed up our files and brought them up to us.

I had a lot of boxes, and once I pulled back the flap on a couple of them I realized why. I had files from not only my office, but Chip's as well. The momentary flash of excitement was followed closely by a frantic yammering in the back of my head.

*But you're ninety percent sure it was something in his cases that got him killed! So if you take over the cases, you might get killed too. Let a vampire take over. They're dead already.*

But I also wanted justice for Chip, and since the personal life angle had been a bust I needed to tear into his files and try to find the reason for his murder. I clicked on the stopwatch program on my laptop and settled down to read. When you have no idea what you're looking for, anything might be significant, so I was concentrating like mad. But it was hard to sustain that amount of focus when most of the reading was boring. Securitech might be a mercenary army, but its financial statements were just like any other company's—dull.

There was another subgroup of papers that was silly rather than boring. My favorite was a six-inch-thick file dealing with increasingly testy arguments over the valuation of an alpaca farm in Taos, New Mexico. Why Henry Abercrombie had owned an alpaca farm in Taos, New Mexico, had never been addressed. Maybe Securitech was training them for secret military missions in South America.

The final category was provided courtesy of our clients, that was the batshit-crazy files.

And I had only gotten through two boxes out of twenty-three.

My cell phone rang. I checked the incoming number and felt my heart lift. I knew that number. For three years it had been the emotional focus of my life. Devon. "Oh, God, you called. I'm so glad you called," I blurted out.

"Linnet, are you okay?" He had a soft baritone and just hearing his voice brought back memories and regrets.

"Physically, yeah. Emotionally, not so much. How did you hear?"

"My mother sent me an e-mail." He sounded very far away. I knew it was probably illusory, based on the many miles and time zones that separated us. My face felt hot, there was a pricking behind my eyelids, and I struggled to swallow past the tightness in my throat. If I had married him, I'd be safely in Dubai. None of this would have happened to me. Maybe I'd been stupid. Could our relationship be repaired? No, too much time had passed, and with it my chance at that life.

"What happened?" Devon asked.

"There was a werewolf. He killed Chip and tried to kill me."

"That's horrible." There was an awkward pause.

"Yes." Another long stretch of silence. "What time is it over there?" I asked. He told me, and we fell silent again.

"Well, listen . . ." I began.

"Well, I better get . . ." he started.

We laughed nervously. "You first," Devon said.

"I better get back to work."

"Me too."

"Thanks for calling," I said softly, struggling to hide the thickness in my voice.

"Sure. You take care."

He hung up. I stared at the phone and longed to call him back. And not just on the phone.

I gave my nose a defiant blow and wiped my eyes. Then I pulled open the top of box number three and dove back into the current of legalese. A soft touch on the bare skin of my arm made me jump and gasp. It was Shade.

"Pardon me, Linnet."

I was suddenly aware of the surprising number of sounds in the normally hushed library. The click, like chickens pecking on concrete, of computer keyboards. Low-voiced conversations and the grind and hiss of an espresso machine disgorging another cup of coffee. It too had been lugged up from the seventieth floor. I forced myself to focus on Shade.

"Our security has informed me that Lieutenant Washington is coming upstairs. The partners would prefer that you offer him no further information. He has your statement. Nothing else is necessary."

"All right."

Shade seemed startled at my meek acquiescence. "Well . . . that's . . . good."

"I'm going to blame you."

"Beg pardon?"

"Well, not you, you. You, the partners. I'm betting the officer won't be happy with me when I clam up, and I don't want him blaming me."

"That's acceptable," the vampire said.

Shade left. I waited, checked my watch, waited some more. Finally I went back to excavating the box.

I opened an envelope from the county clerk's office in Appomattox County, Virginia. I glanced briefly at the letter, picking up a word here and there. *Dear Sir . . . regret to inform . . . document is unavailable . . . fire . . . 1997.* I returned the letter to the envelope and set it aside. I'd figure out what Chip had requested later.

Another envelope and another letter. *Nitrogen . . . viability . . . expected shipment . . .* Oh, God, it was a letter about valuing frozen alpaca sperm. I saw Detective Washington approaching and set aside the letter with relief. Only alpaca sperm could make a visit from the police seem like a good thing.

The lieutenant reached my carrel. "How you doing?"

"Okay. Well, kind of okay. Actually, barely okay."

"And that's okay too," he said, and smiled at me. "You had one hell of an experience." He pulled over a chair and sat down. "You think of anything that might be helpful?"

Nervously twisting a pen through my fingers, I shook my head and said, "Not really. No."

He pushed. "Anything at all? Some offhand remark by Mr. Westin, a phone call he received where he sent you out of the room?"

I shook my head again and added, trying to shove him away from questions about cases, "Maybe it didn't have anything to do with his work. Maybe it was something from his private life." I said it even though I knew it wasn't true.

"We're checking on all that," Washington said gently and patiently.

"Well, duh . . . yes, of course you are. How stupid of me to be telling you how to do your job." I ran a hand through my hair. "I'm sorry."

"No problem. This Securitech case, was it likely that the company was going to have to fork over?" the police officer asked.

"Well . . . uh . . . look, I'd really like to help—" I broke off, took a deep breath, and just said it. "I've been instructed not to answer any questions regarding our cases or clients." I sounded like a bitch even in my own ears.

"Your boss gets disemboweled in front of you, and you toe the company line?" His evident scorn and the reminder of what I'd witnessed only two nights before, set me to shaking.

"I have a duty."

"Obviously not to the dead," Washington said, and stalked away.

If he was trying to shame me, he missed the mark. I had started an investigation, and while one could argue that it might have been better left to the cops, I had a distinct skill set that made me more likely to succeed. The key was in the case and I had the training to find it. Once I figured it out, I'd tell Detective Washington.

Late in the afternoon, the senior partners had coffee and a selection of pastries delivered to the library. The milling crowd of associates was like a herd of thirsty cows heading for water.

Sometimes being small has its advantages. I ducked under a couple of outstretched arms and snagged a slice of Sacher torte and an iced latte that looked like it needed a home.

I took a bite of the chocolate and apricot goody, then spotted Caroline sipping a black coffee. She didn't have a pastry. I swallowed the bite and felt like my hips spread two inches.

David Sullivan walked past. He also had a cup, but his drink left a faint red line on his upper lip. He caught me looking, made a face, and gestured with his cup. "House blend. Half pig blood, half blood bank, most of which seems to have been donated by drunks. Nasty." He glared up toward the ceiling and the seventy-third floor. "They know I'm down here."

"Hey, at least they remembered to order you a drink," I said.

"It's still an insult."

"Okay, fine, have it your way."

The vampire started walking, but stopped after only a couple of steps. "Rumor has it that you fought with the hound."

"If by 'fighting' you mean I wielded the Mighty Can of Hairspray, then, yeah, I guess I fought."

A strange expression flickered across his face, but it was gone before I could interpret it.

"You're in poor odor upstairs," Sullivan said.

"Tell me something I don't know. I'm not exactly sure how being a witness *to*, and a survivor *of*, a murder makes me a pariah."

"We're Ishmael, McGillary and Gold. We're known for our discretion. Now there's a circus out front, and we're all over the papers."

"Yeah, Chip should have thought of that before he got murdered. What is wrong with this place? Chip was *killed*."

Sullivan shrugged. "He was a drone."

"That's an awful thing to say."

"Tell me how I'm wrong."

"Chip was a really hard worker . . . and . . . and . . ." I struggled to add another attribute then finally settled for a feeble, ". . . and a really nice man."

"I rest my case."


The exchange with Sullivan stiffened my spine. I approached the woman who served as assistant to me and two other associates. Mary was in her late thirties and whip thin, with a white streak through her chin-length black hair. It made a dramatic statement against her still young face. I wondered briefly if along with Chip's boxes, I would also inherit his assistant, the intimidating Norma. I hoped not.

"Mary, I need to talk with John O'Shea. Does he have an office in the building, or does he freelance for us?"

"He has an office on Forty-eighth Street. Mr. Gold keeps trying to get him to work with us exclusively, but he's stubborn." She cocked her head, considering. "Actually, I think he just likes frustrating Mr. Gold."

I had just picked up my purse when I noticed the gorgeous receptionist from upstairs wending his way through the crowded desks and chairs. He was coming right at me.

"Mr. Ishmael and Mr. McGillary would like to see you." I abandoned any hope of catching O'Shea. It was already 4:15. Even if the meeting with Shade and McGillary was brief, I'd never get to the detective's office before it closed for the day.

We took the stairs. I was glad. The enjoyment I'd felt while eating the slice of Sacher torte had faded to a dull ache of guilt.

Bruce, the receptionist, took me to McGillary's office, but before he tapped on the door he issued a warning. "Don't take too much of his time. He's on a very tight schedule, and you're a rather low priority."

I just stared at him, gaping. Bruce knocked lightly on the door and opened it after we heard the muffled "Come in." McGillary was behind his desk. Shade was enthroned in a large armchair. I thought Bruce would leave then, but he kept fussing about, straightening papers on the desk and rearranging the cut-crystal glasses on the sideboard. He moved a writing table in closer to Shade's right hand, then he slipped behind the desk to lean in close to McGillary and asked in tones of worshipful adoration, "Is there anything else, sir? Would you like a little pick-me-up?"

"No, thank you, my boy, that will do."

"What about you, Mr. Ishmael?"

Shade just waved him away without comment. A flash of disappointment crossed the young assistant's face, but he finally left, and I was able to study the office rather than watching Bruce's overly attentive ministrations. If Shade's office felt like the study of a European bishop, McGillary's harkened back to the Old West. Three Remingtons graced the walls. There was a large bronze of a cowboy breaking a bronco, and the furnishings were that particular blend of wood and leather known as Territorial.

There weren't a lot of seating choices available—only the couch, which was both tall and wide. I had two choices: I could sit well back on the couch, which would give me back support, but would leave me kicking my feet in the air. Given how short I was, I knew I'd look like a five-year-old. Not the image I wanted to project.

Or I could sit on the edge of the couch, which would allow my feet to touch the floor, but would make me appear to be nervous, jumpy, and ill at ease. Since I *was* nervous, jumpy, and ill at ease, I voted for the front of the couch.

"Linnet, how are you holding up?" McGillary asked.

"Fine. Happy to be back at work." McGillary and Shade exchanged a glance. Maybe the enthusiastic response had been a little too much.

"Glad to hear it." McGillary lined up the edge of some papers on his desk and gave the pens in their holder a minute turn to the right. "It's been decided to turn over all of Chip's caseload to you. Assuming you're willing."

I may not have been in the workplace long, but it didn't take a rocket scientist to figure out that you always step up and accept the challenge offered by the boss. Or you start looking for a new job. *But what if the reason for Chip's death is in those cases?* I pushed aside the fear and said, "I would be delighted."

"Good, well, it's settled then."

He stood. I stood. He began nudging me toward the door. My brief moment in the sun was over. Before he could get me out of his office, I quickly asked, "If I have any questions or problems?"

"Talk to Sullivan." McGillary was already turning away. Then he added, "Chip's cases were hardly vital, but we can't just drop them. . . ."

My heart sank as fast as his voice, dying away as he dismissed the problem of Chip, Chip's clients, and presumably me as well.

"Something was vital," I argued. "Chip was murdered for some reason."

"I'm sure it will turn out to be something to do with his private life. His cases were, at best, slight."

I considered telling him he was wrong, but I was already in enough trouble. Like Detective Washington, he'd find out once I had the answer.

McGillary's dismissive attitude had me fired up, so I dug into the boxes with renewed energy. I would find something in one of those files, or an approach to a case that would elevate it above the designation of *a Chip case*. And I'd be a modern-day Miss Marple—no, not old spinster Miss Marple. Instead, I went back to what the undertaker had called me: a modern-day Nancy Drew. I would solve the murder and win gratitude, fame, and approbation.

As expected, the bulk of the material related to the *Abercrombie* case. One of the first things that needed to happen was meeting my clients. I called Marlene Abercrombie and set an appointment for Friday. Then I called counsel representing Securitech and requested a postponement of the deposition. My counterpart down in Washington was Peggy Waite, and she agreed immediately.

"I was so shocked to hear about what happened." At least on the phone she sounded genuinely upset. "Chip was a nice man." She paused. "But maybe you'll have better luck convincing your clients to accept our offer. They're not going to win, and this is a time sink for our client."

"I didn't know there had been a settlement offer."

"Oh, several. The current one is more than generous."

"I'm just now digging into this. I'll have to unearth it."

"I'll e-mail the latest offer to you so you can at least see it, and fax over a hard copy," Peggy offered.

"Okay. I'm meeting with my clients this week. I'll let you know what they say."

"When do you want to reschedule the deposition?"

"How about three weeks. The twenty-eighth?" I suggested. I heard the quick click of the keys on a computer keyboard.

"Sorry, that won't work for me. I've got a trial and it's scheduled to last a month." There was silence and more keyboard clicks. "Actually, right after Labor Day would be my first opportunity."

*Oh God, Mr. Gelb, don't die,* I thought, but I agreed. There wasn't any other choice.

"Okay, then. September seventh?"

"Sounds good." More clicks. "I'll let the court reporter know. I look forward to meeting you, Linnet."

"Same here."

I went back to scrounging through the boxes. I found something that wasn't part of the *Abercrombie* case, a real estate dispute about the placement of a fence separating two backyards in Queens. Whoopie. I also unearthed a dispute with a contractor over the remodel of a bathroom in a condo in Yonkers. Double whoop.

My computer chimed, announcing a new e-mail had arrived. It was from Peggy, and the settlement offer was attached. I opened the file and looked at the amount. Four million. Not bad for a shit case.

I returned to the boxes and found a stack of pink phone messages for Chip, all of which had come in yesterday while I was out of the office. I riffled through the pile like a card dealer in Atlantic City, just to get a sense of the names. Eleven of the messages were from a Syd Finkelstein.

It was now early evening. I was getting hungry and thought I'd done enough for my first day back. I eyed the last box, and decided to just dig through the final five inches to see if anything interesting turned up.

Apparently, whoever had packed up Chip's office had just thrown things into boxes, because in among the papers pertaining to *Abercrombie* I found a file marked *May Divorce*. I opened it, read the first few statements in Elizabeth May's Petition for Divorce, jumped out of my chair, and let out a shout of excitement. I hastily sat back down, withering under the glares from my fellow associates. Well, to hell with them.

I had hit pay dirt.

Even though it was eight o'clock there was a light shining through the frosted, bumpy glass of the office door. Stenciled on the glass were the words *John O'Shea, Private Investigator.* There was something so forties and Sam Spade about the old brownstone building, the corner office, the old-fashioned door and lettering. O'Shea might deny it, but he was as flamboyant as his Álfar brethren in playing a role.

I knocked, and the lilting tenor invited me, "Come on in, it's unlocked."

I did, and found O'Shea sitting behind a desk in shirtsleeves, tie askew, wearing a shoulder rig. The butt of a gun thrust out of the holster.

"Ms. Ellery, isn't it?" he said. He eyed the folder I was carrying.

"You have a good memory," I said.

"You're a little hard to forget, seeing as how your picture is plastered all over the papers." I blushed, and he laughed. He came around from behind the desk and led me over to a battered old leather sofa. "What can I do for you?"

"I think I may have a lead on who killed Chip." I handed him the file.

"Okay, and you're telling me and not the police . . . why?"

"Because it involves a case, and I've already gotten spanked for giving information about *Abercrombie v. Deegan* to the police."

O'Shea was flipping through the file while I talked. A frown gathered between his upswept brows. "It does seem this hound had a temper, and he wasn't real happy with the missus filing for divorce."

"You'll check for me?"

He closed the file and tossed it across the room. Somehow the papers stayed inside and, even though the edges of the folder flapped like a hurt bird's wings, it still landed neatly in the center of his desk.

"Sure. This should be an easy one. I'll go to the husband's address and see if he answers the door. If he does, we'll know he's not a smear on the top of an elevator. Just tell your assistant to set up a billing file for this case."

"You're not on retainer?" I asked.

"I am, but the firm breaks out my hours between the various cases so they can ding the clients for my services."

"Right, of course, duh. I should have known that."

"Why would you? And besides, I don't mean to be rude, but you look exhausted."

"I am, a bit. I didn't have lunch today, and the blood sugar spike from a pastry mid-afternoon has definitely faded."

"Then we should go get some dinner."

O'Shea stood and pulled his sports jacket and hat off the wooden coatrack in the corner.

My unwary tongue took control. "You really are channeling Dashiell Hammett, aren't you?"

He flashed me a grin. "The dame walked into my office carrying a file. I knew she and it were going to be trouble. . . ." He held the door for me.

O'Shea picked a Chinese restaurant within walking distance of his office. Its linoleum floor, utilitarian metal and plastic tables, and sturdy metal chairs gave it all the ambiance of a bus station. The only attempt at decor consisted of shell paintings of goddesses riding on waves, scholarly old men with long beards sitting in bamboo forests, and panda bears.

"Do you mind if I order?" the detective asked. "I eat here a lot, and I know what's good. Any allergies?"

I blinked at him for a moment, then realized the question was directed at me. "No, just no chicken feet, please, and not too spicy."

"Wimp."

"Hey, I'm an East Coast girl."

"And salsa is the most popular condiment in America now. Where have you been?"

"Growing up in a vampire household," I replied.

"Oh. Yeah, probably not a lot of adventuresome cooking going on there."

The older woman behind the cash register glared at a teenage boy dressed in jeans and a T-shirt celebrating some grunge band. Prodded by the look, he slouched over and grunted, "You ready?"

"Yes." O'Shea rattled off the order, and the waiter went away.

"Wow, that seems like a lot of food."

"We'll split the leftovers," he said.

"I like this plan."

The first things out of the kitchen were soup dumplings. O'Shea had to show me how to hold them in one of the short, sharply bent soup spoons and bite in a way that didn't send hot soup down the front of my blouse. They were wonderful, and all I could manage were grunting sounds of pleasure as I slurped up soup and chewed at the doughy shell of the dumplings.

While we waited for the main course, O'Shea leaned back in his chair and studied me. "So, tell me about yourself."

"Not much to tell. Born in Rhode Island. Dad's a businessman; he owns a big vending machine company. Mom's . . ." I paused, struggling to find a way to describe my mother that wouldn't sound like the stereotypical mother/daughter relationship. "A housewife. She was my father's secretary, and she married him."

"You make it sound like he didn't have a choice."

"He didn't." I flashed him a smile. "I have a younger brother."

"So, how did you end up fostered?" O'Shea asked as he filled my cup with tea. The delicate aroma of jasmine wafted up from the cup.

"My dad's business connections. Vampires like to make money. My dad knows how to make money."

"They normally foster kids from powerful, well-connected families—Kennedys, Rockefellers, Du Ponts, that kind of thing. Pardon me, but what you're describing sounds rather bourgeois."

I feigned outrage, drawing myself up to my full inconsequential height. "I'll have you know that I'm a DAR, and a direct descendent of one of the signers of the Declaration of Independence."

O'Shea laughed. I joined in, relieved to discover that he got irony and sarcasm. Most Álfar seem like they need a humor implant. But maybe that was because the ones I had met were making formal calls on a powerful vampire lord. "It's funny," he said. "In some ways we're a lot alike, and in other ways polar opposites."

"How are we alike?"

A plate of kung pao chicken and a covered bowl of rice crashed down onto the table. The teenager had returned. O'Shea spooned out a large amount of rice and slathered it with the chicken dish.

"Neither one of us knows our actual families very well. I was fostered with humans. You were fostered by a spook."

"Okay, now that really is a pejorative. Is this you being all self-loathing or something?" I asked.

He grinned at me. It was a very nice grin, somehow both mischievous and warm. *It's all snake oil,* the sensible part of my brain reminded me. *He's an Álfar; they trade on charm.*

The waiter returned with our vegetable moo shu. Dumped it and left. John started spreading hoisin sauce on the translucent pancakes.

"I self-identify as human, and my parents—foster parents—are the kind of people who shower after work."

"So, you're a blue-collar elf."

"Yeah, that's a good description."

"I'm confused. I've never heard of Álfar putting up a child to be fostered."

"But I bet you've heard of changelings."

"So you were?"

"Yep, literally swapped in the crib. My human folks realized there was no hope of getting back their real son, so they made the best of the situation. I tried not to disappoint."

"What does your father do?" I asked somewhat absently, because I was fascinated by the performance being made over the construction of the moo shu.

O' Shea's chopsticks darted into the piles of stir-fried vegetables and egg, pulling out large gobs that he deposited onto the pancakes.

"He's a cop in Philly." With deft twists of the chopsitcks, O'Shea folded together the edges of the pancakes to form Chinese burritos. "So, naturally, I became a cop too."

"Oh, that's right, Chip mentioned you'd been a cop. Sorry."

"No problem. No reason you should remember my background."

A moo shu was deposited on my plate. It smelled so amazingly good, my mouth filled with saliva. I picked it up with my hands, took a bite, and mumbled around the mouthful, "You're the strangest Álfar I've ever met."

"And you're not your standard run-of-the-mill lawyer. Name one other lawyer in the firm who would have fought it out with a werewolf."

"All the vampires."

"Okay, *living* lawyers."

"You're making me sound . . . Look, I'm nothing special."

"I think the jury's out on that."

And the smile was back. The devastating, heart-flipping, soul-wrenching smile.

# 7

The next day we were back on the seventieth floor, and I discovered I had been moved out of my cave and into Chip's office. The window gave me a momentary emotional lift, followed immediately by a crushing sense of guilt. I had literally gotten this office over a man's dead body. I also remembered McGillary's words and attitude regarding Chip's cases. *Don't get too excited by this, Ellery. This is not a promotion, not really.*

For a long time I just sat and contemplated my prospects. I muttered my father's mantra. "You make your own luck."

If I could somehow bring *Abercrombie* to a successful conclusion and then start bringing in some business on my own, this still might work out. I spotted the stack of messages I'd unearthed the day before and decided to ask The Terrifying Norma about the caller.

Norma was a woman in her mid-sixties with white hair that had been coiffed until it looked like a helmet and breasts like the bulwark on a destroyer. At every break she headed for the great outdoors, where she huddled with the other cigarette refugees. The odor of smoke and tobacco hung around her formidable person.

"What do you know about this guy?" I asked as I handed over the messages.

My attention was caught by a tall glass jar sitting on the corner of Norma's desk. It was filled to the top with Hersey's Kisses—the gold-wrapped ones, which meant they had almonds in them. I unconsciously reached into the jar, only to have the back of my hand firmly slapped by Norma.

"Uh-uh, buy your own. They keep me from going nuts between smokes." I stuck my hand behind my back like a naughty child reprimanded by her governess while Norma looked through the stack. Her lips pursed in a moue of disgust. "Finkelstein, dreadful little man. He's an ambulance chaser. I can't imagine what he had to say to anyone in *this* firm, but Mr. Westin would never send him packing."

"Okay, thanks. I'll call him back when I have a free moment. Could you book a conference room for me on Friday at three p.m.? Marlene Abercrombie and her children will be coming in."

Norma made a note on a legal pad. It was filled with scribbled notes. I glanced over at her computer. The keyboard was really, really clean. It looked like Chip hadn't followed the usual pattern in a vampire law firm and dictated his correspondence. Which meant Norma was not accustomed to typing, and she probably wouldn't want that situation to change just because I'd inherited her. Or maybe she'd inherited me. That certainly seemed to be her attitude.

The next few hours were spent trying to separate the materials relating to the *Abercrombie* case into organized files. Chip might have had everything filed properly in his head, but out here in the real world it was like a giant tangle of yarn.

Eventually I had everything related to the alpacas rounded up and in its own file. I had a file for real estate. In addition to his home in Virginia, Abercrombie had a house in Portugal, a shooting lodge in Scotland, apartments in Paris and Istanbul, a condo at the Taos Ski Valley (maybe that was where he got interested in alpacas), and a beach house on the Big Island of Hawaii. I could see why the ex was unwilling to accept a lump-sum cash settlement even when she didn't have a snowball's chance in hell of winning control of the company.

I was holding a copy of the title to the 166-foot yacht and trying to decide whether it qualified as a floating house or if it needed to go into the vehicles file along with the Ferrari, the Bugatti, and the vintage WWII Jeep, when I was interrupted by a knock.

I jumped up, wondering if it might be John O'Shea, and my heart gave this curious little swoop. I squeezed my eyes shut and said out loud, "Oh, no." I really was getting a crush. But it wasn't the detective in the doorway. It was Ryan, and he was holding a beautiful calla lily plant. The blossoms were a delicate peach, and the fluorescent light glowed on the leaves.

He gave me the close-lipped vampire smile. "How are you settling in?"

"Okay." I shook my head. "But it's not the way I'd want to get a better office."

"Come on, you're a lawyer. You need to hone those shark-like instincts." This time a bit of tooth showed. I laughed, but it felt a little hollow.

"Here's an office-warming present," he said, offering me the plant.

"Thank you. It's beautiful." I took the pot and set it on a low filing cabinet beneath the window.

"I'm afraid your ficus didn't survive four days without water. I tried to resuscitate it, but I have a black thumb. That's why I wanted to get this to you right away." He gestured at the calla lily. This time my laugh wasn't so forced. "I'd also like to invite you out to Long Island to ride. We've got long days now, and riding near twilight is easier for me."

I wanted to leap at the chance, but caution about interoffice involvement made me hesitate. "This isn't a date, right?" I asked.

"No, no, a trade—horses for coaching," he said.

"Well, in that case . . . it sounds lovely. Could we do it on Friday? That gives me a little more time to pull order out of chaos." I gestured at the stacks of papers. "I'm going to meet my clients on Friday, and I have a feeling I'm going to need to blow off some steam."

"Friday it is. What say we leave from here at 6:30?"

"Sound good."

"Don't forget to pack your boots," he added with a smile, and left.

I found myself thinking less about private detectives and more about a rewarding relationship with a colleague as I plunged back into the mess. I wondered if Ryan had a hostess. Since there were no female vampires, male vampires tended to recruit older human women to fill that role. In addition to arranging social events and overseeing the care of the house, a hostess offered cover to any young woman who might be a guest in a vampire's home. It was charmingly archaic, but it served a deadly serious purpose. It protected a vampire and a human woman from any accusation that there might be a Making. Vampires and werewolves could associate with human women—sleep with them (though the act was tougher to accomplish for a vampire) and even marry them, as shown by the May file. What they could not do was turn a woman into a vampire or a werewolf. Ever.

I thought back on the two women who had filled the hostess role for Meredith Bainbridge during my childhood. Mattie had been fifty-eight when she took the position, sixty when I arrived. She had held it until her death from breast cancer seven years later. Susan had been next, and she had been sixty-three. She was still managing the Bainbridge household, and at seventy-four she showed little sign of slowing down. I thought about Shade's hostess—Debra, age sixty-eight.

I decided I would be fine. Ryan probably had a hostess, and even if he didn't, I'd be mostly in the barn. No problem.

Marlene Abercrombie looked like an animated and angry strip of beef jerky topped with a shock of dyed red hair. I knew from the files that she was eighty-four years old, but fury had apparently held off the effects of aging. She moved toward a chair in the conference room with the energy of a whirlwind.

Her three children were with her. Andrew and Angela, the twins, were sixty-one. Andrew was fat, with fleshy lips set in a perpetual pout. Angela was plump and sported a perky haircut that was too young for her face. Her hair was dyed blonde. Then there was Natalie, age fifty-five. She had the look of a "lady who lunched." She took after her mother in that she was whipcord thin, and her eyes had all the warmth of pieces of flint. Her hair had been highlighted by an expert, and her clothes were of a higher quality than those of her siblings. It looked like Natalie had married well.

They got settled, Norma went off to fetch coffee, and I settled into the chair at the head of the table. The four Abercrombies stared at me.

"Aren't you a little young to take on a case of this importance?" Andrew asked. His voice didn't match his bulk. It was high and rather reedy.

*This case is shit and a nuisance to boot, and I can tell already that I'm going to hate you all.* But I didn't say that. Instead I said, "I worked very closely with Mr. Westin on this case. I'm confident, and the senior partners are confident, that I can see this through to a mutually successful conclusion."

"And are we getting any closer to that conclusion?" Natalie asked.

"Well, it was a definite setback when Mr. Meyers died, but I'm hopeful that Mr. Gelb will be able to attest to the conversation." I took a deep breath and plunged on. "The problem is that time is against us. Memories grow hazy, and people are getting old and dying." I removed a paper from one of my files. "Have you given any more thought to the latest settlement offer from Securitech?"

"What's to think about? It's crap," Natalie drawled.

"Four million dollars. It's chicken feed to these people," Marlene said in a voice like a crow's caw.

"We have our children to consider," Angela whined.

"Maybe you shouldn't have had so many," Natalie snapped at her sister.

"Just because you're a dried-up old—"

"Stop it!" Marlene rapped. They subsided.

I cleared my throat and tried to take back control. "However you might feel about the fairness of this offer, we should at least respond. Perhaps we can present something that better reflects your—"

"All of it!" Marlene snapped. "He spent half our marriage overseas, leaving me alone with the kids. And then he abandoned us. He owed me."

"He did support you quite generously during their minority, and he paid for their educations." I looked at my notes. "Even when Andrew changed majors three times and took nine years to graduate."

"Whose side are you on?" Angela asked, while Andrew puffed like an outraged bullfrog.

"Yours, of course, but I'm trying to make you consider the

arguments from the other side. It's unfortunate that Mr. Abercrombie founded his company and made his fortune after the separation, but those are the facts we face. You should be glad he didn't do it after the divorce. Then you really wouldn't have a case." My tone was hard enough to break rocks. "The reason this case was sent to arbitration is because there really isn't an issue of law at stake. We're trying to find some grounds for an agreement so you can get on with your lives and stop gnawing at this old injury. Locked in litigation is not a good way to live."

Marlene stood. Her face was twisted as if she'd bitten into a rotten lemon. "I don't need psychological counseling from you, young lady. These are his children." She swept out a ring-bedecked, age-spotted hand to indicate them. "Flesh-and-blood children. *Real* children. Not some monster conceived in a disgusting act. I was his wife. I washed his socks and smelled his farts and fucked him. I want what's mine. Come on, kids."

She swept out of the conference room trailed by her dispirited progeny. I leaned back in the chair and let out an explosive breath.

"And I'm supposed to establish that he loved *that*," I said aloud to the empty room.


Ryan whisked me away early, turning up in my office at barely 4:00. I gestured helplessly at the files and demurred, but he just laughed and told me that he was a partner and arguing was not allowed. I surrendered. A partner's order was good enough for me, and I had found my first week back to be exhausting and depressing. There were no treasures hidden among Chip's cases. There was just *Abercrombie,* and more *Abercrombie,* and a potentially murderous husband in a low-rent divorce case. We stopped by the break room fridge so I could grab the carrots I'd brought.

"So, you're of the bribing school of riding?" Ryan asked, his voice catching on a laugh.

"I'm of the spoil-them-rotten school of riding," I answered as we rode the elevator down.

I had thought we'd take the train, but Ryan had his car and driver. "Which is why I wanted to leave early," he said as we settled into the backseat. I tucked the bag of carrots on the floor beneath my feet. "Friday afternoon traffic is always terrible."

"The train—" I began, but Ryan interrupted me.

"Tell me the last time you've seen a vampire on public transportation."

I thought about it. "I guess never. Just too déclassé for you?" I teased.

He smiled back. "Well, that's part of the reason, but mostly it's because we can't pass as human, and we make you uncomfortable. Maybe in another generation the discomfort will pass, but for right now . . . well, it's better not to tempt fate. There are still enough people in this country who think we're devils incarnate, and if violence occurred, somebody would get hurt. Maybe even a vampire," he added with another smile.

"Hence the fostering program," I said.

"That's the primary reason, but don't discount the medieval tendencies of some of the old white-mustache vampires. *It worked in 1260; why shouldn't it work fine now?*" Ryan said in a quavery old-man voice. He shrugged. "They like things to stay the same." I absorbed that, then laughed. "What?"

"You're giving me a totally different image of vampires. Instead of elegant traditionalists, I'm picturing you as crabby old men yelling at the neighborhood kids to *get off their lawn.*"

"Please, don't include me in that categorization. I'm the very model of a modern vampire."

"And a man who likes Gilbert and Sullivan, which sort of undercuts your claim," I said dryly.

"And you are a pearl among humans because you recognized the reference."

The traffic gods were kind—and aided in their efforts by Stephenson's aggressive driving—so we reached Ryan's Long Island house in a little over an hour. Stephenson dropped us at the front door. A maid came down the stairs, gathered up my small case and boot bag, and carried them into the house. There was no sign of a hostess as we walked up the curving staircase to a second-floor bedroom. It was a bit worrisome, but horsey lust had me pushing aside my concerns.

Ryan was waiting at the foot of the stairs when I came out of the bathroom, and damn he looked good in a pair of skin-tight fawn-colored breeches, high black boots, and a white shirt. The lenses of his dark glasses were almost black, and he finished off the outfit with a broad-brimmed Tilley hat.

He gave a whistle as I descended the stairs, and I felt pretty good accepting the accolade. As hard as I try to be chic, I seem to look best in riding togs. I had picked a pair of blue breeches and a sleeveless white shirt with a high collar. My handmade Konig boots made my legs seem longer, which made me seem taller. My helmet swung from my hand. Ryan looked at it.

"You wear a helmet."

"Yes, because I'm not an idiot."

"But you're a good rider."

"Which makes it more likely I'll get hurt, because I get stuck with rank horses, young horses, and the worst of all, ponies. Also, I do more difficult things then a beginning rider. So, yes, I wear a helmet. My best asset is my brain; I don't really want to scramble it."

Ryan gave me a slow look. "Oh, I don't think that's your *only* asset."

I could feel the blush crawling up my neck into the tips of my ears. Okay, so it looked like Ryan was interested in something more than a good working relationship. Getting involved romantically with vampires was always risky. The relationships tended to end quickly, often leaving the woman feeling hurt and abandoned and the vampire unable to offer much in the way of comfort, because realistically she was just one in a long line of women across the centuries. Finally, there was the risk that the woman would hook up with the one vampire who, through either an epic lack of self-control or a nihilistic desire to end it all, would decide to turn her into a vampire and then they both would get killed.

I didn't know how to respond to Ryan's flirting so I hurried past him. "Hey, let's go. Time's a-wastin'."

The barn was behind the main house and some distance away to cut down on smells and flies. Personally I loved the smell of horses, hay, and manure, but I suspected that might be unique to horse-crazy girls. Ryan had tricked the barn out with wood paneling on the six stall doors and brass rather than steel bars. There were nice big runs off all the stalls and huge automatic waterers, a tack-up area, and a wash rack.

I was about to choke with envy. It was a perfect jewel of a barn, and the five heads thrust over the stall doors watching our progress were just beautiful.

The occupant of the sixth stall stood placidly in the cross ties. He was a large black Friesian who had already been tacked up. His ears pricked forward at the sight of Ryan. The groom fished a peppermint out of his pocket and handed it to Ryan, who tucked it in the corner of the big horse's mouth. A look of bliss filled his liquid brown eyes as he crunched the candy.

"This is Maarten. He's my big guy." I reflected that it was a good choice of a mount for a vampire. Friesians were big horses with gentle temperaments, and they would be less likely to be bothered when ridden by a dead guy. Ryan continued, "I thought I'd let you pick your horse."

He led me down the central aisle of the barn. "This is Widestep, Steppi to his friends. He's a sixteen-year-old Hanoverian, trained to Grand Prix." I stroked the horse's velvet black nose and straightened his forelock so it hung straight down over his white blaze.

"This is Unitario. He's a ten-year-old Lusitano stallion. He's a solid fourth-level horse, training to Prix St. George." Unitario was a dark black/bay, taller and leggier than the usual Lusitano. His liquid dark eyes had a golden circle around the edges, and he had a wary look on his long face. Like most stallions, he tested me by trying to nip me, and got slapped on the muzzle for his trouble.

"This one is Lily. She's five and a pill."

"Of course she is. She's a mare *and* a pony." Lily was an Icelandic with a golden coat, black stockings, and a thick mane that blended stripes of black, gold, and white. *Just like O'Shea's hair,* I thought. I toyed with riding her just to feel that weird gait that was something between a trot and a canter, but I wasn't going to waste my chance here on riding a pony, no matter how cute. *And you shouldn't waste your time getting a crush on an Álfar either.*

"And finally my desert queen, Flames Sirocco." She was an Arabian, copper-penny red with a flaxen mane and tail.

"Great, a red-headed mare *and* an Arabian."

"She's exciting," Ryan said.

"I'll just bet."

I turned back to Steppi and Unitario, considered. "How's Steppi on the trail?"

"Nervous."

"And Unitario?"

"The Lusitanos are bullfighting horses. They're brave," Ryan said with a smile.

Both horses stood with their heads thrust over the stall doors. My head swung back and forth between them. Ryan solved my dilemma.

"Del, please saddle both horses for Ms. Ellery. We'll take a trail ride, then come back so she can ride Steppi in the indoor."

"You have an indoor arena," I breathed in awe.

He shrugged. "It was here when I bought the place. I wasn't going to tear it down."

I assisted the groom as he tacked up Unitario. Horses are tactile creatures, so I introduced myself by stroking him and breathing softly into his flaring nostrils. The groom handed me the reins, and I led the horse out of the barn and toward the mounting block. But Ryan came up behind me and laid a hand on my waist.

"Let me give you a leg up." He bent down and cupped his hands. I placed my left knee in his hands, and he tossed me up into the saddle.

You forget how strong vampires are. They're not werewolf-strong, but they way outclass even the strongest human. *They're all predators, even the Álfar. They just prey on your mind and heart,* I thought. *No wonder the Powers are ending up on the top of the food chain even though they only went public thirty-some years ago. They outclass us in so many ways. No, they've probably* always *been on top, we just didn't know it before.*

Ryan swung up onto Maarten, then led us out of the stable yard and down a path through the trees. Unitario's ears swiveled from side to side, and he kept his head up. The raised head wasn't an indication of fear but rather curiosity.

It was cooler under the trees. With twilight coming on there was a soft chorus from little tree frogs. The only other sound beyond the breathing of the horses was the occasional *crack* as they stepped on a fallen branch. I knew I should probably be making small talk, voicing my appreciation of the opportunity to ride, but I just wanted to feel the play of Unitario's shoulders beneath my knees. Feel the way my hips moved in time to his walk. Breathe in the rich smell of horse as he started to sweat in the humid summer air. Watch Maarten's big black hindquarters hitching up and down and his thick black tail swishing from side to side. Notice the hindquarters on the man too. A person either looks great in riding britches or it's a sight to strike you blind. Ryan fell into the first category.

We emerged from the trees into a large meadow. Ryan cranked around in the saddle and grinned at me. "Want to gallop?" I grinned back, shifted my right leg behind the girth, sent my left seat bone forward, and gave a brief half-halt on the right rein. Unitario rocked into a canter. I touched him lightly with both calves. His ears twitched back in a *do you mean it?* gesture. I gave him more rein and clucked to him. I felt his tail flick up like a pennant being carried into battle, and we were off and running.

We caught Maarten in four leaping strides and shot past. The big Friesian was surprisingly light on his feet, meaning his plate-sized hooves didn't hit the ground like thunder, but he couldn't match the quicksilver speed and agility of the Lusitano. I threw back my head and laughed out loud.

We circled the meadow twice before pulling up. Ryan checked his watch. "If we're going to get you on another horse, we'd better head back."

We took a different route back, covering the ground in an easy posting trot. I gave Ryan a few tips about using that outside rein, inside leg connection that helped him keep Maarten's head down.

Back at the barn, I fed Unitario carrots while he was untacked. Steppi, standing patiently in the cross ties, gazed at the carrots with naked longing.

"Your turn will come," I said, and slipped him a peppermint. Which he promptly spat into my hair.

Ryan laughed. "I should have warned you. He hates peppermint."

"Great, helmet head and candy goo," I said. "What an attractive combination."

The indoor arena was behind the barn. It wasn't big enough to be a regulation dressage arena, but it would be a godsend during New York winters. Ryan wasn't kidding. Steppi really was a Grand Prix horse. I rode bits and pieces of the Grand Prix test. Ryan sat in an observation deck and clapped each time we did one of the elaborate moves. Each time he heard the applause, Steppi became more engaged and even more flashy. I ended with a piaffe, a cadenced trot in place directly in front of Ryan.

"He's a ham!" I called out to Ryan, the words catching on my laughter.

"I had no idea. I should have you show him for me," he replied, snapping on the lights.

"Oh God, I'd love to." I shortened Steppi's stride, going for one more piaffe. He got stuck behind my leg and he stopped thinking about moving forward smoothly over his back. I don't know why I did it, but I tapped the horse on the shoulder with the whip. He froze, then carefully lifted his front end, tucked his knees beneath his chin, and held there in a forty-five-degree rear for several heartbeats.

Ryan stood up in surprise. "Good God, what's that?"

I urged Steppi with my lower leg, and he dropped back to the ground and trotted off. I brought him back to the observation stand. "Somebody's trained him to do the levade. This horse is a treasure."

"I think you might be too. You're one hell of a horsewoman."

I blushed and managed to thank him, and we returned to the

barn. Steppi got his carrots, and I held back a few for Maarten, Lily, and Sirocco.

Back at the house, I hesitantly asked if I could take a quick shower and get the sweat and candy out of my hair. Ryan's response was instant—*of course.* I kept listening for the bedroom door while I showered. The lack of a hostess still had me jumpy, but Ryan was a perfect gentleman. Apparently there was no expectation that I would pay for the privilege of riding his horses. I put on the rather crumpled sleeveless white linen dress I had been wearing at the office, realizing I should have packed civvies.

Ryan was waiting in the entryway when I came downstairs. He took my arm and escorted me out the front door and back into the town car. As we rolled down the driveway, he said causally, "I don't know about you, but I'm starving. Shall we have dinner when we get back to town?"

I dithered. Were we getting into date territory? That was dangerous for so many reasons. He was my superior. He was a vampire.

Or maybe he was just hungry. I certainly was.

*Oh, for God's sake, Linnet, you've eaten lunch with him. How is this any different other than the time of day?*

"Sure," I said.

# 8

During the drive back into the city, I burbled about the horses.

"Unitario has the most comfortable trot. Wish I could say the same for Steppi, but he makes up for a bone-rattling trot by knowing *everything*. I love Grand Prix horses. Their idea of an evasion is to piaffe." I suddenly realized I had been going on and on and on about horses. I shut my mouth, my teeth closing with an audible *click*.

"What?" asked Ryan, laughing.

"I'm sorry. Me and horses. I become such a bore. What would *you* like to talk about?"

"First, you're not boring me, and I find the bond between you and horses to be fascinating."

"Oh, please don't lay all that old Freudian shit on me. It has nothing to do with repressed sexuality," I said.

"I still think Freud was right. You feel empowered because you're in control of a large animal."

I made a sound indicating *wrong*. "Nope. It's about communication."

"I don't follow."

"Well, with a horse I don't have to talk. It's like telepathy. Total understanding. Within a very short time on a horse I can think *turn*, or *trot*, and they'll do it. Of course I know they're actually reading minute changes in my muscle tone, but it feels like they're reading my mind. Also, horses are the only species to give you back precisely what you give them. If you show affection to a horse, it will reciprocate. If you're abusive to a horse, it will fight you. There are no hidden agendas with horses." The memory of those final, painful months with Devon came crashing back. Me trying desperately to explain why I couldn't go to Dubai. Him not responding—or, worse, telling me he understood, when I knew damn well he didn't, because he was assuming I would, in fact, go to Dubai. Ryan was frowning at my sudden silence. I gave him a bright and brittle smile. "And I did it again, off on a rant about horses."

Ryan laughed, slipped an arm around my shoulders, and hugged me close. "You are quite adorable."

Okay, this was not a friendly meal between colleagues. Definitely verging into date territory. But I'd already accepted. I couldn't gracefully back out now, and he was very good company. I was enjoying his conversation, quickness, and interest.

We rolled into Manhattan. Ahead of us, brake lights flared and dimmed as the cars proceeded in fits and starts between traffic lights. The blare of car horns was muted but still audible, and the city seemed to thrum beneath millions of tires. Above us, the skyscrapers looked like spires of light, and the top of the Empire State Building glowed a rich blue.

We sat through a light for a third time, advancing only a couple of car lengths. Ryan began drumming his fingers on the door.

"Sorry, sir. The traffic is really bad tonight," Stephenson offered. He sounded nervous, which surprised me. Ryan had struck me as a very reasonable boss.

"Why don't we hop out and walk?" I offered.

Ryan opened his door and stepped out. He extended his hand. I took it, and he helped me slide across the leather seat and out onto the street. We darted onto the sidewalk as the traffic jerked forward.

The pavement seemed to exhale heat, but I didn't care. It was New York on a Friday night. I was out with an interesting vampire, I'd ridden a couple of great horses, and I was starting to get control over my cases. Ryan tucked my arm beneath his and we stepped out, weaving through the other pedestrians.

We passed a clarinet player pitting his music against the car horns and engines. He was good, and I paused, dug in my purse, and placed a five-dollar bill in his open case.

Ryan gave me an odd look as we walked on. "Generous of you," he said.

"It's a habit I picked up from my grandfather, though he would have put in a twenty."

"Really?"

"He was a jazz musician back in the thirties and he said he and his band survived on tips. He taught me to dance when I was a little girl. We used to always dance to the Fascination Waltz." Memories of that short, upright figure, his iron-gray hair and brush mustache, his resonant baritone, and the smell of his aftershave swept over me.

"He'd go broke in New York with all the street-corner musicians," Ryan remarked. "He must not come here often."

"He died shortly after I went to live at the Bainbridge house," I said, and found myself suddenly sad. Chip and my grandfather had somehow become entangled in my head. I gripped Ryan's arm more tightly.

"I'm sorry," he said.

"He was very elderly, and he always said the good Lord didn't owe him a thing. He'd had a great life. It's just that I didn't get to say goodbye, because I was living in Sag Harbor by then."

Ryan guided me down a side street, and we walked up to a cherrywood and brass door beneath a scarlet awning. He paused with a hand on the door. "Do you like Asian cuisine?"

"Very much."

"This is Asian fusion, and it's been getting very good reviews. They also keep a nice selection of hosts for people like me."

"Sounds good."

The decor continued with the redwood and brass theme established at the front door. We sat in a booth upholstered in black leather that faced the bar. The bartender was cute, with shaggy blond-brown hair and a crooked grin. The cocktail menu was long and varied. In keeping with the decor, I decided to go with the Brass Monkey. It arrived with an umbrella and a plastic swizzle stick with a monkey clinging to the top.

I studied the human menu and went with the tasting platter. I'd always loved dim sum because you get to try small bites of many things, and I'd been known to make a meal of appetizers. The maître d' brought Ryan the vampire menu. It was tastefully done, with thumbnail-sized photos of the hosts as well as descriptions of their diets and the nuances of their blood. The prices varied depending upon the amount drunk and the expense of the diet used to maintain the host.

The maître d' leaned in close to Ryan and said softly, "Do you wish to cup, or will this be a natural feeding?"

Ryan cocked an eyebrow at me. "I grew up in a vampire household," I said. "I'm used to seeing vampires feed."

Ryan snapped shut his menu. "Natural, and I'll try Javier."

"Excellent choice, sir. Highly oxygenated blood. Also, for the comfort of other patrons we do screen for a natural feeding. I trust this won't offer offense?"

"Not at all," Ryan said. "Not everyone can be as relaxed as Linnet here and not be bothered." He smiled at me.

I noticed that he hadn't picked up on my actual wording. I had said I was *used* to it, not that it didn't bother me. There was a subtle difference.

The timing of the service was perfect. I was just finishing when the waitstaff set up a beautiful ebony and red silk screen around our booth. Javier arrived. He was of a medium height with the long, lean muscles of a runner, and his lustrous black hair was brushed back from a high forehead. He was dressed in slacks and a vest that left his arms, chest, and neck bare.

"Hello, sir," he said. His voice had the soft echo of his Spanish ancestors.

"Hello, Javier." Ryan's tone was bluff and hearty. "How are you this evening?"

"Fine, sir." He knelt down at Ryan's side. "Which vein do you prefer?"

Ryan studied Javier's bare arms and exposed throat. He saw the pinprick red bite mark on Javier's neck and shook his head. "Let's go with the elbow." He glanced at me. "It's sort of like eating off someone else's plate if you go to the same site this close to another's feeding," he explained.

Feeling that this fell under the category of TMI, I excused myself and headed to the ladies room as Ryan took Javier's arm and bent over the vein in the crook of his elbow. I really took my time in the bathroom. I slowly washed my hands, then used the wet skin to help pull up my panty hose. I reapplied lip liner and lipstick, fluffed and combed my hair. But they were still at it when I returned. Ryan was really gorging.

Javier's eyes were drooping, his mouth slack, wearing an expression halfway between ecstasy and terror. Ryan raised his head, quickly picked up his napkin, and dabbed at his lips. The restaurant used black napkins, so the blood didn't show too much. I suddenly realized that white table linen was becoming less common in upscale restaurants. Just another way the world had changed.

Javier shook his head and groped in a pocket for a press-on Band-Aid to place over the bite. He then nodded to us both and slipped away.

"Do you want dessert?" Ryan asked. His eyes were drooping too, and his cheeks were plump and ruddy from the ingested blood.

I shook my head, and Ryan signaled for the check. As we walked to the door, Ryan used his cell phone to call Stephenson. We stood under the awning outside and waited for him to arrive.

"Ryan, I want to thank you for this evening. It's been wonderful."

"My pleasure." He was smiling down at me, and his hand slipped around my waist.

Ryan's hand actually felt warm because of the recent feeding, and I was very aware of the raw power he exuded. His eyes locked on mine. I reacted as if an electric current had jolted through my veins, then sagged with a sudden lethargy.

"Linnet, you're a very special person," he said softly. "When you connect this quickly with someone, it seems like the universe is telling you something, and you should listen." His car was rolling up to the curb.

I stepped back out of his reach. "First, don't do the Lure on me. Say what you want."

Ryan's eyes narrowed a bit, then he smiled and nodded. "Okay, fair enough. Come home with me, Linnet. I don't want the day to end."

The feeling of warm molasses in my veins was gone. I could make this decision dispassionately. I thought of my apartment, of the nights I woke up drenched with sweat, heart pounding from nightmares. I wanted to go with him. I didn't want to wake up alone.

"Yes."


Ryan lived in a brick apartment building on West Seventy-third street. The doorman touched his cap as we entered, then hurried to summon the elevator for us. Ryan lived on the fifteenth floor. He unlocked the door and allowed me to enter. I was met with the smell of leather and lemon wax—pleasant and very male.

The furnishings had the feel of an English men's club. My feet wouldn't reach the floor if I sat well back in one of the big armchairs. The were lots of bookshelves and an entertainment center with a turntable, speakers, and an amplifier, as well as an old portable television. At least it was color. I guess when you don't die in the conventional sense, you don't have a lot of interest in getting the newest, hottest thing. I had expected Ryan to be more modern than this room indicated.

He took my hand and drew me toward him. He cupped the back of my neck with his free hand, then bent to kiss me. The smell of blood on his breath brought back memories of that night chip had been murdered, and I turned my face away.

He straightened abruptly. "What's wrong?" he asked.

"You're a partner, which makes you my superior. And you're a vampire and I'm a woman. Do we really want to risk this getting out of hand with a really bad outcome for both of us?"

"I won't bite you. It's why, frankly, I gorged at the restaurant."

"So, you were planning this all along?"

Ryan gave me a smile. "I was hoping I'd get lucky. Look, we share so much. Let's share this too. And it's not the Middle Ages. It's time for us to create new patterns of behavior and put aside superstition."

This assertion made sense. It also ran counter to what his apartment said about him, but maybe this was how he fought the tendency to become hidebound. I thought about Ryan's constant lunches with the human associates. Now he'd brought me home. I was really getting in deep here. I thought about leaving but again remembered the nightmares. I decided to stay. Ryan read the capitulation in my face, and he smiled. "The guest room's in here. There's a robe in the bathroom." He led me to a door. "I'll be right in."

It was a prosaic room. A queen-sized bed with a plain wood headboard, a dresser made from the same wood, and a bedside table with a lamp. It had a Holiday Inn feeling. But then what did a vampire need with a bedroom? It wasn't like he slept.

As he said, there was a very plush terry cloth robe in the closet, and a toothbrush, still in its packaging, resting on the counter next to the sink. The sight of the toothbrush irritated me. He had been very confident. Which made me want to leave, except I couldn't figure out how this late in the game.

I availed myself of the opportunity and brushed my teeth. I unzipped the dress and let it slither down over my hips and legs. I stepped out and hung it up. As I unhooked my bra I realized that I liked the act of undressing a lover. The slow unbuttoning of his shirt when you can feel the heat radiating off him. Pushing the shirt off his shoulders and feeling the bulge of muscle in his shoulders and biceps. The slow rasp of a zipper, and the gasp as you slip your hand inside. It was like a Christmas present. This seemed . . . I groped for a word. *Clinical? Distancing?*

I must have been standing there longer than I realized, because there was a gentle knock on the door. I quickly shed my panty hose and shrugged into the robe.

"Come in."

Ryan was swathed in a magnificent dressing gown that brought out the blond highlights in his brown hair. He was very handsome, and he had been an ally and friend at the firm over the past few weeks. This was going to be okay.

"You're adorable." He crossed to me and pulled me into his arms. This time when he sought my mouth I smelled toothpaste and mouthwash, and I relaxed into his embrace.

He kissed me, but didn't push to go past my lips. He dug his hands into my hair and kissed my cheeks, nose, eyes, and ears. He made a conscious effort and breathed so he could allow the breaths to flutter my hair and tickle my ears. I chuckled.

"That's better. You're all right," he murmured.

"I know. It's not you. It's just everything. And I worry that I'm using you. Just coming to you for comfort," I said.

He drew back and his expression was quizzical. "Using *me*," he repeated. "If I can offer you some comfort I'm happy to do it. Now stop worrying. Let's just be together."

He picked me up in his arms, carried me over to the bed, and deposited me gently on the mattress.

"We're not going to your bedroom?" I asked.

He laughed. "Actually, there isn't another bedroom. I've turned it into my office." He gave me a comical look. "Not like I sleep."

"Of course no . . . ot." My voice caught on the last word because he slipped his hand into the robe and brushed his fingers across my crotch. Fire raced along my nerve endings.

He pulled back, untied the belt, and threw open the robe. His belly was distended from the amount of blood he'd ingested. It was disturbing. "You have a diabolical look," I said as he studied my body.

"Just enjoying the view."

This time when he kissed me he demanded access. His tongue dove between my teeth, thrusting deep into my mouth. He reached down again, flicking his fingers across my clit. There was a sensation like warm honey low in my belly. I gasped and arched against him. He slid down so he could take a breast in his mouth. I cringed a bit, thinking of those long, sharp canines, but he was careful, just running his tongue around the nipple. I hardened and pressed my hips against him while reaching down to cup his penis. He shifted off to the side, and I couldn't reach him. Then his fingers were probing deep inside, but it felt more like an examination, testing the level of moisture between my legs.

And then he entered me with one hard lunge. I gasped, but it wasn't from pleasure. I opened my eyes. He hung over me, taking his weight on his forearms. His brow was furrowed with concentration, but his expression was blank. With hard thrusts of his hips, he drove deeper and deeper into me. I tried to match his rhythm, but he made no accommodation for me.

He shuddered and I felt him go limp inside of me. There was no warm flow of ejaculation—of course there wouldn't be with a vampire, just a loss of tumidity. I realized he had been concentrating to send the blood flow to his penis so he would stay hard. Once he'd banged me, he stopped trying. He pulled out, rolled off me, and swung his legs off the bed.

"I'm going to take a shower. It's late. You should go home. There's cab fare on the coffee table in the living room," he said, and he walked into the bathroom and closed the door.

I pulled the robe around me and got out of bed. My body ached, both from his pounding and from my unspent orgasm. My chest felt tight, and I couldn't decide whether to scream or cry. I had thought I had a friend. He had played on that to convince me to do this stupid thing.

I pushed back my hair and looked around the room. No clothes. They were in the bathroom. I tried the door. Ryan had locked it against me. I pounded on the wood. The door flew open. He was wet, lather clinging to his body.

"What?"

"I need my clothes."

"Oh." He disappeared behind the seeded glass of the shower door.

I grabbed my clothes and rushed out. I didn't bother with the panty hose. I just threw on my bra and dress, jammed my feet into my sandals, crammed the stockings into my purse, and ran for the front door.

There were bills on the table. My attention was drawn to another door across the living room from me. I went over and opened it.

It was a bedroom. A spectacularly beautiful bedroom featuring a king-sized bed with a carved ebony wood headboard and footboard, flat-screen TV on the wall, exquisite Chinese watercolors of horses on the other three walls, and a small fountain offering its water music to the room.

I fled. I did pause long enough to scoop up the wad of money, carry it into the granite-walled master bathroom, and toss it into the toilet. I didn't flush. I didn't want him to think I'd actually taken his money.

I rode the subway home and sat up for the rest of the night, wondering when I'd become so stupid.

The weekend passed in a frenzy of self-flagellation. I couldn't even talk to anyone. As fond as I was of Ray and Gregory, I didn't want to discuss my sex life with my gay friends; my mother was right; and fathers never think their daughters are having sex. My best friend from college had gotten married and moved to France, and while I'd had friends in law school, they weren't the kind of friends you called up to discuss bad sex.

Summer heat lay like an anvil over the city. The floor fan was having no effect in my apartment, so I took myself to the movies. When one feature ended I simply moved down the hall to the next theater. It was summer, so I watched a lot of things explode/collapse/crash. Girls ran screaming from masked knife/saw/ax-wielding killers. Men exchanged fart/bathroom/impotence jokes. Animated animals exchanged wisecracks and songs.

On Sunday afternoon, I finally unpacked the bag containing my riding clothes. The rich smell of horse filled my small bedroom. In addition to everything else, it so totally sucked that Ryan owned such wonderful animals. I fantasized about winning the lottery and buying them so they wouldn't have to belong to such a total turd.

On Monday morning, I had to make a detour out to Brooklyn to file my petition to practice before the federal bench at the U.S. District Court on Cadman Plaza East. As I was walking back to the subway, the odor of coconut and almond wafted out the door of an Italian bakery and snared me. I bought another box of macaroons to take back to the office.

It was almost 10:00 a.m. before I rode up the elevator and stepped out on the seventeenth floor. A weird hush fell over the secretarial bullpen, and my cheerful announcement, "I've got cook . . . ies . . ." stuttered away into silence in the face of the stares, the smirks, and the guilty looks. The worst was David Sullivan, who glared at me as if I'd crawled out from beneath some particularly slimy and loathsome rock. He entered his office and closed his door with enough force that it almost qualified as a slam.

I had the feeling my weekend amour was now common knowledge, and I wondered if it was possible to shrink down to the size of a dust mite and vanish. Ellery and Bainbridge training took over. I kept my chin up and my back straight as I went into the kitchen to deposit the cookies. I then walked to my office and closed my door. I did it very, very quietly in the hope that maybe everyone would forget I was there, or maybe even that I existed at all.

I pulled papers out of the final box but I couldn't concentrate. It was going to be painful, and my self-esteem was going to take a big hit, but I had to know what Ryan had said. I keyed the intercom. "Norma, could you come in, please."

She did and stared down at me with an inscrutable expression. I clutched a ballpoint pen. "Okay, if there's one thing I know about you it's that you're not overawed by lawyers. I know you'll level with me. So, level with me," I said, faking a confidence I didn't feel.

"You cost me twenty bucks."

"Beg pardon?"

"Whenever a new female associate comes into the firm we have a betting pool on how long before Ryan has them in bed."

I had been part of a sick sexual betting pool. Nausea, driven by shame and humiliation, gripped my gut. But Norma wasn't done kicking me yet.

"I thought you'd last longer." Disapproval iced the words.

The criticism lit a small fuse of anger that began to gnaw away the shame. "Sorry to disappoint," I said waspishly.

Norma shrugged. "I guess you were vulnerable because of Chip."

"Do you think?" A new grievance rose to the surface. "Why the hell doesn't somebody warn the new hire?"

Another shrug. "We figure you girl lawyers won't listen to a secretary, and the other associates want the next one to fall just the way they did."

"Well, that stinks! Whatever happened to female solidarity?"

"In this shark pool?" Norma asked. "Is there anything else?"

"No."

She left, and I sat frowning at the closed door, flipping a pen over and over while I considered. Good news: I wasn't the only one. Bad news: I wasn't the only one. I had been used and tossed aside, and I hadn't even gotten an orgasm out of it. So, what were my choices? Pretend it had never happened, like every other female associate? Leave the firm and work for a nonprofit? Hang out a shingle and open my own firm? Or get even? I liked choice number four.

# 9

I skipped lunch, continued to work, and thought about my situation. During the course of the afternoon I ran across a scrawled note in Chip's big, looping handwriting. *Join the two cases for the arbitration? Marlene = ballistic.*

Clearly this had something to do with *Abercrombie,* because of the reference to Marlene, but I had never heard of a second case. Maybe it was buried in one of the boxes, but whoever had cleaned out Chip's office had just thrown stuff into boxes without any effort to categorize. This was in addition to Chip's file management strategy, of keeping everything in his head. I muttered an expletive, then felt immediately guilty. *Cussing out a dead man—yeah, I'm a real good person. I'm also the idiot who got snookered by a sexual predator and made a fool out of herself.*

*So stop feeling sorry for yourself and own it!*

I straightened in my chair and considered the wisdom imparted by my inner Linnet. The only reason Ryan had gotten away with it for this long was because female associates, isolated and humiliated, had slunk around pretending it hadn't happened and kept silent. As my dad had reminded me, I was an Ellery. We didn't back down from fights.

First, I had to make it not okay for the human associates to talk behind my back, and then I had to put Ryan on notice that war had been declared. Even though he was a partner, I wasn't worried about him having any power to affect my job. I assumed all the partners knew about Ryan's little sex games, but since no human woman was speaking out they could all pretend it wasn't happening; since his behavior hadn't crossed the line into biting, they turned a blind eye.

If I went public, they were going to have to suddenly be (with apologies to Captain Louis Renault in *Casablanca*), and paraphrasing, *shocked—shocked to find that such behavior is going on in here.* Not because sex was happening, but because Ryan was placing himself in close proximity to human women. That meant biting might happen, which could lead to a Making, the ultimate vampire taboo. Ryan was going to be too busy defending himself to the top partners to go after me.

I waited until I heard the bustle of people preparing to leave. Then I picked up the calla lily, opened the door to my office, and emerged into the central office space. As I suspected, conversations stuttered like backfiring cars and several men uttered amused snorts.

"Hi," I said to the assembled lawyers and secretaries. "Yes, I slept with Ryan, because I'm an idiot." I pinned the balding Doug with a look, daring him to react. He didn't have the guts. Instead he looked away.

I continued. "But guess what? It's not going to happen again because I'm going to warn the next female associate who gets hired at this firm. And you"—I raked the women within sight—"should be ashamed that you didn't."

With that, I dropped the calla lily in the nearest trash can and walked back into my office. There was an explosion of conversation behind me and the sound of one lone set of hands clapping.

I glanced back. It was Norma. She smiled at me, fished a Hersey's Kiss out of her jar, and held it out to me. I walked back and took it.

John O'Shea turned up in the early evening. There was a soft tap on my office door, then he stuck his head around the door. I promptly bit it off.

"Well, it took you long enough," I said, knowing I sounded like a peevish bitch but unable to control myself.

"Hello to you too." He gave me that smile, and my heart did a little cha-cha, but after what Ryan had pulled I had to wonder if I was actually attracted or if this was just Álfar shit.

I pinched the bridge of my nose, trying to push back a headache. "So, tell me you have good news. I could really use some good news."

"Sorry, no joy in Mudville. The hound's alive."

"Damn, that would have been so simple."

"Life rarely is," John said. "So, where does that leave you?"

"Back to Securitech since the bickering Mays crapped out." I tapped my pen against my teeth. "But it doesn't make any sense. It's a nuisance case. Chip was never going to win."

"Maybe he found out something. Something that changed the equation," John offered.

I laid a hand on the nearest box. "If he did, it's buried in here."

"Which puts you at risk if you find it," John said.

"Yeah, I thought of that, especially when I couldn't turn up anything questionable in his personal life. Hearing somebody else say it, though . . ." I shivered, and it felt like ten thousand butterflies had been released in my stomach. ". . . makes it feel more real somehow."

"I'll give you something else to worry about. That hound is stalking his wife."

That brought me out of my personal funk. "What?"

"I had trouble finding Jake, because he's moved out of his apartment and changed jobs three times. Looks like he's trying to beat the court-ordered child support during the separation. But when I asked his former coworkers about him, I got the picture of a really angry guy who hates his wife but still wants to control her. So, I staked out her apartment. Turns out he's been staking it out too. Fortunately I'm better at this than he is, and he didn't see me."

"By that I infer that you didn't talk to him."

"Hell no! Domestic disputes are where cops get killed. My assignment was to find out if he killed Chip and then splatted. He didn't." John dropped into the chair opposite me and propped his feet on the desk.

"Is this woman in danger?" I asked.

"Probably not until the divorce is final. Then all bets are off."

"Restraining order?"

"Bad idea. In my experience their usual effect is to incite the guys they're trying to restrain."

"So, what's the solution?"

"Get the money out of him. Get her to relocate and not leave a forwarding address."

"Tough to do if he ends up with joint custody."

"So, keep that from happening."

I made a face. "Thanks, I would never have figured that out without you." He grinned at me, but his fingers were tapping out a nervous tattoo on his knee. "Let me guess, you want to talk about my Night of Shame."

"That became the Day of Retribution," he said.

I leaned forward. "What have you heard? What's going on?"

"Winchester's been on the carpet in Gold's office, getting reamed. Don't know if it's going to go so far as to get him banished down here with Sullivan, but the brass ain't happy."

"Well, good, but I hope they don't banish him. Think how uncomfortable that would be."

"I'd call that an understatement." He cocked his head and considered me. "You're an odd little duck."

"Thanks," I said sarcastically.

"No, I mean that in the best possible way. You're the first woman to even acknowledge this, much less take it to DEFCON Three like you did."

"Why didn't anybody do this before? Or at least warn a new hire?" I asked.

"Because the women fervently pray the next woman will be a victim too, so they can feel better about themselves. And the men admire him and hope some of it rubs off." He stood up.

"Men are pigs," I stated.

"So I've heard."

"Where do you stand?"

"I make it a policy never to get crossways with a vampire."

"Words to live by," I said.

"I don't notice you doing that," John said.

I just shrugged and turned my attention back to my papers. Then I realized he was still standing there. "What?"

"It's quittin' time. Want to grab some dinner?" John asked.

One part of me really wanted to go. I liked him. He was gorgeous, but he was male, and right now I was feeling emotionally raw. I shook my head. "Thanks, but no."

"Why not?" he asked.

I considered him and decided not to play it safe. "Right now I don't feel very charitable toward males of any species."

He nodded. "I can respect that." He left.

———

The next day I had Norma call to arrange a settlement meeting between Elizabeth May, her soon-to-be ex, Jake, his lawyer, and me. I asked that Elizabeth come in an hour early so we could talk about her situation. Then I tried to figure out how to tell a woman that she was going to have to leave behind everything she knew and build a new life. It was never easy. Divorce was the primary reason women fell into poverty. Children always compounded the problem. I tried to work out a system where the child support would be paid into a trust, and the trustee would then forward the money to Elizabeth while agreeing to never, ever, ever release her address to her ex-husband.

Deciding I needed a walk to clear my head, I rode the elevator to the ground floor. The security guard at his desk started to call my name, but he was interrupted when a pudgy little man with a tonsure of graying black hair around a shining bald pate bounced out of a chair and accosted me. He didn't offer his hand. He just got right in my face and said, "Syd Finkelstein. And I'm gonna talk to you right now!"

The fact that his face was thrust pugnaciously into mine gave me a clear indication of his height—short. This close I could see the limp, frayed quality of his shirt collar and the shine off his cheap suit.

The security guard was at Finkelstein's elbow. "Sorry, Ms. Ellery. Your assistant said not to let him up, and he wouldn't leave," he added in an aggrieved tone.

"Damn straight I'm not! Not until we talk," Finkelstein said.

"And I should talk to you why?" I asked.

"Because Chip and I were working together on a case."

"I never heard about it," I said.

"Okay, that tells me all I need to know." Finkelstein turned and started for the door.

I grabbed his arm. "Oh, no, no, no, no. You're coming up to my office and telling me what this is about," I said. I punched the button to call the elevator and looked back at the guard. "And next time call me directly."

"Bypass the dragon?" he asked.

"Yes."

"Will you protect me?" the guard asked plaintively.

The elevator arrived and I indicated for Finkelstein to precede me. We rode in silence. The little lawyer studied me.

"You look younger in person."

"Thanks, I guess." Then I added, "How did you—"

"Recognize you? Your mug's been all over the papers, and if you Google *Linnet Ellery, breast*, you get about fifty thousand hits. Sometimes they show your face too."

"Great."

"Hey, there's no such thing as bad publicity," Finkelstein said.

"Yes, yes there is. Especially when you're in a White-Fang law firm. They don't like notoriety."

"The Powers can't go public and expect to keep doing their work in secret," Finkelstein said with a shrug.

I was surprised he didn't say *spook*. If anybody was the type to toss out the slur, Finkelstein seemed like that guy. We stepped out on the seventieth floor, and it was instantly obvious that my guest wasn't from around these parts. The cheap suit, the too-pointed toes on his highly polished shoes, and the big, gaudy cuff links all screamed *ambulance chaser*.

As I led Finkelstein to my office, Norma glared at me and gave a loud sniff of disdain. I shut the door firmly behind us and took my chair behind the desk.

"Now, what can I do for you?"

"I represent Chastity Jenkins and her child, Destiny."

I blinked at him. "Okay."

"Destiny is Henry Abercrombie's daughter." I sank back in my chair.

"How old is Destiny?"

"Twenty-seven."

"Oh God. I take it Henry didn't marry Chastity?"

"Nope, but just before he died, Henry told her he was having a new will drawn up leaving everything to her and her daughter."

"Do you have a copy of this will?"

"No. Not the executed will. Henry wrote out the broad terms on a napkin one night at Hot Lips."

"Hot Lips?" I said faintly.

"That's the joint down in Roanoke where Chastity used to strip."

"Oh," I said. I then went to the salient issue. "Forgive me, but without a will you have no case."

"Chastity is sure the will was real, because Henry hired a lawyer down in Virginia. She just didn't know the guy's name. I've been trying to track him down, but haven't had any luck. I told Westin about this, and since he had a lot more resources than me, we decided he'd look into it. The last thing he told me was that the courthouse where Henry kept his important papers burned down. We both thought that was pretty fucking convenient."

Now the letter from the Appomattox County Clerk made a lot more sense. Chip had been looking for a copy of this reputed third will. Which made no sense, because if the will was real and had been witnessed and executed, it kicked the crap out of our case. Chip had been working against his own clients' interests. I remembered the phone conversation when Chip had abruptly hung

up. He must have been on the phone with Finkelstein. I also remembered the conversation when he seemed to indicate that he
didn't want Marlene and the kids to get the company. It was all so
unethical it left me breathless.

I desperately needed time to think, so I stalled. "Look, I'm just
getting into Mr. Westin's files and obviously he didn't tell me
about you and your clients. So why don't you fill me in?" Then I
promptly interrupted him by adding, "And why did you and Chip
work in secret? Why not join the cases and have the clout of an
IMG behind you?"

"I considered that, but Chastity didn't want to be associated
with Marlene. Not even a little. She said Henry talked a lot about
his ex, and everything he said led Chastity to believe that Marlene
was a world-class bitch. Chastity said Henry used his wolfism as
the excuse for the separation and later divorce, but he couldn't
wait to get away from the bitch."

Note to self—do not call in testator's stripper girlfriend to offer testimony about the state of the Abercrombies' marriage. Further note—hope to hell that the attorneys representing Securitech
don't call said stripper. That would kill our case dead.

"And why are you just turning up now? It makes your client's
claim seem very questionable."

"Chastity wasted years on some two-bit lawyer down in Virginia. He took her case, but all he did was fart around for years,
run up bills, and then tell her Securitech is incorporated in New
York State so she was in the wrong venue. The big firms kept
blowing her off, but then she found me." I guess my face gave me
away. Finkelstein bristled. "Look, I'm not some fly-by-night, ambulance chaser." He paused. "Okay, I have been known to take
the occasional personal injury case, but I've got an instinct about
people. I can tell when they're being straight with me."

"Your client is a stripper who spent years having an affair with a married man. She waits seventeen years before showing up. Forgive me if I don't share your instinct."

"She's not a gold digger. Henry told her he was getting a divorce, and for probably the first time in history, it was actually true," Finkelstein replied.

"So, why didn't he marry her after he *did* get the divorce?"

"That dickhead Deegan convinced Abercrombie that marrying a stripper would hurt their chances to land federal contracts. They do a lot of work for the State Department. Henry bought Chastity a house and a new car every year, sent Destiny to private schools, and paid for her college education."

"And what did Destiny study?" I asked cautiously. I didn't want to sound like a snob, but . . .

"She got a degree in comparative literature—Soviet gulag and Cuban shit. I'm actually kind of amazed. When you name a kid Destiny she's gonna end up on the pole, but so far she's resisted," Finkelstein said in his blunt way.

"And what about Chastity? Presumably she's not still . . ." I was finding that a lot of my sentences were ending by just trailing off.

"Stripping? Nah. There is definitely a sell-by date on strippers. Not that Chastity isn't a fine-looking woman, but I don't want to look at a fifty-two-year-old ass, and sagging fifty-two-year-old boobs. She's the manager at Hot Lips now."

I was beginning to see why Norma had such a low opinion of Syd Finkelstein. This kind of earthiness and political incorrectness was not going to sit well with her.

"Look, I can tell when there's something to a case," Finkelstein said. "This case is solid."

"You don't have a will. Not the usual definition of solid," I countered.

"In our last conversation, Chip said he was onto something and he'd get back to me after he'd dug a little deeper. Next thing I know I'm reading about Chip's murder. I figured the worst had happened. So, was he actually killed by a werewolf?"

"Yes."

"You can bet your ass Deegan's behind it."

This matched my own conclusion. A conclusion that had become even stronger now that Finkelstein had entered the picture.

"Look, Chip's files are a mess, and I'm just starting to dig out. Give me a little time. And could you not say anything to the senior partners until I get back to you? If this got out it would . . . well, it would really damage Chip's memory, and it could blow back on the firm."

I stood and extended my hand. Finkelstein took it. He had an oddly limp shake for such a dynamo. He hesitated, ran a hand across his bald spot. "Look, Ms. Ellery. Chip wasn't a very good lawyer, but he was a really good man. He knew if we could find this will, the biggest private army in the world wouldn't be in the hands of greedy shits or crazed jingoists like Deegan."

He left, and I sat down and stared at the closed door while I analyzed the situation. Deegan had control of the company, had gotten control seventeen years ago, and nothing we'd done had affected that. Yes, it cost him money to deal with the arbitration, but he had money. So what had changed?

Well, Chastity and Destiny were a change, and Chip had thought there was enough to the story that he was making inquiries about a document in Virginia and working with another lawyer against his own clients' interests. It wasn't impossible to assume that Deegan, with his resources, had found out. Deegan could safely ignore Finkelstein, since he was a sole practitioner with no resources, but Chip . . . He might have been a drone in Sullivan's unkind estimation, but he was with IMG, and we did have resources. Deegan must have thought there was something to the stripper's story, so he had had Chip killed.

*Now prove it,* came a nasty, snarky little voice in my head.

To do that, I would need to finish pawing through the boxes, take another look at everything in light of this new information, and decide if I was going to continue Chip's inquiries. The case from hell had suddenly gotten a lot more interesting, and *potentially really fucking dangerous.* But right now I was hungry, and I decided to head out to lunch.

There was a hole-in-the-wall deli a few blocks from the office where the food was plentiful and good. I ordered lox on a bagel, then settled down at a table by the window. Caroline came stalking past the deli, long blonde hair swinging, the hem of her dress kissing her knees. She must have sensed my stare, because she suddenly looked over. Our eyes met. She hesitated. Then she shocked me by walking into the deli and taking the chair across from me.

I tried to marshal my rattled thoughts. The cool girl had sat down at my table. *She* couldn't have succumbed to Ryan. She was too beautiful, elegant, poised—

"I'm sorry," she said.

"For what?"

"For not warning you."

"*You* slept with him?" I asked.

"I did."

"So why didn't you warn me?" I asked. I was genuinely curious, which kept my tone from becoming accusatory.

"They throw us into competition with each other, until we're like a bunch of caged badgers. We're trained to think *if you're up, I must be down.* I almost said something after Chip was killed."

"Because you knew I'd be vulnerable?" I asked.

"No, because I admired you. I would have hidden that night. I wouldn't even have tried to help."

She looked so miserable and ashamed that I found myself reaching out a hand and saying, "You don't know that. No one knows how they'll react in a crisis." I looked down at my plate and fiddled with my bagel, centering it exactly in the middle of the plate. "So how did Ryan woo you?"

She sighed. "I majored in fine arts before going on to law school. I always wanted to be a painter, but Daddy said that was foolish. Anyway, Ryan took me to the most prestigious gallery openings. To artist's studios. It was all very flattering."

"Wow, it sounds like you held out longer than I did. It just took one afternoon of being bribed with horses, and I fell into bed with him," I said, and shame was like an oily taste on the back of my tongue.

Now Caroline reached out and touched my hand. "After what you'd been through, you *were* vulnerable, and he played on that." She paused and fiddled with the salt and pepper shakers on the small table, a frown between her perfectly plucked brows. "Why does he have a bunch of horses anyway?"

"He likes horses?" I said a little quizzically. I couldn't understand how anyone could ask that question. I would own a horse again in a heartbeat. "Or the barn was on his property and he had to accessorize?" That made her laugh a bit, though she quickly sobered and said, "And what you did today was incredibly brave too. You've just killed any chance you ever had of making partner."

I shrugged. "I don't think there was much likelihood of that anyway. The old white-mustache guys prefer that partners be vampires, and since there are no women vampires, it's a hard climb for us to overcome that prejudice. I only know of a handful of White-Fang firms that have female partners, and that only happened because of a bunch of EEOC law suits. Most White-Fang firms elevate just enough women to keep the accusations of discrimination at bay."

"So, we're all just wasting our time trying to out-compete the men." Caroline sounded bitter and weary.

"Maybe not. Shade seems more progressive."

"Yeah, but *all* the partners get to vote before taking on a new partner. He's just one vote." She paused again. "What do they have against us?"

"I don't think they have anything *against us*, per se. They're just antiquated. Ryan said something in the car about the medieval tendencies of white-mustache vampires. Think about it. How well is your grandfather coping with women in the workplace?" Caroline's eyes were widening as I talked. "And many of these guys are hundreds of years old. Their attitudes hardened in 1730, or 1260, or maybe even earlier."

"But why would they . . . I don't know, limit themselves? They could bite us and make us vampires too."

"The official party line for both the vampires and the werewolves is chivalry, but I think it's more about self-preservation, and not upsetting the peasants by going after their womenfolk. If you start threatening wives and daughters, you're going to end up with an angry mob outside your house waving torches and pitchforks."

"But women aren't cherished little flowers any longer. The world has changed."

"But they haven't," I countered. "Of course none of this applies to the Álfar. They seduce humans all the time. The difference is we can't become Álfar. They're a different species."

"I don't buy it." She sounded a lot more like the woman who

had dissed me than the new, complimentary Caroline. "The vampires and werewolves were hidden for thousands of years. Most people didn't believe they existed, thought they were myth. There could have been plenty of female vampires and werewolves over the centuries. We would never have known."

Yep, Caroline was smart. She had made the same analysis I had. "Look, I've asked the same questions about the party line, but I was living in a vampire household at the time, and when I voiced those doubts I got a very bad reaction."

"So you just let it go," she said, sounding disgusted.

"I was thirteen, and no, I didn't drop it totally. I snooped a bit, but whatever the real reason for the taboo on women vampires, it's buried deep. It began to feel . . . dangerous, really dangerous, so I let it go." I paused and studied her disgruntled face. "You're not happy."

"No, I'm not. We're being denied the chance to reach the top in our profession because of some taboo that has a bullshit explanation. The point is that times change, circumstances change. The Powers went public, which was a big damn change. People change and adapt." She was ranting now.

"Sure, *people* can." I stressed the word *people*, then stared at her for a long moment. She squirmed under my serious gaze.

"What?"

"Caroline, you have to remember something—*they're not people*. Not anymore."

She shuddered and looked away, then said with some heat, "I hate this. I was first in my class at Harvard. I deserve to be a partner. What can we do?"

"Open our own firm?" I joked. "And no, I'm not seriously suggesting that, at least not at this point in my career, but we *do* need to do something about Ryan. Starting with warning any new hires, and looking for every opportunity to humiliate him. If there's one thing I know about vampires, they're all about pride. They *hate* to lose face."

"Well, you went a long way toward doing that yesterday. I expect it will blow back on you," she said coolly.

"Hasn't yet," I answered with a bravado I didn't really feel.

I spent the afternoon placing every bit of paper on the *Abercrombie* case in chronological order. That meant I had seventeen discrete (but huge) piles, and I wasn't just pawing aimlessly through paper. I concentrated my search on the past year, assuming that whatever happened to get Chip killed must have occurred recently. I tried not to remind myself of that overused and really irritating saying that pompous and annoying people just loved to throw at you: *When you assume you make an ASS of U and ME.*

I looked up when there was a soft knock on the door. "What? Yeah. Come in."

It wasn't who I expected. David Sullivan stood in the office door. He had his usual sour and supercilious expression firmly in place. I braced myself.

"You just love hopeless fights with impossible odds, don't you?"

I blinked at him. "What?"

"Figure it out." He walked into my office, and eyed the leaning towers of *Abercrombie*. "What are you doing?"

"Looking for a motive," I said.

"So you think *Abercrombie* is the reason for the murder?" he asked.

"Yes."

"Want some help?"

"And why would you help me?" Suspicion sharpened the words.

"Because it will royally piss off their highnesses upstairs, who

sent me down here and let a jackass like Winchester stay up there."
He jerked his chin toward the ceiling.

"Okay, that's a good reason and one I can buy," I said.

"You don't think I'd offer to help you just because I wanted to
help you?" he asked.

"No."

For a moment he looked taken aback, then he nodded. I handed
him a stack of papers.

# 10

The *clackity-clack* of the wheels on the tracks was nicely hypnotic. I dropped my iPad onto my lap, half-closed my eyes, and just let the sway of the subway take control of my body. I felt guilty for taking the weekend to visit my two homes, but Mother and Charlie had returned from Europe, and both my real and my foster dads had indicated a visit to both homes would be appreciated.

Since I didn't have a car in New York, I was taking the Long Island Rail Road to Sag Harbor. I would spend Friday night at the Bainbridge house. On Saturday, mid-morning, I would take the Long Island Ferry to Newport, Rhode Island, where someone in my human family would be meeting me. Then back to NYC on Sunday afternoon. Just thinking about it made me tired.

I had loaded a number of mystery novels onto my iPad, hoping that the brilliance of fictional detectives would help me in my efforts to untangle Chip's death and the reputed existence of the missing third will. But my brain was tired, and I didn't want to think about knotty puzzles. I had dipped into a science fiction novel and a fantasy, but I had the same problem. I kept having to do mental work to envision the planets and aliens, or the mythical kingdoms and elves—

Well, actually, I wasn't having a hard time picturing elves. One in particular kept floating to the front of my mind. I hadn't heard from John since his report about Elizabeth May's werewolf husband, and since I presently hated and was eschewing all men of any type and description, I hadn't called him—though I wanted to.

I picked up the iPad and brought up a Georgette Heyer novel. The problems of a Regency heroine—how to make an impression during the season, how to capture and marry the man of one's dreams—seemed quaint and charming, and I felt a certain nostalgia for the era. Life was simpler for women back then.

*It was also confining, difficult, incredibly dangerous—death during childbirth was common, and women were the property of their spouses,* the sensible part of my brain reminded me.

"Yeah, those were the days," I muttered to myself.

Georgette did her magic, and I soon forgot about work as I lost myself in the problems of a young lady who had, scandalously, driven her phaeton down a public street, past gawking gentlemen in their clubs.

One chapter later, we pulled into the Bridgehampton station. I grabbed my overnight bag and hopped off the train. Douglas was waiting. I noticed he was grayer and a bit more stooped, but he still touched the brim of his cap, then gave me a wink and a grin before taking my bag and laptop. He was still driving the same old black Lincoln Town Car that had picked up a terrified eight-year-old seventeen years before. I knew it was the same car, because the initials that brat Stanley Delvechio had carved in the wood around the door handle were still there.

A lump in my throat threatened to choke me, and my vision was blurry with tears as a memory swept across me, ash gray and cold.

I remembered the grilled cheese sandwich and ice cream cone

Daddy had bought me in Newport, Rhode Island, before we'd boarded the ferry for Long Island. It had seemed like a good day because I had him all to myself. No Mommy and no squalling baby brother. We had stood on the deck of the ferry as it chugged its way across the sound. I knew intellectually that I was being taken away to live in another place, but like most children I had the capacity to think the moment would last forever, and that Daddy would never leave me behind.

When we reached Long Island, Daddy had knelt down in front of me with his hands on my shoulders. He had been very serious as he said, "Lennie, you must be very, very good and make Mr. Bainbridge very happy. Don't do anything that might upset him and make him send you back. This is very important. But I know you won't disappoint me. You're my good girl, Lennie. You'll make me proud."

It had been a summer day, and the air reeked of diesel, fish, and rank water. Daddy stood up and Douglas took my suitcase. His hand replaced my father's on my shoulder. Daddy turned and walked back onto the ferry. I started to scream, the sound mingling with the harsh cries of the gulls.

Daddy had turned back and called, "You're not making me proud."

I had swallowed the tears, but what I had learned on that day was that ferry rides end and people leave you behind all the time.

"We read about those terrible events in the city. The entire household is very relieved that you weren't hurt, Miss Linnet," Douglas said with quiet formality.

"Thank you, Douglas, I appreciate that." I paused and added, "And I'm very glad to be home, even if only for a night."

Inside there were more greetings. Susan, Meredith's hostess, looked very chic in a lemon yellow dress and low heels, her perfect pageboy dyed to a rich chestnut. She hugged me tight. "I'm so glad you're safe," she whispered. "I've put Jessica in with Amy tonight so you can have your old room back."

"Can I still escape out the window using the tree?"

"No, Meredith had it moved after a fosterling less agile than you took a tumble and broke his arm."

"How many fosterlings do you have right now?" I asked as we walked up the grand staircase and Douglas followed behind with my case.

"The usual five, but when they're released in three years we're only going to take two. I'm slowing down, and Meredith agreed not to burden me with too many youngsters. This bunch will probably be the last fosterlings I see to adulthood."

I gave her a hug. "Don't say that. You're still young."

"That's sweet, Linnet, but no, I'm not. And it's all the more apparent when you live in a vampire household."

Mine had been the last room on the left. As we walked down a long hall, we heard screams of female terror from one room, and a boy's voice cried out, "Oh gross, how cool." It had the tremor and crack of a boy in the throes of adolescence.

Beneath the shrill cries of fright, there was the eerie thrumming sound of a Hunter. Susan stormed over to the door of the room. I couldn't resist. I followed her.

Seated on the bed and on pillows on the floor were five teenagers, two girls and three boys, in front of a TV. The girls sported the latest fashion affectations, and the boys slouched as if they'd suddenly become too tall and they didn't know when or how it had happened. There was the usual spray of acne across their faces, which were turned to us as we entered. My skin wanted to break out in sympathy.

On the screen a Hunter shambled after a teen couple. Its face was a pale oval, and its only definable feature was a strange, red mouth. How it breathed or saw was a mystery. The worm-like digits that passed for fingers stiffened into claws and thrust into the boy's chest. Then Susan snapped off the television.

"Justin, you know better than to show a Hunter movie in a vampire's household."

"Ah, Susan," came multiple cries in tones of consternation.

"It's just a movie," Justin said, but he climbed to his feet and ejected the DVD. It was one of Roger Corman's low budget efforts from the early seventies. The lurid title *HUNTER HORROR* splashed across the front of the case.

It was an interesting irony that while vampires had bred or created Hunters to do God knows what, even vampires couldn't stand to have them around. According to various sources, they stank like rotting meat, and their blind gaze was disturbing even to their makers. It turned out they were the source of all the walking-dead legends that permeated human cultures. Only vampires with their mesmerizing powers could fully control Hunters, and a special class of vampire enforcers handled the creatures.

Of course, I'd never actually seen one except in the movies— and there were a lot of movies. Once the Powers went public, Hollywood had dumped zombies and taken up Hunters, because there was a great story associated with them. Supposedly they were bred to smell and kill an unknown predator that had the ability to destroy the Powers. All of them.

Susan confiscated the DVD, and we continued down the hall to my old bedroom. It offered a view across the manicured and colorful garden, past the hedge, and off toward the small barn. For a moment I remembered the horses that had filled my ten years with Meredith—Suncloud, Delila, and Miss Patti.

A new girl's treasurers had replaced mine on top of the bookcases. In place of my giant collection of Breyer plastic horses, the new occupant had dainty china and inlaid boxes. On the walls were posters of the latest crop of teen heartthrobs, none of whom I recognized, and I suddenly felt very old. But it was still my room, and the memories hung in it like cobwebs.

"Dinner is at seven thirty, and Meredith would like to have sherry with you in the library at seven."

"I'll get changed." Because of course you dressed for dinner in a vampire's house.

Meredith was flipping through the *Wall Street Journal* when I entered. He held a glass whose contents were too red and too viscous to be anything but blood. I wondered if he was still buying from a local cuppery, or if he had decided to use his meal hosts for cocktails as well.

I braced myself for the inevitable conversation about IMG. Instead he asked, "What do you think of the Santa Fe Opera? Worth a trip all that way?"

I had to reset my brain. "Uh . . . yes. It's a beautiful setting with world-class singers. They always do very innovative stagings at Santa Fe," I offered, and Meredith made a face. Clearly not a selling point. "And Santa Fe is a cool little town. It feels . . . European."

"Ah, interesting."

"But why Santa Fe in August?" I asked.

"Steven Ogden is reprising his role as Tonio in *The Daughter of the Regiment,* and I'd like to hear him sing again."

"Are you going all star-struck opera groupie again?" I asked.

He pretended to bristle. "Show some respect, young lady. And yes, I am. Ogden is a sensation. The finest voice I've heard in many lifetimes. I've been following him from opera house to opera house for the past year."

"Are you going to Make him?"

"It would be a shame for the world to lose that voice. Breath is the essence of singing. We have to force ourselves to emulate breathing. His voice would never be the same. Maybe I'll wait until he makes a lot more recordings. . . ."

IMG never came up once during the evening, and for the first time in a long time I slept without nightmares.


The next morning I stood on the deck of the ferry. There was only the tiniest amount of roll, and I caught it in my knees and swayed softly with the motion. I sniffed the salt air, watched the gulls swooping like feathered sky writers, and ignored the people jabbering on their cell phones.

Up ahead, the buildings in Newport looked like LEGO toys. I wondered which member of my family would meet me. I prayed it wasn't going to be my mother. Eventually the buildings stopped looking like sets in Munchkinland, the big diesel engines roared and strained, and the ferry bumped to rest against the pier.

I grabbed up my overnight bag and computer case then headed down the gangplank and into the building. None of my family was there. I wove past the Starbucks and the sandwich shop, and my stomach gave a growl. I hoped dinner wasn't going to be late.

Out in the parking lot the door on a Corvette Stingray flew open, and Charlie waved at me. It looked like my brother had received the obligatory going-off-to-college car gift.

My dad was a mass of contradictions. He was a fifty-something, sober businessman who loved to gamble—never for large amounts, but all games of chance fascinated him. And he loved fast cars. They were always *American* fast cars, and he told his fellow members in the Chamber of Commerce and at the country club that he was buying them for his children. The statement was always followed with an eye roll that said how silly he found the whole thing. Maybe his colleagues were fooled and never knew how much he enjoyed test driving sports cars before making his recommendations. I was pretty sure he drove my car when I wasn't around. He was getting a lot of use out of it now.

I got my first car when I returned home from Meredith's, and I still had it. Daddy had offered me a choice between a Ford Mustang and a Corvette Stingray. I'd opted for the Mustang because of the whole horsey thing. I also thought the Stingray was very much a "boy's car," and back then I was in my girly phase.

It looked like Charlie had opted for the "boy's car." It worked for him because he took after our tall mother, being damn near six feet tall. I took after Dad, who lied and said he was five foot eight. I put him closer to five-six on a tall day. I also lied, saying I was five foot two. Charlie took after Mom in other ways too. While I had inherited dad's blue-black hair, Charlie's was a dark brown thanks to the mixture with my mom's red hair.

Charlie grabbed my case, dumped it into the trunk, held the passenger door for me, and then took us out of the parking lot like we were starting at the Indianapolis 500.

"You are so going to get a ticket," I said as we hit the Centerdale Bypass doing about sixty.

"Am I making you nervous?"

"No. I just think you're stupid to speed while you're still in town."

"Oh, okay." He lifted his foot off the gas, and we slowed to within five miles of the actual speed limit as we turned onto Highway 44. Charlie glanced over at me. "You look okay."

"Meaning what?"

"You were kind of a basket case when we talked," he said.

"It's been a few weeks, and I've had other things to occupy my mind," I said. "How did you like Europe?" I asked, eager to change the subject.

"I loved it. I want to go to school over there."

That surprised me. "Oh. Where would you go, and what would you study?"

"I don't really care where. Maybe not Germany. I didn't like Germany all that much. Switzerland, France, Italy." He gulped in a breath, and his hands convulsed briefly on the steering wheel. "I'd like to study architecture. The buildings were just amazing. And not just the old stuff. In Paris they've done an amazing job of placing modern buildings next to eighteenth-century chateaus, and it *works*. The modern buildings sort of suggest some of the old styles, and—" He broke off as if embarrassed by his passion. "Well, blah blah." He fell silent.

"Wow. I did not see that coming." He gave me a pained and worried look. "What? You know Mom thinks you walk on water, and Daddy always supports any educational goal."

"I also know he really wants me to take over the business," Charlie said.

"True, but he's always supported us," I repeated in my most reassuring tone.

"Yeah, but you did what he wanted. You always have."

*You're my good girl, Lennie. You'll make me proud.* Spoken to an eight-year-old. Repeated over and over through the years. Most recently a few weeks ago. Had it all been about him? About making me a mirror for his ambitions? It was a horrible, grating thought that left me feeling like my skin had been peeled away.

Had I picked this life because I wanted it, or because Daddy had pushed me into it? Had there been other dreams? Yes. To ride professionally. Go to the Olympics. But those other goals had been dismissed with a smile. I was an Ellery. An Ellery had been one of the first Federal Court judges. He had signed the Declaration of Independence. Being a mere horse trainer was the equivalent of failure. I felt like a pawn. My father had sent me away because it helped his business. He insisted I aim for a White-Fang firm. Why? For access? The thoughts were so devastating that I didn't hear another word Charlie said to me. I just kept worrying at this revelation, trying to find some other interpretation of my father's behavior.

We turned off the highway and headed for the family home on the western edge of the Pascoag Reservoir. It was the usual New England affair: two stories, white siding, blue shutters, pitched shingle roof. Our dad's Lincoln Continental was parked in the driveway behind our mother's Volt.

It was time. I had to prepare myself to face my father. Charlie pulled up next to the other cars and hit the garage door opener. I forced a smile. "The Corvette rates the garage?"

"Of course. Do you think Dad would let rain, snow, or sun hit this precious artifact of American engineering?" Charlie asked.

We came out of the garage into the kitchen, and I smelled shrimp and gazpacho. Saliva filled my mouth. Our mother was preparing cocktail sauce, and the pungent bite of horseradish tickled my nostrils. She left what she was doing and enfolded me in a perfumed embrace. Her dangling bracelets caught in my hair, and her trailing Turkish scarf, which she wore like a shawl, nearly smothered me. People have described my mother's fashion sense as an explosion in a UNICEF store—cruel but accurate.

We finally untangled, and I helped myself to a glass of lemonade from the fridge. It was hot and muggy, and there were some promising-looking clouds off to the east. Maybe a thunderstorm would blow away the oppressive heat and humidity. I have this weird kink—I love violent weather. Wind, rain, snow, thunder, and lightning—I think they're all great.

"*Are* you hungry?" my mother asked. "Because *it's* an hour *to* dinner."

"I'd accept a snack," I said, knowing that's where she was going.

I helped her pull out a round of brie, some crackers and grapes, and an open bottle of white wine. I finished off the lemonade and switched to alcohol. It was a Vouvray, light and fruity, but still complex and not sweet. I sat on a stool at the large central island in the kitchen, nibbling and sipping wine while my mother rattled on about the trip, making every story about her. It was as if Charlie hadn't even been along. It was one of the many things I hated about my mother—people were just props in the play of her life. We'd gotten to the couple she had met in Paris, and how she and Charlie were invited to visit their home in Provence, and she rather thought the husband fancied her, *"But of course absolutely nothing happened, darling, don't look so shocked."*

I actually wasn't looking shocked, more bemused. My mother has always fancied that every man she meets is fascinated, enchanted, and enthralled by her. Nothing could be further from the truth, but none of us have the heart to break this to her, least of all my father.

He and Charlie entered the kitchen at that moment. Daddy smelled of mown grass, sweat, and gasoline. "The backyard is tamed," he said as he gave my mother a kiss on the cheek. "So we can sit on the deck for dinner, admire the lake, and you won't be offended by the shaggy grass."

"Thank you, you are a *dear.*"

"A smelly dear. I'm going to grab a shower. Save me a glass of wine," he said with a wink to me.

I saluted him with my glass. "No promises."

Charlie poured himself a glass, and we munched and sipped wine until Daddy returned. He hefted the bottle, inspected it, then went to his small wine cellar in the basement and returned with another bottle.

The cork released with a satisfying *pop*, and Daddy topped off our glasses. He held up his and saluted me with it.

"You look good," he said. "I knew you could handle this. Get back to work."

"I wouldn't go as far as *good*, but I am back to work."

"But things are better now?" he asked, and he gave me a concerned look. "You're not thinking about quitting any longer, right?"

I wanted to shriek at him, *Stop reminding me of what happened. Let me have my time away. Like Meredith did.*

But I didn't say that. Instead I just shook my head. I needed to say something to keep the conversation going, and I didn't want that conversation to be about the office, so I pivoted to Charlie. "Okay, which country had the prettiest girls?"

He leaned back and tugged at his upper lip like an art connoisseur considering a wall of Monets. "The French girls are chic, but man, there are a lot of cigarettes and piercings, and the short-cropped hair thing kind of got old. The Scandinavian girls are all six feet tall. The German girls, at least the ones I met, were into heavy political conversations, which dropped their pretty quotient way down." He paused, then said, "I've got to give it to the Italians. I loved the way they talked with their hands. And I loved the language. It's like water running over rocks."

Our father stared at Charlie. "My son, you reveal hidden depths."

"I actually think it's fairly clichéd," I said. Charlie threw me the bird.

"Charles Grantham Ellery!" Mother yelped.

"There's a reason clichés happen," my brother said.

"You don't need to further them," I said.

By the time dinner was ready the house was blocking the setting sun, so we decided to eat out on the deck. Cormorants, their long necks ducking and winding sinuously, uttered their soft grunts. While mallards quacked and splashed in the rippling water. At the lake's edge blue herons stalked through the cattails and grasses like dowagers stepping over cow patties. Mother chattered nonstop about people I didn't know, and events I wouldn't normally care about. This time the inane babble was perfect, because it kept the conversation away from the office and the murder.

The chilled gazpacho was perfect at the end of a hot, muggy day, and I had to give my mother credit for being a really good cook. I finished off my last shrimp and picked up a handful of oyster crackers to nibble.

"So I said *to* her. You can't be seriously *thinking* of using chrysanthemums on the *altar* in June." Charlie's eyes were locked on our mother's face, his expression interested. I wondered where his mind really was, and how he managed to keep the appearance of total attention.

My father's and my eyes met, and he gave me a rueful little smile. There was something very poignant about a sensible man married to a vastly silly woman. I choked on a cracker and wondered when I'd started to channel a poor imitation of Jane Austen.

And acknowledging that my mother was silly was not a comforting thought since daughters inevitably begin to resemble their mothers. I vowed to avoid that fate, wondering once again why on earth he and Mommy had ever gotten married.

"There's homemade *peach* ice cream," mother said. "*Who* wants some?"

"Everybody," I said.

Charlie jumped up. "I'll help carry bowls." He and our mother disappeared through the French doors.

Daddy leaned over and rested his hand on mine. "How are you doing? Really?"

"I'm okay." Irritated, I shook off his hand and pleated my napkin for a few moments. "I always wanted to be in a big firm, handling big cases, but I've got to admit it's not what I expected, and I'm not sure I like it."

"What would you rather be doing?" Daddy's tone was carefully neutral, but I could hear the tension just below the surface.

"I still love the law. It's just the atmosphere in these big firms, and I'm not sure how much opportunity there really is for advancement. Another associate and I talked about maybe opening an office together," I said, joking.

It obviously wasn't received that way. A strange expression crossed my father's face. He took a quick sip of wine. "I think that's a really interesting idea, but I also think it's way too early for you to be thinking about setting up your own office. Work a few years, and then see how you're feeling. You'll also have a better reputation to attract clients. I really don't want you coming home. So many of my friends have adult children who have crawled back into the nest." He gave a small laugh. "And I'm rather afraid that Charlie is going to be one of those. After he's done nine or ten years as a professional student. He doesn't seem strongly drawn to anything."

"Not true. He was pretty passionate on the subject of architecture during the drive home."

"Architecture?" I was glad Charlie wasn't at the table to hear the incredulity. "He hasn't said anything to me."

"He's afraid to. He knows you want him to take over the company, and he doesn't want to disappoint you."

"If he's found something that interests him, I'll support him to the hilt."

We heard Mother's and Charlie's voices approaching. I hurried to ask, "What would you have done if I hadn't wanted to be a lawyer?"

"Supported your decision," my father said. But I caught the minute hesitation before the answer.

I slept that night in what had been my bedroom up to the age of eight. Once I was sent to the Bainbridge house to live, it had been turned into a guest room. I looked around, trying to find a vestige of the child who had slept here. There was nothing.

The bookcase offered a selection of bestsellers placed there for the enjoyment of a guest. I wondered where my collection of children's books had gone, and the collection of Breyer plastic horses. Over the years, as I'd outgrown childish things, my little treasures had been packed up by the servants in the Bainbridge house and sent back to my parents. My mother had probably thrown them away, or put them in the church rummage sale. Or perhaps my father had rescued them. I'd have to ask.

I really hoped the Breyer horses were still around. I had always planned to give them to my daughter someday. Though given the perversity of children, any kid of mine would probably end up hating horses.

I sat down on the edge of the four-poster bed. There wasn't a scrap of warmth or personality in this room. It was like I had never existed. I realized that vampires had defined my life. There had been visits home during the holidays, when my human family was always distracted and never at their best. Because of their business ties, my father had been a frequent visitor at Meredith's house, which meant I ended up closer to him than either my mother or my brother. I had tried to bond with them while I was in college and law school, but had I really succeeded?

I felt totally disconnected from all the relationships that should matter. Normally a rootless person builds relationships at work, but I was the dogsbody of Ishmael, McGillary and Gold. Sadness lay like a stone in the center of my chest. But slowly my spine began to stiffen. I was the lowest of the low at the firm, which meant I had nothing to lose. You can't fall further than rock bottom. What was the worst that could happen? They could fire me. Big deal. I had a great education. I was a good lawyer, and I knew how to work hard.

I was going to figure out who killed Chip. And I was going to humiliate Ryan, if it was the last thing I ever did.

# 11

Back at work on Monday morning, I stopped in the bathroom to retouch my lipstick and found Caroline there. She whirled at my entrance, treating me to a ferocious frown that knitted her brows and wrinkled her forehead.

"What? What have I done now?" I asked, defensive and paranoid.

"What are you talking about?" Caroline demanded.

"The look."

"Oh, it's not meant for you." She took a quick glance under the stall doors to make sure we were alone. "Ryan has put together one of his little luncheons," she told me. "I realized after our talk that I'm sick of this, and I don't want to go."

"Then don't go."

"It's not that simple. Every office has politics. We have to play by them. To just refuse would be completely in his face. I need an out. A prior engagement."

"How about a women lawyers' luncheon?" I suggested. "Do you think we could get every female associate?"

"Everyone but Jane. She'll never stop kissing Ryan's butt."

"Wow, that's cold. I thought she was like your best friend," I said. "You're always together."

Caroline gave me a predator's smile. "Just keeping an eye on her so I don't find a knife in my side."

"Keeping your friends close and your enemies closer?" I asked.

"Exactly. Why don't we book our table at the same restaurant where Ryan will be entertaining the boys and Jane?"

"I thought you weren't down with the whole in-your-face thing," I said.

"I changed my mind. And nothing makes men more nervous then seeing a bunch of ex-girlfriends with their heads together. Especially if they're laughing."

"Remind me to never get on your bad side . . . again," I amended. She headed for the door. "Will you pass the word?" She nodded and left. I pulled out my lipstick and lip pencil. *Warpaint*, I thought as I outlined my mouth.

In my office I pulled out the *May* file, made sure my pens worked, and gathered up a couple of yellow legal pads in preparation for the settlement meeting. Elizabeth May arrived twenty minutes late.

"I'm sorry. So sorry. My babysitter was late," she said in harried tones, and pushed her hair back from her face.

She was a pretty woman in her late twenties with fine brown hair that lay limply over her skull. Her haunted brown eyes held that cringing expression you see in the eyes of abused dogs. Her features were round and soft, and in old age, with no cheekbones for support, her face was going to look like a wrinkled apple. She wore a pair of brown slacks and a pink shirt with a Peter Pan collar. None of it was flattering.

"No problem," I said, as I stood and came around the desk to meet her. "Sometimes life just intrudes. Please, sit down. I'm Linnet Ellery. I've taken over Chip's cases."

"I was very upset about Mr. Westin." But she didn't sound like it. She sounded beat down, as if any emotion was an effort. "But I'm glad you're a woman. I think I'll be more comfortable with a female lawyer. But Jake is going to hate you."

"Because I'm representing you?"

She shook her head. "Oh, that's part of it, but he'd say you were taking a job from a man who has a family to support. He hates uppity women."

"I take it you didn't work during the marriage?" I asked.

"No, Jake would have gone ballistic."

"Have you ever worked?"

"No, we got married right out of high school."

*Great*, I thought. *That means she has no social security built up, and zero job skills.*

"When did Jake get infected?"

"He did ten months in jail. He said the only way to stay safe was to join a gang. So he picked the meanest gang he could find."

I had heard that werewolf infection rates in prison were on the rise. Short of putting everyone in solitary, it was tough to prevent. It also meant that most of the guards had to be werewolves too.

"What did Jake go to jail for?" I asked.

"Assault and battery. It was a bar fight," she added, as if that made it better.

"And you didn't think you should get away from him right then and there?"

She gave me a wounded look. "You're not as nice as Mr. Westin."

I clutched a handful of my hair. "No, I'm probably not, but I know that men who use their fists to solve problems always take that problem-solving method back home. So, when did he start hitting you?"

Elizabeth flushed. "Last year. After he lost his job."

"Because of course that was your fault," I said acerbically.

"Ms. Ellery, I'm really scared. Jake said he'll infect the boys if I don't stop the divorce proceedings. And if I do go ahead and divorce him, is the court going to make me share custody with him after what he said?"

"Normally a court will opt for joint custody. My job is to make sure the court realizes how dangerous that would be for your children. Especially given Jake's gang involvement. Once in, never out is the general rule with those guys." I picked up my pen and beat a tattoo on the top of the legal pad. "There's another issue. You need to get out of the tristate area. We've established that Jake is watching you."

At this news, the woman went so white I was afraid she was going to faint. Alarmed, I keyed the intercom. "Norma, please bring me a glass of water."

"Oh God, what am I going to do?" She clasped her hands over and over, knuckles whitening with strain. "Maybe I should forget this. Just go back to him."

"No! If you go back the abuse will just get worse, because then he knows it works. I'm going to ask for a large settlement, but you've got to help me by moving away." *And I've got to get her sole custody of the two boys.*

"I don't know. My friends, my family—"

"Your children's safety."

There was a quick knock, and Norma entered with the water. Elizabeth took the glass and gulped down a few sips.

"Mr. May and his attorney are here," Norma said.

"Okay." I gathered up the file, the pad, and my pen. I looked down at Elizabeth. "You ready?"

"I guess."

We headed upstairs to a conference room.

We had been given the smallest room, which meant we were all breathing each other's air, and my knees came perilously close to touching Jake May's. I had taken one look at his twisted face and made sure Elizabeth wasn't seated across from him.

I could see how May might have swept a young girl off her feet. He had red-gold hair, blue eyes, and a fit, trim body. He also had one of those complexions that went blotchy red when he was angry. He was angry now, and his eyes kept switching from blue to the wine red glint of the werewolf.

May's attorney, Kevin Phenrod, was sweating, and he kept looking at his client instead of meeting my gaze. That seemed odd, so I took a long look at the man. May's hands were balled into fists and pressed against the table—and the reddish hair on the backs of his fingers was slowly thickening and lengthening. No wonder Phenrod was sweating.

I introduced myself to May and Phenrod. The other attorney shook my hand. I had to force myself to extend my hand to May. He didn't take it. He muttered something that might have been words, but seemed more like a growl.

"If there are no objections, I'd like to tape this meeting so we can be sure we have an accurate transcript for the court," I said.

"How do I know you won't doctor the tape and make up some bullshit?" May asked.

"How about if we use my phone? It's got video recording," Phenrod said hurriedly.

"I have no problem with that," I said.

Phenrod set his BlackBerry in the center of the small table "First, I'd like to say on behalf of my client that he opposes this divorce. He loves his wife and children, and he feels counseling and mediation would resolve their problems. He's willing to do both."

Elizabeth stirred in her chair. I didn't want to be one of those lawyers who ramrodded people into divorces, but I also knew Elizabeth was an abuse victim, and if they don't have help, they have a hard time breaking with their abusers. I hurried into the conversational break.

"Noted, but my client is resolved to move ahead with the divorce." Elizabeth retreated to the very back of her chair.

"Cunt," May said succinctly.

"Yes, he does seems very loving," I said in a cool tone. I was amazed I pulled it off. My belly muscles were quivering. There was the faintest musk of wolf in the room, and it was bringing up a whole lot of unholy memories. "Given Mr. May's refusal to pay basic support during these proceedings, we have no expectation that he'll honor an order for child support, so we're going to ask for a lump-sum payment of seven hundred thousand dollars."

"If I don't have access to my kids, I'm not giving that bitch a fucking dime," May said.

"You've threatened to turn them!" Elizabeth's voice spiraled toward dolphin-whistle range. "They're nine and five. They're scared of you!"

"Because you turned them against me!"

"And it's because of these threats regarding the children that we're going to petition the court for sole custody," I said, before the fight between them could escalate any further.

"You fucking bitches!" May roared, coming halfway out of his chair. The nails on May's hands were thickening, lengthening into claws. Phenrod laid a hand on his client's bulging forearm and was shaken off.

May lunged across the table, his face only inches from mine. I had a real good view of the transformation that was beginning. Elizabeth chittered with fear. I wanted to gibber in terror too, but there was also part of me that was rejoicing—we were going to get everything we wanted.

I gave Elizabeth's chair a hard shove to the right at the same time that I shoved my chair back from the table. The wheels rolled really well on the stone tile, and Elizabeth's chair careened away and crashed into the credenza. Glasses, the pitcher of water, and the phone went tumbling to the floor. The glass shattered, and the phone let out a faint, unhappy *ting* of protest. My escape from May wasn't as successful, because I only had a few inches. All too soon I slammed against the wall.

The picture above my head bounced and flew off the wall. I cringed, waiting for it to land on my head, but it arced out and hit the table, shattering the glass. Several small pieces nicked my arms and face, but a large shard flew straight at May and sliced across his eye and cheek. Like all face wounds, it gushed blood. He screamed, pressed a hand against the cut, and recoiled away from me, falling to the floor on the other side of the table. Moaning and writhing, he shifted back toward human.

The commotion brought partners, assistants, and security running. The room wasn't big enough for the crowd. It was like being at a cocktail party from hell—not enough air to breathe and bodies pressed way too close for comfort. Shade grabbed May by the back of the neck, hefted him off the ground, and just held him there.

Gold and McGillary arrived together, and Gold took charge, roaring, "What the hell is going on in here?" He was glaring at *me* rather than at the bleeding man.

My hand was trembling a bit as I pointed at the BlackBerry, now covered with May's blood. "It's all there. It was being recorded."

McGillary snatched up the phone, wiped away the blood, and

casually licked it off the palm of his hand. I found myself wondering if werewolf blood tasted different. And shouldn't there have been courtesy between monsters? I wasn't sure where that nasty little thought had come from and hurriedly pushed it aside. McGillary set it to play back. I watched his eyebrows climb up toward his hairline. He offered the BlackBerry to Gold, who watched, then forced a snort of disgust and walked out.

Shade, still holding May, turned to Phenrod, who was just standing there, his expression akin to a poleaxed bull. "Give me one reason why I shouldn't call the police right now and have this man"—he gave May a shake—"arrested."

"Because your associate just won everything she wanted in the settlement. There's no way we want this played in open court. Whatever you want, we agree," Phenrod said, this time directly to me. "Now let me get this guy to a hospital to get sewn up."

McGillary and Shade exchanged glances, then Shade sat May down. Client and lawyer left, the client trailing blood. I was suddenly aware that Elizabeth was crying. I put an arm around her. "Shhh, it's okay. It's all over."

"What happened?" She sniffled.

"You're getting an uncontested divorce, and anything else we want. I'll write up a settlement agreement this afternoon. Look, while Jake is at the hospital get your kids, pack up, and move. There's a battered women's center that will take you in while we get this finalized."

"But—"

"Just do it!" She squeaked and tried to reach the door, but the crowd was too tight. "Okay, it's over! Get out of the way!" I ordered. Amazingly, a number of people filtered out of the conference room.

A handkerchief was held out to me. I looked up. It was

McGillary. I took the square of fine linen and blotted at the cuts on my arms and cheeks. "You are certainly an . . . interesting new hire," he said, and left.

I sat back down and realized I had just won my first case.


With all the excitement I'd forgotten about our ladies' lunch. Caroline turned up in the door of my office and gave me one of her cool stares. "You've got to stop making a habit out of fighting werewolves. Are you ready?" I stared at her, puzzled.

"Ready for what?"

"Our women's solidarity lunch." There was more than a little sarcasm in the words.

"Oh God," I groaned. "I forgot. I'm not sure I'm up to this."

Caroline grabbed my arm and hoisted me out of my chair. "Nonsense. And you need a glass of wine. It's all over the office what you did," she continued. I dropped my face into my hands. "No, it's a good thing. McGillary is bragging about you. Practically acting like he invented you."

"Gold won't like that," I said a touch bitterly.

Our girl posse was gathered in the lobby. There were congratulations offered, and many mutterings about male assholes. Caroline had timed our reservation so we arrived before Ryan and the boys. We were ensconced at our table and decided to get a bottle of wine. With fourteen of us, it amounted to a sip each, but that was okay. We were celebrating and declaring war at the same time. We also began to compare notes on Ryan.

Like me, Delia had experienced the cab fare on the table. "Oh, I wish I'd thought of the toilet, but I felt so fuzzy once it was all over," she said. "I ended up just leaving it there."

"I felt like I was floating in this romantic dream. Then I woke up and realized I'd been treated like a hooker," Nancy said, and shame laced the words. Caroline put a comforting arm around her shoulders.

As they talked, I realized their ordeals had lasted many hours longer than mine. Because I'd been fostered, Ryan hadn't used his mesmerizing power on me, which meant I was fully aware of his rough treatment. I also realized that the game he was playing was dangerous as hell. Had the senior partners known? And if so, why hadn't they shut him down? I was furious with them for risking us in this way. It was pretty clear now that Ryan was a thrill seeker. He skated on the edge of what was safe. As far as I was concerned, the Convocation, a gathering of senior vampires almost like a court, could execute Ryan, but not these women. They had been victims.

"Hookers would have done better," Cecelia, big and blonde, declared. "One cheap-ass dinner and cab fare? With our looks and education, we are an escort service's wet dream," she added with a grin. And I added *charmingly brassy* to the *big and blonde* description.

Juliette, a beautiful black woman who had the soft music of Jamaica in her voice, took a fortifying sip of wine and detailed how Ryan had used a vacuum erection device to get it up when he slept with her.

"Time to puuump you uuuup," Kathy, a pert redhead, drawled in imitation of a decades-old *Saturday Night Live* skit.

We erupted into gales of laugher. That's when Ryan swept in, trailing associates like a cloak. Jane bobbed around the edges of the group like an overactive puppy vying for attention. Ryan froze and the basso rumble of pontificating men stuttered into silence. He glared at us.

The women with their backs to him cranked around in their chairs. We were all looking at him. And then it happened. We didn't plan it. It was just one of those perfect moments. As one, all fourteen of us lifted our glasses toward him, and then burst out laughing.

Ryan was a man and a vampire. Neither beast can be ridiculed with impunity. He spun on his heel and left the restaurant, shouldering aside and scattering associates as if they were bowling pins.

David Sullivan was in my office, sitting on my ball chair, behind my desk. Since I was just coming off an hour and a half of women's empowerment, I was annoyed.

"That is *my* chair."

He shrugged. "Get a more comfortable client chair. And by the way, this chair isn't exactly a bed of roses either. And congratulations on your victory."

"Small beer for this firm," I said, with a shrug of my own.

"A win's a win. I found something interesting." He held out a scrap of paper torn off a legal pad. I recognized Chip's round, fat handwriting.

*#28 24th Street, Bayonne, NJ, two mil,* I read.

"Any idea what this means?" David asked.

I sat down on the client chair. He was right. It was pretty uncomfortable. "Not a clue. Where did you find this? I've never seen it before, and I've been pawing through those boxes for days."

"It was stuck on the back of a folder. It would have been easy to miss."

" 'Two mil.' That's got to mean two million, right?"

"Seems logical."

"But two million what?" I asked.

"Oh, come on, Linnet, you're not that dense," David said.

"Okay, I was being deliberately obtuse, because what does it say about Chip if he was scribbling notes to himself about two million bucks?"

"The question is whether he was the payee or the payer," David said.

"If he was the payer, that would imply Chip was into somebody for two million, and that just doesn't fit. Chip's only vice that I could see was food. And I know. I checked on his personal life."

"The other option is that he was the payee, he was blackmailing somebody. That would explain why he was killed," Sullivan said.

I shook my head. "I just can't see that. Chip wasn't that kind of guy."

*But he was actively working against his client's interests by helping another claimant to the estate. Was this money he was demanding from the stripper and the daughter once they got control of the company?* I just couldn't see it. Chip had been concerned about putting the power of a private army in the hands of assholes.

I was pretty sure this had something to do with the *Abercrombie* case, and since it might reveal Chip's unethical behavior, I wanted David out of the loop. Cautiously I asked, "Did you Google this address?"

"Yeah, it's a crappy, rundown house in a crappy rundown neighborhood."

"Did you find out who owns it?" I asked.

He handed over a piece of paper. "It's a rental property. The owner lives in a condo down in Florida. I haven't been able to reach them to find out the current renter."

"You've put a ton of work into this. Thanks, but I've got to ask—why?"

He rolled the ball chair away from the desk. "I need to get back to my own work. Let me know when you reach the owner, and what you find out."

He left, and I realized he hadn't answered the question.

I tried five times to reach John during the afternoon, but every time I got his voice mail. I wanted to send him off to the mysterious address, but obviously he was working on something else.

At six, I decided I'd had enough. Facing down an angry werewolf and dealing with Ryan had me exhausted. I headed to the elevators. A car arrived, the doors opened, and as I met Ryan's cold-eyed stare, I realized what really confronting him meant. After the day I'd had, I didn't really want to get into it with him, and from his expression it was clear he wanted to.

"I'll wait for the next one." I stepped back. The doors closed, cutting off my view of his expression.

I was on the next elevator when it stopped on the sixty-third floor and Ryan got in with me. I wasn't sure how he'd done that. Gotten off on sixty-nine and run down five flights? Or had he used some vampire power to know which elevator I was riding?

He got close, invading my personal space. "You're smart, but not very wise, Linnet. You shouldn't have picked a fight with me. I can make your life very unpleasant."

Outrage gave starch to my spine. "Gee, I thought you'd already done that," I snapped. "Silence and shame were your allies, Ryan, but the word is out now."

The elevator's stomach-dropping descent slowed then stopped at the ground floor lobby. The door opened, and I stepped out. "And I know you used your power on those women. If you make a move against any of us, I'll go to the Convocation."

"I'm going to destroy you."

Heat coiled in my chest. I turned back to face him. "Darth Vader threats? Really? And in front of security." I pointed at the wide-eyed guard at the front desk. "You are so pathetic."

I walked away, the wheels on my case chuckling over the seams in the tile.

# 12

A few days after the May affair, I began getting casses assigned to me. They weren't big, and they weren't terribly important, but they were *mine*. It also meant I was busy and so hadn't headed to New Jersey, since I still hadn't reached John. But that was about to be rectified. I'd decided to go on my own.

Today, I was waiting for a Mr. Joylon Bryce, due in at 2:00 p.m. I was feeling guilty, because exercise hadn't been high on my list of priorities for almost a week. I kept a bag with workout clothes under my desk in the hope (so far unrealized) that I would either exercise in lieu of lunch, or go to a gym after work. I decided to spend my lunch hour at a nearby gym.

I ended up on a rowing machine next to a woman who insisted on critiquing my technique for the entire time, and then as I was headed toward the dressing room for a quick shower, after my sweat-inducing workout, I heard a female trainer advising her client that she really needed to hit the gym at 5:00 a.m. before she went to her office. "It will be painful for the first week, but then it will just put you in the zone."

"Yeah, the zone of total exhaustion," I muttered to myself. The locker room smelled of sweat, steam, hair spray, and perfume. I ran through the shower, styled my hair with one of the provided hand hair dryers, put on my makeup, and headed back to the office. By the time I walked back through the summer heat I needed another shower.

My stomach was sending up emergency signals to my brain. *Hey, we're empty down here.* I stopped in the kitchen for a big glass of water, averted my eyes from the half a donut that remained in the box, and went back to my office.

I worked a bit on an environmental case I'd been assigned and then it was two o'clock and Mr. Bryce arrived. He was in his forties, with graying brown hair, bright blue eyes, a long face, and a prominent nose. He was also in a wheelchair. I jumped up and hurried around the desk to push the client chair out of the way.

Once Bryce was situated in front of my desk, we exchanged handshakes. "Ms. Ellery," he said in a clipped, upper-class British accent.

"Mr. Bryce. Nice to meet you." I returned to my chair.

Norma inquired about beverages. Mr. Bryce went with a Coke. I asked for coffee. She left.

"Now, Mr. Bryce, what can I do for you?" I picked up a pen and prepared to take notes.

He had a slim black attaché case tucked between his hip and the arm of the chair, which he pulled free and laid on the desk.

"I just purchased the license to run a venerable old riding facility in Brooklyn, and a pair of developers are agitating the city to turn over the land to them. I'm determined to resist. Would this be of any interest to you at all?" he asked rather anxiously.

"Oh, definitely. I've ridden my whole life, and everybody always forgets quality of life in this town in favor of the pursuit of the Almighty Dollar." I broke off, blushing. "Sorry, didn't mean to go on a rant."

"Quite all right. I prefer to have someone with passion handling the case, and Mr. Ishmael thought you might be the right person for my little problem."

"Do go on." I waved the pen.

He continued. "It was built in 1867, it's on some prime acreage, and the pond scum—"

"Meaning the developers?"

"Yes. They're telling the city they could be making so much more tax revenue if the property was changed into high-rise offices or condos."

"Developed by the pond scum, I presume?" I asked.

"Exactly."

"Does the pond scum have a name?"

"The Kellog Group."

I wrote it down. "Is the city going to try eminent domain?"

"I think that's where they are going."

"That's not good news, because it may be tough to beat. The Supremes handed down a case a few years back, *Kelo v. City of New London*, that basically gave a city the power to condemn land for just such a purpose."

"Oh, dear."

He looked so upset that I hastened to add, "But that case caused such an uproar I'm not sure a city, even Brooklyn, would want to risk it. Is there community support for the stable?"

"Very much so. People like to walk through the woods on the property, and jog and ride bikes on the riding trails. The current management wisely banned motorized bikes, since some horses find bicycles quite terrifying enough, but I digress. It's powerful business interests that find us offensive. And I do have something that might be of help."

He opened the flap on his case and pulled out a document. I took it and had a sinking sensation when I read the opening words. *I, James Harris, being of sound mind and . . .*

I couldn't help it. I blurted, "Oh God, not another will."

"Beg pardon?"

"Sorry, sorry. I'm working on a long and ugly case over a contested will," I answered.

"And you'd prefer not to have another."

"That about sums it up."

There was a discreet tap on the door, and Norma brought in my coffee and Mr. Bryce's Coke. She left again, closing the door behind her. I began flipping through the pages of the document.

"The relevant section is on page eleven, about midway down," he offered.

I flipped to that page and found the relevant section. I read it and reread it, then looked up at my client.

"According to this, Mr. Bryce—"

"Please call me Jolly, or Joe."

He just didn't look like a Joe, and the Brits seemed to be all about silly nicknames. "Okay, Jolly, according to this document the underlying land already belongs to the city."

"Yes, it was deeded to them at the time of Mr. Harris's death in 1883."

I went back to reading. "And it states that the property can only be used for a horse facility, and if it ever ceases to be a horse facility the property reverts to the Harris heirs."

"Quite so."

"Well, they can't claim eminent domain on something they already own."

"Could they let it go back to the heirs so the developers could then buy the property from them?" Jolly asked.

"Very unlikely. Once a property has been left to a state or a municipality, they never give up the asset. Political opponents would charge them with squandering an asset, violating their fiduciary duty, and being in thrall to special corporate interests."

"All of which would be true in this case," Jolly said with a smile. "So, it sounds like we're home free?"

"I think so. It's an unusual clause. It grants a license to someone to use the improvements on the property. It states that the license can be transferred so long as the transferee continues to operate it as a horse facility." I looked up at Jolly. "Is that what you did?"

"Yes, I bought the license from Mrs. Maddy Unger. She's been running the facility and giving children riding lessons for fifty-eight years. But she decided to retire."

"Good God, how old is she?"

"Eighty-seven," Jolly said with a smile. "And she rode up until last year."

"Okay, that's an inspiration." I read through a few more sections of the will, but it looked like the lawyer who had drafted it back in—I flipped to the final page and read the date—August 31, 1877, had done a good job. "Okay," I said. "I think we're good. I'll contact the Brooklyn city attorney and point out this little fact." I waved the pages of the will. "But it wouldn't hurt if you marshaled public support."

"I'll get on the press and public opinion angle right away," Jolly said as he maneuvered back from the desk and turned his chair around so he faced the door.

I could tell from his expression that he wanted to say something more. "Was there anything else?" I asked.

My encouragement worked, because he turned his chair around to face me and said, "This will probably sound strange, but I was wondering if you would be willing to ride my horse for me?" He gestured down at his legs. "Obviously I'm no longer able to ride in any meaningful way, and this is a magnificent creature who needs a job and a partner. Mr. Ishmael told me you are quite the horsewoman. I don't know if that would be some sort of conflict of interest. . . ." He allowed his voice to trail away.

"If I were representing Brooklyn in this dispute, then yes, it would be a conflict. But for us, no. And I would love the chance to ride regularly. What style? Tell me about the horse? How much training?" I pressed my lips together so I'd stop babbling.

"He's a young Lusitano stallion, Vento. Blazingly white, ready to show Prix St. George. Once he has his tempi changes he'll be ready for the Grand Prix."

"So he has the passage and the piaffe?"

"They will amaze you. He's very sensitive and sensible. It's like dancing a tango with the perfect partner. So it's settled?"

"Absolutely! When can I start?"

"How about this evening? There's an indoor arena, so once winter comes you can still keep riding. Even after one of your very busy and long days."

"I'm sorry, I can't tonight. I'm going to see a show. Friend of mine is in the chorus. Rain check?"

Bryce handed me his business card. "Call whenever you want to come, and I'll have Vento ready for you." He began to roll his chair back so he could get into position to head for the door. I jumped up to open it for him. He looked around the office, at the lighter squares on the walls that marked where Chip's diplomas and pictures had hung and the stacks of *Abercrombie* files. One eyebrow quirked up and he said, "I love what you've done with the place."

It took me a moment to grasp his meaning. Then I looked at my space and realized that there was no touch of my personality. My diploma was on the wall to my left, and that was it. I hadn't even unpacked my wind-up Godzilla yet.

"Hmm, yeah, I guess it is a little . . . stark, isn't it?" I said.

"You might say that."

"I haven't had this office all that long, and things have been . . .'"

I groped for a word and settled on "hectic." I paused and then added, "I can't thank you enough for this opportunity."

He smiled up at me, and there was an expression in his eyes that made him look like an impish ten-year-old. "It was all part of my cunning plan. Once you ride Vento, you're going to want to continue, and you won't be able to do that if we can't keep the stable open."

I debated whether to be offended at the implication that I wouldn't work hard without a bribe, but I decided that wasn't his intention. Sometimes men of a certain generation can be a bit clueless where professional women are concerned.

"Don't worry if you come late. If you ride past sunset there are lights on the outdoor arenas as well as the indoor."

"Sounds good."

"Do you want directions?"

I shook my head. "Google Maps and HopStop are my friends."

"Sometimes I don't understand my world," Jolly said as we headed for the elevators.

"Now you sound like a vampire."

"Meaning what?" David called, his acute, undead hearing allowing him to pick up my words even though I was on the opposite end of the room from him.

"That you're dinosaurs and eavesdroppers," I said in a normal tone of voice, assuming David would hear. Judging from the way his mouth twisted, he did, but I couldn't interpret the expression.

Once Jolly was on the elevator and on his way, I headed back to my office with a decided spring in my step. I had a horse to ride again. And cases of my own.

————

Ray was dancing in a revival of *Auntie Mame*. I emerged from the subway and headed toward Forty-fourth Street and the St. James Theater. Occasionally people in the flowing crowds would stare down their noses at my roller bag since I was now a double obstacle on the crowded sidewalks. I realized I could have left it at the office, and I cursed myself for an idiot. It was too late now.

I went around the corner onto Forty-fourth Street, where marquees on various theaters presented a lot of revivals of older hits interspersed with musicals based on Disney movies and TV shows. I wondered when audiences had lost their taste for anything new and innovative. Was it because the audiences for Broadway shows skewed older? But why not embrace some rock-and-roll musical based on the antediluvian music of the Stones or the Beatles?

Or maybe it was the emergence of the Powers. Given their conservatism, it wasn't surprising that they weren't interested in a hip-hop Broadway musical or a show built around Facebook or online dating sites. But that generalization didn't really fit either. Werewolves tended to be found in the world of business and finance, and creating a successful new business meant you had to be forward leaning, not worrying about making better buggy whips. I chuckled out loud. Yep, vampires were definitely buggy-whip guys and werewolves were definitely killer-robot guys.

Or maybe it was about people retreating to the familiar in a desperate attempt to find some sense of security.

Or maybe the new shows and music just sucked, and that was why people wanted to see *My Fair Lady* or *Oklahoma!* over and over again.

I reached the theater, got my ticket from the will-call window, checked my bag with the bored coat-check boy, and headed to my seat. I loved the atmosphere in the old theaters, many of them built back in the 1920s and '30s. I could picture gentlemen in tuxedos opening the doors to Packards or Dusenbergs and as-

sisting women in fabulous furs, long gloves, and sparkling dia-
monds as they stepped out.

At the curtain call, Cole Porter or George M. Cohen would
step out onto the stage and take a bow with the cast members, and
then you and your date would head off to some club with an improbable name—the Copacabana, Clam House, the Nest—and
eat supper and dance until three in the morning.

I watched a very large couple trying to wedge their enormous
rear ends into the narrow velvet upholstered seats and made
another extrapolation—people were a lot smaller in 1930. Then
the conductor walked into the orchestra pit, accompanied by a
ripple of applause, and I settled back to enjoy. Act One ended
with the fox hunt and the big *Mame* production number.

Ray looked really cute in his red hunt coat, white britches,
and tall black boots. Of course the "boots" were pliable so he
could dance. Not like my dressage boots, with the steel rod up
the back to keep the boot stiff and my leg in the correct position.
Boots made me think about riding, which made me think about
Ryan. I banished him from my thoughts.

The show wound down to the reprise of "Open a New Window," the curtain rang down, curtain calls were taken, and the
crowd began to disperse. I recovered my roller bag case, went
around to the side of the theater and the stage door, and talked
my way inside.

There was the smell of hot lights beginning to cool, grease
paint, cologne, flowers, and sweat. Ray was in the chorus members' dressing room. People were running in and out in various
stages of undress. There were kisses and hugs, and the roar of conversation as excited performers relived the performance and began
to come down off their performance highs.

Ray was talking with friends while Gregory tried to wipe off
the excess cold cream smeared around Ray's ears. Ray spotted

me, let out a shriek of delight, bounded over, and hugged me hard. His skin was greasy against my cheek, and I just knew my makeup was also falling victim to his cold cream.

"Oh, sweetie, you came. I'm so glad. Are you coming to the party?"

I shook my head. "It's a school night, I've still got to do some work before I get to bed, and I have to go to New Jersey tomorrow."

"Okay, that's just horrible," said Gregory. "You should get a lot of sleep before you face that."

# 13

Around 4:00 p.m., the lobby guard called to tell me my rental car had arrived. I packed up my bag and headed down.

Since I wasn't sure the company would reimburse me for the rental, I went for a subcompact. What waited for me at the curb was a Chevy that looked like a cereal box on very tiny wheels. The young man from the Enterprise office handed me the keys, opened the trunk, and insisted on lifting in my roller bag. He then asked if I wanted any guidance on the car's features. I resisted the impulse to ask, *What features?* Instead, I accepted the keys and climbed into the cramped interior.

It was the last day of July, and sizzling. I cranked up the air conditioner to maximum and tried to listen to the radio over the roar of the fan. With my usual impeccable timing, I had managed to hit rush-hour traffic. I had thought I was being clever going up to I-95 to cross over into New Jersey rather than taking the Lincoln Tunnel, but the traffic was terrible there too, so my journey into the wilds of New Jersey took forever.

———

Gentrification and urban renewal had definitely not reached the part of Bayonne where the rental house was located. Deserted factories and warehouses gazed out across the waters of the Newark Bay on one side of the peninsula and the Upper Bay on the other. The rusting struts, girders, and unknown equipment looked like relics of an ancient and alien civilization. Mr. 2 Mil's address was a couple of blocks inland from the rotting buildings.

Older-model cars, many showing dings and dents, were parked on the streets. The houses were narrow, three-story affairs with steep steps leading up to porches. Some had been screened, but the mesh showed tears, and there were no people sitting on the porches enjoying a summer evening or children playing in the unkempt yards.

I located the address, found an empty space along the curb, and parked. My phone chimed. I opened the large metal clasp on the front of my purse and pulled out my phone. I had a new text message from Kevin Phenrod, May's lawyer, telling me the settlement check would be ready next week. I texted back to tell him that was okay, and that I'd send a runner for it when it was ready. Then I got out of the Chevy and slammed the door. The loud *clunk* briefly silenced the droning cicadas. In the distance I heard the faint sound of cheering. I looked around for the source, then spotted the tall lights and backstop of a city sports facility.

I locked the car and started up the stairs to the front door. The curtains were drawn on the windows. I heard the sound of a car passing in the street, then silence aside from the cicadas that had resumed singing.

The doorbell was broken. I pulled open the sagging screen door and hammered on the wooden front door. I was just about to turn away, assuming no one was home, when a strange, buzzing mechanical voice responded from the other side of the door.

"Who is it?"

It seemed male, so I said, "Sir, my name's Linnet Ellery. I found a note among my boss's files with this address and an interesting notation. I'd like to talk to you about it."

"Who's your boss?" the robot voice asked.

"Chip Westin."

I heard multiple locks being thrown and chains rattling. I had thought that amount of security was only found in Manhattan, but apparently Bayonne was also a hotbed of crime. The door opened to reveal an old man—make that an ancient man—dressed in slacks and an undershirt that had once been white but was now gray, scuffs on his feet, and a tatty plaid bathrobe over the clothes. The hand, holding an artificial larynx to his throat, was ropy with thick blue veins that wound between dark brown age spots. He was nearly bald, but a few wisps of white hair were draped across a scalp also mottled with age spots. The eyes behind thick-lensed glasses were cloudy with cataracts.

"You his secretary?"

"No. I'm—" He interrupted before I could continue.

"Girl lawyer?" Even through the buzzing mechanical sound I could hear the disdain.

"Yes, 'fraid so," I said. "You are?"

"Thomas Gillford," rasped the robot voice. He gestured toward the mechanical larynx. "Throat cancer. It was worth it. Loved my cigars."

A sensible response was hopeless. I settled for "Okay."

"Come in. Your boss send you?"

He moved aside and I stepped into the dim interior. There were trails through piles of magazines and newspapers, none of which bore recent dates. Some of the piles were over my head. In addition to the papers, every available flat surface was covered with tchotkes, and shelves, similarly filled, covered the walls. The dust that covered every surface was so thick that it resembled brown felt, and the room smelled both musty and sour.

"Not exactly. Mr. Westin is dead."

"Heart attack? He was fat as a pig." He patted his sunken belly. "Me, I'd never let myself get in that kind of shape."

*No*, I thought. *You just smoked until your throat fell out.*

But I stayed polite. I also saw no reason to lie so I said, "No, he was killed—"

The reaction was startling, and if Gillford's frailty hadn't been enough, this made it clear he wasn't the person behind Chip's murder. Gillford slammed shut the door, then frenziedly threw the bolts and hooked the chains. He then twitched aside the dusty curtain and peered out. Apparently satisfied, he allowed it to fall back into place and gestured toward the stairs.

"Come upstairs. More room up there."

There were shelves on the wall next to the staircase, and my eye kept being drawn to the gaggle of Hummel figurines, the big jar filled with marbles, the grinning Ho Tai figures with their arms upraised in celebration, dollhouse china tea sets, and porcelain-headed dolls with their legs hanging limply over the edge of the shelves. Above the shelves was a collection of reproduction shields, swords, and daggers, both Asian and European, a set of nunchakus, and a fighting staff.

He noticed the direction of my gaze. "My wife. God rest her. She loved to collect and couldn't throw anything away. I keep it to remember her. And it's also too damn much effort to get it cleaned out. It'd take a backhoe."

"And the papers and magazines?" I asked.

He looked back over his shoulder. "Okay, that's me."

"Looks like you suited each other." He grunted in assent.

I had plenty of time to study the junk, because the pace set by

Mr. Gillford was glacial at best. Frankly, I was afraid he'd die before he made it to the second floor, but he hung in there. He led me to a bedroom. If he hadn't been a thousand years old, it might have made me uncomfortable. As it was, I was grateful to reach the room because it was reasonably uncluttered. The sheer volume of stuff was making me claustrophobic.

There was an unmade double bed shoved against one wall, a bedside table loaded with library books, and against another wall a rolltop desk and a chair. Gillford waved me toward the chair and lowered himself stiffly onto the bed.

"Did you bring my money?" he rasped.

"So, the notation did mean two million dollars," I said.

"Yeah, and it's taken so damn long for you people to respond I just may raise the price."

"And what exactly are we paying for?" I hedged. "Remember, Mr. Westin died before he could bring me up to speed on all his cases."

"The will."

It felt like something had exploded behind my eyes. "Will?" I managed weakly. "And which will might this be?"

"Abercrombie's, leaving everything to Chastity. I drafted it."

"Ms. Jenkins has a lawyer. Why didn't you contact him? Why contact Mr. Westin?"

"Because you're fucking Ishmael, McGillary and Gold, and the firm is loaded. I checked out Finkelstein. He's a pisher. An ambulance chaser. He wouldn't pay me what I want. Oh, he might claim they'd give it to me after they got control of Securitech, but I know how that game is played. I'd never see a dime, 'cause once they had control of the company they'd say it was my duty to reveal the will. But you guys—you'd pay to keep your case alive and making billable hours, and wait for Securitech to finally offer enough money that even that bitch of an ex-wife would take it."

"We'd have an obligation to reveal the other will," I said weakly.

"Yeah, right. When this much money's at stake, nobody plays by the rules."

"I don't think there is another will. If there was, you'd have made this offer to Securitech," I challenged.

"What? You think I'm stupid? They're a mercenary company, and there have been rumors about how Deegan handles competitors and whistleblowers. No, the bloodsuckers were the safer bet."

"Why are you doing this now?"

"Because I'm old, and I'm sick, and my wife is dead, and I want out of this rattrap house. I want to live out the rest of my days in comfort in an assisted-living joint, with hot and cold running nurses"—he attempted a leer—"clean sheets on the bed, and meals I don't have to cook. I got one all picked out. Down in Florida." He shuffled over to the desk, picked up a brochure, and thrust it into my hands. "See."

I looked down at the glossy flyer, at the picture of the fit, tanned, silver-haired couple holding tennis rackets, and I felt enormous pity for the old man. He wasn't going to be swinging a racket or attending the Saturday night luau. He was going to be in his room rejoicing in his clean sheets and flirting with his nurses. Was this the result when we no longer had extended families? Warehouses for the old.

Gillford pulled me back. "Now, do we have a deal or not?"

"Where is the will?" I asked.

"Uh-uh, not until I have my money. You think I'd give up my leverage? Not a chance."

I stood up. "I'll have to talk to the senior partners, but I don't think they'll agree."

"Then I'm going to give the will to Finkelstein and blow up your case—"

I interrupted. "You won't get your money if you do that."

He gave me a rictus smile. "*And* I'll tell the court how Westin was working against his own clients, and how you were preparing to pay me in exchange for a kickback. It'll sure as hell get you censured if not disbarred."

Suddenly I didn't feel so sorry for him. He was a vile, evil, horrible old man, and it was going to be his word against mine, and the evidence against me was the fact I had rented a damn car and drove to New Jersey to meet with him. And I knew what would happen at the firm. The senior partners would rally around me until the State Bar had taken action, and then they would fire me.

I was trying to decide whether to cry or throttle him when I heard the sound from downstairs of chains pulling out of the wood with a rending shriek and the front door crashing open.

# 14

In that moment, all animus was forgotten and Gillford and I were allies. I didn't know who was downstairs, but it was pretty clear they weren't magazine salesmen or proselytizing Mormons. I pulled out my cell phone and dialed 911. Nothing happened. Then I noticed the icon in the upper left corner. *No service.* Which was crazy. I'd had service thirty minutes ago.

There was an old-model Princess Phone on the bedside table. I ran over and snatched it up. There was no dial tone. I stood there with a phone in each hand and wondered what kind of burglar cut the phone lines. *Not a burglar.*

I dropped the landline phone and stuck the cell phone in my skirt pocket for easy access. I then slung my handbag so the strap hung across my chest, leaving my hands free.

"Is there another way out other than the stairs?" I asked. Gillford shook his head. I ran over and heaved him to his feet. "Come on. We can't get trapped in here."

He moved, but *very* slowly. I could hear crashes and bangs from downstairs as the home invaders searched the downstairs rooms. We reached the head of the stairs. My mind was screaming at me that it was stupid to go down to meet them, but I also knew we couldn't just cower and hide. They would find us. We had to get outside and scream for help or hope like hell my phone started working again.

We'd managed only a few steps when a man peered up through the bannister and spotted us. He had brown hair in a crew cut and a neck as wide as his head. "Got 'em!" he yelled, and he brought up a pistol.

The barrel seemed overly long, but I'd seen enough movies to realize the extra length was a silencer. My yammering brain wondered why he'd bothered with a silencer after breaking down the door. If that hadn't roused the neighbors, I doubted a gunshot would.

I pushed Gillford hard in the chest. He fell backward, but I was too late. I heard the gun give an odd coughing sound, and blood blossomed on Gillford's chest. He hit the floor. The mechanical larnyx fell from his suddenly slack hand and went bounding and rolling down the steps. I tried to retreat, but the gun made another coughing sound and something slammed into my chest. The force sent me careening into the wall beneath the display shelf. My chest felt like I'd been kicked, but somehow, miraculously, I was still alive. I glanced down at my purse. The big metal medallion that covered the clasp was dented and deformed.

The wall shook, dust fell like brown snow onto my head, and the big jar of marbles teetered and then fell. I managed to catch it before it brained me, but the weight of it bent me over, which meant the intruder's second shot flew through the space where my head would have been. My fingers were locked around the jar, and I couldn't loosen them. I lifted my head and saw the shooter starting to run up the stairs toward me. I was weirdly fascinated with how each steel-toed boot landed on each stair tread.

I was going to die. This time he was making sure of his shot. I was both terrified and angry. The swirling colors in the jar caught my attention, and my rigid fingers moved, twisting off the lid of the jar. I jammed my hand into the jar and pulled out a big handful of marbles. I forced myself to look at approaching death, timing his steps. He was six steps below me. As his foot came up to stop on the next tread, I threw the marbles beneath his boot.

The shooter had no time to react. The ball of his foot hit the marbles and flew out from under him. With his arms windmilling wildly, he looked like a drunk from a silent movie as he tried to keep his balance. As he fell, his hand convulsed, sending another bullet into the ceiling.

Fur sprouted from his face and hands, his nose and mouth began to elongate into a snout, and claws replaced his fingernails. In his wolf form, his agility would have been increased, but the transformation didn't happen fast enough to save him. He struggled to keep his footing and careened against the wall. Miniature tea sets, antique dolls, and a curtain of dust cascaded to the floor, and the weapons on the wall bounced on their hangers. He careened back in the other direction and hit the bannister. The wood gave way with an ear-splitting crack, and a long splinter drove into his side. He fell to the ground floor. I peered over the broken bannister. As the intruder's body had begun to morph, his clothes had ripped, giving me a view of his half-transformed body. It was almost as disturbing as his neck, which was bent in a most unnatural position, and the bloodstained splinter protruding from his side.

I kicked off my high-heeled shoes and started down the stairs. I wanted to run down as fast as I could, but instead I picked my way carefully through the scattered marbles and shattered china, not wanting to end up like the shooter. A werewolf in full wolf form appeared at the foot of the stairs and stared up at me. Bunny-like, I froze on a step. Belly low, lips drawn back to expose his fangs, he crept up the stairs toward me. The growl erased rational thought and brought back only primal memories. I began backing up the stairs. He was closing on me. When he was three steps below, he launched himself at me. It was pathetic, but I used the only weapon to hand. Locking my fingers around the edge, I swung the marble jar and caught the hound on the side of the head. The heavy glass shattered with a boom, and marbles flew in all directions.

Like a baseball player going for a high ball, I had timed my swing to hit when the werewolf was at the apex of his leap. The blow affected his trajectory just enough that he missed landing right on top of me. I dodged, stepping on a glass shard. It dug painfully into the sole of my foot. I yelped and hopped, feeling the wet flow of blood.

The elongated snout wrinkled, the lips drawing back even more, and saliva dripped from the fangs. The rank scent of were- wolf filled my nose. I cringed back, preparing to die. In my pe- ripheral vision, I caught a glimpse of something falling. It was more instinct then conscious thought—I threw out my hand, hoping to ward it off, and ended up catching it.

The werewolf, jaws snapping, leaped at me. I threw one arm across my face and thrust out my hand as if I could fend him off. It didn't work. The creature landed on me, but almost immediately went limp. Sticky, warm wetness flowed over my hand and arm, and a new smell joined the rank animal scent. It was cloying, cop- pery, and almost sweet. The werewolf lay on top of me. Gagging, I pushed him aside. A dagger protruded from his chest. That was what I'd caught. I would never have had the strength to drive home the dull replica weapon. The werewolf had done it himself with inertia and his own weight. I stared down at the blood coating my hand and arm.

*I killed somebody! I killed somebody! I killed somebody! Oh, holy fuck, I killed somebody!*

I went hobbling down the stairs, wincing when I landed on marbles and broken china, and blinded by tears. *The werewolf at the office was an accident. Not my fault. He killed himself when he attacked me. Not my fault. But this time . . .* I laid a hand over my bloodied arm, covering the palm of my once-clean hand with blood.

Then I was down the stairs, in the living room and among the paper towers. Some had been knocked over in the frenzied search for Gillford and me, but most were still upright. I began wending my way toward the front door. I tried to step lightly, to keep the papers from crackling underfoot. I glanced back and saw a bloody footprint. Even if I was quiet, they would find me, track me. How many were there? Were there still more in the house? Panic was a vise around my chest. I fought the urge to just run screaming for the front door. To combat the terror, I advanced in short sprints and then froze, listening hard. Truthfully, all I was hearing was the blood rushing in my ears, the hammering of my heart, and my short, shallow breaths. Then a blood-freezing howl went up. It ended with an almost questioning warble. There was another one, and he was between me and the door, and this one was obviously wondering where his friends were.

I reversed course and headed toward the kitchen. There would be a back door. There had to be a back door. There was the crackle of paper: the hound was moving. I tried to hold my breath and step softly. Then I realized how stupid that was. The werewolf could smell me, his hearing was acute in his wolf form, he knew by now something had happened to his buddies. The time for subtlety was over!

I broke into a run and heard a paper wall fall to the floor as the hound leaped over it. I risked a brief glance over my shoulder. His back legs were tangled in the falling wall, and his front paws found little purchase on the slick covers of the magazines. He actually tumbled onto his side. I had a small head start.

I felt a wash of heat as I ran past a wall heater proving old people must get cold to have this on in the summer or else it was broken. The grill was bent, and I had a brief glimpse of the pilot light burning brightly.

Into the dining room, running like a maniac. Only one small area wasn't covered with junk: the place where Gillford had eaten his solitary meals. At the far end of the room was a lovely built-in cabinet filled with china. All of the sets where colorful, and the patterns tended to be floral. On one wall was a collection of large bronze disks etched with Mayan figures. The chandelier over the table, made of deer antlers and hanging unevenly from the ceiling, was clearly a replacement for an older fixture. The base didn't fully cover the hole in the ceiling. I saw it all in a flash, and then I was in the kitchen.

The walls had once been a cheerful yellow, but now they were so coated with grease and smoke and dirt that they had turned a dull brown. I ran past a scarred and stained chopping block with an upright cleaver driven point-first into the wood. On the stove was a large iron skillet filled with congealing Crisco. The grease was darkened and flecked with bits of breading. A single chicken leg lay like an ice-bound ship in the solidified grease.

I spotted the back door and put on a final burst of speed, only to be tripped up by the frayed and trailing extension cord stretching from the old refrigerator to a wall plug on the far side of the kitchen. I fell down and felt liquid soaking into my skirt and blouse. Water had leaked from beneath the fridge and was forming a puddle on the warped linoleum. The frayed electrical cord rested in the water. I tensed, waiting to be electrocuted, and looked toward the back door. It was lined with locks and chains too. My heart sank. I'd never get it open in time.

Then I realized there was a doggie door cut into the wood. Not small. Not large. Sort of medium sized. Since I was already on the floor, I just started crawling toward that possible escape. Lifting up the flap, I tried to shove my way through the doggie door, and I felt my blouse and skirt rip on the top edge. My purse, still flung around my neck, was stuck underneath me, impeding my progress. I pulled back into the kitchen, ripped it off, and thrust it through the door. Then I dove through. It was much easier without the bulky purse. I was almost out when I felt a clawed hand tearing at my ankle. I kicked back hard, feeling something wet and cold on the sole of my foot. Nose. The hound yelped. Noses are sensitive. *Good to know,* I thought in a burst of irrational analysis, but the kick had caused the werewolf's grip to loosen, and I was able to get outside.

I heard the howl of frustration from the other side of the door as the hound fumbled with the chains and locks. Unless he changed back to human, he wasn't going to open the door. My knees were trembling, but I managed to get to my feet. The door shook as the werewolf flung himself against the wood. Then rational thought seemed to once again take control of the creature, and I saw the shaggy head thrusting through the dog door. Snatching up my purse, I took off running around the side of the house and bashed into a set of wind chimes on a freestanding hook, setting them to ringing wildly. I raced on toward the street and my car. The bells seemed to keep ringing. I shook my head and fumbled frantically through my purse, searching for the car keys.

Naturally they had fallen to the very bottom of the bag. Sobbing with exhaustion and frustration, I upended the purse. Out fell hairbrush, makeup kit, lipstick, lip pencil, pen flashlight, dental floss, breath mints, house keys, wallet, pens, pad, cell phone, package of Kleenex, my card case—the metal was dented—and finally the car keys. I bent to pick them up.

I got an excellent, if upside down, view of the werewolf rounding the building and closing on me with massive, ground-covering leaps. The leaps seemed to be in time to the calliope music. I straightened and blindly ran into the street. The hound was right behind me.

A rush of air fluttered my hair. Calliope music filled my ears. My peripheral vision caught a glimpse of white and garish colors. There was the blare of a car horn. A loud *thump*. A shrill *yelp*. Followed by screeching as a handbrake was pulled.

I half-turned to see what had happened, but my legs gave way and I collapsed in a heap in the street. My nose was filled with the scent of hot asphalt, gasoline, and blood.

"Oh, Jesus, oh, Jesus, oh, Jesus." It was a young male voice shaking with anxiety. I forced my eyes open. And found myself staring at a clown. Or rather, the painted visage of a clown grinning at me from the side of a white-paneled ice cream truck. The calliope music was still tinkling away.

A young man in a white suit and a silly little hat came around the truck. He was shaking, and his eyes were rimmed with white.

"Are you okay, miss?"

I opened my mouth to give the obligatory response, but then I shut my mouth and shook my head. "No."

"Are you hurt? Did I hurt you too?"

"No. Not exactly." I pulled the foot that had been grabbed by the werewolf into my lap and looked at my abraded, bloody, dirty sole, the long claw marks on the ankle, and my shredded panty hose. "Would you call the police? Please."

"Oh, right. Police. I was gonna call my boss. I think I killed your dog," he added.

"Oh God, I hope so."

# 15

This interview wasn't conducted in the lush comfort of an Ishmael, McGillary and Gold conference room. The police station in downtown Bayonne was rundown and stank of burned coffee, unwashed bodies, and old vomit. The driver of the ice cream truck was seated at one scarred and battered desk, giving his statement while I sat at another. I had given my statement, and now Sergeant Balfour, at whose desk I was seated, was in the lieutenant's office with the door closed, a phone to his ear, and my wallet in his hand.

When the cops had arrived, I had gasped out "Bodies, house," and pointed. The two patrolmen exchanged alarmed glances, went through the open front door, and came back out in a really big hurry. One had gotten on the radio while the other checked the crumpled pile of fur. The ice cream man had indeed killed the hound.

A little while later a whole lot of cops and ambulances had arrived, and then the ice cream guy (whose name was Salvatore Balduini, and who was a student at Ramapo College) and I were taken to the station.

". . . I barely missed her, and then there was the dog . . . er . . . wolf. I tried to brake, but the brakes failed. I tried to miss him, but I just couldn't. There wasn't time. And that's why I ran over him. The only way I stopped was because I pulled the handbrake and threw the truck into park."

"Yeah, but you had to have been speeding." The cop posing the question was middle-aged, with stooped shoulders and a walrus mustache.

Sal looked to one wall and then the other. "Well, maybe, but only a little. There was a soccer game over at the community center, and it was about to let out. I didn't want to be late. I knew there'd be a lot of hot kids and parents. I sell a lot at those games. I get paid on how much I sell, and I'm short paying my fall tuition." He looked hopefully at the cop, who seemed unmoved by Sal's sad story. Sal sighed and continued.

"But I *was* late, so I might have gotten a little lead-footed. But it's not like there's traffic or kids or anything on that street. In fact, a lot of the houses are empty."

"Still, you were speeding, and you killed a hou—" The cop's mouth twisted beneath the mustache. "Power."

I was beginning to realize that outside the cocoon of my upper-middle-class life and ivy league university, there was a lot of ambivalence, if not out-and-out hostility, about the Powers.

"You could be in a lot of trouble," the cop added, and Sal looked green against the white of his shirt.

I wasn't sure if I was about to help or hurt him, but I couldn't just sit by and let my inadvertent rescuer get thrown to the dogs— or the wolves. "Officer, that wolf was trying to kill me. If Sal hadn't been there, I'd have my throat torn out right now." I gave the officer a smile, hoping it didn't look like a grimace.

The sergeant hung up the phone, then made another call. More time passed. Sal's boss showed up. He was a big, red-faced man, and things didn't look good for Sal in terms of keeping his summer job.

They started to leave. I stood up and took Sal's hand between mine. "Thank you so much. You really did save my life." The boss split a suspicious look between the two of us. "I'm sure my dad would be happy to get the brakes of the truck fixed."

"And the front grill?" the boss asked in a pugnacious tone. "It got all bent to hell. And a piece even broke loose and got blood all over it."

"I'm sure the grill too." The boss looked a bit mollified.

I stepped a little closer to the older man, wincing at my sore feet. I lowered my voice. "You know, there's a story here. About how your driver saved someone from a rogue werewolf."

He looked thoughtful. Sal threw me a grateful look, and they both left. Sergeant Balfour finally emerged from the lieutenant's office, but he didn't say anything to me. Instead he sat at his desk and typed out a report on an ancient PC.

It was nearly nine, and the final rays of the setting sun were stabbing through the glass and wire-mesh windows. I was suddenly ravenously hungry, and my clawed leg was hurting like crazy. I risked a question.

"Sergeant, is it going to be much longer?" He stiffened, but I wasn't in the mood for any more cop authority bullshit. "I've given my statement, and now I want to go home." I paused and inspected my shredded ankle. "And to a doctor. So please return my personal effects, and—"

"No," the sergeant said.

"Am I under arrest? If so, I want my phone call and I want a lawyer, and I'm not saying another word until both of those things happen." I folded my arms across my chest, and we glared at each other.

"I'm waiting on a cop from New York to show up. He says this case may be related to one he's working on."

"That's crazy. I'm not involved in—" I broke off even before the cop interrupted me to say,

"When I typed your name into the ViCAP system it spit out a big fucking report about you and a murder and a dead were-wolf."

"Well, okay, that's true. But I was a victim—"

"Like this time." His tone dripped with irony.

"Yes. Who's this cop?" I asked. "Is it Detective—"

Sometimes life does unspool like a movie, because at that moment the door to the station house opened, and Detective Washington walked in. For a moment I vibrated between relief at seeing him and concern because I was starting to feel like the criminal in these events.

Washington and the New Jersey cop introduced themselves and shook hands. Balfour jerked his head toward me. "Report's on the desk. I'll leave her to you," he said, then walked away.

Washington sat down and carefully and slowly read over my statement, alternating between the typed pages and photographs of the inside of the house and the carnage in the street. My possessions were laid out on the desk. Washington carefully studied the dented metal clasp on the purse and the dented business card case. All the while, my knee vibrated in impatience and tension. He finally looked up at me. "You realize the bullet hit the clasp and the card case, and that's why you're not dead."

"Oh" was all I could muster.

"You realize how unlikely that is?"

"I guess."

He gestured at the statement and pictures. "You know this is a highly improbable series of events."

"I know." I sniffed, looked around for a Kleenex, and had to settle for dabbing my nose and eyes with the tail of my blouse.

"Once again, you are lucky to be alive."

"I know." My voice was a miserable mew.

"Who was this man . . ." A glance down at the papers. "This Gillford?"

"He said he had information about a case."

"But you're not going to tell me which case."

"I can't." My leg was starting to throb in time to my heartbeat, and I felt faint.

"Did he have information?"

"He just made the claim. He never backed it up, and then . . ." I gestured helplessly. "All that other stuff happened."

"Who were they there to kill?" Washington asked.

"Both of us. I'm pretty sure."

"Werewolves again. And before you clammed up, you told me about Securitech."

"So shouldn't you be talking to Securitech?"

"There's nothing linking any of these bodies to that company."

"They had guns."

"Guns are easy."

"They cut the phones."

"Any two-bit home invasion artist will do that."

"You just don't want to brace Securitech," I accused.

"Not without something more. My pay grade isn't that high."

"Maybe after I get killed you'll work up the nerve." I only resort to out-and-out bitchiness in extreme circumstances. This seemed like one.

Washington matched me. "That doesn't seem likely to happen, does it? Given your extraordinary luck in cheating death."

He took me through the events again. Just thinking about it made my stomach clench, and I wasn't hungry anymore. I was clinging to the last shreds of my patience and control when he suddenly focused on my torn ankle. "Why didn't you get that taken care of?"

"Because I've been sitting here for hours."

"The ambulance drivers should have dealt with this. Come on." He handed me my purse, took my bloodstained jacket off the back of the chair, and led me out of the station and to his car. He then drove me to the hospital.

Maybe it was because I had a cop with me, but I didn't have to sit in the emergency room for hours. Since there weren't any people actively dying, I got moved to the front of the line. The young Indian doctor numbed the area, cut away the curling edges of the drying skin, cleaned out the wounds, and bandaged my ankle. He then wrote me a prescription for antibiotics, saying, "The claws on those creatures can be very dirty. If it starts to hurt, and you see red streaks above the bandage, go immediately to your regular doctor."

It was now 10:30 p.m., and I was dropping. Washington looked down at me. "Do you need me to take you home?"

"I have a rental car. I've got to get it back to the city."

"It's at the police station."

"Then take me there."

"Are you sure?"

"Yeah," I said, but I really wasn't.

Washington parked next to the tiny rental. The lights in the parking lot threw round flares of light on the pocked asphalt. The night was sticky hot, and out toward the Atlantic Ocean lightning played fitful tag on a line of clouds.

"I'll probably have more questions for you."

"Okay." I unlocked the trunk and threw the bloody jacket in on top of my roller bag. I really just wanted to throw the thing away, but there wasn't a trash can handy. I fumbled a bit trying to get the key into the front door lock.

"You're sure you're okay to drive?"

"Yes." I wanted to scream at him *Just go*, because what I wanted right now was silence and the inside of my own head.

He waited until I was in the car and started to drive out of the lot before he got back in his car. For a while we traveled in the same direction, but then he turned off. I found a parking lot in front of a strip mall, turned in, stopped the car, and rested my forehead on the steering wheel. I pictured driving on the New Jersey Turnpike, making my way across the George Washington Bridge onto I-95, and then into Washington Heights. I pictured trying to find a place to park the car near my apartment. I had been wrong. I couldn't make it home.

I knew I shouldn't let the senior partners find out about this latest misadventure from Detective Washington. I should call Shade's answering service. That thought exhausted me too. But if I couldn't face the drive home, who could I call to come and get me? Ray and Gregory? They didn't have a car. My dad? Too far away. Finally I dug out my cell phone and called John. He answered on the first ring.

"O'Shea."

I almost hung up when I heard a woman's voice muttering in sleepy irritation. Instead I burst into tears. "John," I sobbed. "It's Linnet. I need your help."

"Where are you?"

I looked around, but I was in the middle of a block and couldn't see any street signs. "I don't know. Somewhere in New Jersey."

"Okay, that's dire."

"Let me drive to a corner. Find a street sign—"

"No, stay put. I can find you. Just don't turn off your cell phone." He hung up. I leaned the seat back as far as it would go, closed my eyes, and waited.

———

My phone rang, jerking me awake from a sleep I hadn't intended to take. "Hello?"

"Hi, it's me," came John's voice.

"Where are you?"

"Parked next to you."

I looked out through the driver's side window. There was a non-descript four-door sedan parked next to me. I opened the car door and got out. John did the same. The sight of his crazy-quilt hair, and the cleft in his chin, and the way the corner of his mouth always quirked up as if he were secretly amused, almost overcame my control. I started to run to him, then froze.

He sensed my need, because when he reached my side he put his arms around me. "What the hell happened?"

"It's a long, long story." I sighed.

"Okay. Is this piece of shit your car?"

"No, it's a rental."

"Okay, we'll leave it here and come back for it tomorrow." He checked his watch. "Later today."

"What if it gets stripped?"

"Oh, please, nobody would want parts off this thing. But if you have any personal items, you better get those out."

I opened up the trunk and, with a shudder, tossed aside the jacket. "Sorry about interrupting your evening."

He didn't pretend not to understand. He shrugged. "She'll get over it. Or she won't."

I started to lift out my roller bag, but it was heavy and I was tired, and my arms began to shake. John quickly took it out of my hands and put it in the trunk of his car. He then held the passenger door for me. I paused.

"What?" he asked.

"I've got blood on me. I don't want to get it in your car."

He touched the bloodstain on my skirt. "First, it's dried, and second, this car has been bled in more than a few times. Come on. Let's go."

I leaned back against the headrest and briefly closed my eyes. When John turned the key the radio started up, a pulsing salsa beat. He snapped it off, turned up the air-conditioning, and pulled out.

"Okay, we've got a drive ahead of us so tell me the long, long story."

So I did.

After I finished, John drove in silence for a while. He frowned out the front window, chewing a bit on his lower lip. The strobe of oncoming headlights periodically brought the angular planes of his face into high relief.

"Linnet, there is something going on with you. Something strange. Nobody has luck like yours."

"What, shitty?" I asked.

"No, good. You should be dead four times over."

"What are you saying?"

"I don't know. I just know it's not normal. But let's get to what I *do* know. You are *never* to go off alone like this again." I shrank back at the tone. "You call me and take me along."

The injustice of that put starch back in my spine. "You might recall that I tried. I called you a number of times, and you never called back."

He had the grace to look embarrassed. "Yeah, well, now that I know what you're dealing with that won't happen again."

"What am I dealing with?" I asked.

"I'm not sure. I've got suspicions, but no certainty."

"Are your suspicions like my suspicions in that they all center on Securitech?"

"Pretty much," he said. "So you didn't tell anyone where you were going?"

"No." I amended that. "Well, David Sullivan knew. He's the one who found the address."

"So you think Sullivan set you up?"

"No, of course not." I hesitated. "I don't think so."

"Or you don't want to think so." John chewed thoughtfully at his lower lip. "If this other will exists, the old guy should have been dead weeks ago, before he could tell anyone."

I pondered on that for a moment. "The fact that he wasn't implies they didn't know his identity or where to find him." I slewed around to face him. "So, how did they find him now?"

"Because you led them there," John said, his tone grim. He suddenly spun the steering wheel, sending us cutting across four lanes of traffic and down an exit ramp onto a street called Edgewater Ave.

As the sound of furiously honking horns died away behind us, I swallowed my heart again and gasped out, "Are you nuts? You could have gotten us killed!" I had no idea where we were going or what we were doing.

John pulled into the parking lot of an all-night burger joint. He jumped out and ran around to my side of the car, opened my door, and pulled me out. He was muttering to himself.

"Okay, it probably wouldn't be on you." He pressed the car key and the trunk popped open. He lifted out my roller bag. "Do you take this everywhere?"

"Pretty much."

His clever, long-fingered hands flew across the surface of the case. He unzipped the pockets, reaching inside each crevice. "Have you left it unattended recently?"

"In the office when I go to lunch or the bathroom." My tone was waspish. I was still shaken by his crazy driving, and low blood sugar was making me cranky.

"Outside the office," he said, with the kind of patience you reserve for the very young or the very old and senile.

I opened my mouth to say no, then remembered *Mame.* "I checked it when I went to the theater."

"Aha!" It was a cry of triumph. His hand emerged from inside a pocket of the case. He was holding a small disk.

"What's that?" I asked.

"Tracer."

"Oh God," I moaned as I sank down to sit on a concrete tire stop. "I led them to him. I got Gillford killed, didn't I?"

John knelt down in front of me and gripped my shoulders. "No, the guys who killed Gillford are the guys who killed Gillford."

"But—"

"No buts. You didn't do anything wrong." He paused. "Other than going alone, which . . . You. Are. Never. Ever. Going. To. Do. Again." He gripped my shoulders and gave me a little shake. "Right?"

"Yes, yes, I promise." A new, and very unwelcome, thought intruded. I craned my neck and looked all around the parking lot. "Are they following us now? Do you think they'll come after us? Why didn't they come after me while I was waiting for you?"

"Who ever sent those guys may not yet know the plan went tits up. Also, if you fetch up dead right after this other incident, the cops are going to start taking a real hard look at events surrounding you, your life, and your work. I don't think our killers want that much scrutiny." He tossed the tracer into the air and caught it several times. "You said your cell phone didn't work in the house?"

"Yeah."

"But it worked when you called me."

I nodded. "And it worked fine until I reached the house."

"Okay, I'm becoming more convinced about Securitech," John said.

"Because of the trace?"

"No, those are easy to buy. But blocking a cell phone signal—now we're starting to get into real sophistication." He dropped the tracer and ground it under his heel, then picked it up again.

"So, this means David Sullivan's off the hook, right?" I didn't know why, but for some reason it was important to me that John agree.

"Yeah. He knew the address. He could have made a phone call. There would have been no reason for all this cloak-and-dagger shit."

At that moment the door to the burger joint opened, and the smell of grilling meat and French fries wafted out. My stomach clenched down into a painful ball because I was so hungry.

"I know this is just really awful of me, and I shouldn't want food after what happened, but I'm fucking starving. I haven't had anything since lunch."

John stood up and held out his hand. "Come on. I could do with a cheeseburger too." I gave him my hand and he pulled me to my feet. "And look, they do chocolate malts. Do you like malts?"

"Um-hmmm," I managed as my mouth filled with saliva at the very thought.

We started across the parking lot, and even though I tried to hide it, John realized I was limping. He looked down at my bare feet and shredded stockings. Next thing I knew, he had swept me up into his arms. Despite his willowy build, he was incredibly strong. I clasped my arms around his neck, and he carried me into the restaurant.

The air was redolent with the smells of grease and chocolate. It was wonderful. John deposited me in the plastic chair at a plastic table and leaned in. "What do you want?"

"Cheeseburger, fries, chocolate malt."

"Look, I don't think you ought to be alone until we figure out exactly what's going on. Either you can come to my place, or I'll stay at yours. No funny business. I'll sleep on the couch."

"Hasn't your bed already got somebody in it?"

"I doubt it after the way I blew out the door." He gave me a somewhat rueful grin and shrugged.

"Then I'll take you up on your place. All I seem to do is have nightmares at mine."

And he surprised me by leaning in and giving me a kiss on the cheek.

# 16

After our grease-and-carbs dinner (John got a large order of onion rings, and I ended up eating way too many of them), we climbed back into the car. As we pulled out onto the street and headed for the entrance ramp to the freeway, I watched John's eyes flicking up to the rearview mirror, over to the side mirrors, and back again.

"What are you . . . ? Are you—" I began.

"Yep, there they are."

"Somebody's following us," I squeaked.

"Yeah, I figured they would get a little closer once the trace went dead."

"Are you going to . . . lose them? Chip said you could go into this . . . other world . . . Fairy . . . are you going to do that?" I felt like an idiot even saying it.

"Nope." The word was a harsh single syllable. "I don't go there." He took a deep, steadying breath and shook his head. His tone was normal when he continued. "Look, they know who I am. By now they probably know where I live. It's not worth the effort."

"Not worth the— They might try . . ."

"Trust me, they won't. They're not that desperate—yet."

I found that more ominous than comforting, but John was

right. Nothing happened. I occasionally looked in the mirrors and even turned around in my seat to look back, but I never saw anybody following. John laughed at me. He had a good laugh, full throated and filled with joy.

I gave him a suspicious look. "Did you just say that? Because I don't see anybody," I said.

"Oh, no, they're there. They're good, and you don't know what to look for. And now they're dropping out because they know where we're going," John said as he turned down city streets and drove into the Village.

Amazingly, he found a place to park only a few cars down from his building. He carried me and the bag up three flights of stairs. The smells of dinners long past lingered in the air, but they were nice smells—lemongrass and curry. We went past a tricycle and a bicycle chained to the bannister, and a squeak toy on one step.

I pointed at it. "Is that an early warning device so you know when someone's coming?"

"Neighbor's dog. A pretty whippet, but she forgets where she leaves her toys."

We approached a door painted bright blue, and he set me down. He took out a key, inserted it in the lock, and let us in. The door to his apartment opened directly into a long, narrow kitchen. A wrought-iron potholder hung from the ceiling, and it was festooned with copper pots and high-end cookware. A gigantic spinning spice rack stood on the meager counter space. Another counter was swallowed by an espresso machine. At the end of the kitchen there was a half bath.

There was the faint odor of orange and ginger in the air. Either it was something he'd been cooking or a really lovely sachet.

A left turn took us into a postage stamp–sized living room. A flat-screen TV hung on the wall opposite the Territorial-style sofa and armchair. There were a number of bookcases (all filled), several pieces of decent art (all landscapes), and a Bose wave radio/CD player. A large, bright orange cat sat on a perch suspended in front of the windows. It *twurted,* stretched, jumped down, and ambled over to be petted.

Its fur was deep and silky, with a soft undercoat that gave it the feel of a plushy toy. The cat wove, purring, between our legs, arching its back to receive our strokes.

"This is Gadzooks. He'll sleep with you, if you let him."

"I'd love that."

There was a half-open door. John led me through it and into the bedroom. The bed was rumpled, covers tossed aside and half-dragging on the floor. John sighed.

"Yep, she was pissed."

"Sorry."

He gave my back a quick rub. "No, it's okay. There's a full bath to your left. I'll change the sheets while you clean up. There's a bathrobe hanging on a hook on the door, and I'll leave a T-shirt for you to wear."

"Thank you," I gulped past the lump in my throat.

I left my purse on the dresser and admired the collection of Native American fetish figurines, especially the white buffalo with turquoise horns and the white bear with a heart line outlined in some kind of red stone. I wondered how it was that Gadzooks hadn't decided they were really awesome cat toys. Maybe the supposed deep affinity of the Álfar and animals was true. I headed into the bathroom.

An overly deep tub, shaped like a triangle to accommodate the small space, was tucked into a corner. There was a large rain-style shower head directly overhead, and shower curtains with a decided South Sea Island theme. The hooks had tiny, brightly colored palm trees on them. While the tub was filling, I stripped out of my torn and bloody clothes, wadded them up, and crammed them into the trash can. I'd worry about what to wear tomorrow when tomorrow arrived. Except it was already tomorrow. That thought was just too confusing. I shook my head. The steam began to occlude the mirror until I could no longer see the wan-faced girl looking back out at me.

The hot water stung my cut and abraded feet. Too late, I realized I probably shouldn't have gotten the bandage wet. The water lapped at my chin as I sank down low. A quiet knock made me splash and jerk upright.

"Wha . . . what? Yes?" I stammered as I jerked awake.

"Didn't want you to drown in there."

"Thanks. I probably would have. I fell asleep."

"I thought you might," John said with a quiver of laughter in his voice. "The bed's changed. T-shirt awaits. I've got a pillow and blanket, and I'm going to embrace the couch. Call if you need anything."

"Okay."

I washed up, scrubbed my hair, and climbed out of the dirty, soap-scummed water. John bought nice towels, thick and soft, bath sheets rather than regular towels. I limped out, wrapped in one. The door between the bedroom and the living room was closed, and Gadzooks was taking a leisurely bath in the center of the bed. I admired the black lacquer Oriental-style headboard with lots of nooks for books and drinks, and even his and her reading lights.

I dropped the towel, pulled on the T-shirt, and crawled between the crisp, clean sheets. Gadzooks determinedly marched up the bed and plopped down against my stomach. His purrs rumbled in my gut. My head sank into a down pillow, and I was gone. I didn't have any nightmares.

———

I awoke to the intoxicating smell of blueberry pancakes, bacon, and coffee. Gadzooks, standing at the door, heard me stirring and let out a plaintive *twert*. I pushed the hair off my face, stretched, and climbed out of bed. The sounds of the city greeted me: trucks rumbling past, car horns, a yapping dog, a garbage truck's hydraulics whining as it pushed trash into its interior.

The cat was making ever more tragic and desperate sounds. I cracked the door as I staggered past on my way to the bathroom. He darted through the opening. I hit the bathroom and peed. While I was sitting on the toilet, I noticed the bandage had come off my leg during the night. The claw marks were no longer raw, the edges had begun to seal, and there were no red streaks, so I figured I was out of the woods. I snagged the bathrobe off its hook and donned it. It covered my toes and it smelled of John and cinnamon. Both very nice scents.

I headed into the kitchen. As I walked through the living room I noticed a pair of slacks and a blouse that I recognized as mine draped over the back of the armchair. Clean underwear and a bra were folded on the seat. Set neatly in front were a pair of sandals with really pretty multicolored agates on the straps that I'd bought on sale at Bloomingdale's. I frowned at them and completed the journey into the kitchen.

John was flipping pancakes on a griddle placed over two of the stove's burners. He set aside the spatula and opened the oven door. The odor of bacon became much stronger. He grabbed a fork and turned the strips of bacon on their cookie sheet, then turned to greet me with his devastating smile.

"Morning. How did you sleep?"

"Like a rock," I answered. I pushed back my hair nervously. "I saw the clothes. How did you . . . ?"

"I slipped into the bedroom, took your house keys, got your address off your license, and drove up to your apartment. I didn't think you'd want to put back on your dirty clothes, and our only other option was to go shopping with you dressed in a bathrobe."

The image disarmed me, as I suspected he thought it would. I laughed. "Well, thank you."

"Coffee or espresso?"

"Espresso."

He set a cup under the tap on the espresso machine and punched a couple of buttons. There was whirring, grinding, and then a groaning as it deposited a thick black brew into the white cup. It finished, grumbling to itself a few more times. John handed me the cup. A beautiful rich cream floated on the top.

"Do you take anything?" he asked.

"No, this is perfect." I blew on it, then took a sip. It was, in fact, perfect.

I helped by draining the bacon and setting the small two-person table in a corner of the kitchen. We then tucked in. I inspected the graceful curving glass bottle of Canadian maple syrup. "Nothing but the best," I said as I poured it across my short stack.

"Damn straight."

We ate in silence for a few minutes, then I took a breath and pushed back my chair. John gave me an inquiring look, which changed to alarm.

"Not good?" he asked anxiously.

"No, it's great, the food I mean. It's the day I'm dreading. By now the partners will have heard about the latest hideous killing that has me at its center. Securitech is out there. . . ." I waved vaguely at the window. "Are they out there?"

"No," John said, and ate a slice of bacon in three quick crunching bites.

"But I can't mention Securitech because it's an ongoing case, and because . . ."

"We can't prove anything," John supplied the end of the sentence. "Suspicions. No proof."

I studied my folded hands. Looked back up. "Can we get proof?"

"Say, by having Securitech try to kill you again?" he asked.

"Maybe something a little less drastic."

"That's harder. If Securitech is behind Chip's murder and this latest killing, they've been very careful to put a lot of daylight between them and the killers." He nervously beat out a rhythm on his plate with the fork. "We'd need them to make a mistake."

"When people get desperate, they make mistakes," I said.

"*Sometimes* they make mistakes. These guys are professionals. Maybe all that happens is that you get dead, and we *still* can't prove a thing." He drank some coffee, then changed from drum practice to drawing pictures with the fork's tines in the syrup that lined his plate. "The only way I can think to make them desperate is to go find the other will. Assuming the other will exists."

I shook my head. "But then I'd be working against the interests of my clients. I can't do that."

"You went to New Jersey to talk to that old lawyer."

"I didn't know he was the lawyer who drafted the other will. It was just a cryptic note."

"But now you do know that the other will exists. Don't you have an obligation to find out the truth?"

"No, I have an obligation to my clients. Right now all I have is the unsupported word of a senile old coot who is now dead. I don't think I have any obligation to follow up on this."

"A minute ago you wanted to get the goods on Securitech. You can't have it both ways, Linnet."

I sat and dithered, pulled first in one direction and then in the other. "I need to be a good lawyer."

John nodded. "That's probably the smartest approach. Certainly the one best suited to keeping you alive. And I like the idea of keeping you alive."

"Probably not as much as I do."

We cleaned up the kitchen together. I was startled to discover it was 11:20 in the morning. I was really going to be late to work. Then I decided, *fuck it*. After what I'd been through, I figured I was entitled to a few hours of personal time.

"If you're done in the bathroom, I'll just nip in and take a shower," John said.

"Sure. I'll get dressed in the living room. I don't suppose you packed up any makeup for me?" I said jokingly.

Deadpan, he pointed at the small cosmetic bag underneath the coffee table. I swept it up, pulled back the zipper, and stared at my Bare Minerals makeup. John was leaning against the bedroom doorjamb, grinning at me. "Okay, you are practically perfect in every way."

I finished dressing and checked my cell phone. The battery was stone dead. I looked around for a landline, but didn't find one. It seemed Álfar—or at least this Álfar—were hip and with it. I leaned against the closed bedroom door and called, "May I borrow your cell phone and check in with the office?"

The door opened. John wore a towel wrapped around his waist and nothing else. I had wondered if his chest hair was going to be as motley as the hair on his head. Now my question was answered. He didn't have hair on his chest. *Of course he doesn't; that would be way too déclassé.* What he did have were ripped abs and a flat belly. Water glistened in the hollow at the base of his throat. I had a desperate urge to press myself against him and kiss away the dampness. Tangle my fingers in his amazing hair, feel his hands on my back. My eyes wandered to that mobile mouth, the soft curve of his lips. I wondered how he tasted.

"Sure," he said, and padded over to the dresser where he recovered the phone. He tossed it to me. I didn't embarrass myself; I caught it. "Let me get dressed, and we can go in together. I've got to make a report to Cecelia on a personal injury case she's handling."

The door closed again, and I settled on the sofa, bare feet resting on the coffee table, and called Norma.

"Linnet Emery's office."

"Hi, Norma, it's me—"

"Where are you!? The office is like a stirred anthill! Mr. Ishmael even sent the police to your apartment. Daniel Deegan is going to be here in forty minutes!"

It took a moment for the name to penetrate and get placed. Once it did it sent me jumping to my feet. "Deegan? The guy who runs Securitech?"

"The same."

"Why's he coming to the office?"

"I don't know. His assistant called this morning, requesting a meeting with you."

I paced around the living room. Gadzooks twined between my legs and nearly tripped me. "Oh God, oh God, oh God. What does this mean? What does he want?"

Norma's tone was waspish. "I'm sure I don't know. Why don't you come to work and find out for yourself?"

The tone and the unspoken criticism snapped my control. I got angry. "I nearly got killed yesterday!" I yelled into the phone.

"What, again?"

The deadpan delivery snapped me out of the irrational rage. Why had I assumed that my secretary would know what had happened, and even if she did know, why would I assume that this was going to be as big a deal to her as it was to me?

"Sorry. Thanks," I mumbled.

"You weren't close enough for me to throw a glass of water on you," Norma replied.

"Are you ever sympathetic?" I asked.

"Rarely."

"I'm on my way." I hung up the phone and rushed toward the bedroom door. It opened before I could knock, and John stepped out. I gripped the front of his shirt.

"We've got to go now. Daniel Deegan, the head of Securitech, is coming to the office. To see me. I don't look very professional. He called for an appointment this morning. I wish I had time to change. Guess I don't. I'm going to die."

John disengaged my hand from the crisp material of his shirt and, holding my hand, led me through the kitchen and to the front door. "Probably not at the office."

"Why not? That's where it nearly happened last time."

"Murderers don't normally make appointments."

I opened my mouth, shut it again firmly, and looked up at him. John was smiling warmly down at me.

"Sorry, I'll stop being nuts."

"Actually, I think you're remarkably sane for someone who's survived two close brushes with death within a three-week period." And he bent down and gave me a quick, soft kiss on the lips.

He tasted as good as he looked.

# 17

We set a speed record getting from Greenwich Village to the office. Sitting tensely in the front seat next to John, I asked if we were being followed. He didn't answer, just shook his head.

He dropped me in front of the building. I paused to pull up the handle on the roller bag and went running through the lobby. I hit the elevator call button about twenty times until a car arrived. I checked my watch. *Fifteen minutes until Deegan time.*

I dove out of the elevator on the seventieth floor and headed straight for the bathroom. I had been waiting until John finished his shower to put on my makeup, which meant I was barefaced against the world. I might be dressed in slacks, an Oxford shirt, and sandals, but I was at least going to have on my face when I faced Daniel Deegan.

A few people must have seen me blow past, because suddenly Caroline, Juliette, and Cecelia were in the bathroom with me. I took out the brushes and the little jars of makeup. Conversation rattled around me like machine-gun fire.

"Detective Washington came to the office."

"Went into a private meeting with the senior partners—"

"Well, it was supposed to be private—"

My hands started shaking, and I set down the lid holding a tiny dollop of base and the brush on the edge of the sink.

"But that little turd Bruce was serving coffee—"

"And he heard some of what happened, and told the secretaries—"

Caroline picked up the makeup and pressed it back into my hands. Instinct took over, and I feathered the base over my face.

"After that it spread through the firm like viral video—"

I moved on to the blush while Cecilia said, "When the news reached David Sullivan, he became a walking, stalking, snarling monster—"

"He actually lifted Norma out of her chair, demanding to know where you were."

"Have you got a comb?" Juliette asked. I pointed at my purse. She dug through until she found it, then handed it to me. I began to lightly tease and fluff my hair, trying to defeat my stubborn center part and cowlick.

"The senior partners called *all* the partners in for a huddle in the big conference room—"

"But not David. He wasn't included."

"And then the call came that Deegan wanted a meeting with you—"

"And Norma's been burning up the phone lines trying to reach you."

"So, the partners don't know about Deegan coming in?" I asked.

"No, they told everyone they weren't to be disturbed," Caroline answered.

"We can guess what they're discussing," Juliette said grimly.

"Me," I said bleakly.

"And I'm sure we all know how Ryan's going to vote," Cecilia added.

"Right now, whether I keep my job is the least of my worries." I brought up my left wrist and looked at my watch. "Deegan will be here any minute."

Cecelia stepped back. Juliette handed me my lip pencil and lipstick tube. I outlined and painted my lips. Opened my arms in a *what do you think?* gesture.

"You're ready," Caroline said.

"Knock 'em dead," Cecelia added.

At the word *dead* I shuddered, but I squared my shoulders, picked up my purse, grabbed my roller bag, and left the sanctuary of the ladies' room.

As I crossed the central lobby, all conversation ceased and the secretaries and assistants stared at me. Behind me, I heard the *ding* of an elevator arriving. I headed toward Norma's desk. She handed me the usual clutch of message slips. She then gave an imperceptible head nod and muttered, "He's here."

I turned, bracing for what I would face. Whatever I'd pictured it wasn't this. Deegan was of medium height and slight build. He had a slightly receding chin, and his jawline had started to soften. Soft brown hair flopped boyishly over his forehead, and while it might have been charming fifteen years ago, now it looked incongruous against the crow's feet and the two deep gouges on either side of his mouth. He was very well dressed in a bespoke suit, Italian loafers, and a crisp maroon dress shirt.

Flanking him were an older man with a thick waist and quivering jowls, also dressed in a suit, and a woman in her late thirties carrying a slim briefcase and dressed in the woman lawyer's uniform—skirt, sensible heels, blouse, linen jacket.

For the briefest instant Deegan's eyes rested on me, and I saw the barest flash of recognition, then his gaze flicked away, and he addressed the room.

"I'm looking for Ms. Ellery."

*Nice save, asshole,* I thought, but clearly he'd recognized me, which lent support to John's and my belief that Securitech was behind the attacks. Then I remembered my picture plastered all over the papers and the Internet. *Of course he would recognize you, dumbass.* Yes, I would be a terrible cop.

"I'm Linnet Ellery." I stepped forward and forced myself to extend my hand.

He smiled as we shook. "Pleased to meet you." He indicated the man and woman with him. "Stan Buchanan and Peggy Waite."

Buchanan shook my hand, but his expression was sour. The lawyer from Gunther, Piedmont, Spann and Engelberg towered over me. Peggy was six feet if she was an inch, and very thin. She had kind brown eyes and a warm smile.

"I've booked the small conference room on the seventy-third floor," Norma said.

That was the room where I'd had my lovely confrontation with Doug May. I hoped this wasn't going to be a repeat.

As we rode up in the elevator, Peggy initiated a bland conversation, I reciprocated, and we chatted about the difficulty, despite hourly flights, of air travel between DC and New York, the weather, and the latest Broadway shows. Deegan occasionally added a comment; Buchanan just continued to glower.

Upstairs, the awful Bruce showed us into the conference room and asked if anyone wanted anything. No one did, but he still lingered until I almost physically pushed him out and shut the door. Deegan, Waite, and Buchanan were already seated when I turned back. Peggy snapped open her case and pulled out a sheaf of papers.

"Mr. Deegan has authorized me to make an offer of twenty million dollars to your clients." Buchanan emitted his first sound, something between a growl and a snort. "He has further authorized us to pay Ishmael, McGillary and Gold's share of that settlement amount so that Mrs. Abercrombie and her children will net five million each."

I dropped into my chair, going down like a poleaxed cow in a slaughterhouse. I opened my mouth several times, but I couldn't force out a sound. *From four million to twenty million. What the hell?* Finally, I reached over and accepted the sheaf of papers. I read quickly through the terms. They were very clear, and there appeared to be no bombshells hidden in the language.

I looked up. Deegan smiled at me. Or at least his lips curved. The expression never reached his eyes. They were all calculation. Once again my mouth took on a life of its own, and I said pretty much what I'd been thinking. "What brought this on?" I asked, though I was pretty damn sure what had happened. Thomas Gillford had happened. My silence and acquiescence were being bought.

"This case has been a time sink for our firm and a monetary drain for Mr. Deegan," Waite said. "He came to us and said he wanted to get it settled and off his plate, so . . ." She made an eloquent open-hands gesture.

Deegan spoke up. "I also know that Henry felt bad about Marlene and particularly about the children. I think this is what he would have wanted me to do."

"You couldn't have come to this conclusion seventeen years ago?" I responded dryly.

Deegan's smile stiffened, but he remained smooth. "Probably a poor decision on my part."

"So, do we have a goddamn deal?" Buchanan finally spoke, and he was as charming as I'd expected.

"I'll need to talk with my clients." I stood. "I'll call them now, but they might want a few days to consider."

"Well, that's where I am going to play a little hardball," Deegan said.

I looked inquiringly at his attorney. Peggy looked faintly uncomfortable, but her voice was firm as she said, "There's a time limit on the offer. Mr. Deegan wants an answer in two hours or he's withdrawing the offer."

It took me aback. It wasn't how negotiations were normally conducted. I gave Deegan a thin smile. "Well, then I'd better make that phone call."

My footsteps were slow and leaden as I made my way to the elevator, but there was no way out of it. I had to make that call. "Get Marlene Abercrombie and her brood on a conference call," I ordered Norma when I reached my office. "Right now."

I entered my office and closed the door. I sat at the desk where Chip had plotted to give the company to the woman Henry Abercrombie had loved, and I felt like shit. A few minutes later, my phone rang. "I'm connecting you with Ms. Ellery," I heard Norma say. "You're on with Mrs. Abercrombie, Andrew, Angela, and Natalie," Norma said, and there was a click as she left the line.

I plunged in without any preamble. "There's a new settlement offer from Securitech, and you'd be crazy not to take it."

"What is it?" the son said, overriding his mother's knee-jerk statement of "No settlement! I want it all!"

"Twenty million dollars. That's five million to each of you."

The daughters gasped. "No," Marlene snapped.

"Hell, yes," said Andrew.

"Yes, take it," said Angela.

"No!" It was almost a howl from Marlene.

"Oh, Mother, shut up! You're old and you're going to die soon. This money will make a real difference in our lives." A lovely comment from Natalie.

"Mommy, you've just been fighting for the sake of fighting, but Daddy's been dead for seventeen years. He doesn't care. Let it go. Take the money and enjoy the rest of your life," Angela implored.

"She's giving you really good advice, Mrs. Abercrombie. If you continue with this, the odds are that you and your children will end up with nothing. Your position is incredibly weak. This is a gift from Deegan. Take it."

It took another twenty minutes of cajoling and yelling between the siblings and Mrs. Abercrombie while I sat silent, but it was finally done. I headed back upstairs to where Bruce had brought in beverages and a cheese platter for Deegan, Waite, and Buchanan despite my order not to. They looked at me as I paused in the doorway. "We have a deal."

There were handshakes all around. Deegan signed five copies of the agreement, and Peggy left them with me to get the Abercrombies' signatures. I said I'd have their copy back to Peggy by week's end.

We parted at the elevator. Deegan held my hand for a fraction of a second too long and said, "I'm glad to have had the opportunity to actually meet you."

*Yeah, if you'd succeeded in having me killed you would have missed this magical moment.* But for once in my life I didn't say what I was thinking.

The elevator arrived and the trio got in. Deegan held the door. "Are you going down?"

"Thanks, but I think I'll take the stairs."

"That's how you stay so slim," he said, and allowed the door to close.

I wanted to take a shower. I opened the door into the stairwell and started slowly down toward the seventieth floor, trailing my hand along the cold metal bannister. I considered my reaction, and whether it was only due to my suspicions. *It's more than a damn suspicion when Chip was killed by a werewolf and Gillford was killed by the concerted efforts of* three *werewolves.*

David was prowling in the small lobby by the elevators. He

jumped when I pushed open the stairwell door, and rushed over. "What happened? What's going on?" They were couched as questions, but they were really commands.

"They made a settlement offer, and the clients accepted."

"A big settlement?"

"Yeah, really big."

And that's when it hit me. The case that had been dragging on for seventeen years was over, and our clients, despite deserving jack shit, were going to walk away with twenty million dollars. And Deegan assumed that, since he'd bought me off, there would never be justice for Chip.

I realized David had been saying something. "What?" I asked, trying to focus.

He gripped my shoulders. "I said, how much?"

"Twenty million."

His release was almost a push. I struggled to keep my balance, opened my mouth to object, and watched him go sprinting toward the door to the stairwell. "Wait. Where are you . . . ?"

The door swung shut. I went back to my office and groups of female associates trooping in to ask me what had happened. I was in the midst of the fifth explanation when Bruce walked, unannounced and unheralded, into my office.

"You're wanted upstairs," he said, his tone snotty. The other women and I exchanged glances. "They don't like to be kept waiting," Bruce added, his tone huffy.

I followed him to the elevator, and we rode up in silence as Bruce glared daggers at me. He led me to Gold's office and actually gave me a push into the room before shutting the door behind me.

The three senior partners and David were all waiting. Gold's office was about what I'd expected. Heavy wood desk and bookcases, large British men's club armchairs, oil paintings of stormy landscapes and distant castles on the walls.

"David tells us you've settled the *Abercrombie* case," Shade said.

"Yes, sir."

"And you didn't see fit to tell us," Gold snapped.

"I knew you were in a private meeting and not to be disturbed. I figured it would wait until you were finished."

"May we know the terms?" McGillary asked.

I handed over the settlement agreement. Shade, in the middle, held the papers while Gold and McGillary read over his shoulders.

"Good lord," McGillary said faintly.

Shade handed back the paper and gave me a wide smile, his canines flashing under the florescent lights. "Bravo, Linnet. Well done."

"But what did she *do*?" Gold asked in a complaining tone.

All three looked at me. I set aside the settlement and considered what to say. I couldn't say I'd been following Chip's lead in locating another will. I temporized. "I'm not sure."

David, hanging back at the door, rolled his eyes. I shot him a glare, then arranged my features into a conciliatory expression and faced the senior partners.

"I'm not trying to be glib, really. I honestly don't know what brought them to the table with . . . with . . ." I gestured helplessly at the pages.

David stepped forward. "She's been digging into this case ever since Chip died. Following leads that perhaps Chip didn't exploit."

"Would one of those leads involve a dead man in New Jersey?" Gold asked.

"Yes, sir."

"Did you find yourself in scrapes such as this at Yale?" he asked.

"No, sir."

"So are we likely to continue to . . . enjoy these adventures?" Gold drawled.

"I'm glad somebody's enjoying them," I muttered resentfully. Once again, David cast his eyes up toward heaven as if imploring it for patience. "And God, I hope not."

Shade laid a hand on Gold's forearm. "She's brought to a conclusion a case that has plagued us for years and made a great deal of money for this firm. I think that answers the question we were debating."

For a long moment Shade and Gold locked eyes. Gold looked to McGillary, who gave an imperceptible nod. Gold made a conscious effort to breathe so he would have enough air to emit a gusting sigh. "Very well. She stays."

David jerked his head toward the door. I followed him out. I stood in the hall outside Gold's office and I tried to parse all the emotion I'd experienced in the past few hours. Fear when I'd learned Deegan was coming to the office. Shock at the offer. Anger while dealing with Marlene. Triumph when the deal had been inked. And now . . .

"Pick a feeling," Sullivan said.

I looked up at him. "Exhausted. Defeated, and I shouldn't feel that way." My hands clenched and I started to pace. "And damn angry. I accomplish something and they"—I pointed a shaking hand at the blank face of the door—"make me feel like shit. Well, fuck that! I'm good at this."

"Yes, you are, but you're also . . ."

"What?" I demanded, and I could feel the pugnacious thrust of my jaw as I uttered the word.

"I don't exactly know. Smart, yes, you wouldn't be here if you weren't smart, but indefatigable? Unexpected? Blunt to a fault?"

"Careful, it's starting to sound like you like me."

"I wouldn't go that far," he said, dampening any pretension on my part.

"Then why did you bring the news to them? About the settlement."

He made a sound somewhere between a growl and a mutter and turned on his heel. "Because I hate that asshole Winchester." He walked away toward the front lobby.

Which brought me back to the old lawyer adage: *Never ask a question to which you don't know the answer.* Here I thought I had made a new friend and ally, and instead I was just a pawn in a battle between David and Ryan. Vampires sucked. Or maybe lawyers sucked. Actually, *people* sucked.

I shook off my reverie and walked toward the lobby and the elevators, only to be intercepted by Bruce. He looked pissed, and he pushed in on me until our faces were only inches apart.

"Why are you doing this?" he hissed. "Why do you draw their attention when it won't do you a damn bit of good? They have meetings about you. They argue about you, and you're just a woman. There's no reason to notice you."

I was on the verge of just letting loose on him for the dismissive, sexist bullshit, but then I realized that underneath all the attitude was fear and grief and desperation. "You want to be Made so badly it's killing you. Forgive the gallows humor."

Bruce jerked away from me. "Oh, fuck off!"

I went after him, touched him lightly on the shoulder. "Bruce, listen to me. I was fostered in a vampire household. You're doing this all wrong. Yes, you're incredibly handsome, and you try to be useful, but that's not what makes them pick a man. They are connoisseurs. Why spend thousands of years in the company of ugly people? But it takes more than looks and a willingness to please. They look for brains, training, accomplishment, and life experience. How old are you?" The response was too muffled for me to understand. "What?"

"Twenty."

"Get out of here. Go back to school. Get a degree. Excel at something, Make them notice you for who you are, not how you look. Become a man first."

He kept his back to me but gave a sharp little nod. I felt a quivering in his shoulders, and I hurried off to the elevators while he ran for the bathroom and a chance to compose himself.

Downstairs, I sat in my office for another twenty minutes pretending to work but unable to concentrate. Finally I emerged to a round of shoulder pats from the male associates and hugs from most of the women. There were many congratulations. Some of them were even sincere. I was in a bleak fog, however. I had been checked and mated by Deegan.

At seven p.m., my phone rang. Norma sounded sour.

"It's that Finkelstein character."

"Put it through." She sniffed but complied.

"Well, it looks like we established what you are," Syd said, disdain dripping off every word.

"Excuse me?"

"So, Deegan found your price."

I lowered my voice. "He offered a settlement. I had to take it to my clients."

"You just took money away from Chastity and Destiny!" he yelled.

"They're not my clients. I represented my clients!" I snapped back, my tone rising to match his.

"Yeah, well, Deegan's leaning on us now. He offered us a shitty half a mil. What did you get?"

"You know I can't tell you that."

"Westin would have."

I slumped. "Yeah, he probably would have, but I'm still trying to be an ethical lawyer."

"That tells me all I need to know. You did a shitload better than half a mil." I remained silent. "Well, we're not backing down."

"You're not going to take the offer?"

"Fuck, no. Abercrombie loved Chastity. She was the love of his life. He left her everything."

"But you don't have the will."

"I'll keep looking. I have to." I didn't pry, but I heard the sorrow in Syd's voice, and I wondered what he wasn't telling me about Chastity and Destiny.

I knew I was under no obligation to reveal what I'd learned from Gillford, but it felt shitty not to. And now my clients had their settlement, so what could it hurt?

"Look, Syd, meet me at the Algonquin. We'll have a drink."


I slipped through the sliding doors just behind a filled luggage cart with the hotel's long-haired white cat riding proudly on the top suitcase. The Japanese tourists who owned the luggage were giggling and snapping photos, delighted by this touch of New York flavor.

Syd was sunk down in one of the big upholstered chairs. His sport coat was hung on one side of the high back, and its loud windowpane pattern seemed fluorescent in the muted, subaqueous lighting of the bar. He wore a short-sleeved shirt, limp with sweat, and his tie was loosened.

I took the chair opposite. A small table separated us. A highball glass with only dregs of ice shed condensation, and moisture rings dotted the table like the sucker tracks of an invisible octopus. The waitress came over.

"What are you drinking?" I asked Syd.

"Gin and tonic." He held out his glass. "I'll take another."

"Nothing for me, thanks." The girl left. "Though it does sound refreshing. It's so hot."

"You didn't ask to meet me so we could discuss the weather," Syd said shortly. "What's up?"

"Look, I'm going to give you a name. Thomas Gillford." I stood and threw down two twenties on the table to cover Syd's drinks and a tip.

"What does that mean? Who is this guy?" Syd called as I started to walk away.

"You're energetic enough. I'm sure you'll figure it out."

I paused to give the cat a stroke on the back and left feeling all smug and Mata Hari–ish.

# 18

On Saturday afternoon, Caroline and I met up at the coffeemaker in the kitchen. She grimaced down at her mug. "I think this will be my eleventh cup."

"Yaagh, you're going to wreck your stomach," I said.

"I know, but Johnson is going to trial in two weeks, I'm the second on the case, and I'm making sure everything is ready."

I checked my watch. "Look, I've been getting up to speed on this environmental case since eight this morning. What say we take off, get some lunch, and do some shopping? We can get back to breaking rocks tomorrow."

"It's tempting. . . ." She started to shake her head.

I jumped in. "Come on."

"Oh hell, why not?"

We left our dirty coffee mugs in the sink, raced back to our offices for our purses, and met at the elevators.

"Did you ever ditch school?" I asked as we got on the elevator.

"Oh God, no! I'm the quintessential good girl. You?"

"No way. And from fourth grade until I graduated from high school I was fostered with a vampire. You do *not* want the truant officer calling your vampire liege."

Caroline laughed. We nodded to the lobby guard and stepped out onto the street. The heat seemed to shimmer off the sidewalks. We found a small restaurant that specialized in soup and salad, and we both went for the chilled cucumber and almond soup and a small side salad resplendent with roasted red peppers, piñon nuts, and feta cheese. Fortified with food and buckets of iced tea, we headed off to Bloomingdale's.

Hangers *shush*ed along metal bars as we flipped through a rack of silk blouses. "You've been at the firm longer. What's the story with David Sullivan?" I asked Caroline as she held a deep purple shirt under her chin and critically inspected herself in a nearby mirror.

"I have no idea. What do you think?" she added, waving the blouse at me.

"Wrong color with your skin tone."

She sighed. "I knew that. I just hoped you'd convince me otherwise. I love this color. But no, I don't know. He'd already been demoted when I started four years ago."

"Wow, it must have been some offense if he's still in human purdah."

"He's always a real shit to everyone." Caroline returned the purple blouse to the rack, and we moved on toward my downfall—the shoe section.

"I can understand why. You're a superior being: stronger, tougher, faster, and pretty much immortal." I shook my head. "At that point you don't worry too much about being polite to the noisy monkey throngs that spring up and die around you."

"You mean us humans, right?" Caroline asked.

"Yeah, think about it. Our lives must pass by vampires like a DVD on fast-forward."

"Unless they drag. Would life become a burden after centuries? Is it the certainty of death that gives us drive?" Caroline mused.

I considered that while I inspected a pair of winter boots that had just been put out on display. It was hard to imagine needing them when it was ninety outside. "Well, they're not big on innovation, that's for sure. You don't hear about a vampire Einstein or Steve Jobs."

"Hey, you want to get an iced coffee and continue this conversation sitting down?" Caroline asked.

"Sounds good."

We headed for the escalator, and Caroline asked, "What about werewolves? Are they more creative?"

"They're certainly more violent." I couldn't totally suppress the shudder. We glided up to the seventh floor and 40 Carrots. "If they're not in the military, they tend to gravitate toward the financial sector—bond traders, that sort of thing."

"Maybe they sublimate the violence with competition," Caroline said.

"Yeah, that's possible, and I think they like to keep score, and toys and money are an easy way to measure success." The hostess seated us.

Caroline leaned across the small table, her expression intense. "Okay, since you've been raised around vampires, maybe you can explain something else to me."

"I'll try."

"Why didn't Ryan bite us? Not enough to make us vampires, but as a way to show his dominance over us. That's what the crappy sex was about, and the sex act is intrinsically difficult for him."

"It's what I told you before—they don't bite women."

"I thought you were just talking about turning someone into a vampire and making partner. You mean they never—"

I interrupted. "No, they won't lay a tooth on us, and if they do, the punishment for both parties is very severe. As in *make you dead* severe."

"Wait a minute. What about Bram Stoker—Dracula, the vampire brides, Lucy Westenra, and all that?" Caroline argued.

"Stoker was a Victorian man with real hang-ups about sex. He had syphilis, and supposedly Dracula was all about his disease. My guess is that he knew someone who actually knew the secret—that vampires existed. Stoker then took that knowledge and created a work of fiction. Real vampires don't bite women for fear that sometime, one of them might go too far." Caroline opened her mouth, then closed it, but she still looked like she wanted to argue. "Have you ever seen a female vampire?" I pressed.

"No."

"There you go. If I order an ice cream, would you help me eat it?" I asked, trying to change the subject.

"Using me to assuage your guilt?" Caroline snapped.

"Forget it," I said, and wondered how somebody could seem so nice one minute and bite the next.

She was frowning and fiddling with her silverware. "Do you think they might ever reconsider the taboo?"

"Probably not in time to do *us* any good."

"I wish I could change. Become a man." The words burst out of her, harsh and ragged.

"Well, that's just stupid, and no, you don't. You're brilliant and talented, and also happen to be beautiful, and you shouldn't beat yourself up over your gender, or allow yourself to be judged by it—"

"But I *am*."

"And you're buying into it: assuming that the fact that you're a woman is going to limit you or make you less than vampires. Think how they're limited. No children, no family. No, I wouldn't want to be a vampire."

"Why not? A chance to make partner. Eternal life. Not getting old. Some people would find that wonderful."

"First, I want children, a family. Second, you don't suddenly get young when you're bitten. You stay the age you were when you were Made. And finally, you might not stay all that pretty as the decades and centuries pass. Vampires don't heal all that well. There's an old adage in the community—read the years in the scars."

"I haven't seen that with our partners," she argued.

"We haven't seen beneath their clothes. Well, except for Ryan, and he seems to be a very young vampire. Mr. Bainbridge has a terrible scar on his shoulder. One of my foster brothers told me about it. He had the nerve to ask about it, and Meredith said it was from a battle-ax."

"Okay, we have officially gone into too-much-creepy-information territory."

Our coffees arrived, and we dropped the subject of vampires.


On Monday morning, the Abercrombies came in and signed the settlement agreement. I put a set of the documents in the pouch heading to Washington DC, and set a runner to file the executed copy with the court. Now there was no way for Securitech to back out.

With everything that had happened I hadn't followed up on Joylon Bryce's offer to come and ride. I decided to remedy that. I called and asked him if I could come out around six. He assured me that would be fine.

After the subway, there was a bus that dropped me off almost at the front gate of the Bella Luna Riding Stable. Large trees over-hung the crushed gravel driveway, and their shade helped blunt the force of the sun. A group of five giggling girls rode past. They looked to be in their early teens, and they were mounted on a mixture of horses—a Connemara pony, an old quarter horse, a pinto mare, a fancy chestnut thoroughbred, and a dainty Arabian.

I remembered being that age, when I'd slipped away from the Bainbridge house to a nearby stable. I had worked as an unpaid stall cleaner to cadge rides on other people's horses. Then Mr. Bainbridge had found out and bought me a horse, and the old barn on the property had a resident again. Suncloud, a black-and-white paint of indeterminate breeding. He was such a sweetheart that he would let me sit under his belly to get out of the rain, and I rode him bareback and pretended I was an Indian.

Mr. Bainbridge had stood in an upstairs window and watched me jumping fences, and suddenly I had a coach, and more horses joined Suncloud in the barn. Delila, Miss Patti, and Excalibur. I tried everything—western, jumping, eventing, even sidesaddle, but I'd settled on dressage. There was something about the precision and total communication that matched my personality. Then I'd gone off to college, and it was back to working for rides and riding "problem" horses. And now, it seemed, I was doing it again.

Jolly was waiting for me when I arrived at the wood and stone barn. Unlike Ryan, he did not have a groom tacking up the horse. Instead he showed me Vento's saddle, bridle, and tack box, waited for me to change into riding clothes, and then led me down the barn's center aisle. Beautiful heads thrust over the stall doors, their liquid brown eyes filled with pleading looks. And Jolly responded with a treat and an affectionate croon for each horse. The air was redolent with the scent of hay, dust, and horse. Dust motes spun in lazy golden circles in the still air. At the end of the barn was a double-sized stall. Jolly gave a strange little whistle. There was a *chuff* from inside and a white head was thrust over the door.

Like may Iberian horses, Vento had a Roman nose, but there was more than a hint of his Arabian ancestors that had come across with the Moorish conquerers. His forelock hung over his eyes. Jolly reached up and brushed it aside, revealing a bulging forehead bisected with a deep *V* between Vento's eyes. Legend said that horses with that configuration on their forehead were smart. In my experience, legend was right.

I stepped up close and noticed the ring of blue that surrounded Vento's dark eyes. He looked like a baroque painting, all compact ovals. He wasn't big, maybe fifteen hands, which was fine by me. I'd ridden more than my share of seventeen-hand warm-blooded monsters, and at five foot one it was not fun.

"Vento, meet Linnet. Linnet, meet Vento," Jolly said with grave courtesy.

I extended a hand. Vento lipped it, then lifted his head and regarded me seriously. I leaned forward and gently blew into his nostrils. He *whuffl*ed back. Jolly rolled his chair back a few feet and gestured at the stall door.

"Okay, he's all yours."

I took the black leather halter with its silver nameplate off the hook by the stall door and stepped into the deeply bedded sawdust of the stall. Vento dropped his head over my shoulder and pressed me against his neck and chest in the equine version of a hug. Then he obediently dropped his head into the halter.

As I led him down the aisle toward the tack-up bays he chuckled at one of the mares. Without thinking, I smacked him on the shoulder and said, "Cut it out. No trash talking."

Jolly gave a small laugh. "Yes, you are a horsewoman. He is very well behaved for a young stallion, but occasionally he has to be reminded of his manners where ladies are concerned."

I took my time picking out his feet and grooming him. I even braided his long silver, white, and gray mane. I wrapped his legs with polo wraps, placed the saddle, and was pleased to discover he wasn't a bit girthy.

I plucked the bridle off its hook and fingered the bit. It was a French snaffle with a nice lozenge in the center, but it was the type of bit you use on a young horse just starting under saddle. "This is a pretty fat snaffle for a stallion," I said, not wanting to sound critical.

"He's not your average stallion. And he doesn't like to be uncomfortable. When I first got him, I tried him in a thinner bit. He was fussy. When I went to the big, fat baby bit he was much better."

I nodded and held the bit with my left hand while my right hand slipped the headstall over his ears. Vento took the bridle with the same eagerness and good humor with which he'd embraced the halter.

"He's just been started in the double bridle," Jolly said. "If you two suit, and if you'd like to keep riding him, I'd appreciate it if you'd ride him in it once a week."

"Sure."

"He's ready to show fourth level now, and I'd like to bring him out Prix St. George and intermediaire one next spring."

"So, did you get to ride him before—I mean, you didn't . . . this happened . . ."

"Three years ago. Car crash." The smile stayed in place, but I noticed that Jolly's hand tightened convulsively on one knee. "At least I got to ride him for a few months."

"I'm sorry." I didn't know what else to say.

"It's all right. I've almost accepted it."

I tightened the girth another hole and led Vento toward the mounting block just outside the barn doors.

"Oh, one more thing. He puffs up like a toad. You'll need to tighten the girth again after you've trotted."

I nodded my thanks, led Vento up to the block, and mounted. We headed down the lane toward the outdoor arena.

After a walk and long and low trot work, I tightened the girth for the final time, shortened the reins, and suddenly I had an upper-level horse beneath my seat. There was so much air time in Vento's collected trot that it felt like my heart beat a couple of seconds before the next foot fall. With the barest shift of my seat we were cantering, a cadenced, floating motion that felt like riding a carousel. I couldn't resist. I brought him down to the walk, asked for the *passage*. I had never felt that much suspension on a horse before.

I rode over to where Jolly sat in his chair by the gate. "Okay, he's world-class, and I don't know if you should trust him to me. This horse should be with one of our Olympic riders."

"But then I wouldn't get to see him. No, I'm very happy to keep him here, and after watching the two of you together, I think you're the perfect rider for him."

I felt myself blushing. I tugged down the brim of my helmet so maybe it wouldn't show so badly and went back to riding. Forty-five minutes later, the sun was a red smear on the horizon and I realized that Jolly was gone. Feeling guilty, I headed back toward the barn. I had essentially taken the guy's horse and hadn't even noticed when he left.

Jolly was waiting at the barn. His eyes were heavy lidded and he seemed vague. I wondered if he was stoned, then decided it wasn't any of my business.

"Did you enjoy yourself?" Jolly asked as he rolled over to a switch and turned on the lights. I glanced toward the double doors and realized it was now full dark.

"Very much. Thank you, thank you. He's wonderful." Vento gave me a shove with his head as if to say, *Hey, lady, my dinner is waiting.*

I hurriedly slipped the rubber bands off his mane and undid the braid. I brushed him down, and Jolly held out a hand for Vento's lead rope. "I'll take him."

I handed over the rope and watched the man in the wheelchair and the gleaming white stallion, pacing next to him, glide down the aisle. For an instant there seemed to be a nimbus of light around them both. I gave my head a shake, and it was gone. Apparently just a trick of light on dust.

"Are there carrots?" I called after him.

"In the feed room."

I found them and threw a large handful into a bucket. Vento eagerly left his hay once he saw the carrots.

I leaned on the stall while Jolly sat silently next to me. The sound of munching filled the barn. It was very peaceful. I finally moved. "I should get home. I'll try to come tomorrow, but expect me both days of the weekend."

"I look forward to it."

We shook hands, and I decided to travel home in my riding clothes. When I emerged from the subway station near home, my phone chimed to indicate a missed call. In fact, there were seven missed calls. I was relieved to see it wasn't the house number up in Rhode Island, or any family cell number. It wasn't any number I recognized. I hit callback, and a few rings later someone answered.

"Flushing Hospital Medical Center, Dr. Bush speaking," said a woman's voice.

Sudden gut-loosening terror gripped me. "This is Linnet Ellery. I have a number of calls from you."

"Yes, thank you for calling back. We have a John Doe admitted here. His identification was gone, but our ER found a crumpled piece of paper in his pocket with your name and number. If you could help us identify this man, we would very much appreciate it."

"John Doe. Is he dead?" Panic had closed my throat, and the words emerged as a croak.

"Not yet. He's in a coma."

"What's he look like?" I asked, picturing Charlie or John.

"Short, balding, a bit rotund."

"Pointed-toe shoes?" I asked, just to be sure, though I was pretty sure I knew who she was describing.

"Yes."

"His name's Syd Finkelstein. He's an attorney with an office in Queens. What happened to him?"

"Unless you're a family member, I can't release that information. Let's just say it was bad enough that his survival is in some doubt."

My legs were suddenly boneless, and I leaned against the wall of the local Italian bakery. "I'll be there as soon as I can," I forced past lips that felt like bars of ice.

I ended the call and sat there for a few minutes. I remembered my last meeting with Syd. I'd been so cocky. Well, I didn't feel like Mata Hari any longer. I felt like a heel.

# 19

"Do you think this is my fault?"

"I don't know." John said as he pulled the car into the parking lot of the hospital. It wasn't the most comforting answer.

I had called him right after I hung up with the doctor. He had answered, heard my voice, and then offended me by asking in a joking tone, "What kind of trouble are you in now?" But when I told him what had happened, he had stopped teasing and rushed to pick me up.

John wheeled into a parking space and stopped as I said, "Maybe I should have warned him."

We got out. John leaned on the roof of the car and gave me an exasperated look. "From what you've told me, it sounded like Finkelstein already didn't trust Securitech."

"But if I'd told him about the attack on me and the old lawyer he might have been *more* on his guard."

John pressed the lock button on his car keys. The car dutifully honked and blinked its head and taillights, sending red and white light strobing across the other cars in the lot.

"For all we know Securitech had nothing to do with this and he was hit by a bus. I mean, he had no ID," I said, and then jumped nervously, thinking I saw a shadowy figure hunched among the cars. It turned out to be a low bush in one of the dividers. "It could have been just a mugging."

"You don't really believe that," John said.

"I could hope. Oh God, that sounded horrible."

"You need to calm down until we get some actual facts," he said.

We were approaching the sliding glass doors that marked the main entrance to the hospital. I shook my head. "I should never have told him about the other will."

"And then you would have felt guilty about withholding that information. You cannot singlehandedly keep the universe in balance, Linnet," John scolded as we entered the hospital.

We checked the board and discovered the ICU was on the third floor. As we rode up in the elevator, the air had a taste that was both antiseptic and rotten. I took a seat in the waiting room.

"Aren't we going to . . . ?" John gestured at the nurse's station.

"No point. They won't tell us anything, and we can't get in to see him."

"Then why are we here?"

"Because they will have called his family by now. They'll show up and I'll find out what I need from them." I glanced at my watch. "They may even be here now."

John dropped into a chair, slouched, and stared up at the television. It was turned down so low that no words could be distinguished, just a bass drone. It looked like some kind of game show. I picked up a magazine, its cover tattered by too many nervous fingers, and added my own bends and tears as I flipped through the pages, not really focusing on anything.

Twenty minutes later, I saw a petite, white-haired woman wearing a white lab coat and a stethoscope around her neck walking with a tall, slender woman with expertly highlighted brown-blonde hair who looked to be in her fifties. A man about her age had his arm around her. They were surrounded by five very tall young men.

The conversation concluded, the doctor peeled away, and I stood up as they headed into the waiting room and asked, "Mrs. Finkelstein?"

"No, Mrs. Messinger. Finkelstein was my maiden name."

"You're Syd's sister," I said.

"Who are you?" demanded one of the giants.

"Caleb, don't be rude," said the older man. He held out his hand. "Nate Messinger."

"My name is Linnet Ellery. I'm an associate of Syd's. The hospital called me because they found my number in Syd's pocket."

Mrs. Messinger fell on my neck, crying and hugging me. "Thank you. Oh, thank you so much. If it hadn't been for you, Syd might have lain here for days all alone."

John joined us, and I introduced him. The Messingers introduced their sons Joshua, David, Aaron, Izaak, and Caleb. We all sat down.

"It was so good of you to come," Mrs. Messinger said. The boys were eyeing John and me with some skepticism. Their father masked it better.

I took a deep breath. "I don't mean to pry—" I saw the male Messingers stiffen, and John stepped in.

"But she's going to. It's what she does." He softened the words with an inclusive smile. "Look, Syd and Linnet had a case in common."

"A case that led to me being assaulted. Then I got a call that Syd was in the hospital. I want to know . . . I need to know what happened to Syd to see if it's related." *And if I'm responsible*, my hindbrain added. *Please don't let me be responsible.*

"Our uncle was attacked," Izaak said.

"He was mauled pretty badly," David added.

"Mauled," I repeated. John gave me a significant look.

"They had to amputate his right arm at the elbow," Mr. Messinger said. His wife shuddered, and he hugged her again.

"How did he survive?" I asked, thinking of my own close calls.

"Dumb luck," Nate Messinger said. "A delivery truck pulled down the alley and the driver saw him lying there. There was a guy bending over Syd. The delivery man took out after him, but he got over a wall and escaped."

"Was he human?" John asked, and the Messingers gave him an odd look.

"What time did the truck pull down that alley?" I asked.

"It was after dark," Joshua said.

I looked at John. "He would have been clearly visible in the headlights. It was a human."

"All that means is that he had transformed back to human so it would be easier to get at Syd's wallet," John argued.

"And it could have just been a mugging," I countered. I ignored him and turned back to the family. "Was he coming from work?"

"Yes," Mrs. Messinger said.

"Did they find his briefcase?" John asked.

"No."

"People sometimes carry money and valuables in a briefcase," I said.

"Why are you insisting on making this a simple mugging?" he demanded.

"And why are you trying to prove this is something more?" The Messingers were staring at us. John stood up, took my arm, and pulled me to my feet.

"Linnet wanted to tell you to tell Syd to get better soon."

He started to march me away. Then he called over his shoulder, "I'd get security for Syd!"

We rode the elevator in simmering silence, me on one side of the car with my arms folded definitely across my chest, and John on the other with his hands thrust deep into his pockets.

John keyed the car's lock from across the lot. The headlights flashed, and it was almost as if the car had winked at us. It was a warmer and friendlier response than I was getting from my silent companion.

We reached the car, but I didn't get in. I rested my hands on the roof and said (I hoped) firmly and professionally, "Don't treat me like a brainless twit."

"Then stop acting like one." It wasn't the response I'd been expecting. It actually took my breath away.

"How have I been brainless?"

"You didn't have to tell Finkelstein about Gillford and the other will, but out of some weird sense of honor you decided you had to. But it never occurred to you that if Securitech was watching *you*— and you were just representing lunatics with no realistic claim on the estate—they were sure as hell going to watch the guy representing the stripper who actually has a real claim to the company."

Put that way, I no longer looked so noble. I looked like . . . a brainless twit. I looked back at the storied bulk of the hospital, windows gleaming like yellow eyes. There was no way to cast this as a mugging and excuse myself. Syd was in a coma, missing half his arm, and because he'd managed to survive he was still in danger. And all of it because of me. I lost it and started to cry. There was an aching weight in my chest, and my muscles vibrated with the desperate, futile wish that I could go back and do things differently.

John came around the car in a flash, and gathered me in his arms. "Oh shit, Linnet, I'm sorry. I didn't mean to make you cry. I'm just angry because that could have been you in that hospital."

"No, you were right. I didn't think. I didn't consider all the ramifications. I had found out information about the other will, and I guess I just wanted to show off."

"No, that's not it. You have an instinct for justice, which, sad to say, isn't all that common among lawyers." Even though I didn't totally buy what he was saying, it was nice to hear. "Let me take you home," he murmured. "Are you hungry?"

"I couldn't eat."

I stared unseeing out the side window as we made our way back to my apartment. I finally stirred and looked over at John. "Do you think Chastity and her daughter are in danger?"

"Oh, probably, but not tonight. Deegan may think he's home free with Finkelstein in the hospital."

"But when he finds out Syd didn't die . . ." I couldn't finish the sentence. The consequences were too dire.

"We'll burn that bridge when we get to it. The hospital isn't going to give out information to just anybody. We've got a little breathing space."

We turned down the side street that separated my building from a small park enclosed by a wrought-iron fence. "You can just drop me off. It's a bitch to park—"

I broke off when I saw the space directly in front of the steps and doors of my building. John wheeled up next to the space and executed a perfect parallel park. I decided if it happened a third time I was going to assume it was some kind of Álfar power.

He turned off the car and cranked around to look directly at me. "I don't *drop women off.* I escort them to their door the way Big Red taught me."

"And who's Big Red?" I asked as I got out.

"My dad."

"Guess the training didn't extend to opening car doors," I said as he took my gym bag and roller bag out of the trunk of the car. I grabbed my boot carrier and slung it over my shoulder.

"Oh hell yeah, it did," he said as we crossed the street. "But in this feminist society a guy's gotta pick his courtesy battles." I flashed him a wry look as I fished for my key. "I don't open doors for women anymore—that gets me dirty looks—but I hold elevators, carry heavy things, and escort them to their doors."

He was trying to make me smile, and he succeeded for a few moments, but then the problems and worries pressed in again. Inside the vestibule I headed for the stairs.

"Hey, there is an elevator," John said.

"It's my workout plan," I said. "You can take the elevator. I'm on the seventh floor."

"I don't think that qualifies as escorting," he said as he hefted the bags a bit higher and followed me up the stairs.

We were almost at the top when my toe caught on a tread, and I nearly took a header. With lightning-fast reflexes, John dropped the bags and caught me under the armpits, keeping me from a nasty face-plant.

"Easy there. You okay?" His hand was resting on my back. I nodded, but he was frowning. "Good lord, woman, your back is like an iron girder."

"I'm tense. So sue me."

"Tense doesn't begin to cover it," he grumbled as he recovered my bags and we made it to my floor. I opened the door to the apartment, and we entered. John set down the bags and looked around appreciatively.

"Nice." He moved over to the secondhand bookshelves lining the wall under the windows and began looking through the books. "You have very eclectic taste."

"Is that polite-speak for 'bad'?" I asked.

John turned to face me. "No. Why would you think that?"

"Because you called me a brainless twit."

"Correction. You called yourself that. I merely agreed."

"And that's better how?" I was embarrassed to discover that tears were pricking at the backs of my eyelids. I turned away.

John was suddenly there, gentle hands on my shoulders, turning me to face him. "Hey, hey. I'm worried about you. Okay? Now sit down." He guided me to the sofa and pushed me down. He then got behind the couch and began to massage my neck and shoulders. He was really, really good, and it was heaven. I let out a sound that was half-groan, half-sigh.

"That's better." His voice was soft and low and sounded like a caress.

His hands became gentler, stroking down my arms. It seemed that electricity danced on his fingertips, making my skin suddenly hot. A shivering began somewhere deep in my core. He leaned down, and his breath fluttered my hair. I breathed in his scent, spice with a touch of sweat. I felt my thighs convulse and tighten as I anticipated a kiss on the nape of my neck, but he withdrew. I sat there, considering. I could feel the heat coming off him in waves and the answering heat in my own body, but he was holding back, resisting.

I knew if I looked back at him he would kiss me. Now I just had to decide if that was a good idea. *To hell with whether it's a good idea. It's what I want.* So I looked back over my shoulder, and sure enough, he kissed me.

His mouth tasted of vanilla and honey. I wondered if he'd managed to chew a lozenge or if that was another Álfar trait. If so, it wasn't fair. I hated to think what I might taste like after a day at the office drinking coffee, and hours on a horse, and then more hours until we reached this point. I was probably disgusting. He sensed my withdrawal.

"I'm sorry," he began.

"No, I'm not objecting . . . it's just . . . let me brush my teeth—" He silenced me by pressing his mouth firmly down on mine. His tongue teased at my lips. I gasped and opened to him. Our tongues touched, fenced. I pulled back again. "Look, you're an Álfar—"

"I try to forget about that—"

"So I feel gross and gauche and—"

"Shut up," he said, amusement lacing the words. He swept me up into his arms and started carrying me toward the bedroom door. "You're smart." He gave me a kiss. "Funny." A kiss. "Brave." Another kiss. "Loyal." Kiss.

"Woof," I said.

John started laughing and lost his balance, and we went down in a tangled heap on my bed. Once we'd untangled we lay side by side, gently kissing, our fingers exploring each other's faces. I especially liked running my fingers through his hair. It was incredibly thick and surprisingly coarse. I had thought an Álfar's hair would be like silk dipped in silicone.

We didn't seem to be moving toward any other body parts, so I reached down and began unbuttoning his shirt, exposing his chest. I ran my nails from his sternum to his belt buckle, making him gasp and arch his back. I felt perversely pleased with myself, and his excitement elevated my own anticipation.

I sat up, and he grabbed hold of the bottom of my tank top and pulled it over my head. I leaned into him, and his hands sought the clasp of my bra. I wasn't terribly well endowed, and I wondered if he'd be disappointed. But he didn't rush. He rubbed the palm of a hand across my nipples, then cupped a breast in each hand and bestowed feather-like kisses while his thumb continued to flick across my now painfully erect nipples. I gasped and cried out, and he pulled me against his chest, bare skin to bare skin, and just stroked my back.

I reached down, undid his belt, unzipped his slacks. His erection was very evident, pressed against the white cloth of his boxer shorts. That was another thing I hadn't expected. I thought an Álfar would be a jockey kind of guy. It was like John had read my mind. He pulled back a bit and smiled down at me. His eyes were dancing, filled with mischief.

"A real Álfar would go commando," he said, and I choked on a laugh. "Remember, I'm the blue-collar elf."

I slipped my hand beneath the waistband of his underwear. My exploring hand noted the ripped muscles in his abdomen, and then I gently cupped his penis. He groaned, his eyes rolled back, and he bucked against me. I drew my fingernails down the back of his member and gently touched his balls. This time the groan became a growl, and he flipped me over and began kissing me. His lips were hard and demanding now, his tongue like a rapier.

I was gasping, burning up, and my clothes felt way too tight and confining. I wanted to press myself against that lean body and feel John's warmth. He seemed to feel the same urgency, because we tugged and wriggled until we were out of our pants and underwear.

There was another pause while John pulled back, leaned on his elbow, and let his eyes explore my body, taking in every inch. And I felt every inch blush. I tried to cover myself, but he grabbed my hand.

"You're beautiful."

"No. I'm cute."

He shook his head. "Never argue with a connoisseur. You're beautiful."

I threw my arms around his neck and hugged him close. His skin was hot to the touch, and the heat seemed to enter my body. Something deep in my groin gave a flip, and I gasped. Never in my life had I been this aroused, this quickly.

I discovered he was very sensitive on his throat and ears. Kissing him there made his eyes roll back and hoarse gasps puff from between his lips. He kissed the hollow at the base of my throat, then took one breast in his mouth. His tongue teased across my nipple. I struggled to take a breath, and my back arched like a stroked cat's. His erection pressed against me, tumescent and sticky. We were both so ready.

I tried to guide him inside me, but he resisted, and instead he flipped me onto my stomach and began kissing and nibbling along my shoulder blades, paying special attention to the small of my back.

Somehow he had known that I loved to have my back fondled. Maybe he really *was* telepathic.

"You have such a beautiful back." His finger traced the line of muscles.

"Horses," I managed to gasp, and I gripped the pillow with both hands and writhed beneath him, emitting little mewing noises. He put his lips next to my ear and whispered, "You sound just like a kitten."

"Oh, great, so much for sexy and seductive."

"Oh, you're that too." John gently rolled me over, and looked down into my face. His expression was serious. "Do you want this?"

"Yes."

"Are you ready?"

"Oh God, yes."

He still held back, gently brushing my clitoris with the tip of his penis. It was wildly arousing. I let out a cry of frustration, clutched him tightly, and pulled him against me. He slid into me, all the while murmuring endearments. We fit together very well, and we found each other's rhythm almost instantly.

Over and over John brought me to climax, thrusting deep into me, then slowing to a tickling caress. Each time he tried something new he asked: How was it? Did I like it? Did it feel good?

Half the time all I could manage was a nod and a strangled "Uh-huh."

I started to stress over his lack of an orgasm. He must have sensed the subtle tensing in my muscles. He slowed down and ran a hand through my hair. "Too much? Am I doing something you don't like?"

"No, I just worry that you—"

"Don't worry about me. I'm having a *very* good time."

"But you haven't come yet."

"I will. I want this to last for a while. You don't mind, do you?"

"Oh God, no. You're wonderful, you're amazing. I just want it to be good for you too."

"Stop worrying about everyone else, Linnet." He gave me a devil's grin and began to pick up the pace.

My hips rose to match him. An orgasm later, John began to groan and gasped out, "I can't hold back any longer."

"Don't," I cried, clutching at his shoulders.

He drove in deeper, and my cries matched his. He gave a final, shuddering yell. I felt his release, a wash of warmth deep inside me, and John collapsed onto my chest. I tightened my core muscles, closing my vagina around him. He gasped and shivered.

"What are you doing? And how are you doing it?"

"Horses," I said again with some smugness.

"Jesus, woman, that feels amazing."

We lay together for a long time, still connected, my hand stroking down his back. He played with my hair, and I dozed off. I awoke to find him looking down at me with amusement.

"What?" I said defensively.

"Isn't it supposed to be the man who falls asleep?" John teased.

I made a face and pulled his hair. "You're just not typical because you're not a man."

"Really? What am I?"

"Annoying. What time is it?"

He lifted up an arm, canting it to catch the light from the window, and checked his watch. "Three thirty."

"I'm going to be wasted at work tomorrow . . . today."

"You could not go in," John said.

"I don't want to get in trouble."

"Linnet, have you not noticed that you are the Golden Child?"

"Yeah, maybe, but pretty soon they're going to be asking *What have you done for me lately?*"

"So take advantage of it now."

"Why? What did you have in mind?" I teased.

"More of this," he said, with an expansive gesture that encompassed the bed.

"That sounds good," I said, and snuggled in close to him. He spooned me against his belly, and this time he slept too.

# 20

But I awoke with a different plan. John was still sleeping. I set some cinnamon-raisin bread to soak in a mix of cream, eggs, orange juice, orange zest, and Grand Marnier for French toast, put bacon in the oven to bake, brewed a pot of coffee and got a cup, and sat down with my laptop to do some research on Thomas Gillford.

Everybody's on the net, whether they use it or not. It didn't take long to locate Gillford's old office address in Red Oak Hollow, Virginia. Securitech had its headquarters and training facility on 700 acres between Red Oak Hollow and Roanoke, where Chastity had danced and won the love of Henry Abercrombie.

When lawyers retire, they have only two choices regarding the files they've accumulated over the years—return them to the clients, or store them. Even after lawyers die, the files have to continue to be stored, or their heirs have to try to return the papers to the clients. I realized lawyers were rather like Marley's Ghost, dragging behind us vast reams of paper instead of cash boxes.

There had been no sign of filing cabinets in the rented house in Bayonne. Granted, I hadn't seen every room, but Gillford's bio in *American Lawyer* gave his birthdate, and when I did the math

I figured out he had been eighty-five at the time of his death. He had started practicing law at twenty-three by doing an apprenticeship and then taking the Bar, something that was permitted in certain jurisdictions. Judging by the length of his career, he would have had a ton of files, and I didn't think they could have been stored in the remaining upstairs rooms of his house.

Large law firms rent warehouses to store the files, but small firms and sole practitioners often go with storage units. It's an expense, and many human firms were in the process of scanning and storing these files electronically. I figured there was no way a White-Fang firm would ever part with the paper. I pulled back my wandering thoughts and took a sip of coffee. Gillford had been a sole practitioner. I figured he was more likely to have rented a storage unit, and going digital seemed unlikely. Somewhere in those files would be the executed copy of Abercrombie's will.

John wandered in, a towel wrapped around his waist and another in his hands, vigorously drying his hair. The thick thatch stuck up like a rooster's comb. It made me smile.

"Something smells good," he said.

"Bacon. My coffee isn't as fancy as yours, but there's a pot ready. Let me start the French toast."

I left the table and turned on the electric skillet.

"How are you doing this morning?" John asked as he sat down.

"I have had sex before."

John actually blushed a bit. He shook his head. "I thought you might have. No, I was talking about Finkelstein. You were feeling pretty bad last night."

"Not so much now. Now I'm just mad," I said as I watched butter melting on the hot skillet. "And when I get mad, I get even." I looked over my shoulder to give John a smile and found him looking alarmed.

"What does that mean?" he asked.

"We're going to find the other will, take the company away from Deegan, and give it to Chastity Jenkins."

John dropped his head into his hands and groaned. "Jesus, Mary, and Joseph, she's a madwoman." I presumed he was talking with the Holy Family, since this clearly wasn't directed at me. His next remark was, "And just how do you propose to do that?"

"Thomas Gillford."

"I've got a news flash for you—he's dead."

"Yes, but our works live on after us." I slid the soaked bread slices into the skillet. They sent up a merry sizzling, and the rich smell of cinnamon and frying food filled my small apartment.

"Hello. Not your case. Syd getting hurt . . . also not your fault."

"Last night you implied it was."

"Last night I was a dick."

"Yes, you were, which is why I need you to find out if Gillford had a storage unit rented for his files. It's probably in Red Oak Hollow, Virginia. He probably wouldn't have wanted to move them to New Jersey when he and his wife moved." I frowned at that and turned the toast. "One wonders why they moved to a colder, uglier place? Maybe she had family in New Jersey." I shrugged. "You can check on that too."

"I'm not checking on nothin' because nobody is going to be paying me."

"Chastity will pay you after she gets control of Securitech. I'm going to contact her and explain that Syd has been hurt and that I'm taking over for him."

"You are so in conflict-of-interest territory. Assuming you succeed, Chastity is not going to be happy that you took twenty million of her money."

"Okay, good point. So I won't be the attorney of record. But I'm still going to find that will."

"Do you have a death wish, or are you just interested in seeing if you can cheat death for a third time?"

I dished up the French toast and set down our plates. "Would you get the bacon out of the oven?" I asked John, then said, "I thought you were like super-detective or ninja-detective. You can make sure we're not being followed."

John grabbed hot mitts and pulled out the cookie sheet. "If you think Deegan hasn't had an army of investigators looking into Gillford's background, you're smoking opium." The bacon sizzled and popped as if to contradict the harsh statement.

But his words deflated me. I sat down abruptly. "So, you're saying it's hopeless. They will have already found his storage unit and destroyed the will."

"That's what I would do," John said as he placed the bacon on paper towels to drain.

"Yes, but you're clever, and Deegan has been more of a blunt instrument. Burning down the courthouse in Virginia—"

"You know for certain about the courthouse?"

"No, but it seems likely. Killing Chip, killing Gillford, attacking me, attacking Syd."

"He can't be that stupid," John said as he brought over the bacon. He grabbed a few pieces, slathered his toast with butter and syrup, and tucked in.

I doctored my toast and began to eat. "No, but he is arrogant, and he thinks he's dealt with all the problems. And sometimes arrogant can be dumber than stupid. Or something," I finished lamely as I got tangled up in the sentence.

"You're really determined to go to Virginia, aren't you?"

"Yes."

"Then I guess I'll have to go with you so you don't get killed."

"Thank you," I said, and I meant it.

John tossed his napkin on the table, leaned back, and gave me a look that was both ironic and leering. "Well, there goes my dream of a day spent in bed."

I had thought that John would handle this online and with phone calls, but he had given me a smirking grin and said, "Oh, no, this gets done the old-fashioned way. Legwork."

Which is how I found myself telling the office I was taking a few days off. Fortunately, Shade seemed to think this was reasonable. He peered at me from behind his desk and said thoughtfully, "Yes, I suppose you should, given that you were attacked . . . again. And you've earned it with that settlement."

I was relieved he had filled in the reasons so I didn't have to invent one—meaning lie, because I couldn't very well tell him that I was setting off to do the work of another lawyer.

"Detective Washington is quite . . . interested in you," Shade added.

I didn't like that significant pause. "Why? I didn't do anything. At least anything wrong."

"So he has concluded. But he does think you are a nexus around whom interesting events swirl."

"If he actually said 'interesting,' I'm going to kick him if I ever see him again. I can tell you it was anything but *interesting*."

I left the office and hurried to my apartment to pack an overnight bag. I was actually down on the sidewalk waiting when John's car pulled up. I hurried toward the passenger door, then stopped—there was a stranger behind the wheel. As I stood there dithering, four more cars identical to John's pulled up. He was in the last car. He jumped out and tossed my bag into the trunk. While it was open, I noticed two Kevlar vests in the back.

I blanched. "Do you actually think we'll need those?"

He didn't answer. Instead he took my arm and hustled me

into the car. All four identical white cars pulled away at the same time. We drove to a particularly snarly intersection where five streets bisected each other, and the cars began an intricate weaving dance.

"What are you doing?" I gasped as the cars cut each other off, and the drivers used the extra streets to duck away and come back together like an elaborate street-sized square dance.

"Three-card monte with five cars. With luck, they won't know which one to follow."

"How did you. . . . ?"

"Rented four cars identical to mine at Avis. Hired four limo drivers. Gave them their instructions." John lifted a hand and clenched his fist, and all five cars exploded in opposite directions down the five different streets.

"Securitech," I said hollowly.

"We know they're watching you" came the grim reply.

We drove in silence for some time while John constantly checked the rearview mirror and the side mirrors. He relaxed against the back of the seat and gave a nod of satisfaction. "We're good."

"Okay, well, maybe now you'll answer my question. Why the vests?"

"I'd rather have them and not need them than need them and not have them."

"Makes sense," I said, then added in a smaller voice, "Will Kevlar actually stop a werewolf's teeth . . . or claws?"

"It slows them down and keeps you alive for a few seconds longer so you can shoot them."

"Well, that's a relief," I said in a teasing and sarcastic tone. The grim lines around his mouth didn't ease. In a very tiny voice I added, "Is something wrong? I mean, I know you didn't want to do this—"

"I drove over to Bayonne to see about looking through Gillford's house. That would have saved us some time, because he was bound to have had receipts for his storage unit. But the house is gone."

"Gone? What do you mean, *gone*?" I had this vision of guys jacking up the house, loading it on a big flatbed truck, and driving away, leaving only a hole in the ground with pipes sticking out.

"Blown up. Burned to the ground. The cops said it was a gas leak ignited by a spark from an extension cord in the kitchen, but . . ."

"It seems very convenient," I finished for him.

"It also means the Securitech guys probably found what they wanted and destroyed the place to make sure we couldn't find it too."

"They couldn't have just stolen the receipts?"

"There were too many other ways for us to find the location—old tax returns, canceled checks, address books. The point is, this is probably a useless trip. You sure you still want to go?"

I considered, then nodded. "Yes, I owe Syd that much."

We flew out of a tiny airport south and west of New York. John had chartered the plane, and I gulped at the price, but this was my quixotic mission, so I couldn't very well complain. He paid in cash, and I promised to keep track of all our expenses and write him a check when this was all over.

The pilot took us into Roanoke, and John had found a cash-only rental car company. John handed me a few pages of printout, then wrestled a GPS out of its case.

"What's this?" I asked as he got the boxy little machine and its screen secured to the dashboard.

"A listing of all the self-storage places in a fifty-mile radius of

Red Oak Hollow. I figured we'll start with the ones in town and
radiate out from there. You can be my navigator and put in the
addresses."

"Okay." I typed in the information, and a bland female voice
said, "Calculating." She then began to feed us directions.

As we made our way through Roanoke, I spotted Hot Lips,
the strip club where Abercrombie had met Chastity. The sign
consisted of lots of different-sized and -shaped lips that seemed to
be flying in space. All the lips were very red and very lush.

I pointed it out to John, who gave me a grin and said, "Strip
joints usually have good value on food. We could have lunch
there."

"You speak from experience?" I asked.

"I've been in a few."

"Mostly in the line of duty, I'm sure," I said.

He cast me an impish look out of the corner of his eye. "You
can think that if you want to."

I waved a hand in front of his face. "Hello, irony. But if we do,
I insist on equal time, and lunch at Hunk-O-Mania when we're
back in New York," I said, referring to the club that featured hard-
bodied young men dressed in tight pants and long duster-style
jackets with bare chests.

"Oh, goody, us and the gay guys."

"Hey, I went to a bachelorette party at the Chippendales in
Boston."

"Thus proving my point. Women go to strip joints for special
occasions. Men would happily live in one."

The GPS soon had us out of town driving through a country-
side that was multiple shades of green. We passed a lot of white-
fenced pastures with horses grazing on the lush grass. I couldn't
help it: my eyes kept going to those sleek bodies, tails swishing

at flies, and pricked ears as they occasionally looked up to scan for danger.

I looked back down at the printout. There were a depressingly large number of storage places. "How long is this going to take?"

"Not long." He paused then added, "If we get lucky." He shot me a grin. "Welcome to the thrilling world of the PI. Legwork and stakeouts. That's my life."

"We couldn't have just called?" I asked plaintively.

"Most people won't give out that kind of information over the phone. But in person . . ." John flashed me that amazing Álfar smile.

"That's not going to work on a guy unless he's gay," I said dryly.

"That's why I have you along."

Our navigator robot guided us into Red Oak Hollow and began issuing ever more stringent commands. *"In four hundred yards, go left and prepare to make a turn. Turn left."*

John chuckled. "She's got that whole dominatrix vibe going, doesn't she? I think I like her."

I looked over the instructions. "You can change languages and voices. How about this one?" The next command was uttered by a male voice with a strong Australian accent.

We made a few more turns while John and I switched the voices between Barbara the Dominatrix and Wally the Aussie, and we pulled through the gates of U-Store-It. Inside we found a middle-aged woman with brassy bleached-blonde hair, deeply tanned skin, and a net of wrinkles that made her look like an aged turtle head had been transplanted onto a human body. She was slumped behind the counter, smoking. At her feet was a very fat Labrador retriever. As we entered, the dog's tail beat out a slow cadence on the linoleum floor.

The manager looked up, and perked right up at the sight of John. "Help you?" she drawled in that soft Virginia accent.

I opened my mouth, but John was there before me. "Yes, this young lady's grandfather recently died under tragic circumstances." He leaned across the counter and lowered his voice. "Home invasion. Murdered."

I have an absolutely useless talent—I can cry on cue. I thought about my first horse dying, and the tears filled my eyes and spilled over to run down my cheeks. John gaped at me but recovered quickly.

"We're trying to locate his assets, because Sarah is his sole heir."

"What's the name?" the dyed blonde asked, turning to her computer.

"Thomas Gillford."

The dog rose ponderously to her feet, waddled over to me, and pressed her body against my legs. It seemed like the dog was trying to comfort me. I patted her and felt like a shit. It was one thing to fool a human, but taking advantage of a dog . . . The woman typed and clicked on the computer, then finally shook her head. Gillford hadn't stored with U-Store-It even though this location was less than a mile from the former site of his office.

We thanked the woman and left. John slipped an arm around my waist and guided me to the passenger door. "Are you okay?" His tone was warm and solicitous.

"Oh yeah. I can cry when I want to. I just think about something sad."

"If you ever decide to stop being a lawyer, you can come to work for me," John said as he opened the door for me.

We hit five more self-storage companies before deciding at one o'clock to take a break and find lunch. We had been slowly circling outward in search of Gillford's elusive storage unit, and there weren't a lot of restaurant choices out on these country roads. Finally we spotted a small diner on the outskirts of another small town.

As we walked through the door into the icily air-conditioned dining room, the smell of frying food and baking bread folded around us. The walls were hung with photos and plates that had been autographed. I didn't recognize most of the names, but then I spotted a few jazz and blues greats.

"Somehow I think ordering a salad would get me tossed out," I whispered.

"Live a little. Just don't think about your arteries," John whispered back.

We settled into a booth. The Muzak was blues and bluegrass. Our waitress, a pretty young woman with cocoa-colored skin, a cloud of jet-black hair, and a name tag that read *Julie,* delivered our menus. John quizzed her for a few moments about what was good. She said everything. John went for the chicken-fried steak. I went with fried chicken.

The food arrived. I appeared to have half a chicken served with garlic mashed potatoes and cream gravy, a mound of hush puppies, and a side of greens that looked but didn't taste like spinach. There was also a plate of cornbread and biscuits to share. The iced tea was heavily sweetened, which surprised me. The waitress correctly interpreted my expression.

"Are you from up North? I bet you want unsweetened tea," she said with a smile.

"Because that's going to make *so* much difference in the calorie count," I said as I stared at my overflowing plate.

The girl laughed, went away, and soon returned with my unsweetened tea. I began to eat. John had already made inroads in a breaded steak that seemed to cover his entire plate and was swimming in cream gravy.

The food was wonderful, but I only managed to eat a thigh, a leg, and a wing. The girl packed up the leftovers, saying, "It's really fine when it's cold. It'll make a nice snack for you folks. Anything else I can get for you? We've got peach cobbler and blackberry pie."

I shook my head, but John ordered peach cobbler à la mode. When Julie came back with the dessert and my packed chicken, I regretted my self-control. The crust was perfectly browned and dusted with sugar, and the rich syrup, bubbling at the edges of the bowl, made the ice cream melt like a late snowfall on a hot spring day.

John pulled out the sheaf of papers and asked, "Is Chipmunk Storage near here?"

"Yeah, it's not far," Julie replied.

She gave us quick and concise directions and handed John the bill, which I promptly took away from him. I went up front to pay so I would be removed from the temptation of the cobbler.

Back in the car, with the smell of chicken filling the space, John gave a gusting sigh. "I feel like a python that just swallowed a goat. Can I go hibernate now?"

"No. You're the one who ordered the dessert."

"And it was reeeally good."

He put the car in gear, and since Julie's directions had been so clear we dispensed with Barbara/Wally. It was kind of a relief not to have them nagging us.

Ten minutes later, we spotted a large billboard sporting a giant chipmunk, the tail rising even higher than the top of the sign. It was holding a nut between its paws and had a faintly crazed expression. Next to the squirrel the sign read CHIPMUNK STORAGE.

We pulled in and went to the office, housed in a double-wide trailer. A young redheaded man with an impressive paunch and suspenders to keep his pants from falling below his belly stood up as we entered. John dropped back behind me, my cue to take the lead.

"Hi, my name is Sarah Hall." I almost began our usual patter, but something made me change it to say, "An elderly relative of mine was recently murdered, Thomas Gillford—"

"Wow, that's strange."

"Excuse me?"

"I've been dealing with that account. The rental checks stopped coming three months ago. I'd send letters to Gillford, but there was no response. Guess this is why. And somebody broke into his unit."

My spirits dropped like a stone at these words. We were too late.

"Lucky for you, we had already moved his stuff out. But Mrs. Dannforth is gonna be pissed." He grinned. "Oh Wow, that's kinda funny."

"What is?" John asked, stepping in.

"Whoever broke in just ripped the door off, but when they got inside they didn't take anything. They just peed all over her furniture." John and I looked at each other.

"So, you still have Mr. Gillford's possessions?" I asked.

The young man eased his bulk out from behind the counter and picked up a large set of keys. "Good thing you got here when you did. The file cabinets, bookcases, and that big old desk and chair were going to be put up for auction on Saturday."

"And the papers?" I asked anxiously.

"I called to have them hauled away to a recycling place, but they haven't shown up yet."

"Oh, thank God."

"Come on."

The manager led us out of the trailer and over to a Quonset hut. The steel had been painted white, but it was still an eyesore. He unlocked the door and waved us in. It was breathlessly hot inside the metal building. A fat fly buzzed lazily in a shaft of sunlight pouring in through the high, narrow windows. John's hand shot out, so fast it was almost a blur, and knocked the fly out of the air.

"Wow," said the manager. It seemed to be his general catch-all word for surprise and wonderment. "There are the files." He pointed at several rows of mixed metal-and-wood filing cabinets.

"And the contents?" John asked.

The manager pointed at a pile of large and bulging black plastic garbage bags. John and I exchanged another look. So much for going right to the year when Syd had said the will was drafted. "Oh, yippee," I said.

We moved toward the pile but suddenly the kid got a crimp in his conscience. "I don't know, maybe I shouldn't be letting you go through this stuff."

John reached into his coat pocket, pulled out a leather wallet, and flipped it open. It showed a flash of gold before he quickly flipped it shut again. "You're helping us with a criminal investigation."

I wondered if he had just kept his badge from when he'd been a policeman or if it was a prop. Either way, it made me uncomfortable. I would clearly suck as a private eye. I waited hopefully, but the kid didn't seem impressed.

"You're not a cop in this jurisdiction."

Damn *Law & Order*, I thought. John and the manager measured each other's gazes, and it seemed a nonverbal conversation was taking place. John stepped in close and laid a hand on the manager's shoulder. I drew in a breath, expecting John to sucker punch him or something equally macho. Instead I saw a fifty slide from John's free hand into the kid's. I realized I'd watched too many movies too.

"Now that's the kind of badge I can get behind," the redhead said. "I'll leave you to it."

He left, closing the door behind him. "Is this your world?" I asked.

"Pretty much."

"Does it depress you?"

"No, it's just left me with few illusions about human nature. Open that door, or we're going to die from heatstroke," John said as he loosened his tie and took off his sports jacket. When the jacket came off, I realized he was wearing a gun in a shoulder rig. I spent a moment admiring the way his Italian-cut shirt hugged his body, and I had a sudden, sharp memory of those abs and running my fingers down his side. It got a few degrees hotter in the hut.

I propped open the door with a small rolling filing cabinet. John grabbed the first bag and untied the plastic drawstring.

I sat down on the concrete and started sifting through the mess. I reflected that, for me, the *Abercrombie* case had begun in a welter of paper, and it seemed it was going to end in one too.

# 21

Gillford had practiced law for a looong time. There were fifty years of files all jumbled together. I tried very hard not to absorb anything from the non-*Abercrombie* files. I tried to just look for key words, like—oh, *Abercrombie*. I also knew that a lot of clients, or heirs of the clients, were about to have their documents consigned to the shredder. This wasn't really my problem, but I found myself wondering if I should inform the State Bar of Virginia.

Judging by the letterhead, the watermarked paper, and the silk ribbons that tied shut some of the folders, Gillford had been a pretty old-fashioned kind of guy. So I told John to look for large folders of thick parchment-colored paper with ribbons and Gothic type that read *Last Will and Testament*.

With fifty years of active practice, there were lots of Last Wills. A couple of times we heard the whine of the electric gate opening, and cars pulling in. Each time John would tense, go to the door, and peer out. Every time it turned out to be a tenant and not the Securitech goons returning.

"What if we don't find it before dark?" I squinted up toward the ceiling, but the Quonset hut didn't seem to have been wired for electricity. "Have you got a flashlight?" I added.

"Have I got a flashlight." John stood up and took a penlight out of his pocket. "A good PI, like a good Boy Scout, is always prepared."

"So, what else have you got in your pockets?"

John dropped down next to me. "You know, that sounds faintly suggestive."

I gave him a slap on the upper arm, but his nearness and the spicy scent of his sweat and aftershave had me once again very aware of my pelvic area. I could tell I was blushing, and I wanted to say to hell with this search and go find a hotel. But I didn't think the kid would be as amenable to our search after he had a day to reflect. We had to finish today.

As if my thoughts had summoned him, the kid wandered in, bringing with him the scent of pizza. My stomach gave a growl. It had been five hours since lunch. I thought about the chicken in the car. Then I thought of the heat and decided a dose of food poisoning would not improve the day.

"Hey, the night manager's going to be coming on at eleven. I don't think he's going to be too cool with you going through stuff, so you better finish up before then."

"Okay, thanks," I said. He slouched out again, and I tackled the second-to-last trash bag.

"You know it's probably going to be in the last bag," John said.

"The way our luck has been, yes, that's probably true."

"Oh, I don't know, I think your luck has been pretty damn spectacular," John said.

"What?" It emerged as an outraged shriek. "I've been attacked and nearly killed by werewolves *twice*. I've come *this* close"—I held up two fingers a millimeter apart—"to getting fired—twice."

"Yes, and you've survived, both literally and metaphorically. And you're leading a women's revolt in the office."

"I am not."

"Are too. But be careful. Ryan has a nasty streak."

"Gee, I hadn't noticed," I answered, sarcasm dripping off each word.

"Using you is one thing. He hasn't actually gone after you."

"What can he do to me that he hasn't already tried? He tried to get me fired and failed."

John was staring at me with an expression of bemusement. "For somebody who was raised by a vampire, you seem awfully naive. Or you must have been fostered with an exceptional vampire."

"Yes, I guess he was . . . is. He started me riding, supplied my horses, and gave me the horse I was riding when I turned eighteen and went off to college. He and Shade are close friends."

"Okay, that explains a lot. Shade Ishmael seems closer to human than most of them, and I suspect a friend of his would be the same. But let me assure you, that is not the norm. Most of them are distant loners with a narcissistic streak. They'd have to be because what other kind of person goes out looking to live forever, leaving behind all the people who were important to them in life?" His tone was harsh and ragged, and his gaze seemed to turn inward. I had a feeling this had less to do with vampires and more to do with him. It didn't seem like the right time to point out the obvious, but this was me, so of course my mouth engaged before my brain.

"You're going to live forever too."

A flash of corrosive grief filled his eyes. He dropped his lashes, veiling those betraying eyes. "Not forever. The Álfar die too, but slowly, very slowly." He paused, then added so quietly I almost missed what he said, "I just don't know if I have the courage to deal with that."

"Courage? What does that mean?" Then understanding hit like a punch. "Oh no, don't you tell me you're thinking about suicide." The papers I'd been inspecting lay forgotten in my lap.

"What other solution do I have? I'll watch my parents die—"

"That's a burden all children bear."

"My siblings. If I marry, I'll bury her too, and our children, and their children." John fell silent, and his face was so immobile that he reminded me of the effigies on tombs in Westminster Abbey.

The future he was describing did sound horrible, but I was twenty-seven and dying seemed pretty horrible to me too. "John, how old are you?" I asked.

"Forty-three."

It startled me. He looked like a man in his twenties. I picked up the papers and nervously shuffled them, shifting them front to back.

"Then you've got a lot of time before—" John's hand shot out and closed on my wrist.

"Linnet, look."

I did. I was staring down at a heavy parchment folder that read, *Last Will and Testament of Henry Lee Abercrombie.* My fingers were trembling as I untied the ribbons holding it closed. There were only two typed pages inside. It was a very short and simple will, and it was as Syd had described. Henry had left all his worldly goods to Chastity Rose Jenkins and her daughter Destiny Star Jenkins, whom he formally acknowledged as an heir of his body.

"Oh, this is fucking dynamite," John breathed, and I noticed that his hand went up to touch his pistol in its holster. I don't think he was even aware of it, but for an instant, and despite the suffocating heat of the Quonset hut, it felt as if a bead of ice water had run down my back.

We hurriedly stuffed the papers back into the trash bag, then rushed over to the trailer and told the manager that we were finished. In a voice that was *way* too casual he asked, "Did you find what you were looking for?"

John's hand tightened on my arm. I gave the manager big eyes filled with total sincerity. "No. I don't think the will—" I broke off suddenly as if I'd given something away. "The document we were looking for ever existed. Thank you for letting us look though."

John gave him another fifty and we jumped into the rental and hit the highway. John kept checking all the mirrors, and he seemed to be taking a circuitous route, much to GPS Barbara's annoyance. Every time he ignored her instructions we would hear a huffy "Make a legal U-turn and proceed 400 feet to—" Or an even more annoyed "Recalculating route."

"You think Securitech talked to that guy," I said.

"You think so too," John said.

"Why are they always a step ahead of us?" I grumbled.

"They're not, but they are definitely only half a step behind us. They're breathing down our necks. We need to get a copy of that will faxed to the office."

"We can do that." I checked my watch. "Though I doubt any place will be open at six p.m. in Red Oak Hollow. But it really won't make any difference. This is one area of the law where the courts aren't keeping up with technology. A fax or a scanned document will not be considered binding. Since property's on the line, the court demands the original document."

"So we book it for New York," he said.

"The only other option is that we hang around here and hit a court in Roanoke in the morning," I said.

"Securitech will be all over us before morning. I think we've gotta keep moving. They'll expect us to take the direct route through Roanoke, so I'm going to head south for a little while. Try to throw them off the scent."

We drove in silence as I clutched the satchel containing the will. This document represented a life change for two women I had never met. I wondered how they would react. Then it hit me, and I sat bolt upright.

"John, we've got to go to Roanoke."

"No, we don't."

"Yes, we do. Chastity and Destiny are there." His head snapped around, and he stared at me. "We know Securitech talked to the manager. They now know the papers were still on site. They'd be stupid to assume we *don't* have the will. Which means Chastity and Destiny are in danger, and we know Deegan won't hesitate to kill people. We need to take them with us."

"Oh shit," he moaned as he beat his forehead against the steering wheel.

I was hurt and piqued by his reaction. "Tell me if you disagree—"

"No, no, you're right. Goddamn it."


We reached the outskirts of Roanoke. "Okay, do you remember where this place was?"

"We passed it when we left the airport. I remember that much. Wait."

I dug out my phone, went to the browser, and Googled Hot Lips, Roanoke, VA. Soon a map appeared. I keyed the address into the GPS, and Barbara came out of her sulk and began to guide us. John pulled into a driveway marked with a sign containing a big red arrow and more lips that read PARKING IN REAR.

"There's something so crudely suggestive about that," he remarked as he pulled into a space. Since it was a little past seven at night, I figured the place would be hopping. Surprisingly, there were only four cars in addition to ours parked in the lot—two pickup trucks, a beat-up Nissan, and a low-end BMW sedan.

"Seems pretty dead," I said.

"They probably have a big noon crowd, and it's still early for a titty bar," John said as we got out of the car.

The main entrance appeared to be in the back, facing the lot. Which made sense. Maybe the men frequenting the place didn't want to go parading down the street, and it was a much shorter walk. The door was big, metal, painted black, and very heavy. John pulled it open, and I walked into an entryway that had a coat-check area, a sofa against one wall with some magazines— *Field & Stream*, *Guns & Ammo*, *Popular Mechanics*—and the doors to the bathrooms.

In front of us were big double doors padded in red leather with large brass pulls. They were also very heavy, as evidenced by the sudden definition in John's biceps. Past the double doors was a large room with curving walls, mirrors, a disco ball (I couldn't believe my eyes), a raised stage with the obligatory pole, and cages on either side. Four men were seated at tables as far apart from each other as possible. Two were powerfully built men whose T-shirts revealed bunched muscles in their arms and burgeoning paunches. They were drinking beers out of bottles. In the very back was an old man who seemed more interested in the plate of prime rib than in any activity on the stage. Seated at a table closest to the stage was a man who looked like a banker. He was dressed in a decent suit, the coat draped over the back of his chair, and he was nursing a highball.

He was staring at the girl going through a desultory bump and grind. She was decked out in cowboy boots and a fringed red bikini bottom, and her long hair clung to her sweaty shoulders and back. She leaned down and shook her breasts in the banker's face. His only response was to blink slowly.

John leaned down and whispered in my ear, "You sure take me to classy joints."

There was a woman bartender wiping down the bar. She was pretty in a sort of hard way, with long red hair pulled back in a ponytail and breasts that had cost her a fair bit. I had a feeling that not too many years ago she had been on that stage. It seemed like the owner of Hot Lips believed in job security.

We walked over to the bar. She gave the bar one final swipe. "Well, you're not missionaries dressed like that, and I haven't heard about any recent lawsuits. Jeb won't hire runaways or anybody under eighteen, so you can't be PI's looking for a lost daughter. So what can I do you for?"

"We need to speak with Chastity Jenkins. Is she here?" I asked.

"Yeah, in the office going over the weekend accounts." She picked up a phone behind the bar and dialed an extension. "Hey, it's Ruby. There's a couple of people out here looking for you." She listened for a moment. "Guy and a girl." She eyed John. "Make that a *gorgeous* guy and a girl."

A few minutes later, Chastity Jenkins came through a door near the edge of the stage. She wasn't what I expected. She was blonde (men do seem to pick a physical look and stick with it), but very petite. She had a good figure, big blue eyes that gave her a neotenous look, and a narrow upturned nose. There were a few wrinkles around her eyes and the corners of her mouth, but Botox had smoothed her forehead.

"Hi, I'm Chastity," she said in a husky voice that had an odd little catch to it.

"I'm Linnet Ellery, and this is John O'Shea. Is there someplace where we can talk privately?"

"Sure, come on back to the office. Jeb won't be in until nine. We'll have the place to ourselves."

We followed her past the stage, where the bored dancer was now eating a banana as she gyrated, and through a flimsy door. It seemed odd, given the bulk and heft of the other doors.

John correctly interpreted my frown. He leaned down and said, "You want to be able to hear if a fight breaks out."

We went down a hallway past dressing rooms for the dancers until we reached the office. It was small and cluttered, but furnished with surprisingly comfortable armchairs. Then I realized that if you had to be in a place all night long, you probably wanted comfort. It also had a printer/copier/fax/scanner machine on the desk.

Chastity sat down behind the desk. "Okay, what can I do for you?"

"I'm an attorney from New York, a colleague of Syd Finkelstein."

"Oh, Syd. I've tried to call him for the past few days, and he never calls back." She gave us a brave but rueful smile. "I guess he's given up on me, or at least on my hopeless little case, too."

"Actually, no, Syd was hurt, and he's been in the hospital. I've been helping out with his cases, and your case isn't hopeless. You're about to win it." I took out the will and gave it to her.

Chastity read through it slowly. The farther she read, the more tears gathered in her eyes until they spilled over and ran down her cheeks. "He did it. He didn't lie. Oh, Henry, I miss you so much." The final words were a whisper, and she hugged the will to her chest.

John stirred and leaned forward. He gently worked the will loose from her grip. "Look, Ms. Jenkins, we think you might be in danger. We're here to take you and your daughter back to New York. But first, can we use your machine?" He nodded at the multipurpose printer.

"Sure . . . go ahead . . . in danger?" She looked confused.

"Where is Destiny?" I asked.

"Who do you want this sent to?" John asked as he lifted the lid on the printer.

"David Sullivan," I answered.

Chastity answered me. "She works at the Sephora cosmetic counter over at Penney's." I found myself reflecting that a degree in comparative literature wasn't much of a career starter.

Chastity leaned down, pulled her purse from beneath the desk, and took out her cell phone. "She should—"

She never got to finish the sentence. There was the sound of high-pitched female screams and basso bellows that escalated into high-pitched screams almost indistinguishable from the women's. Then came the *boom* of a shotgun blast and high-pitched yelping.

# 22

"Is there a back way out of here?" John demanded, grabbing Chastity's wrist, while I lunged across the desk, grabbed the will, and crammed it back in my satchel. She shook her head. "Damn! Okay, stay behind me and when I say *run*, you *run*! Got it?"

We both just nodded mutely. We hurried down the hall to the door that led into the club. John pulled his pistol and paused at the door, hand on the handle, ear to the wood. The handle started to rotate. John stepped back, the door opened, and a werewolf confronted us. The beast and John were only the width of the door swing apart. John raised his arm, leaned forward, pressed the barrel of his gun against the creature's forehead, and pulled the trigger.

Brains and blood flew out the back of the hound's head. Chastity shrieked and started to collapse. I grabbed her under the armpits and dragged her in John's wake. "Come on!" I screamed, and I could barely hear myself because my ears were ringing from the too-close gunshot.

The scene in the club wasn't pretty. The banker was on the floor by his table with his throat ripped out. Ruby was firing her shotgun without a lot of thought about aiming. As we entered, I saw one wild blast hit one of the burly construction workers. He went down with a scream. Two werewolves were scanning the room. One of them spotted us and leaped up onto the stage. The door to the offices was just off the right side of the stage, and this meant he was closing on us fast. It also meant he could jump down on top of us. *He was going to have the high-ground advantage,* I thought, terrified by how fast the creature was bounding across the stage.

Chastity started to collapse again, and the sudden weight hitting my arm pulled me to the left. I threw out a hand to steady myself and hit the sound board and controls for the stage. The volume on the CD player went way up, the disco ball started whirling, and the pyrotechnics that had been embedded in the edge of the stage flamed to life—just as the werewolf gathered himself to jump off the stage and onto us. The rush of hot sparks whooshed up against the beast's belly and set his shaggy coat alight. The sound as the hound burned was part human, part animal, and totally horrible. He began to run wildly through the room, biting at the flames and setting alight the tablecloths.

Another poorly aimed shotgun blast took down the disco ball. It hit with a crash and shattered. Another shot, and the mirrors on the far wall fell into pieces. I wasn't sure which was more dangerous, the wolves swirling around us or Ruby and her shotgun.

The light from the flames meant I had a much better sense of what we were up against. It wasn't encouraging. It was hard to get an exact fix on the numbers because the werewolves were moving so fast, but it seemed like there were three or four more of them. The fire alarm began blaring.

The other burly man ran for the door, but a wolf's jaws closed on his ankle, severing his Achilles tendon. He collapsed with a wail, and the wolf landed on him, teeth savaging his neck.

John, moving with incredible speed and grace, leaped across the room and onto the back of the wolf attacking the construction worker. He locked his knees around the creature's shoulders, gripped the elongated skull with one hand, jammed the barrel of his gun into the base of the skull, and pulled the trigger. Even over the bass beat of the rock song I heard the report. The beast collapsed.

A wolf came flying from another direction. I screamed a warning, but the beast landed on top of John, who lost his grip on his pistol. The gun went skittering across the carpeted floor. John rolled fast, and for an instant he had the wolf beneath him, but he gave a wild twisting buck and dislodged John. Then he was on top of John again. John had a grip on the creature's head, struggling to keep those snapping jaws away from his face and throat.

Dragging Chastity after me, I ran for the gun. My eyes were watering from the smoke and the stench of burning plastic. It was getting hard to see, and the heat was singeing my exposed skin. Then, with a pop and a hiss, the sprinkler system came to life. Water ran into my eyes, and the strands of hair that had fallen across my face plastered themselves to my skin. I scraped them off and looked desperately for the gun, but I kept looking back to watch John and the werewolf. The muscles in John's arms were like iron cords beneath the skin, his face was red, and his jaw was set in a grimace. *Where is that goddamn gun? What can I do if I can't find the gun?*

I looked back just in time to see John release his grip on the wolf's head. I screamed. John, his hands moving so quickly they were almost a blur, smacked his palms hard against the wolf's ears. The creature screamed and brought up his front paw to scratch at its ears. John flipped both of them over, placed his knee in the creature's back, grabbed the wolf's head, and gave it a sharp twist. The beast went limp.

John jumped to his feet. His nose was bleeding, and he had a cut on his cheek. "Run, run!" he screamed at us, waving his arms like a man shooing chickens.

Chastity and I ran for the double doors. John sprinted past us and slammed into the door, pushing it open. We stumbled through. A hound was right behind us. John gripped the handle and slammed the door into his snout. He fell back with a whine. I don't know how John made that heavy door move that fast.

We started running across the parking lot heading for the car when Chastity collapsed and started having loud hysterics. John snatched her up, threw her over his shoulder, and kept running.

"What about Ruby? And that old man?" I gasped.

"They're probably dead" was the cold response. He dug in his pocket with his free hand and emerged with the key. The car honked as he unlocked it.

"But—" I began.

John yanked open the back door and literally threw Chastity into the backseat. "I'm trying to keep us from joining them."

I glanced back at the door to the club as a werewolf lunged out. I scrambled into the passenger side and hadn't even gotten the door closed when John sent us roaring out of the lot. Sirens were approaching. A cop car, its lights spinning, went racing past us. We passed a fire engine. An ambulance, more cops.

"Where's the Penney's store?" John shouted back to Chastity.

"Mwwaaaaa" was the ear-splitting response.

"Can you get sense out of her?" John snapped.

I slewed around in my seat to look at her, turned back around, and shook my head. "Probably not." So I unlimbered my phone again, got the address, and keyed it into our GPS.

John took a corner almost on two wheels, and I grabbed for the panic strap. "Don't get pulled over," I warned.

"I don't think we have to worry. Every cop in Roanoke is probably at Hot Lips," he answered tersely. He had a point.

Ten minutes later, we were pulling into the lot at the mall. "I'm going to drop you at the door."

"I don't know what this girl looks like," I said.

"How many people can there be behind the cosmetics counter?"

"Oh, yeah, duh. Sorry."

He gave me a wan smile. "It's okay. We're all a little frazzled." He rolled an eye back toward Chastity, still keening in the backseat.

"I'm sure as soon as I have time to think about it I'll be in the same shape as her."

"I doubt it," John said as he pulled to a stop. "I'll circle the lot and keep coming by to collect you."

"Okay," I said, and headed into Penney's.

The door opened into the housewares department. I rushed past beds decked out with multicolored duvets and lace-edged pillows. I reached an aisle and glanced in both directions. There was no clear sense which way led to cosmetics. I randomly picked left and found myself in the infants' and children's department, where there were a surprising number of shoppers. Many of the women were pregnant, carrying babies, or towing toddlers. There appeared to be a baby boom underway in Roanoke.

I was getting a lot of weird looks, so I hurried past, looking for the women's department, figuring Sephora would be located there. I found another aisle crossroads and took a look. To the right was hardware, with gas grills lined up like tin soldiers and lawnmowers, their bodies bright red or yellow, arranged like the petals on a flower. There were also shelves and shelves of tools. I saw five men entering from the mall side of the store. They didn't seem like they were looking to buy a new chainsaw, and they had a look I had come to recognize—broad shoulders, necks as wide as their heads, shorn hair, and flinty eyes. I pulled back among the frilly first-communion dresses and continued my search, using the racks for cover.

As I hunkered down among the flounces, I tried to think. How to find the cosmetic counter? I drew in a deep breath and smelled the faint odor of perfume. I moved left and it faded. I moved right and it seemed like the scent became stronger. I decided to follow my nose.

Using racks for cover, I made my way to the other side of the store. I passed a mirror and got a glimpse of my face streaked with soot. No wonder people were staring. I had left my purse in the car so I didn't even have a tissue to scrub it off. My only hope was to find Destiny before somebody alerted security about the madwoman in petites.

I pulled aside a couple of blouses and peered through the opening at the cosmetics counter. A beautiful black woman was behind the counter. In front of the counter, a fortyish woman sat on a tall chair getting a makeover. The woman applying the makeup was blonde, and while she was taller and not as buxom, there were enough similarities to Chastity that I was willing to bet she was Destiny.

I looked back and saw the big men walking down the aisle. I jumped up and ran for the counter.

"You can see how creamy it is. Very moisturizing, and it slides on so smoothly," Destiny was saying as she shook the bottle of foundation.

"Destiny! You've got to come with me. Your mother's been hurt!" I felt bad for the lie, but I had to get her moving with a minimum of conversation.

She stood, foundation bottle in one hand, sponge in the other, and gaped at me. "Mama?" she said faintly.

"Come on!" I grabbed her hand and felt the sponge squish makeup on my palm.

"She's doing my face," said the woman in the chair. I ignored her and began dragging Destiny toward a door.

"I can't just leave. I need to tell someone—" Destiny argued. Her voice held the soft lilt of a Southern belle.

"No, no you don't. Come on."

"I'll lose my job."

"You can afford to," I said.

I heard a male bellow from behind us, and the pounding of feet in heavy shoes hitting the linoleum. I ducked off to the left and into the women's clothing section. Fortunately, the recent trend in department stores was to cram in massive numbers of racks tightly packed with clothes. It made a great obstacle course that women were trained to negotiate and that baffled men.

"What's happening? Who are those men," Destiny panted.

I glanced back at the flushed, angry faces of our pursuers frantically knocking aside racks and shoving people out of the way. Women were starting to scream. "Not friendly, and they're the guys who hurt your mother," I said, ducking through a rack of tacky formal gowns. Destiny was tottering after me. "Kick off your shoes," I snapped as we rounded a checkout counter.

"They cost a hundred dollars."

"Trust me. You'll be able to replace them."

Ahead of us was the exterior door, and please, God, John, waiting. I kicked into a full-out run. Destiny ran out of one shoe and ended up abandoning the other because of the discomfort. I could hear a pursuer closing fast. It was more instinct than any rational thought—I snatched the foundation bottle out of Destiny's hand and flung it wildly at the man. I missed by a mile. It hit the floor well in front of him and shattered, sending foundation splattering everywhere.

The man stepped in it, his feet flew up in front of him, and he landed hard on his tailbone and lower back. I guess it *was* really creamy. We hit the door handle, and it flew open violently, clocking a woman in the face. She fell back with a scream, clutching her face.

"Sorry, sorry!" I yelled. I frantically scanned the parking lot. No John. Tears of fear and frustration clogged in my chest.

The Chevy turned the corner at the end of a line of cars. I jumped up and down, screamed at him, then started running for the car. I risked one look back. The men were trying to get past the infuriated woman I'd knocked down, but she was hitting them with her very large handbag and screaming at them.

Destiny yelped in pain as her feet hit the hot, rough asphalt. We reached the door. I released her and yanked open both the front and back doors. Destiny, eyes wide and rolling with terror, scuttled backward away from me.

"You're cr-crazy," she stuttered.

Thank God Chastity had regained her shit. She leaned out the door and yelled, "Destiny! Get in the damn car!"

The girl dove into the backseat and into her mother's arms. I slammed the door behind her, scrambled into the front, and closed my door. John floored it, and the car jerked forward just as the glass blew out of the rear window. The two women screamed and I ducked down.

"Linnet, grab hold of me! Tell them to grab my shoulders! We have to get *out* of here!"

"What are you—"

A big black SUV was speeding to cut us off, and a man was running at us from between the cars waving a gun.

"I don't have time to explain. Just fucking *do it!*"

I grabbed his thigh, Chastity and Destiny laid their hands on his shoulders, and the air seemed to wobble and flex. The mall vanished, and we were in a roundabout with an equestrian statue of an Álfar on a pedestal in the center. Carriages, drawn by glossy-coated horses like Arabians crossed with Irish hunters, and touring cars jostled for position all around us.

And the passengers weren't people. They were Álfar, with their exotic multicolored hair and beautiful, sharp-boned faces. The clothing of the Álfar in the carriages and cars looked like a mash-up of art deco, Edwardian, and twenties style clothing. There were a lot of startled looks as we joined the parade on the roundabout.

"Oh, shit," Charity moaned.

"What . . ." I began, and the word ended on a gasp because John was no longer dressed in slacks and a polo shirt.

He was decked out in a white linen suit with a white duster-like coat over the top. And we were no longer in a rented Chevy. We were seated in a twenties-style touring car with a long, long hood and the top folded down. I was wearing a pair of old-fashioned jodphurs, high boots, a scarf knotted at my neck, and an oxford shirt. A pistol was holstered on my hip.

"What did you do?" I asked. I barely recognized my voice because of the thin edge of hysteria held in check by rigid control.

"You're in Elfland now, baby," John said, and he sounded tense and exhausted. "They can't follow us here."

We left the roundabout on a road heading north. "Won't they react to the human interlopers and throw us out?" Destiny asked a little nervously. I was glad to hear her voice. She seemed to be recovering her composure.

"First, you're with me, and I'm clearly an Álfar, and they keep human pets around." His voice sounded grim.

"I didn't think you had anything to do with . . ." I made a vague gesture at our surroundings.

"I don't." Curt, short.

I subsided for a few moments, but I was burning with curiosity. "Then how did you learn to . . ." Another random arm wave.

"When I hit puberty, I started to switch between realities without meaning to. It would happen when I was asleep. It was causing fits, both for my folks and on this side. So my mother sent over a tutor. He worked with me for a few days and taught me control. This is the first time I've ever done it—deliberately."

"I'd think it would be incredibly useful in your line of work."

"Which is why I don't do it. Too easy to start relying on it. Too easy to draw *her* attention." He was looking even grimmer.

"Who's her?"

"My bitch of a mother."

"So why risk it now?" John just turned his head and looked at me. The frown faded, the harsh lines around his mouth softened, and he smiled without saying a word.

It was the expression in his eyes as they rested on my face that made my chest tight and made me want to laugh and cry and shout all at the same time. Was I in love? Yes, I'd fallen in love.

We drove on. Once John had the car purring along in fourth gear, he took my hand again. Occasionally I felt a flutter of wind lift my hair as if another car had passed us. The greens of the forest seemed greener, the air seemed to sparkle as if I were breathing champagne bubbles, and through the trees I caught an occasional glimpse of beautiful homes outlined in graceful columns or topped with delicate spires and towers. We didn't talk. I was too rattled, and I could tell from the set of his jaw and the frown line between his brows that John was really concentrating.

"So are we just going to pop out in New York in a few minutes?"

John shook his head. "No, geography is geography. We still have to cross the same number of miles from Virginia to New York."

"So, this isn't a different world . . . or . . . or dimension or something?" Chastity asked.

"Nope, same world. Their rules."

"How does that work?" I might have been raised by a vampire, but this was totally new to me, because people and even vampires were always warning you against the Álfar and their realm.

John shrugged. "Damned if I know. Sometime back in the early seventies a scientist crossed over all ready to figure it out based on quantum mechanics or some damn thing."

"And?"

"And nothing. He went native, bought into all the Unseelie Court shit, and died in this reality."

"So, why do you look like Jay Gatsby if you think all of this is shit?"

The grin he gave me was rueful. "Because this place lets you play out your deepest fantasies and make them real. Your secret sense of yourself is revealed."

"So, my vision of myself is . . . is . . ." I gestured helplessly down at my body.

"Very Laura Croft. Or a female Indiana Jones."

"Great," I muttered.

"I'd rather have that sitting next to me then some woman who sees herself as Cinderella. That puts *way* to much pressure on a guy to make everything all Happily Ever After."

I glanced into the backseat to see how Chastity and Destiny saw themselves. Chastity looked like the country club ladies who played golf or bridge with my mother. A sort of Talbot's sport look with a red blazer, slacks, and a silk tank top. *This is what she thought her life would be if she had become Mrs. Henry Abercrombie,* I thought.

Destiny looked like she ought to be strutting the runway in Paris or Milan, with a short silver skirt, white thigh-high socks with silver embroidery on them, stacked-heel shoes, and a glittery, almost transparent lilac-colored blouse. Her hair was spiked into a wild do. They both looked stunned, but Destiny gave herself a shake and asked, "Okay now I want an explanation. Who are you people, and what is going on?"

"I'm Linnet Ellery. I'm a lawyer. This is John O'Shea, a private detective who works for our firm, and he is also an elf, which is how we got here."

Keeping a grip on John, I used my free hand to open my satchel and tease out the will. I handed it back to Destiny, and she read through it.

"So, this is why you said those things about replacing the shoes and not worrying about losing my job," Destiny said.

"Yes."

"How much are we talking about?" Destiny asked.

"The company's been valued at just over seven hundred million dollars," I answered. Destiny made a small choking sound.

"Definitely worth killing you to hang onto it," John said in his blunt way, and Destiny made a somewhat louder choking sound.

That roused Chastity out of her shock and fear. "I'm not risking my daughter's life, or mine, for that matter, over money," Chastity said. My respect for her climbed. I had a feeling Marlene Abercrombie would have handed her kids to Deegan to be killed and eaten if it meant she got the money.

I shook my head. "You have to see this through now. Deegan will never believe that you won't come back looking for a payout. It's the only way to be safe," I said.

"Yeah, and Deegan's losing his shit big-time. These kinds of public attacks are crazy," John added. "At this point I think he'd just kill you for the hell of it. Impulse control is not a werewolf's strong suit."

We drove on. The mother and daughter were deep in a

whispered conversation. I tried not to listen in, but occasionally phrases would reach me. " . . . *take that screenwriting course.*" *"Move away . . . meet someone."*

Several hours later, a twenties-style touring car roared past us. Seated in the rumble seat behind the Álfar driver and passenger was a plump human man dressed like a butler. The female Álfar turned her head to look at me. She was dressed in a flowing peach-colored frock, and a twisted necklace of pearls and silver lay on her porcelain skin like windblown flowers. She wore a cloche hat and actually looked beautiful in that singularly unattractive headgear. Her expression poured disdain over me like an acid bath.

She leaned over and said something to the driver. He jerked the wheel, and he would have sideswiped our car if John's reflexes had been a second slower.

"Shit!" he shouted.

The other car tried again to force us off the road. John floored it, and our car leaped ahead. The sudden acceleration sent Chastity and Destiny falling against the backseat, losing contact with John. The landscape began to waver and dissolve. Just before we dropped out of Fairy, I flipped the bird at the Álfar bitch. I had my hand slapped hard by John.

"Why—"

"Because on top of everything else, I really don't want to fight a duel today," he said.

"You have got to be kidding me," I said.

He shook his head. "There's nothing an Álfar hottie likes better than males bleeding over her."

"Why were they so pissed?" Chastity asked.

"Maybe because I'm in a car with three human women," John said. "Maybe for no reason at all."

"That's just crazy," Destiny said.

"Yeah, that pretty much sums it up. Everything in their world has to be much bigger, much more dramatic, and all about *me*." He shrugged. "Basically the Álfar spend their lives in a psychological state of amplified hysteria."

"But you're not like that," I said.

"No, because I had a no-nonsense father who wouldn't put up with that kind of crap. I still have the tendency though, so I watch it every minute."

We took hold of John again, and he pulled back out onto the main road. An hour later, we reached the outskirts of a gold and crystal city. In the distance a castle sent twisting spires toward the sky. There was more Álfar traffic now. Fortunately no one seemed inclined to start a fight with us. John rotated his neck, stretching out taut muscles.

"I'm having trouble holding my concentration for this many people. I wasn't raised here, and I'm not very good at this, which is why you have to keep touching me. I need to drop out. Walk around, stretch my legs. Maybe get something to eat."

I removed my hand, Chastity and Destiny leaned back with sighs of relief, and our world returned. The spires of the castle turned into the smoke stacks of a distant factory. Immediately around us the view was bleak, with warehouses, factories, and sad little narrow houses decked out in dull-colored siding. In my human reality the sky didn't seem as blue, the leaves as green, or the setting sun as golden bright. Melancholy settled like a weight behind my eyes. I plucked irritably at the fabric of my jeans. It felt harsh and rough against my skin.

"And that's why people get trapped in Fairy," John said gently as he turned on the GPS unit and scrolled to the map function. "Go there too often, and you lose all ability to see beauty in the world unless you're seeing it through their eyes."

We left the freeway and headed into a neighborhood in search of a restaurant. My cell phone came back to life and chimed to indicate voice mail. I had three—one from my mother, one from David Sullivan, and one Syd. My heart lifted.

"Syd's back," I said after listening to the message. "Sounding weak, but very feisty. He told me not to steal his clients."

John had just begun to play back a message on his phone when we heard the single whoop of a siren, and a police car, lights flashing, pulled in behind us. John began gliding over to the curb to stop.

"Damn, what did we do?" I asked.

"Our rear window is blown out. Here." He thrust his phone into my hand. "Listen to this message while I get out my license."

I held the phone up to my ear and heard a gruff, basso voice saying, *"Hey, Elf, it's Carson. There's a BOLO out for you. You're a suspect in a series of murders. What the hell you been doing?"*

"John!" My voice was approaching a shriek. "There's a BOLO out on us."

His head snapped around. "What?"

"What's a bolo?" Destiny asked. We ignored her.

"That was somebody named Carson on the phone," I said.

John glanced up into the review mirror. I used the mirror on the inside of the visor. A cop was cautiously approaching, gun drawn. Another knelt behind his car holding a bull horn in one hand and a gun in the other.

"Shit, shit, shit! Linnet, take my hand. Ladies, grab hold."

"We're running," Chastity gasped. "That's never a good idea."

"Normally I'd agree with you, but not this time." John shifted the car back into drive. We all grabbed for some part of his anatomy.

"GET OUT OF THE CAR AND LIE FACEDOWN ON THE GROUND!"

John floored it, and we were back in Álfar World.

"Why did we run?" Chastity asked.

"Because we're murder suspects. Which meant when they caught us they would search us, we'd get locked up—"

John picked up my tale of woe. "And the will would just somehow disappear out of the evidence room." He took a deep breath.

"Are you going to be okay?" I asked, alarmed by his paleness.

"I'll have to be."

We drove in silence for a few minutes. "Do you think the firm can get us out of this?" I asked in a small voice.

"Guess we'll find out how good they are, and how much we're worth to them" came the comfortless reply.

# 23

We finally reached the Álfar version of New York, which seemed to consist of fluted spires constructed entirely from crystal, gold, and silver. There was a lot more greenery between the buildings, and the Álfar strolling the boulevards moved with languid grace quite unlike the hurly-burly of my human New York.

The Álfar were also gorgeous, with exotically colored hair, tall, slender bodies, and clothing in fabrics that took my breath away. The humans, almost all clearly servants, stood out like frogs cavorting in a flight of butterflies.

I didn't see as many vehicles on the Fairy roads. Once I heard dimly, as if muffled by a vast distance, the blare of car horns that was the music of human New York.

A taller than average Álfar, dressed in what looked like livery, was followed by six other Álfar as he hurried through the etched glass doors of a building and waved urgently at us. The stone of the building seemed to have been inlaid with silver lines in swirling patterns, and many of the stained-glass windows threw jewel colors across the crushed white gravel that formed walkways around the structure.

John made a sound like a growl and shook his head. "I don't have time for her right now."

"Who?"

"My mother." John drew in a deep breath and released my hand. "Ladies, please let go." There were lines of tension around his mouth, and dark circles rimmed his eyes.

I was back in my jeans, the ladies were back in their day clothes, and we were once again seated in a Chevy, and around us was human New York. I realized we were on Seventy-second Street, opposite the Dakota, New York's premier residence. We were surrounded by honking rush-hour traffic. The Álfar servant and his minions had emerged from a building that was the Fairy analogue to the Dakota, and now that it was the real Dakota they were still there. They had followed us into the human New York.

"They're still there," I said unnecessarily.

"Shit." There was an edge of panic to the word. John tried to maneuver through the other cars, but it was six o'clock and the traffic was wedged tight, held in place by a red light.

The Álfar swarmed the car. The doors were locked, but something they did affected the electronics and the locks snapped up. They yanked open the doors. The tall one pulled John out of the driver's seat. Two more lunged into the back on either side of Chastity and Destiny.

I made a frantic dive over the backseat and snatched up the will just as an Álfar slid into the driver's seat. Another one basically sat on my lap, and they drove us through the arch and into the courtyard of the Álfar Dakota.

Where prancing horses were led past by liveried servants, and a Dusenberg was parked against one wall. Servants, all of them Álfar, rushed to open the car doors, and we were pulled out.

John was struggling desperately against the grip of his captor. He said something, and the tall Álfar let him come to me.

He took my hand, I stuck the will into the waistband of my jeans, and we were all escorted into the building.

An Álfar operated the elevator, a fantastic creation like a hollowed-out diamond. Occasionally a glowing facet would break the light into a prism of colors. On the top floor a servant waited and threw open crystal inlaid double doors. I took a tighter grip on John's hand as we entered, and the servant announced, "Sindarhin and humans."

"John O'Shea and friends," John said to the living Erte figurine who stood before us.

John's mother was draped in a gold-trimmed green silk gown that exposed a lot of chest. A necklace of emeralds and gold lay against her golden skin, and her black-and-white streaked hair hung to her waist. John had inherited her deep green eyes. She wore an odd little cloche hat like a golden helmet that formed a false widow's peak on her forehead. She opened her arms to John, and the tassels of gold chain with moonstones and emeralds threaded on them clashed and rang.

She kissed his cheek. "Always so huffy. He doesn't mean to be rude," she said. Her voice was pure music, as if a celesta played in the background.

"But you always are," John said. She ignored the insult.

"Please, sit, have tea."

She walked over to a sofa upholstered in white leather, which sat between two end tables of polished cherrywood that doubled as cabinets. All the hardware was chrome. A very angular modernist tea set rested on a Macassar ebony coffee table with wide curved legs that extended above the edge of the top; they looked like battlements protecting the table's surface. There was a tray of small pastel-iced cakes and finger-sized sandwiches.

John refused to move, but the Álfar holding him forced him forward and shoved him down on a couch. John's mother waved a languid hand at Chastity, Destiny, and me.

"Oh, bring them too." We were frog-marched forward and pushed down.

"Don't eat anything," John warned us.

His mother's beautiful and youthful face assumed a pout. "Do you think I'd trap them?"

"I wouldn't put it past you."

Her eyes glittered, and suddenly she didn't look so beautiful. She seemed very alien and very scary.

"Be careful defending them. You might want them to stay with you here."

I felt a cold, coiling pressure in my chest and a stiffening in my spine as I realized we were on the verge of a kidnapping. The Álfar behind me had a light hand on my shoulder. Was that necessary to hold me in their reality, or was he just being prudent and figuring (rightly) that I was about to tear this woman's face off?

"What are you talking about?" John asked.

"You've walked in our world for much of a day. You reject us except when you need us. Now you must pay the price. You will remain. I want you home."

"You should have thought of that before you dumped me in a Philly hospital and took John—which would have been his name if you'd left him with his family." My John was raging, and his face had the same inhuman coldness of his dam's. There was a visible struggle, but he got himself under control, leaned back, and said with studied casualness, "Where is Parlan, by the way?"

"Off." She waved vaguely in the air. "Pursuing a girl. Or hunting. I don't remember which. He's no longer interesting."

"So, what? You're just going to dump him out of the only world he's ever known and slot me in his place? Well, it won't work. I'll never agree."

"Fine, leave, but I'll keep your women." She tapped a perfectly manicured nail against the tabletop and gave Destiny, Chastity, and me a predator's smile.

Anger flared deep in his eyes, and I felt my jaw clench. There was no way in hell I was going to let this happen. I just had to figure out how to wrench us out of this world and back to our own.

I looked over at Destiny and Chastity huddled together on a fainting couch. They were clinging to each other, slumped, battered by events. Two Álfar loomed over them, hands on the backs of their necks. They were in this mess because of me. *They would be dead if you hadn't gotten involved*, said the whining, bargaining voice. *Leave them. Take John. He can probably get you out.*

My vampire upbringing surged to the fore. *They're my responsibility.* I released a pent-up breath and looked up at John.

"We have to agree," I said softly.

"I know," he said, and he kissed me softly on the lips. I wanted to be strong and brave, but a small sob burst out, and I wrapped my arms around his neck. He held me hard, burying his head against my neck. I felt his shoulders shaking, but when he straightened and stared at his mother there was no hint of distress. Instead he gave her a look of pure loathing. I would not have wanted to have been on the receiving end of that look.

"Okay, I'll stay. Now let them go."

"Happily," his mother said, and the room began to fade around us. I heard her begin to sing. Gleaming ice crystals appeared in the air with each note. She gathered them into her hands, formed them into a splinter, and drove it deep into John's eye.

I screamed, a cry of rage and denial, and then we were in someone's apartment in the Dakota, and there was a pair of King

Charles spaniels yapping and jumping around the three of us, the smell of cinnamon incense, and a Spanish-accented voice calling from the kitchen.

"Who is it? Who's there?"

"We've got to get out of here!" I spun Chastity and Destiny around and shoved them toward the door of the apartment.

A puzzled-looking maid in a uniform came into the living room, stared at us, crossed herself, and screamed.

We threw open the door and ran for the elevators. There was a doorman in the lobby who just stared at us. We must have looked a sight. Chastity and I were caked in soot, and Destiny was shoeless.

"Hey!" he shouted, but I hit the door running full out.

We dodged between the cars in the courtyard and rushed out onto Seventy-second Street. Night had fallen while we'd been in Álfar World. I threw up my hand to flag down a taxi, then realized I didn't have my purse. I looked over at Chasity and Destiny. No purses. No cell phones. We were bag ladies with a multimillion-dollar piece of paper that was totally worthless in the current situation, but could sure as hell get us killed.

It wasn't too many blocks to the office, but we were on the wrong side of the park, and the mother and daughter looked like they were at the end of their strength. Destiny was grimacing with every step. I kept us moving until we reached Central Park West, then walked up to Seventy-third Street. Destiny was leaning on me so hard I felt like my shoulder was breaking. I stopped, assumed my best damsel-in-distress face, summoned the tears, and accosted a middle-aged man walking past with a cell phone pressed against his ear.

"Sir, we were carjacked and robbed. I really need to make a phone call. May I use your phone? It's a local call."

People say New Yorkers are rude. I've never experienced it. The man took one look at our bedraggled persons, ended his call, and handed me the phone. "You should call the police," he said.

"I will. I just want to get us off the street first." I checked my watch. 9:30 p.m. The office switchboard would be closed, voice mail only. I knew the number for the guard desk in the lobby. I called that.

"The IMG Building," came a male voice.

"Hi, this is Linnet Ellery. Is there anybody still in the office at Ishmael, McGillary and Gold? Preferably a partner, but I'll take anybody."

"Just a minute," the guard said. Then I heard his voice, faintly now because he'd obviously turned away from the phone. "You work for the law firm, right?" I heard a faint acknowledgement. "There's a Linnet Ellery on the—" His voice broke off, and then I heard David Sullivan.

"Linnet, this is David. Are you in trouble?"

I felt a flash of annoyance that his first thought would be that I was in trouble. But I *was* in trouble. There was a painful lump in my throat. I swallowed past it and managed to say, "Yes. I need help. We're on the corner of Central Park West and Seventy-third Street. I have no money. I've got the will, but no money. I've got to get—"

"Stay there! I'm on my way." And he hung up the phone.

I returned the cell phone with many passionate thank-yous, then pulled Chastity and Destiny under the awning of an apartment building. The doorman chased us off. So now I had experienced one incident of rudeness, but I probably would have chased me off too.

Eventually we crossed over to the park side of the street. The grass was easier on Destiny's feet, and it wasn't private property. A cop might roust us, but hopefully not before David found us.

———

Daniel Deegan found us first.

I saw the big black Hummer driving slowly down Central Park West accompanied by a chorus of honking horns and shouted insults. The big car suddenly dove into a no-parking zone, and Deegan leaped out. *How?* my tired and frightened brain cried. All I could think was that somehow the abandoned Chevy had turned up in the courtyard of the Dakota, and that it was linked to the BOLO. However it had happened, he was here now.

He was smiling, but the expression was somehow murderous. *John was right—he's losing it.* The thought of John made tears sting my eyes. I wanted him here to help me, protect me. Now I was on my own.

*Maybe he'll suggest a settlement,* the lawyer part of my brain suggested. Deegan turned into a wolf. *Or not.*

Destiny and Chastity screamed. So did a lot of other people. I swung my head wildly, looking for a weapon. The garbage cans were chained down, and I probably didn't have the strength to lift one and throw it even without the chain. Even the damn lids were linked to the cans with little chains. *Cars.* I could hit him with a car. Except I didn't have a car, and in the time it would take me to carjack someone, Chastity and Destiny would be dead. And me, shortly thereafter.

A taxi pulled up on the other side of the street. David jumped out, flinging money like confetti. He scanned the street, spotted us, and plunged into the traffic. He didn't run between the cars; he leaped onto the hoods and the roofs and used them like stepping-stones. Brakes screeched, horns honked, and people shouted.

Deegan gathered his haunches beneath him and leaped.

Chastity and Destiny ran deeper into the park. I stood my ground. The thought of having that mass of fur and teeth land on my back was somehow more horrifying than seeing it coming, and maybe I could fend him off long enough for David to reach me.

David landed on the roof of the car closest to us and threw himself into an arcing dive that landed on Deegan's back. The sudden weight broke Deegan's trajectory, and they crashed to the ground almost at my feet. I scuttled backward, tripped on a sprinkler, and fell down hard on my butt.

David gripped Deegan's elongated muzzle and tried to snap his head around. The wolf gave a violent buck and dislodged David. The vampire tucked and rolled, coming smoothly to his feet. He danced backward, out of reach of those massive claws.

It was surreal. Here was David in a two-thousand-dollar suit, power tie, and Gucci loafers fighting a shaggy beast. Since the fight was illuminated only by streetlights and headlights, I couldn't see any evidence of tears or grass stains on the suit. The only sign the lawyer was locked in a life-and-death struggle was that his perfectly combed hair was mussed, a curl falling over his high, white forehead.

*I've got to help him,* I thought, and I staggered to my feet and resumed my search for a weapon.

Deegan began to howl, the keening sound of a hunter closing in for the kill. It froze my blood, but David just looked even more bored and contemptuous. Deegan leaped at David. At the apex of the jump David caught him, one hand gripping Deegan's arm/front leg, the other on his pelvis, and tossed Deegan over his head. As the werewolf sailed past I heard the sharp *crack* of the creature's arm breaking.

Deegan howled in pain, then yelped again as he crashed into the trunk of a tree. I spotted a trash can with a broken lid chain.

I ran over and grabbed the lid, then ran back toward the fight. I wasn't exactly sure what I could do with my misshapen metal Frisbee, but it made me feel less helpless.

Regaining his feet, Deegan surprised me by not going after David again. Instead he bounded into the street. Traffic was hopelessly snarled. Nothing was moving except for a small van with a satellite dish on top, bearing the logo of a local television station. It was driving down the sidewalk while the driver and passenger leaned out of the windows shouting at pedestrians.

Deegan bent and gripped the undercarriage of a small convertible. The muscles beneath his hulking fur-clad shoulders bunched and strained. He flipped the car onto its roof. I heard a desperate screaming from the two girls inside, saved by the roll bars. But what in the hell was he up to?

My attention was briefly distracted by the men in the van. They jumped out, yanked open the side door, and pulled out a camera and microphone. One helped the other heave the camera onto his shoulder, and they started weaving through the cars. Their focus was on Deegan, which brought mine back to the werewolf.

Deegan gripped the gas tank and yanked it off the car. His powerful claws pierced the metal. Dread like liquid iron flowed into my belly. The pungent scent of gasoline overcame the smell of exhaust. Deegan, gas dripping off his claws, advanced on David carrying the gas tank. For the first time I saw a flicker of uncertainty on the vampire's face.

Only two things could kill a vampire—decapitation and fire. Deegan, hulking, misshapen, and huge, advanced on David.

The reporter and cameraman wove and danced back and forth, trying for the best angle on the action. I screamed at them, *"This is not a fucking movie! Help!"* They gave no reaction.

At the last moment, Deegan ripped open the tank and went

to splash the gas over the vampire. I didn't know how he intended to ignite the gas, but I was willing to bet he had that detail covered. I ran forward, raised my garbage can lid, and caught most of the liquid on my makeshift shield. Some splashed on me and on David, but the bulk fell harmlessly onto the grass.

Deegan gave a scream of rage and slashed at me. His clawed paw ripped the lid out of my hands, nearly cutting it into two pieces. I was helpless before him. David stepped forward, caught me around the waist, and swung me aside. The blow meant for me took the vampire full in the face. The skin on his cheek hung in shreds, but there was only the tiniest trickle of blood.

Another TV station van arrived.

Fire seemed to flicker in the back of David's eyes, and he bared his teeth, revealing his fangs. With the gore on his face, he didn't look human any longer. Then he put on a burst of vampire speed, and in an eyeblink he was chest to chest with the werewolf, his hand on Deegan's throat and his knee pounding the hound in his nuts. Deegan screamed at each blow, and with each scream he began to sound less and less like a wolf and more and more like a man in extreme pain.

David had forgotten to breathe. His mouth moved, but no words emerged. He realized he had no air to power sound. He drew in a deep breath and said, "Change," in a voice that cracked like thunder.

The wolf's response was to snap his jaws just in front of David's face. The vampire reacted quickly, thrusting Deegan back a few inches to preserve his nose. David drove his knee one last time into Deegan's crotch, then brought his hand down and grabbed his junk.

"I swear I'll make you a eunuch. Now *change!*"

And he did. David laid Deegan down on his back on the grass, human, naked, bloody, and groaning, his hands cradling his crotch.

That's when New York's Finest arrived. I wanted to tell John that his cop buddies sure timed that well. Then I remembered, *John is lost.* Everything washed over me, and I burst into tears.

# 24

One week later I stood in a Manhattan courtroom with Syd Finkelstein, his severely shortened right arm swathed in a bulky bandage, and our clients.

I hadn't intended to be there, but Syd, Chastity, and Destiny insisted, saying that none of this would have happened if it hadn't been for me. Since that was undoubtedly true, I had agreed to be listed as co-counsel.

That meant I had to contact the Abercrombie brood and request a conflict waiver. Since I'd represented them initially, I couldn't now represent the Jenkins women without the Abercrombies' express approval. Naturally Marlene was completely opposed, and she seemed on the verge of reopening the entire case until I pointed out that if she did they might lose the twenty million. That got everyone's head right.

Judge Mandel's nasal and rather high-pitched voice brought me back to my surroundings. He accepted as authentic the last will and testament of Henry Lee Abercrombie and introduced it for probate. He pulled down his glasses and peered over the top, scanning the courtroom, which was filled with press, Syd's family, and, to my shock, Gold.

"Is a Miss Chastity Jenkins present?"

"She is, Your Honor," I said, while at the same time Syd said, "Yep."

"Do you understand you have been appointed as the executor of this will?"

"Yes, sir," Chastity said in a small voice.

"And do you understand that you and your daughter . . ." He pushed his glasses back up and read from the papers in front of him. ". . . Destiny Lee Jenkins are jointed beneficiaries of this will?"

"Yes, sir."

"Then let's get 'er done and off my docket. You're very lucky women," he concluded, then banged down the gavel. A scrum of journalists surged toward the mother and daughter. I slipped away while Syd, who seemed at least an inch taller, helped field questions.

Gold was waiting for me just outside the courtroom doors. He took my briefcase (I had abandoned the roller bag for a sleek underarm portfolio), linked his arm through mine, and tried to walk me away. I held my position.

"I'm not infirm," I said. "And it's not 1850." He gave me an exasperated look and handed back my briefcase. His frown no longer had the power to intimidate me, and that felt good. I gave him a bright little smile. "Thank you."

"So, another financial win for the firm. *Abercrombie* has been very good for you. But I do hope your future cases will be more . . . staid," Gold said.

Outrage stopped me dead in my tracks. "What a terrible thing to say, and no, it hasn't *been good for me.* Chip is dead. A lot of people who shouldn't be dead are dead, and John is trapped. Money can't make up for everything we've lost."

It was as if his skin had become ice as he reacted to my

disrespectful tone. *Watch it, he could fire you,* the cautious Linnet whispered in the recesses of my brain. Then I discovered that the Linnet who lived front and center didn't give a shit. I noticed a man in a wheelchair waiting by the far wall. It was Jolly.

"If you'll excuse me, I see one of my clients. I need to speak with him." I walked away.

I couldn't swear to it, but I thought I heard Gold say very quietly, "Congratulations, Ms. Ellery."

I reached Jolly's side. "You could have come over."

"I didn't wish to disturb," he said. He opened the briefcase that he had tucked next to him in the chair and pulled out an envelope. "I received this today."

He extracted a sheet of paper. The letterhead read *City of Brooklyn.* I read quickly through the letter. *Your analysis . . . correct . . . property shall remain an equine facility . . .*

When I'd finished, I looked up to find him smiling at me. "They agreed with you. Thank you. I get to keep my barn."

"You're welcome, but this one was easy."

He began to push his chair toward an exit. I walked with him. "Unlike your last one. The reports in the papers were frankly terrifying," he said.

"It was not fun," I admitted.

"But you won," he said.

"Yeah, mostly because I'm too stubborn to know when to quit." Jolly looked like he wanted to say something, but he just shook his head. "I know I sort of ran out on you, but do I still get to ride Vento?" I asked, afraid of the answer.

"Of course."

I sagged with relief. "May I come today?"

"Both he and I would be delighted."

We stepped through the broad brass doors and onto the portico of the courthouse. A summer storm was snarling through heavy gray clouds and setting the flags in front of the building to snapping. The air smelled of rain and ozone. We both looked up at the rapidly approaching clouds.

"Thank God for that indoor arena, eh?" Jolly asked. "Well, I'm going to roll for a taxi." He headed off toward the retrofitted concrete ramps and went whizzing down toward the sidewalk.

A few fat drops spattered on the granite steps, and a few splashed against my scalp. I ran behind him for the taxi stand.

Norma beat a tattoo on her steno pad with the end of her pen. "A lot of people have been calling for appointments." She had thrust several pencils into the teased and sprayed hair helmet and obviously forgotten about them, so now she looked like an odd occidental geisha.

"You don't have to sound so surprised," I said. I stood beside her desk riffling through the pink telephone message slips.

"I guess this proves there's no such thing as bad publicity," Norma sniffed.

"Hey!"

There was a whisper of sound like surf washing onto a beach. It flowed across the commons area, and I realized it was indrawn breaths and faint gasps. It was followed by silence broken only by footsteps on the slate tile. I looked over my shoulder.

Ryan Winchester walked through, head high, eyes straight ahead, carrying a box. I could just make out the tops of frames over the edge of the box. Assistants backed out of his way. He was heading for my old office. His eyes fell on me, and it felt like acid had bathed my skin. The only other time I had experienced such a hate-filled gaze was when Deegan had been taken away by the police with a shock collar clasped around his throat to prevent transformation.

I rushed to David's office. It was empty, stripped of diplomas, honors, and pictures. The top of the desk loomed like a desert. I raced back out and went charging up the stairs to the seventy-third floor.

The awful Bruce looked up as I came slamming through the stairwell door. "Hey, is David Sullivan up here?"

Bruce sniffed and made a show of looking down at his phone list.

"He is," came David's voice. It fairly throbbed with pride and excitement. I turned. He stood in the doorway leading to the private offices. "Want to tell me where to hang my art?"

That evening, I begged off from a dinner with Ray and Gregory. Instead I stopped at a little local produce stand and picked up fresh tomatoes, basil, onion, garlic, and oregano. Next I hit the small Italian market for a bottle of red wine, pasta, mozzarella, capers, and olives. It was a warm early September evening, and *spaghetti con pomodoro crudo* sounded like the thing.

When I came through the door lugging my purchases, Gadzooks threatened to send me ass over teakettle as he twined through my legs, mewing piteously. I had used a combination of helpless charm and bullshit on the super at John's building until he let me in. Then I whisked the cat away. For the moment I was paying the rent on John's apartment too, but since it was rent controlled and I'd gotten a nice raise at work it wasn't a big hardship. If his absence went on for too long, I'd consider putting his things in storage. Hopefully that wasn't going to happen.

The cork emerged with a satisfying little *pop*, and dark ruby liquid washed the sides of the wineglass. While I chopped the tomatoes and herbs and waited for the water to boil, I sipped wine and visited with the family who had called to offer their congratulations.

"Not that I particularly like Gold, but I have to agree with him on one thing," I told my dad. "I really, really, really hope my future cases aren't this exciting. I nearly got killed two . . . three . . . well, a bunch of times."

"But you didn't. And you made a lot of money for the firm and brought them a lot of attention," he soothed.

"Yeah, not exactly what vampires like. They're more behind-the-scenes types."

"The world is changing, Linnie," he said, and I wasn't quite sure what he meant by that.

I ate dinner on a TV tray and watched an episode of *The Forsyte Saga*. It proved to be a bad choice because I hit the point where Bosinney gets killed. It took a long time before I stopped dripping tears into the remnants of my pasta. I finally cleared away my plate and kept refilling my glass as I paced the confines of my apartment. Sleep was elusive.

At 1:30 I finally felt tired enough to go to bed. 'Zooks, purring like a diesel engine, crawled in with me and demanded a position against my belly and under the covers. I fell asleep to his warm rumble.

I dreamed I was dancing with John. He was telling me something, but I never fully caught the words. I knew it was important, and the lack of understanding made me cry with frustration. Then he seemed to be pulling away down a long tunnel of alternating gold and darkness.

Gray dawn light was limning the edges of the windows in my bedroom. I sat up and clawed my hair out of my eyes. There was a sweet smell like jasmine and orange blossoms in my room. I looked down at the foot of the bed and froze at the sight of a small branch covered in white and yellow flowers lying on the folded spread.

The bark was cool against my hand as I swept it up and buried my face in the blossoms. 'Zooks bumped his head against my arm and purred and *twert*ed. I hugged him close.

"Your daddy was here," I whispered.

I scrubbed away the tears and threw back the covers. I couldn't storm Fairy like some heroine in a fantasy novel. But there was another lady with a sword who might be able to help me. My friend had been essentially kidnapped. However odd the Álfar reality was, it existed within the geographical confines of the State of New York in the United States of America. Our laws had to have jurisdiction and take precedent.

I was a lawyer. I was going to establish just that and bring John home.